"I hate you, Irish Fitzpatrick," Kenna snarled. "You tricked me."

"You made a deal," Irish answered as he lowered her onto the coverlet. "One night of lovemaking for the return of the envelope. And you're going to pay up."

Kenna struggled harder against the man who imprisoned her in his arms.

"Be still," he ordered, and his lips captured hers. His steel strength immobilized her body under his. The feel of his hand against her soft round flesh as it began a tantalizing exploration brought a moan from Kenna's lips.

"Kenna," he whispered against her mouth, and she found herself trembling in response.

The envelope lay unnoticed on the floor, the cause of their struggle forgotten in the heat of their desire. . . .

PHOENIX RISING

FRANCES PATTON STATHAM

Fawcett Gold Medal · New York

To the memory of the three hundred American nurses who died while on duty overseas during World War I.

Prologue

APRIL 1914

EACH YEAR, FOR AS LONG AS KENNA COULD REMEMBER, the Irish horse traders had come to Atlanta, with the king of the clan riding at the head of the procession.

Today, amid the blossoming of dogwoods and azaleas, they had finally arrived to bury their dead and to marry each other.

Gaudy gypsy wagons—miles of them—and sleek, glistening horses ridden proudly by arrogant, dark-haired men kicked up the dust in the streets, causing businesses to close down and women and children to scamper to safety until the horse traders had passed by with their yearlings and foals, newly come from the spring grazing pastures.

O'Hara, Carroll, McNamara, Sherlocke. These were not ordinary gypsies, but sons of Erin, descendants of a single clan that had come to America in the 1850s and dispersed to the South in a wandering, nomadic life, trading their horses, living off the land, and meeting once a year for their celebration of life and death.

Gold coins around the men's necks caught the sunlight and Kenna, standing on the street corner, shaded her eyes, yet continued to watch for fear of missing even one small portion of the colorful procession.

Her lips curved into a smile at the sight of an awkward, playful foal nuzzling its mother's side and then loping on.

As one wagon passed by, an old woman sat in the back and turned the fortune card—face up. Suddenly, her gnarled hand lifted the curtain. With blue, piercing eyes, she searched the crowd until she saw the small blond-haired girl on the corner.

Crossing herself, the old woman let the curtain drop and returned to her cards.

One

TWIN GUARD BOXES AT THE ENTRANCE TO FORT MCPHERSON towered above the blinding rim of late afternoon sun as the Campbellton Road trolley eased to a stop two blocks away.

Kenna Chalmers stepped down to the pavement and waited until the trolley, its bell clanging loudly, continued on its journey. Then with a quick glance toward the guards, she edged near the evergreen hedge that separated the military post from the deserted sidewalk.

On the opposite side of the street, German prisoners of war, sailors from the captured *Kronprinz Wilhelm,* were out for their evening exercise behind the tall barbed-wire enclosure. They shaded their eyes from the sun and watched the movements of the slender blond-haired girl.

Kenna hurried to escape their stares, quickly pushing herself through the small opening between the hedge and the spiked iron fence surrounding the fort. She gathered up her skirts and with one foot wedged between the spikes, she hoisted herself and jumped onto the government property. Landing agilely on her feet, she sighed with relief and reached down to smooth her rumpled skirt.

"You'd do well to go through the main gate," a male voice taunted from beside her, "especially at this time of day."

Kenna recognized the deep masculine voice before she turned and saw the man astride his giant white horse. Startled, she looked up to meet the contemptuous glower of Irish Fitzpatrick. Her eyes darkened and her cheeks flamed with embarrassment at being caught climbing the fence.

"I'll enter any way I choose, at any time of day I choose," she retorted, her haughty voice disguising the chagrin she

1

felt. When she started to pass, the soldier moved his horse in front of her, blocking her way.

"Not if the guard catches you, Miss Chalmers. You're subject to the same regulations as the rest of us. You could have been shot for your actions just now."

"Please get out of my way," Kenna demanded. "I'm late."

Irish made no attempt to comply with her demand. He remained motionless, his eyes taking in the student nurse's uniform, the slender fingers clutching the scarlet and blue cape, the long, pale moonspun hair with its damp tendrils escaping from the severely twisted knot at the nape of her neck. Kenna felt her anger mounting. How dare he keep her pinned to the iron railing against her will while his eyes devoured her like this.

She stamped her foot and brushed against the horse in a bid to get free. The animal reared at her sudden movement and, dodging a dangerous hoof, the girl darted past.

Kenna didn't heed the disturbance behind her. Totally ignoring Irish's effort to calm his mount, she began to walk briskly down the worn, dusty trail. The sound of hoofs directly behind her told her, without looking back, that she was being followed. Yet, Kenna had no intention of turning her head to acknowledge the presence of either horse or rider.

Suddenly, Kenna's feet left the ground and her body was suspended as a strong, muscular arm encircled her midriff to draw her roughly against rippled sinews of horseflesh.

"Put me down," she shouted, struggling against the iron grip. But the man's arms merely tightened as the ground underneath Kenna swept by with alarming speed.

The jolt of each rise and fall of rhythmic cadence as the horse galloped along the hard trail matched the rapid beating of Kenna's heart. Around her, the landscape spun in a whirl of colors, changing from pattern to pattern.

The man was mad—brutal in his anger—out of all proportion to her burst of defiance. But there was nothing she could do until he finally came to his senses.

Completely at his mercy, Kenna closed her eyes and held tightly to Irish Fitzpatrick, in her fear of falling and being trampled by the surging animal.

As she sensed her body shifting Kenna moaned and clung to the man even more. Then she felt the hard leather of the saddle. She was no longer suspended, but secure, with his arms about her, the gait of the horse slowing from a runaway gallop to a steady trot and finally to a walk.

Irish's breath touched her ear and Kenna arched her back to avoid the closeness. Then, taking a tentative look, she blinked and waited for the trees to stop their unnatural swaying.

She listened for the man to offer an apology, but he remained silent. Kenna turned and looked into brown, penetrating eyes the color of ripe, golden tobacco. She saw only anger. Matching his indignant glare, she accused "You had no right to . . ."

The tightening of his arm around her waist cut off her breath. "*You* had no right to behave so foolishly," Irish interrupted. "You're just an empty-headed little society snob who's determined to play at war but can't be bothered to obey the simplest rules."

The fury that Kenna had fought to control erupted. "Go to hell, Irish Fitzpatrick," she screamed at him, pummeling his chest in an effort to free herself.

His laugh rang out over the deserted trail. "Hardly the Florence Nightingale oath," he commented and waited for her to stop struggling. His smile left his rugged face, and his jaw tightened. "One day soon, we *both* might be in hell," he warned. "I have no choice. But there's still time for you to back out."

He looked down into the mutinous gray eyes and urgently whispered, "Forget about going overseas. Go *home,* Kenna Chalmers. Go home," he repeated, "to your tea dances and your alms for the children of Belgium."

The slap intended for his face was aborted as he caught her hand. In frustration Kenna cried out, "I'll never back out. Never."

"Then heaven help you," he said, a grimness suddenly invading the arrogant brown eyes. He released his hold and immediately she slid to safety.

She stood and watched as he galloped away. A disquieting

3

foreboding caused her to shiver until he disappeared in a cloud of dry red Georgia dust.

Why was he so angry with her? For taking a shortcut over the fence? Or for frightening his horse? Kenna straightened her uniform and wiped her dusty shoes with her handkerchief before hurrying toward the base hospital. But the words spoken by Irish Fitzpatrick still rankled. Empty-headed. Little society snob. That's what he'd called her, as if she weren't capable of anything but wearing satin dance slippers and raising money for relief.

Aware that her effort to save time had failed miserably, and that she was even farther away from the hospital because of Irish's abduction, Kenna quickened her pace. She passed the Victorian red brick barracks where soldiers, finished with duties of the day, lounged on the porches. Ignoring the men, she walked on. The tree-lined avenue of officers' houses appeared on the right and reiterated the color of the trainees' quarters, but with added gingerbread trim and stone turrets and yards filled with spring flowers.

Kenna had no time to stop and admire the residences or oak leaves unfurling in a glory of green on the lawns. Her thoughts and actions were now centered on getting to the hospital and washing up before her supervisor, Miss Dacus, missed her on the wards.

At the corner, the base hospital loomed into view. Walking beyond the hospital sign, Kenna went up the steps and paused at the door. Before her fingers touched the knob, the door was jerked open and the girl quickly stepped aside to avoid collision.

"It seems my last warning was not sufficient for you, Miss Chalmers." The grating voice matched the hostility in the hawk eyes staring at her.

Kenna drew in her breath. "Miss Dacus . . ."

"There'll be no excuses for your tardiness this time, young woman. I've made up my mind. You can come by my office in the morning for your dismissal papers."

Numbed by this unlucky encounter, Kenna remained silent. Yet her expression revealed her disappointment more eloquently than mere words could have. The cape suddenly felt

4

heavy on her shoulders, and the slender girl with the silver-blond hair visibly drooped.

"Did you get the typhoid serum for me, Miss Chalmers?" a man's voice inquired, seemingly oblivious to the tension between the two women.

"Serum?" Kenna repeated. "No, sir. I . . . ."

"You sent Miss Chalmers on an errand, Dr. Grant?" Miss Dacus asked in surprise. "She was due to relieve Miss Hannon on the wards ten minutes ago."

Dr. Grant's eyebrows lifted at the woman's harsh voice. He looked at Kenna and back to Miss Dacus. In a cold voice he said, "I trust Miss Chalmers won't get into trouble for following my orders."

And then, as if the matter were too insignificant to bother with, he strolled past them to the steps and onto the sidewalk.

Miss Dacus, her face flushed at the reprimand, returned her attention to Kenna. She looked her over from the repaired knot of her silky hair to the hastily cleaned shoes on her feet. Kenna forced herself to keep still and waited uneasily for the inspection to end.

"What happened to your uniform? It's dusty."

Kenna's heart sank. For a moment, she had been hopeful that Davin had saved her. But she should have known that her untidiness would not go unnoticed. She was still going to be dismissed. Miss Dacus would see to that.

"It's my fault entirely," Kenna answered with a weariness to her voice. "I got in the way of the cavalry."

"You realize, of course, that you can't go on the wards in a dirty uniform."

"Yes, Miss Dacus."

Disheartened, Kenna turned to leave, but the next words stopped her. "So you might as well report to Jackson to help her scrub the convalescent porch."

"You mean . . ."

"Put on one of the green aprons, Miss Chalmers, and get to work. You're over fifteen minutes late."

Irish Fitzpatrick sat in the officers' quarters, his face shadowed by an intense frown. He couldn't get Kenna Chalmers

5

out of his mind. How could he—with the feel of her body wrapped in his arms and the newspaper clipping burning a hole in his pocket? He pulled out the picture, creased and worn from his constant fingering. PATRIOTIC DEBUTANTES JOIN NURSE CORPS, the headline read. Staring at him was Kenna Chalmers with her dark-haired friend Steppie Hannon. He didn't bother to look at the other girl. He was interested only in the silver-headed Kenna, with her high cheekbones and innocent, wide eyes that denied the sensuality apparent in the shape of her mouth.

He remembered the first time he had seen her up close, when he had been thrown by Godrin before the horse had accepted him as master. He had limped to the post hospital to have his finger set and Kenna Chalmers had been on duty behind the desk. He couldn't believe his eyes, looking at the small porcelain figure before him. Staring at the picture again, Irish felt his rage growing again—at Kenna's family for allowing it and at the army nurse corps for accepting her for training.

Hefty, raw-boned girls from the country were much better-suited to care for the wounded—they were less likely to flinch at the sight of blood, the slaughter and carnage. But it would serve her right—this foolhardy Kenna Chalmers—to be shipped off to Europe.

She wouldn't last long, Irish thought. That was for sure. One battle, and one man with his guts hanging out, would be enough to send her scampering home. With a sense of satisfaction Irish folded the newspaper clipping and pushed it back in his breast pocket.

The hot soapy water and the strong disinfectant took their toll on Kenna's delicate white skin, but she paid no attention to the stinging of her hands, or to the discomfort of her knees on the hard gray boards of the convalescent porch. Kenna didn't even mind that Jackson had disappeared, leaving most of the scrubbing to her. Miss Dacus had not dismissed her. She still had a chance.

Her only companion was a fly that buzzed about the electric light bulb hanging from the ceiling. Off and on the fly, bombarding the screen, frantically searched for some escape.

6

Back and forth from light to screen it went until, exhausted from its fruitless search for freedom, it lit on a wooden slat.

Then the sound of the wet brush scrubbing against the grain of the wooden floor planks took over, marring the silence. Only a few more boards and she would be finished. A strand of hair fell across her face, but when Kenna reached out to push it from her forehead, she collided with another hand that smoothed the wayward curl.

Startled at the encounter, she looked up into the concerned blue eyes of Dr. Davin Grant. He gently clasped her red hand as he knelt beside her on the floor.

"Kenna—Kenna," he whispered.

"Thank you, Dr. Grant," she said, "for rescuing me from Miss Dacus."

He winced at the formality in her voice as she removed her hand from his larger one. "We're alone, Kenna. You don't have to be so formal with me."

"I'm still on duty," she replied and reached again for the scrub brush.

"I should have let her dismiss you. It would have put an end to all this."

"No, Davin," Kenna remonstrated and suddenly looked around to make sure she hadn't been overheard. In a softer voice she continued, "I have to get to France and this is the only way. *You* know that, don't you?"

"He's dead, Kenna. Why do you torture yourself?"

The stubborn jut of her chin caught the harsh glare of the light bulb. "No one saw him die."

"The plane was shot down—"

"But it didn't catch fire," Kenna added, suddenly standing up. "Don't you see? There's still a chance. So many things could have happened—"

"Your brother crashed behind German lines, Kenna," Davin said, his voice sounding brutal.

"That doesn't automatically mean that Neal's dead." Her voice disturbed the fly and once again the buzzing started, back and forth from light bulb to screen. "I . . . I have to finish the porch," Kenna said and sank again to her knees.

A frustrated Davin Grant took one last look at the slender,

7

determined figure and then walked down the hall to his office on the second floor.

The conversation with Davin had effectively taken Kenna's mind off her encounter with Irish Fitzpatrick. Now left alone, she continued her chore mechanically while she reexamined the events that had made her late to the fort in the first place—seeing to the house and taking Neal's black roadster out for its weekly run.

Kenna could still hear the family servant's disapproving words spoken only an hour before at the house on Boulevard, as she hurriedly changed back into her nurse's uniform for the trolley ride to Fort McPherson.

"But I worry about you, Miss Kenna, down at that army fort. If your grandmama was still alive, she wouldn't be al-lowin' you to live there with all those soldiers."

"You sound as if I'm sleeping in the barracks with them, Verbena," she'd protested.

The black woman snorted. "Don't get smart with me, missy. As for bein' in the nurses' dormitory, it ain't much of a step above that. Better for you to be back home where you belong, and where I can keep an eye on you."

"Just keep an eye on the house, Verbena. That's all I ask. I want it to be spotless when Neal comes home," she added.

Kenna smiled and handed the week's wages to the woman. "I'll see you the same time next week."

The plump black woman put the envelope in her apron pocket. Muttering to herself, she walked out of the house with Kenna, parted from her, and trudged down the path to the servant's house in the back yard.

As Kenna continued scrubbing the convalescent porch, a great love welled inside her for the woman who had taken care of her and shared all her joys and her hurts from the moment she was born.

Verbena had been her strength during those terrible months after her parents had gone down with the *Titanic*. And for four years, she had served as a buffer between the rebellious Kenna and her aged, aristocratic grandmother, until that link too had been severed by death.

Now, only her half brother Neal remained. And it was left to Kenna to find him, wherever he might be.

She mustn't forget to make arrangements at the bank for Verbena's wages to be paid while she was overseas.

Two

THE RHYTHMIC CHINK OF THE SHOVEL AGAINST THE DIRT erupted into a sharp, raucous clang of metal against rock. The lantern wavered and the prisoner swore softly at the reverberating sound in the middle of the night.

Hardly daring to move an eyelid, he waited for some sign that he had been overheard. But no alarm was raised by the outside patrol, no barracks doors were bashed in. And so, breathing a little easier, he wiped the grimy sweat from his forehead and began again the slow, tedious procedure of removing the dirt from around the offending rock, and then shoveling once more.

Gott im Himmel! It was like trying to break up cement—this hard Georgia clay. He'd already broken one shovel handle and it had taken him a whole week to make another.

It was a wonder they had not all been caught, especially with all the dirt they had disposed of. But Pershing's regulars, waiting to be relieved, didn't have their hearts in guarding prisoners. Ever since they had been moved from the temporary stockade, the six prisoners had taken turns digging an escape tunnel under the barracks that housed them. A few more days and they would be clear of the fence that encircled the camp, with its layers of barbed wire strung overhead.

He was getting dizzy from a lack of air. But that only indicated how far they had dug and how near to freedom he was.

Boards in the distance creaked, and the prisoner heard someone crawling in the tunnel toward him.

"Fritz," a man whispered a few feet from him. Recognizing the voice, the prisoner lowered his shovel.

"*Ja?*"

"You must come now. The sun will be up in a little while."

9

Seaman Second Class Fritz Rilke left his shovel and, carrying the lantern with him, crawled back to the opening into the barracks. He blew out the lantern and moved the bunk into place over the opening in the floor. After he removed his grimy workclothes, he fell into the bunk.

Only one hour to sleep—yet his mind tenaciously clung to his plans for escape. He'd have to have some money and some other clothes if he were to get to Savannah and make contact with the agent on the coast.

What rotten luck for the raider, *Kronprinz Wilhelm,* to be caught in American waters and for the entire crew to be interned. That was the surprising part—something Fritz couldn't understand. America had been so pro-German at first. Even his cousin, Erich, a naturalized American citizen, had been caught unaware by America's sudden warlike move, and now Erich, too, languished as a prisoner for the duration of the war, but he was at Fort Oglethorpe, with all the other German-born Americans. Only the crews of the *Kronprinz Wilhelm* and *Eitel Friedrich* were here at Fort McPherson.

But one thing for sure, Fritz was determined to escape. Unlike Erich, he had no intention of being caged like an animal any longer than he could help. He would either escape or die trying.

The day began, far too soon for Fritz, tired from the night's digging. Slowly he trudged across the street with the well-guarded work detail that had been assigned to the boiler room behind the hospital.

Past the wrought-iron gates he went, past the chapel and the Red Cross house with its flag fluttering in the mild breeze. The post hospital came into view, and he walked onto the grounds, the hair on his arms prickling immediately as instinct told him that he was being watched.

He looked into hostile gray eyes staring at him, memorizing his every feature. Fritz's blond head rose a trifle higher and he returned the stare, expecting the girl in the nurse's uniform to avert her eyes as anyone usually did when caught.

But this girl was different. Her gaze didn't waver. And it was Fritz who broke the locked stare when the guard yelled, "You! On the end. Get a move on."

She was so blond—Nordic in look—but fine-boned. He could tell, even under that voluminous uniform designed to cover her figure. His thoughts lingered on the girl for a while. Then he dismissed her from his mind. All his energy and thoughts should be directed toward his escape—not toward a girl whose eyes reflected intense hatred.

Kenna, ready to go to class, stood on the sidewalk adjacent to the hospital and waited for Steppie Hannon to catch up with her.

Each morning the two student nurses went through the same ritual, with the nervous Steppie stalling until the work detail passed by before venturing out of the dormitory, and Kenna following the prisoners' movements with an unconcealed animosity.

As Kenna watched, she saw her small brown-eyed friend approach, pausing to glance cautiously over her shoulder at the work detail.

Today, as usual, there was no flamboyance to call attention to Steppie's scrupulously neat figure until the sun, as if by sudden caprice, caught the bright flame of red in the brown tresses that she had tried to hide underneath her heavily starched white cap.

Steppie had changed neither in appearance nor in loyalty since their days together at Washington Seminary. In fact, her loyalty had grown even stronger after her father, a widower, had remarried. It had been a double blow to Steppie to be deposited on her cousin Cricket's doorstep at the age of eighteen, just when Neal had left to join the Lafayette Escadrille in France.

Friendship and their mutual love for Neal had kept the two girls together. Kenna, realizing the tremendous courage it had taken for the shy Steppie to follow her into nurses' training, glanced again toward the disappearing prisoners and hastened to assure Steppie, "The prisoners can't possibly harm you. They're too well guarded."

"I know that, Kenna," Steppie agreed in her soft Southern drawl. "But I'm still afraid. I keep wondering what would happen if some of them escaped."

"That's hardly likely. But one thing is certain. They

11

wouldn't waste time around here. They'd get away as fast as they could.''

"I suppose so," Steppie said and walked in silence for a while. "I heard that two U-boats were sighted off the coast last week," she commented. The dark, velvet eyes widened in fright and Kenna said, "Are you going to believe every rumor you hear, Steppie?"

"But the citizens' committee said . . .''

"The citizens' committee is nothing but a big witch-hunt—looking for Germans under every rock. And they think every one of them is blond and blue-eyed," Kenna emphasized. "They've held so many blond-headed American officers for questioning, it's ridiculous. Can you imagine how angry the officers would be to be mistaken for the enemy? I'd be mad too," Kenna added with a giggle. She touched her silvery hair and said, "Do you think I'll be the next one they arrest?"

Steppie's eyes showed her amusement at Kenna's bantering. "Only if you start speaking in German," she replied.

"Actually, I'm better with German than I am with French. *Parlez-vous français, mam'selle?*" Kenna asked, pursing her mouth to say the words.

"*Un tout petit peu,*" Steppie replied, reacting immediately to Kenna's lightheartedness.

Arm in arm they walked toward the classrooms and along the way they practiced their French—a prerequisite for going overseas.

The next morning the heat of May hung heavily on the horizon as Kenna awoke with a headache. She frowned and rubbed her eyes. Then quickly she climbed from bed and stared out the window of the nurses' dormitory. She saw nothing to indicate that the day would be any different from the previous one.

A shower was what she needed—to clear her head and take away the dullness that plagued her. The night at the hospital had been unusually difficult, with Miss Dacus watching her every move. And she hadn't gotten enough sleep.

Yawning, Kenna closed the window and tiptoed out of the

room she shared with Steppie. With soap and a towel in her hand, she hurried down the hallway to the showers.

By the time Kenna was ready for class, a heavy layer of smoke drifted from the west and fire engines in the distance clanged their alarms. First one—and then another—and another. Kenna took little notice of the work detail of prisoners that morning, for her eyes were searching the sky and her mind wondering what had happened to cause such a huge alarm.

Noise penetrated the classroom and the complicated Dakin-Carrel method of irrigating wounds had to be explained several times to the students. "Please pay attention," Miss Dacus scolded and looked directly at Kenna.

Kenna watched while the method was explained once more, with the rubber supply tubes inserted directly into the wound to allow the chlorine solution to begin its flushing. Kenna shuddered as she thought of the pain that went with the treatment. But, however painful, it would be preferable to gangrene, blood poisoning, and death.

By noon, the horse-drawn steamers with their clamoring bells had multiplied and rumors began to fly with the increasing speed of rolling, clacking wheels of the fire engines.

The city was on fire. Sabotage—Germans—Kenna heard the whispers in every direction and she became caught up in the uneasiness that now gripped Atlanta—the fear of being burned to the ground by an unseen enemy. For as soon as one fire had been brought under control, two in a distant section of the city broke out.

By mid-afternoon, when the paper-thin shanties next to the old pest house caught fire, the fire horses had finally lost their race. The densely packed rabbit hutch of buildings between Edgewood and Houston streets exploded like resinous kindling, igniting the city. And the streets became clogged with citizens seeking escape.

Inside Fort McPherson, soldiers were ordered to patrol the streets, to help the police to bring some semblance of order to the mass exodus of the crowds, and to stop the looting of deserted houses.

Kenna stood and watched as one by one, motorized vehicles, filled with soldiers, rushed through the wrought-iron gates. A truck came to a stop near her and she impulsively called out, "How far has the fire spread?"

"They say it's already down Boulevard," the driver shouted and then drove on.

Kenna's face turned pale. "No," she cried, and closed her eyes, seeing her own home on Boulevard and her precious letters from Neal secreted in the drawer of her Queen Anne desk in the bedroom upstairs. They contained the only clues she had for ever finding her half brother. Verbena would never think to rescue them from the flames. No. She would have to see to the letters herself.

Not taking time to remove her nurse's uniform, Kenna rushed to the trolley stop outside the gates of Fort McPherson. She waited but no trolley appeared on her side of the street. All seemed to be heading in the opposite direction— away from Atlanta. Only the military trucks leaving the post turned left, up Campbellton Road.

Finally, with no hope of getting a ride on a public conveyance, Kenna went back inside the gates, where the last two military vehicles were being loaded.

No one questioned Kenna's presence on the truck as it left Fort McPherson. Her long dark-blue nurse's uniform partially covered by the military scarlet and blue cape was enough to give credence to her journey. Squeezing herself into the small space on the end of the long bench, Kenna ignored the interested looks of the soldiers beside her. Soon they forgot her in the excitement of watching the passing fire engines from nearby cities—Chattanooga, Newnan, Rome.

"The cotton warehouses," one man voiced aloud as white billowing smoke poured into the carmine sky behind the truck. To the north, a denser, blacker cloud greeted them as churches and houses were caught up in a scattered, patternless conflagration. Sparks skipped entire blocks, and then touched down on some unsuspecting rooftop, to smolder for a time and then burst into flames.

Kenna coughed from the density of the smoke and the soldier seated next to her turned. "I hear they're going to use dynamite on some of the houses to keep the fire from spreading," he confided.

14

"Which houses?" Kenna asked, speaking for the first time.

"The ones nearest Druid Hills," the man replied.

Not *her* house. They wouldn't dare destroy the ones on the upper end of Boulevard, where so many lovely homes were located. Or would they? Had fire fighters not done just that in San Francisco, sacrificing a portion of the city to save the rest? And succeeded?

"How soon?" Kenna asked.

"What?"

"How soon," she repeated, "before they dynamite?"

"Whenever they can get the people out, I guess."

Kenna wasted no time in leaving the truck. As soon as it slowed at the next intersection, she climbed out.

Across the street she ran, between two rolling wagons piled precariously high with furniture. At her recklessness, a frightened driver jerked on his mules' reins, and the action jolted a blue enameled chamber pot from its perch on top of the wagon to crash onto the street. The driver's protest was swallowed up in the constant, insistent din of a population leaving the city with as many possessions as it could carry.

"Stop!" a soldier shouted at the girl skirting the street blockade. "You're going in the wrong direction."

Kenna didn't bother to find out if he was shouting at her. She continued to run down Boulevard. Immediately before her, a white-columned house with green shutters suddenly burst into flames. Sparks exploded on the sidewalk at her feet and embroidered the hem of her skirt. She paused just long enough to brush away the embers before resuming her flight.

The firecracker sound of hungry flames gnawing at dry wood was left behind. Now the only sounds came from her own lungs, gasping for fresh air, and her shoes crunching on the sidewalk. With eyes smarting from the heavy smoke, she searched for the familiar house amid canopied green limbs of the giant oaks. As the rising hot wind parted the leaves, Kenna saw her home in the distance—still standing.

She was in time.

Kenna paused at the steps that separated the wide expanse of lawn from the sidewalk. She looked over her shoulder. Striding down the street was the soldier who had tried to stop her at the blockade.

She was too close to her destination to be stopped now. Kenna ducked and ran along the brick path between the tall boxwoods, up the wooden steps of the house, decorated with clay pots of red geraniums, and onto the verandah. Her hand tugged at the brass doorknob, but the front door was stuck. Surprised, she jerked at it a second time, but it didn't budge.

Unwilling to waste any more time, Kenna raced from the verandah toward the rear of the house. She climbed the steps, pushed open the screen door, and walked onto the back porch. The door leading into the hallway stood slightly ajar. Relieved, Kenna ran inside.

"Verbena," she called, once inside the hallway.

There was no answer, but Kenna didn't really expect one. The maid would have been evacuated by the soldiers. She continued up the stairs to her own bedroom, where the white curtains billowed in response to the wayward breeze.

Kenna walked to the Queen Anne desk and, touching the hidden spring, she released the drawer that held her treasured letters. One by one she retrieved them and laid them on the desk top. Her eyes misted with tears at the sight of the familiar writing, the envelopes with foreign stamps, her name scrawled across in bold black writing.

Despite her need to hurry, Kenna removed a thin sheet of paper from one of the envelopes and hungrily scanned the message.

"Our mascot arrived today," she read. "A baby lion named 'Whiskey.' But Tom had a terrible time getting him from Paris to—" And that was where the censor had cut a hole in the paper. Yet Kenna knew it had to be Verdun.

She continued to read. "'A Brazilian dog,' he assured the conductor. But Whiskey evidently was insulted. He growled and showed his claws. After that, the lion *and* Tom had to ride the rest of the way in the baggage car . . ."

Kenna smiled and hurriedly went to the next one, which resembled a slice of swiss cheese because of the censor's scissors. Yes, this was the one she was looking for. It was the letter that Neal had written to her on the day before he was shot down. And it contained the only strong clues as to where he might be found. A feeling of resentment struck her, for in

16

cutting out certain words, the censor had destroyed much of Neal's secret message to her.

A sound of footsteps on the stairs interrupted Kenna's reading. Quickly she stuffed the letter back into its envelope.

It didn't matter now if the soldier had followed her and found her. She had what she wanted. As Kenna turned to leave, a towering blond figure stood in the doorway, blocking her exit.

Not the soldier at all, but—

"You!" Kenna uttered in disbelief.

She stood frozen to the carpet, her legs trembling, while the man with the haunted, desperate look of a fugitive in his cold blue eyes surveyed the girl before him.

"So, *Fräulein*," Fritz said in a low voice. "You recognize me?"

Three

THE SAME PRISONER SHE HAD WATCHED EACH DAY AS HE walked past the hospital was standing before her.

A deadly calm invaded the bedroom. Even the wind had ceased to billow through the curtained windows. Kenna was alone in the house with the enemy.

They stared at each other in total silence, surprise mirrored from gray eyes to blue and back again. Kenna's mind whirled with unanswered questions. How had he escaped? What was he doing in *her* house?

The prisoner recovered first, taking a step farther into the bedroom. Reacting to his movement, Kenna backed away until the edge of the desk stopped her. With her hand groping for the desk top, she tried to release the letter she held before the man noticed it. But she was too late.

"What do you have in your hand, *Fräulein?*" he questioned, frowning at her.

"Nothing important," Kenna replied.

"Let me see."

"No."

"Bring to me," he ordered.

She shook her head and at that, he took another step toward her, grabbed her arm, and forced the envelope from her hand. It fell to the floor and sailed under the desk, to lie fluttering and quivering like some wounded bird.

"Now see what you've done," she shouted, incensed at his action. Wrenching herself from his grasp, she got down on her hands and knees to retrieve the letter.

"Leave it," he ordered.

Kenna, ignoring his order, reached for the envelope. She snatched her fingers away from the toe of the polished black shoe just in time to keep them from being crushed. In an attitude of protection, she held the letter against her cape while her angry eyes traveled from the shoe to the civilian blue suit that the prisoner now wore.

"You have on Neal's suit," she choked, getting to her feet. "You've stolen my brother's . . ."

"Silence," he commanded.

And she was silent.

"We go," he said. "At once." He waved her toward the door and the waiting stairs.

Kenna shook her head. If he thought she was going with him, he was crazy. But then she saw the gun in his hand, pointed at her.

She cast a doleful glance toward the remaining letters and then, reluctantly, left the room with the escaped prisoner on her heels. She paused, but he forced her down the hall, through the kitchen door, and into the back yard.

He evidently knew where he was going, for, without hesitation, he headed straight to the carriage house that served as a garage for Neal's black Chevrolet Royal Mail roadster.

So he had found it. Standing in the entrance of the garage, she looked first at the prisoner and then at the car before her. Now she knew what he planned to do—make his escape in the automobile that she had kept in immaculate condition for her brother's return. And that made her even angrier than his theft of Neal's suit.

"You start," he ordered, pointing to the shiny black roadster with its kerosene cowl lights attached to either side of the windshield.

"No." Her voice was low and angry.

"*Fräulein*," he said, matching the hostility in her voice, "you will start the automobile."

She saw the gun moving toward her face and she stepped back. "It needs gasoline," she hedged.

His eyes swept to the metal can on the floor of the garage. He walked over to it and with his foot, he pushed it. The liquid made a sloshing sound. Satisfied, the prisoner pointed toward the car. "You put in. Now."

Kenna resignedly stepped toward the gasoline can and, picking it up, she poured the liquid into the oval-shaped tank mounted to the back of the car seat. When she started to set the can on the garage floor again, the man shook his head. "We take," he said.

"You won't need it," Kenna protested. "You're not going to get far, you know."

An angry sound came from the prisoner and Kenna, seeing the look in his cold blue eyes, hurriedly strapped the can to the back of the roadster.

"Get in." He motioned her toward the driver's seat.

Kenna suppressed a smile. So he couldn't drive. And he was relying on her. "I can't drive," she lied.

"I see you drive," he answered in a gruff tone. And then Kenna remembered the day she had driven past the barbed wire fence opposite the fort. She sighed. He had called her bluff.

Slowly removing her scarlet and blue nurse's cape, she exchanged it for the beige linen duster and hat hanging from a peg inside the garage. As she took her time in tying the hat's scarf under her chin, the German showed his impatience. "Hurry up, *Fräulein.*"

Stubbornly, Kenna resisted his efforts to hurry her. When she had finished tying the scarf, she reached for the goggles that hung from another peg. And only then, with the goggles in hand, did she climb into the driver's seat. The prisoner followed, settling himself beside her, with his gun in plain view.

"Hello!" a voice called from outside. "Anyone here?"

Kenna turned toward the open garage door, but she wasn't given a chance to answer. The prisoner clamped his fingers over her mouth while he pressed the gun to her ribs.

The voice called out again, but farther away this time, and hope of being discovered died. The prisoner's fingers against Kenna's mouth finally relaxed. "Start the automobile," he whispered.

"You'll have to crank it," she answered. "It's too hard for a woman." She pointed to the front of the roadster and waited for the German to climb out. She hoped that he didn't know what a crank could do to a man's arm if he was unfamiliar with the procedure.

20

"No. *You* crank it," he countered, his patience at an end, and slapped her across the face.

The slap took Kenna by surprise. Her hand reached up to touch the place on her cheek, and her gray eyes glittered with disdain for the man beside her. But he had achieved his purpose. Kenna walked to the front of the car. The backfire produced by the first try filled the garage with a deafening sound. The man's head jerked, but he relaxed as the added noise, mixed with the rumblings and roars outside in the street, went unheeded.

Repeating the trying procedure, Kenna finally succeeded in starting the motor. She climbed back inside the car and, with her hands on the vibrating steering wheel, backed out of the garage into the narrow alley and onto the street.

In every direction the sky shone red. Heavy black smoke with pieces of soot floating through the air surrounded them as the car gathered speed.

A new noise erupted, like a slow rumbling of thunder, and the street underneath the little car began to shift dangerously, forcing the car toward the ditch.

Then one giant explosion split the street in half.

The car hit the ditch while all around them chimneys and walls began their disintegration in slow motion. White mortar, holding bricks together, dissolved into a powdery dust to rain down like a plague loosened from the heavens, invading Kenna's lungs and choking the breath from her. While she coughed, she held her hands over her ears to block out the street noise. But the man beside her pulled her right hand from her ear and shouted, "Move."

The little car groaned its way out of the ditch as Kenna stepped on the gas pedal. On uneven ground the roadster crept until it finally escaped the worst of the holocaust.

All Kenna's efforts to attract attention were thwarted as she became an obscure part of that slow procession of people, wagons, carts, and automobiles down Ponce de Leon Avenue. Everyone else was far too busy trying to save his own possessions to notice a girl driving out of the city with a man at her side.

Tall mansions, still threatened by the wind despite the dy-

21

namiting to produce a firebreak, were being hosed down and bags of sand were stacked to act as barriers against the malevolent sparks. Glancing toward her companion and back to the activity on both sides of the street, Kenna began to get worried. They could go for miles without running out of gas. And it would take forever to get back to Fort McPherson.

She was due to go on duty at the hospital later that evening. And Kenna had been so careful not to get into trouble or cause Miss Dacus to give her a black mark ever since her encounter with Irish Fitzpatrick. His face suddenly loomed in Kenna's mind.

What wouldn't she give to see the soldier's disapproving glare at that very moment? Instead, she had to endure something far worse—as an unwilling hostage of the enemy.

Sullen and silent, she sat by the campfire only a few yards off the deserted road to Macon. Nothing had gone right. Now it was night and Kenna was still a hostage of the blond-headed Fritz. At least now she knew his name.

The coffee in the cup was cold, but Kenna held onto it, occasionally sipping the distasteful liquid while Fritz openly stared at her. Even Verbena's house had not escaped his looting, Kenna saw as she recognized the small cooking pot over the fire. Kenna jumped as an owl hooted in the distance. A splash in the nearby creek echoed through the stillness. Suddenly cold, she pulled her beige linen duster around her.

Who would have thought that her desire to save Neal's letters would land her in such a hopeless situation? And worst of all—to discover the *one* letter that she had been able to save had disappeared somewhere along the way?

Kenna thought of Miss Dacus when she didn't show up for duty. But surely the woman couldn't blame her when she was a prisoner in the German's hands? Would that not be an adequate excuse for not showing up for duty or classes? She couldn't help it if she had been forced to go with Fritz. And yet, the nagging thought remained with Kenna as she huddled miserably under the cloak. How pleased the woman would be when she didn't return in time.

Kenna, caught up in her problems, ignored Fritz until his

sudden movement disturbed her. Seeing him striding purposely toward her with a rope in his hands, Kenna threw down the coffee cup and jumped to her feet. But he was too quick for her.

She screamed and pushed at him as his arms enclosed her. "Be quiet," he demanded. She paid no attention to him, but continued her struggle, landing a kick to his shin that brought a guttural epithet to his lips.

Kenna was no match for him. In a short time, she was trussed hand and foot, like some poor fowl prepared for the roasting spit, while he stood over her.

Tears escaped her silver-gray eyes, closed in humiliation. She was powerless to stop him, she knew. And breathing far too fast, she braced herself for the next assault.

Strangely, nothing happened. Kenna opened her eyes to see the man walking back toward the fire. He poured another cup of coffee and stared into the low flames, as if the episode had never occurred.

Relieved, Kenna stifled her ragged breathing. Fritz had not wanted to make love to her as she had feared, or else he had changed his mind. Perhaps she was more valuable to him as a driver, and he had tied her so she couldn't escape, and then left her alone.

Later that night, in the dim light of the embers, Kenna could see the outline of Fritz's body and hear his steady breathing. But whether he was actually asleep or merely pretending, she had no way of knowing.

She picked at the knots that bound her hands and feet together. The German didn't move or lift his head to see what she was doing. Finally, she gave up. He had secured the rope too well for her to free herself.

As she inched her body into a more comfortable position, a rock grazed her knee and a sound of pain escaped Kenna's lips. Fritz lifted his head and then lay back, as if he knew that she couldn't leave the campfire site until he let her.

Exhausted from the long day and her fruitless efforts to escape, Kenna closed her eyes. Her last thought before going to sleep was on her freedom. Somehow, she had to get away from Fritz the next day when he untied her.

23

"Wake up, *Fräulein*," the voice beside her ordered.

Kenna's eyes flew open as she felt the loosening of the ropes that bound her hands. She looked at Fritz in reproach at this treatment of her—the humiliation of being subjected to him. But he avoided her gaze and began to loosen the knots securing her ankles as well.

Kenna, hating the intimacy of his touch, had a hard time refraining from hitting him over the head. But she knew that would only make matters worse. His glance caught her off guard, and Kenna quickly turned her attention from his blond head to the trees and the pale light that signaled a new day.

Then she heard his voice again. "Don't go far, *Fräulein*. I wait for you. Five minutes."

Kenna looked down at her ankles still tied together but in a different manner—like a horse, hobbled to keep it from galloping away.

How could she get far, like this? Her body ached from the hardness of the ground but she flexed her free hands and got to her feet, slowly and stiffly, while Fritz walked back to the small, carefully laid fire.

He placed the kettle of water over the fire to start their breakfast, but his mind was on the girl. She had behaved well so far, Fritz thought, after she had become reconciled to his authority. But he didn't trust her. At the first opportunity, she would turn him in. That was why he had to decide what to do with her when they got closer to the coast. But as long as the car held up, he needed her to drive it.

At the thought of the car, Fritz suddenly frowned and removed the water from the fire.

In mincing steps, like some Parisian dandy, Kenna tripped through the underbrush. She made enough noise to alert the most amateur hunter or tracker. Even if she *did* decide to run away, Fritz could tell exactly where she was from the noise. And she couldn't get far. Or could she? If she could make it to the roadster without Fritz's intervention, then she could still drive with her ankles tied together.

She changed directions, but in her eagerness, Kenna took too large a step and lost her balance. She landed in a pile of pine needles and her teeth were jarred from the unexpected fall, despite the softness of the needles. Kenna sat up on the floor of the forest and furiously tugged at the ropes that bound her feet together. But the sailor's knots were too complicated. And her five minutes were whirring by—too fast.

Biting her lip, Kenna twisted her body and slid her feet over the ground as silently as she could. She circled the campsite and headed for the automobile hidden from the dirt road by a small copse of plum bushes.

Every few steps, she stopped and listened. But the only sound was the noise she herself made—more like a moose, she thought, than a dandy in high heels.

The tangled vines of honeysuckle, with their yellow blossoms, became an added obstacle in her path—twisting, grabbing at her feet, and running in tendrils from tree to tree—slowing her down. She reached out to brush away the wild vines, and the cloying, sweet odor of the blossoms assailed her, making her suddenly feel sick.

Kenna closed her eyes, and she was not in the woods, but at home in bed—a child again, in the little nursery that connected to her parents' room. Despite the heat of that spring afternoon, the window was closed to keep the odor of honeysuckles out.

She remembered that the tap on the window had awakened her, and she had crawled out of bed. In her long white gown, with her silvery hair tied back with a ribbon, she walked to the window and peered out. Her brother, Neal, older than she by two years, smiled at her. And in his hands he held the offending honeysuckle vines, pulled up by their roots.

In his childlike way, he had thought the honeysuckles growing along the fence were to blame for her illness—not merely the offending odor that had made her nausea much worse. So long ago—

Kenna pushed away the vines as her heart ached in past remembrance. "Oh, Neal," she cried out softly. She walked on in the woods—careful not to be tripped by her own carelessness. She had too much to lose.

In the clearing, the car sat. Kenna looked in all directions to see whether she had been followed. The tiny steps allowed her by the rope finally got her to the automobile. After setting the spark, she took a deep breath. Her hands trembled as she reached toward the crank. Kenna prayed that the car would come alive the first time, for at the sound of the engine back-firing, she knew Fritz would rush to stop her. And she had to have enough time to get into the car and drive away.

Leaning over, Kenna grasped the handle and turned it with all her strength. She jumped back as it spun in the opposite direction, without starting the motor. But no sound came from the engine.

Again, Kenna took the crank, this time using both hands—a dangerous thing to do—but the added strength whipped the motor into action. A sputter, uncertain—then louder—firmer—and steady.

She hurried to the driver's side of the car and tried to step onto the running board. The length of rope would not allow her foot to reach that distance from the ground. So, holding onto the side, Kenna swung herself upward and landed with both feet on the running board. She fell into the car, and as she righted herself, Kenna gasped. She was not alone.

An ironic smile twisted Fritz's face as he climbed in from the other side. "I did not know you were in such a hurry, *Fräulein*. Had I realized it, I would not have bothered to start breakfast."

Two hours later, Kenna wiped the dust and dirt from the goggles that protected her eyes, and she continued driving southward. Her unhappiness grew as the distance from Atlanta increased.

Fritz had removed the ropes from around her ankles, but had offered her no food. With obvious gusto, he had eaten a large chunk of bread with butter on it while she had gone hungry.

The gasoline can strapped to the back of the roadster was as empty as her stomach. And no blacksmith shop with its gasoline pump inside was in evidence on the muddy road.

Kenna rubbed her wrist where the ropes had chafed her skin the night before when she had struggled to get free. She stopped when she felt Fritz's eyes on her movement. Quickly she put both hands on the steering wheel and concentrated on the road ahead.

The windshield provided only partial protection against the

mud, and Kenna became spattered from the red clay slung from the wheels. Fritz drew the leather curtains around them, but it was too late to ward off the ruin of both his blue serge suit and her nurse's uniform.

"The coat. You left it behind, *Fräulein*?" the guttural voice asked as he looked at the mud-stained girl beside him.

Kenna nodded. "Yes—back at the campsite. If you remember," she said, her voice getting louder with antipathy for him, "you wouldn't let me go back to get it."

For a moment, Fritz looked puzzled. "The duster. I asked you to let me get it," Kenna explained. And the puzzlement left Fritz's face.

"Duster," he repeated and nodded.

So he hadn't understood her then. Even though he spoke English well enough, except for the thick accent, he didn't always understand the words she used. Somehow that frightened Kenna even more than if he spoke no English at all.

The muddy hill ahead looked formidable. Kenna raced the motor and got a running start. The car slipped and slid like a crab going for its slanted walk—more sideways than straight ahead. Fritz held onto the side of the car with one hand, the other on the gun at his side as the car zigged and zagged a path through the mud. Kenna was far too busy trying to stay in the ruts to reach for the gun. Fritz need have no worry about that.

Kenna had almost topped the hill when the car slipped out of the ruts, spun half a turn, and began to nose downward in the opposite direction. She pressed the brake to the floorboard but it was no use against the slithery mud. As if on a roller coaster, the car gained momentum, going downhill faster and faster, eating up the yards that had been gained. Finally, the car stopped in a ditch at the bottom of the hill.

Apprehensive, Kenna looked at the towering blond man at her side. Fear gripped her heart for the first time when she saw the intense anger on the prisoner's face.

She looked from the cold, murderous blue eyes to the mud that reached almost to the running board on her side of the car. It would take quite a long time to dig the car out of its mire.

"It wasn't my fault," Kenna started. "The hill . . ."

27

"Take off shoes," he ordered, interrupting her.

"What?"

"Shoes," he repeated, pointing to her feet. And when she was slow in obeying him, he raised his hand as if to strike her again.

Quickly, Kenna leaned down to remove her shoes. Fritz did the same, rolling high the legs of his blue trousers before stepping out of the car into the mud.

"Come," he said. "We dig."

Four

Two days later Kenna, driving along the dry, crusted roadway, glanced at the white blouse and navy-blue skirt that she was wearing. Fritz had taken them from a clothesline, along with a fresh white shirt for himself.

She hadn't wanted to wear the stolen outfit, but her nurse's uniform had been completely ruined when she and Fritz had worked to free the car from its muddy trap.

They were now living off the beneficence of the countryside—goat's milk, berries, and anything else that Fritz could scrounge without being caught. The money that Fritz had stolen before leaving Atlanta was almost gone. There was enough to buy one more tank of gasoline, if they could find it. That was all.

The gradual transformation of hills to flat land, the bleaching of color from the red earth to lighter loam and then to sandy soil told Kenna that they were now past the plateau and onto the coastal plain.

So far, Fritz didn't seem to suspect that she was not headed to Savannah at all, but farther south to Brunswick and the golden isles. The longer she could stay inland, the greater risk Fritz ran of getting caught. At least, it had seemed a good idea when she'd first thought of it. She hadn't reckoned, though, on Fritz's caution, avoiding people who might help her.

Had no one in Atlanta missed her, or wondered what had happened to her? Steppie, of course. And possibly Verbena. But no one else would care. Certainly not Miss Dacus, or Irish Fitzpatrick. They'd be glad to be rid of her. They would never initiate a search for her.

Her main chance of rescue remained with the military authorities at Fort McPherson in their hunt for the escaped prisoner. Realizing this, Kenna's spirits ebbed. Naturally they would assume that Fritz had taken the route to Savannah—and alone. So their help couldn't be counted on either. Well, she would just have to rely on herself, as she had in the past, if she wanted to escape from Fritz. There was no one else to help her.

Kenna's mind remained on her dilemma while she drove along the lonely stretch of road bordered on both sides by tall, stately pines. Suddenly, as she came to a crossroad, she spotted a rundown blacksmith shop with a small dwelling attached to it at one end, just ahead on the left.

"Stop," Fritz ordered, placing his hand on the steering wheel.

His action caused Kenna to jump and the roadster swerved to the side of the road. She glared at him but brought the car to a stop a short distance from the entrance of the yard, where an old plow horse stood under a sweet gum tree. A sign on the shop read BLACKSMITH. And underneath, in crudely printed letters, had been added GASOLINE SOLD HERE.

Pointing to the sign, Fritz said, "Gasoline. You get."

He handed Kenna the last coins in his pocket. She climbed down from the driver's seat and walked to the rear of the car, where she unstrapped the gasoline can.

This might be her opportunity to escape from him. If there were some people in the building, all Kenna had to do was to denounce Fritz as a German prisoner and let the men overpower him. Of course, Fritz still had a gun. That was the only trouble.

Seeming to sense Kenna's restlessness, Fritz got out of the car and walked close to her side. But she needed just a few seconds to get ahead of him. Making up her mind, she threw down the gasoline can and sprinted toward the partially open door.

She rushed inside, slamming the door behind her. Without waiting for her eyes to become accustomed to the change in light, she called out, "Please help me," to the figure seated near the pump. "I'm . . ."

The figure stood and Kenna stopped speaking, for she realized she was talking to a small boy, no older than six or seven

30

years. A chill traveled across her shoulders as the door behind her opened. She didn't look back, but she knew Fritz was there.

"What do you want?" the boy asked.

"S . . . some gasoline," Kenna stammered, for Fritz now stood so close to her that she could feel the concealed gun in his coat pocket. She took the gasoline can from Fritz and walked dejectedly toward the boy.

From the other door of the shed, a woman holding a baby came into sight. "What is it, Ovie?" she inquired of the boy.

"Just some people wantin' gasoline, Mama," he replied. And turning to Fritz, he asked, "How much do you want?"

Quickly, Kenna answered, "Enough to fill the car tank."

The baby began to cry and the woman, shifting the infant to a cradling position, watched the procedure with a frown on her face. She seemed to sense that something was wrong. But Kenna knew her attempt to get help had been effectively stymied. She could not bring herself to put the woman and her two children in danger.

Fritz accompanied her back and forth, until the tank had been filled and all the money was gone. With a frozen smile, Kenna bade the woman good day. Conscious of the angry, silent Fritz walking beside her, Kenna hurried to the car, cranked the engine, and began the next lap of the journey, all the while waiting for some sign of retaliation that, surprisingly, never came.

Slower and slower they traveled south into a sparsely settled area, the highway dwindling with each mile and no other road crossing its path.

All around Kenna, the landscape assumed an ethereal foreboding. Waters, black and mysterious, moss-draped oaks, and a quietness that stemmed from aeons past enveloped them.

There were no people at all—only an occasional deer crashing through the woods, or a rabbit or bird fleeing from the automobile. Alien sounds suddenly erupted on all sides and were gone almost before the ear had recorded them. And then total silence reigned again.

Kenna was lost. She had known that for the past ten miles.

But she kept going, for there was no place to turn around—merely the narrow ribbon of road taking them farther and farther into the wilderness. It was no longer a road, actually, but a trail that finally came to an end at the watery edge of earth beyond the stand of slash pines.

The roadster, sputtering through the quietness like some raucous animal sensing its entrapment, slowly sank into the green, pungent softness of ground and was still.

They had reached the dreaded swamp. They were surrounded by danger softly covered by unfathomable beauty—water lilies hiding the secrets of the waters underneath . . . Okefenokee. Now she knew where she was—too late.

She and Fritz stared at each other as a heron took flight beyond the cypress trees. Kenna knew at that moment that he was aware of her duplicity and that her value to him had ended.

Fritz tightened his hand on the gun. Kenna, sensing the movement, didn't wait to see what he would do next. She jumped from the car and began running wildly without direction. Her only purpose was to escape Fritz. And this time, she was not hampered by ropes hobbling her ankles.

A bullet sang out, breaking into the stillness of the afternoon. Kenna, stumbling on a rotten log in the soft earth, heard a whizzing noise over her head.

She plunged through the unfriendly terrain, while her mind reversed itself to the beginning of the nightmare. The fire, the encounter with Fritz in her own home. Running. She was always running. For four days the nightmare had dragged on and still showed no signs of lessening. She might try to escape from Fritz but he would find her and kill her because of what she had done. And her bones would be hidden forever in the awful majesty of the swamp.

A rustic cabin with its sagging porch leaning toward the waters was barely visible in the twilight. Camouflaged into the landscape, its weathered boards took on the dull patina of the bearded moss swaying in the slight breeze that sprang from the waterside.

Kenna crouched behind a bush and watched the cabin, while her ears listened for sounds behind her. No smoke came

32

from the clay-daubed chimney of the small house. And there was no movement in the yard surrounding it. Yet Kenna knew from stories of the swamp that someone could be watching her from almost any direction. She was in danger here, also, for no one took kindly to being spied upon in the swamp. But she had to take a chance.

"Anybody home?" she called, emerging from her shelter. "Hello!"

Vulnerable from all sides, she stood in the clearing and waited for some acknowledgment. It came sooner than she expected, but behind her.

The sound of the gun and the stinging of her right hand were almost simultaneous. Like a wounded deer startled into flight, Kenna rushed toward the cabin. Droplets of blood on the ground broadcast the direction in which she went.

But the cabin wasn't safe. Her safety, Kenna knew, lay in the dangerous swamp—away from human eyes and weapons—away from Fritz.

On the other side of the cabin, a rickety dock came into view. A small boat, tied loosely, nudged against the pilings supporting it. Kenna didn't hesitate. Down the projecting catwalk she went, the creaking sound of her footsteps matching the rubbing squeak of the boat in the swell of water.

Holding her injured hand next to her body, Kenna jumped into the boat. She untied the craft from its mooring, took up the paddle, and guided the boat through the curtain of moss that served to separate the amber waters from the verdant caulk of land.

Kenna looked down at the small but painful wound on her hand, where the skin had been torn from the flesh adjacent to her little finger. She was lucky that the bullet had done no more damage than that.

Even now, she didn't have time to tend to it properly. Despite the pressure she'd used against it, the wound kept on bleeding as she paddled, seeking to put as much distance as possible between the boat and the dock.

She would have to stop soon and attend to it, to staunch the bleeding with her petticoat. The white linen wasn't clean— not like the sterile bandages at the post hospital. But she'd worry about infection some other time.

Kenna listened for sounds that would indicate she had been spotted and followed. The only noise came from the water lapping against the boat. No voices—no shouts.

Finally, Kenna placed the oar inside the boat and allowed the craft to drift in a meandering pattern at the whim of the current. She tore a strip of petticoat to bind her wound. But before wrapping it, she dipped her hand into the water to wash off the blood.

A sudden lunge in the water made Kenna withdraw her hand. She gasped and held onto the side of the boat as the moving log hit. No—it was not a log at all—but a brown, rough, slit-eyed monster, showing its white underside with the slash of its wickedly long tail.

The boat careened, then righted itself as the alligator passed by. Kenna grabbed the oar and when the alligator turned and headed for the boat again, she was ready.

All her strength was fed into the blow across the alligator's snout. The force cracked the paddle and it flew out of her hands. Kenna had to hold onto the sides of the boat to keep from being catapulted into the water as the craft swayed, dangerously near to capsizing. She saw the oar, her only weapon, drifting out of reach and realized that she was now at the mercy of the alligator.

Unmindful of her bleeding hand, Kenna sat up and with wary gray eyes watched the water for the alligator's return. Moments passed. The only movement came from the thin ripples that widened and then disappeared in the distance.

She felt weak, whether from fright or the violent action with the paddle or the loss of blood, she didn't know. She only knew she was too tired to keep her eyes open any longer. She'd rest a little while and then decide what to do next.

Several hours later, Irish Fitzpatrick stooped and fingered the dried blood on the dock. His eyes, dark and turbulent, gazed into the water. Then fury and frustration seized him.

The rickety wooden planks absorbed the weight of his body, the stamp of his boots, as he moved quickly from the dock to the spongy earth and onto the sagging porch of the cabin.

Inside the weathered old swamp cabin sat Fritz, guarded by two other soldiers. Irish walked across the room, toward the prisoner. He reached out and grabbed Fritz by his shirt, hauling him up from the chair.

"What did you do to the girl? Where is she?"

"Not so rough, Irish," one of the soldiers cautioned. "We're responsible for him, you know."

"Escaped prisoners usually get shot while running away," Irish replied, reluctantly loosening his hold on the man. Fritz fell back into the chair while Irish continued to bait him.

"How would you like that, Fritz? To be released and given the same chance you gave the girl?"

A fearful Fritz, uneasy at the barely controlled violence in the man, looked at the other two soldiers and back to Irish. "I didn't kill her," he replied.

"Where is she then?"

"Out there—in a boat." Fritz's hand pointed in the direction of the swamp.

"God in heaven," Irish said, sick at the thought. She had about as much chance of surviving as a newly dropped foal surrounded by wolves.

"Well, guess we'd better get started," one soldier commented. "It's a long way back to Atlanta."

Irish turned abruptly to the soldier. "You can't leave until we find the girl."

The short, bespectacled soldier shifted his feet uneasily. "We have our orders," he answered, "to apprehend the prisoner and get him back to the fort as quick as possible. The major didn't say anything about looking for a girl."

Irish stared at the two soldiers and, no longer trusting himself to speak, he stormed out of the cabin and walked again down the rickety dock where the setting sun hung low over the water.

Vaguely, he heard the crank of the army motor vehicle as it left. But Irish didn't look back. Instead, he pulled a package of cigarettes from his breast pocket, lit one, and continued to gaze toward the vast wilderness of water.

All around him were the sounds of a swamp coming to life in the night. An eerie, terrified screech reverberated over the water as one animal was trapped by another.

Kenna was out there, alone and hurt, subject to the vagaries of a primeval world. And there was absolutely nothing he could do about it until morning.

Five

"Now I been livin' here in this swamp nigh on thirty years," the old man explained to Irish the next morning as they cruised down the stream where the cypress knees rose out of the water to meet the swell of the swamp buggy.

"You'd think I'd know it all like the back of my hand. But that ain't possible. Parts of it, I know well," he conceded. "But this piece of God's tremblin' earth is so big, it'd take another thirty years just to go through it. A healthy respec'. That's what you got to have," he continued his monologue, "for somethin' this size.

"Take that snake, for instance." The man pointed to the large snake wrapped around a limb ahead of them. "Ain't doin' a thing but what the good Lord put 'im on earth for. Just got to be careful, that's all—to stay out of his way."

The noise of the airplane propeller, attached to the rear of the swamp buggy to give it power, increased as the man accelerated toward the middle of the stream, away from the overhanging branches.

Deep in the recesses of the swamp, morning life stirred. Survival was the priority—a new day for the hunter and the hunted. With hungry eyes, land creatures watched each other, while in the water, large carnivorous amphibians monitored the movements of them all and waited for a chance to strike.

In the darkest dark, where no light penetrated, the small boat, caught on a projecting limb, rocked while the girl continued to sleep. And in the distance, the slight noise of the searching swamp buggy was veiled by layers of green that served as a canopy from the morning sun.

Weak from her ordeal, Kenna lay in the gently rocking

boat. Her eyes fluttered open but darkness still surrounded her. Something was wrong. It should have been morning long ago. That thought gnawed at Kenna's brain. But she soon forgot it and closed her eyes.

Off and on she slept, disturbed by the throbbing of her hand and the constant jolting of the boat. A crevice of light widened and then diminished. Kenna knew then it must be day. But somehow, it didn't seem to matter. And later, when she opened her eyes, she was covered by darkness again.

The breeze touched her skin, but gave her no relief from the burning. And her lips cried out for water, but no one heard her.

A grim-faced Irish continued his search for the second day. Nathan, guiding the swamp buggy, shook his head at the man's persistence.

There'd been no sign of the girl. Take more'n a miracle, Nathan thought, to find her now. Course, she could still be alive, no doubt about that, but she couldn't last much longer—not a city girl like that. Men, now—he'd seen men walk out of the swamp weeks after getting lost in it. But they'd had guns to protect them and get their food.

"You ready to quit for the day?" Nathan asked.

Startled, Irish looked toward the setting sun and his mind protested the waning of the daylight hours.

"One more run, Nathan. How about it?"

"Has to be a short one," the man declared, seeing the formation of rain clouds overhead. He was willing to oblige for another half hour. By that time, it would be dark and the storm was apt to hit.

Once again the cutter made its way through the waters while Nathan and Irish looked hard for some trace of the boat. Fritz had sworn she'd gotten away from him. But the blood was another matter.

Fritz could be lying. He might have killed her and pushed her into the water. Even now, Kenna's body might be wedged between the pilings of the dock. Irish shook his head. No, he mustn't think that. He had to keep looking.

The flash of lightning across the sky came a brief moment

before the clap of thunder. "Got to get off the water," Nathan warned. "That was too close for comfort."

Disheartened, Irish knew the man was right. Water drew lightning. Droplets of rain began to pelt the men while the harsh breeze brushed against the hangings of moss from the trees.

Nathan had turned and was headed back to shore when he suddenly diverted the swamp buggy to avoid a floating limb. And that was when the small boat, sheltered by the promontory, came into view.

The two men saw it at the same time. "Nathan," Irish shouted, as he pointed.

"I see it," the old man replied and slowly edged the swamp buggy through the mass of water lilies.

The boat, a casualty of the constant bumping of the tree limb against the stern, lay low in the water. At first, it looked empty. But as Irish lifted the lantern, he saw the girl inside.

"Kenna." He called her name but no response came. She lay still—oblivious to the water seeping around her, threatening to sink the boat.

Irish handed the lantern to Nathan. Balancing himself with one foot on the boat, Irish leaned over and lifted Kenna from the waterlogged craft. He brought her into the swamp buggy and held her in his arms. Anxious for some sign that she was still alive, he placed his head against her chest.

"Her heart is still beating," Irish announced with relief.

"Good," Nathan responded, glancing at the slender girl. "Close call, though. Poor little mite."

Another clap of thunder swept the wilderness of the swamp. Nathan's attention left the wounded girl and he concentrated on getting to land, while Irish continued holding Kenna in his arms and shielding her face from the sudden downpour of rain.

Nathan finally edged the swamp buggy toward the dock and held it steady long enough for Irish to remove Kenna from the boat.

Anxious to leave, Nathan then cast off, calling over his shoulder, "You'll be all right. The cabin's high enough off the ground to be safe."

39

"Will I see you again?" Irish shouted.

"Nope. Got things of my own to tend to," Nathan replied gruffly over the noise.

He moved on, remaining close to shore until the sound of the swamp buggy disappeared in the promised fury of the storm.

For Irish and Kenna, the weathered gray cabin, rising out of the swamp mist on awkward stilts, became a haven.

Far into the night the rain came down, the wind howled, and the crashes of thunder reverberated throughout the Okefenokee. Water rose and covered the dock in front of the old planked cabin, and soaked the earth surrounding it.

Inside the cabin, the fire that Irish made on the hearth snarled and hissed at the sheet of rain daring to find its way down the chimney. Kenna lay on the bed built into the wall, her hand freshly bandaged.

Her teeth chattered and Irish tucked the blanket around her to seal in the warmth. But a few minutes later, she kicked off the blanket covering her.

Gently, Irish leaned over to place it into position. Near the fire he had draped the tattered skirt and blouse and what was left of her underwear after he had used it for bandages. And so, underneath the blanket, the nude Kenna stirred and moaned in her delirium.

She was so beautiful, with her long, slender limbs, the delicate curve of her breasts—her nipples taut and pointed from the cold. Yet her very vulnerability erased his immediate desire for her. To protect her and care for her—that was all he wanted for now.

Irish sat and dozed until her movements woke him.

"No," Kenna cried. "Please don't tie my hands."

She flailed about as if she were trying to free herself. Against the wall she rolled, and before Irish could stop her, she hit her injured hand on the splintery planks. He swore when he saw fresh blood staining the bandage.

"Kenna, you must be still," he urged, taking hold of her arms. But she kept writhing and moaning.

He'd seen the same wild, delirious behavior before in one of his high-spirited horses spooked by a recurring nightmare.

And he knew the only solution lay in the calming presence of a sturdier, serener companion to allay the nightmares before the animal damaged itself further.

As if he were the calming stall mate of a nervous filly, Irish climbed onto the bed, his body serving as a buffer between the hard planked wall and the restless Kenna. His arm reached around her body and he whispered soothingly in her ear.

Kenna quieted, but her ragged, rapid breathing dispelled any thoughts he might have had of leaving her alone for long. In the dimness of the erratic light on the hearth, Irish lay, listening to the rain and the troubled murmurings of the girl beside him.

Two days passed while Irish waited for the water to recede. Most of the time he spent in caring for Kenna. He bathed her fevered body, changed the bandage on her hand, and forced her to drink a little water.

The hand needed stitches, but there was no one to do it. And so at night, when her fever was highest and her sleep more restless, Irish protected her from harm with his own body.

As he lay beside her, his desire for her grew. Damn! How wrong he was to think he could escape the spell of her closeness. It was even stronger than on that day at the fort when she had rushed by him and he had caught her in his arms.

Kenna turned toward him in her sleep and Irish reached out to touch her cheek. "Neal," she murmured. Irish stiffened and immediately withdrew his hand.

She was warm—dry—not bone-chilling, soaking cold as she had been earlier. Kenna smiled and snuggled closer to the source of her warmth.

Blackberry winter—the phrase twisted in and out of Kenna's mind like a thread winding and unwinding itself. Mother Nature was turning her back on the sun to let her consort, winter, have one last romp. She'd been so cold. But now, Kenna was warm again. It must be summer, not winter.

The girl basked securely under the cover until her nose came in contact with an alien face, studded with whiskered stubble. Alarmed, Kenna lifted her head from the pillow and stared unbelievingly at Irish Fitzpatrick. He was sleeping, stretched out next to her, as if it were of no consequence that they were sharing a bed.

Kenna's involuntary gasp went unheeded. Irish continued sleeping while Kenna's eyes swept the room, coming to rest on the fireside, where her tattered skirt and blouse lay, shriveled and wrinkled, but dry. Then her attention was drawn to her own body, exposed to the waist. Hastily, she lay back on the bed and covered herself.

Her head began to throb in rhythm to the throbbing of her hand and tears came to her eyes. Now she remembered . . . Fritz had shot her. She had fled from him in the boat. Irish must have found her and kept her alive.

"I hope you're feeling better," a voice in her ear said.

Kenna quickly closed her eyes. Barely above a whisper, her voice quivered in reply. "Yes, thank you."

Her eyes remained shut. But she knew he was watching her with those penetrating brown eyes. And she dared not meet his gaze so soon.

"Are you hungry?" he asked.

"No—thirsty."

The movement of the bed told her that Irish was getting up. Aware of her nakedness, Kenna pulled the blanket closer to her chin, as she felt his legs brush against hers.

His bare feet made little noise on the cabin floor. "Here, drink this," he ordered a few seconds later. At his command, Kenna forgot and opened her eyes.

Her lips felt parched. Greedily, she drank the water in large gulps while she held onto the blanket.

"Where is Fritz?" Kenna asked, still avoiding the brown eyes watching her.

"He's probably back in the prison compound at the fort," Irish answered. "The others took him several days ago."

"Were you the one who found me?" Kenna asked, finally unable to avoid looking at Irish, who was putting on his army trousers over his shorts.

"Yes—with Nathan's help."

"Nathan?"

"The old man who lives in the swamp."

42

Kenna, sitting up, struggled with her dizziness. When it lessened, she searched the room curiously, as if seeing it for the first time. She looked at Irish and then back to her clothing near the hearth.

"I'll have my clothes, please," she said.

He brought the skirt and blouse to her without comment, placing them at the foot of the bed.

"I'd like the rest, if you don't mind," she said.

"If you're referring to your petticoat, it was used for bandages."

Kenna's lip quivered. "Then, please leave the room so I can put on the skirt and blouse."

His eyes showed his mutiny at her request.

"It's a little late for modesty, don't you think? Besides, you're so weak, you'll probably need help."

"No. I'll manage on my own."

"You haven't so far," he reminded her.

Angry at his stubbornness, she grabbed the blouse and attempted to put it on under cover of the blanket. But she was clumsy and her bandaged hand wouldn't go through the small opening of the sleeve.

Ignoring her protest, Irish took his knife and cut the sleeve seam. Then he guided the sleeve over the bandage. "It's better not to object too soon, Kenna. You see, you need my help after all."

The girl frowned at her hand. "Well, the bandage is far too large for the wound. That's the trouble."

Irish's next words were caustic. "If you want it to look professional, then you can take care of it yourself."

The old hostility had crept into his voice and Kenna was far better able to cope with that than with his gentleness. She continued dressing, slowly buttoning the blouse with her left hand. When she had finished, she was exhausted. Her eyes closed again and she slept.

By late afternoon, Kenna was much stronger. Something to eat had made a vast difference in the way she felt. Finally, she tackled the chore of changing the dressing on her hand.

Irish watched as Kenna unwrapped the old bandage, made from strips of her petticoat. He seemed to be waiting for some reaction when she saw the angry, inflamed wound. Refusing to be dismayed at the sight, Kenna, with an air of bravado, said, "I'll be seeing much worse than this overseas—on the battlefields."

Irish stared in disbelief at the bruised and battered girl, whose skin still bore the numerous scratches of her flight from Fritz. Hadn't one German been enough for her?

"You won't be going overseas now," he snarled.

"And what will stop me?" Kenna met his angry gaze and waited for him to respond.

"First of all, your escapade with Fritz."

"I don't like your choice of words, Irish Fitzpatrick. For your information, I was held hostage—and that's hardly an escapade."

He went on as if he hadn't heard her. "And added to that—sleeping with a man—an even more damaging offense."

Again Kenna defended herself. "I didn't sleep with Fritz. He only wanted me as a driver to get him to Savannah—not as a . . . a lover."

"I wasn't speaking of Fritz."

So that she would not misunderstand what he meant, Irish took a step nearer and leaned down, his face on a level with hers. "You slept with *me*. Not for just the first night—but last night, too. How will you explain that?"

"But I was ill. Nothing happened."

"Didn't it?" he whispered, standing up. His eyes fell boldly on the curve of her breasts hidden partially by the blouse, now too small from the rain-soaked washing.

Kenna flushed at his scrutiny. She shook her head violently. "No. You couldn't . . ."

Driven by the harsh timbre of her voice, so different from the sweet, yearning tones forming another man's name in the night, Irish taunted her. "Will Neal mind that I made love to you?"

Kenna paled and a look of intense pain crossed her face. "Neal was shot down over Verdun. He's still missing."

A teardrop rolled down her cheek and landed on the fresh strip of cloth. Her hand trembled and her fingers became clumsy in their attempt to secure the bandage. Seeing Kenna

44

in such a state, Irish started to speak but changed his mind. Instead, he left her side and went to stand by the hearth.

Kenna's mind was in a whirl. Being taken hostage by Fritz would be hard enough to explain. But there was no way she could escape the censure of spending these two days alone in a deserted swamp cabin with Irish Fitzpatrick. She saw that now.

Of good moral character. Every nurse had to have a certificate stating she was above reproach. But now Irish was telling her she had lost even that.

Six

THE CONFRONTATION WITH IRISH LEFT KENNA MISERABLE. Although her body had responded to the food and rest, her unhappiness showed in her lackluster eyes. She chafed to leave the cabin, where she now felt as much a prisoner as she had ever been with Fritz.

No. She'd take that back. Irish hadn't tied her with real ropes. His were more subtle. But that was the only difference. Men were all alike—arrogant, rude, accustomed to their own way. She was still at the mercy of a man she didn't trust.

Irish had left that morning, not even telling her where he was going or when he'd be back. If she were only strong enough, Kenna vowed she'd walk out too, and get back to Atlanta on her own. She hated having to depend on Irish Fitzpatrick for everything.

The storm was gone and the sun shone down at the edge of the swamp, where puddles of water remained as tiny vestiges of those furious days. Gone too was the dock, broken apart by the buffeting wind.

Kenna sat on the sagging porch and looked down at her hand and then to her right foot. She hadn't known it was injured until she'd tried to put her weight on it as she got out of bed. The foot was discolored and slightly swollen on the outer edge. A chipped bone, probably. Yet Kenna had no idea how it had happened. The injured hand was bad enough, but at least it didn't slow her down. The foot was another matter. She held it up to check the discoloration and winced as she turned it slightly.

The noise of a vehicle lumbering into the yard ended her contemplation. A momentary panic set in when she heard men's voices. Kenna stood up, and holding onto the rotten railing of the porch, she hobbled inside the cabin and slid the bar into place to secure the door.

She listened as heavy footsteps sounded on the porch. Then someone tried to open the door.

"Kenna," Irish's exasperated voice called out. "Let me in."

Relief at hearing the familiar voice caused Kenna to forget her earlier antagonism toward Irish. She removed the wooden bar and opened the door widely. "You frightened me," she said. "Where have you been?"

"Arranging transportation out of the swamp," Irish replied. He walked to the bed and stripped it of its blanket, then took the first-aid kit from the table. "I'll be back to help you in a moment."

Her face lit up. He must have found the abandoned roadster. Quickly, she gathered the few things that she possessed—the small bit of ribbon, the stockings—her only pair.

"Are you ready to leave?"

"Yes—oh, yes," she answered with such eagerness that Irish paused to stare at her. Not waiting for Irish to reach her, Kenna lurched toward the door. But he caught her up and, lifting her, carried her onto the porch. From the distance, Kenna saw two men who waited with a covered wagon and horses.

Irish horse traders. She recognized them from their trappings and the gypsy wagon painted white, with its wheels in rainbow colors, and bright curtains shielding the window openings.

"Didn't you find the car?" Kenna asked, frowning.

"No," he replied. "It was either washed into the swamp or someone salvaged it. But my people have come to help. You'll ride back to Atlanta in the wagon they've provided."

Kenna looked toward the wagon and then back to Irish. His people? Then Irish Fitzpatrick must be a horse trader, too.

Kenna pursed her lips and pointed to the vehicle with a disdainful finger. "You expect me to ride all the way back to Atlanta in . . . *that*?"

"How else can you get there without being seen?"

"What do you mean?"

"Since only two other people—Fritz and Nathan—can swear for sure that you were ever in this swamp, we might be able to keep your reputation intact. Just do as I say and get into the wagon without creating a fuss."

He whisked her past the two men, hiding her face as he did so, and then hoisted her into the back of the wagon. "There're some fresh clothes for you," he said, pointing to the skirt and blouse folded on top of the small chest. "Put them on."

His imperious manner went unnoticed, for Kenna was too busy registering his words in her mind. Did Irish intend to help her to get back into Atlanta undetected? The night before, he'd made her lose all hope in preserving her reputation. But was it possible, as he intimated, that he could spirit her to Atlanta without anyone's finding out that she'd been held hostage by Fritz and forced to travel with him? Or that she'd spent three days alone in the swamp cabin with Irish himself?

Kenna smiled. Yes, it might be possible. All she had to do was stay out of sight. And what better way to ensure anonymity than to travel in a gypsy wagon?

Why was Irish doing this for her? Had he had a change of heart? Yes, that must be it. He was now sorry for his actions.

But what excuse could she give for having been away an entire week? Kenna bit her lip in concentration as she changed her wrinkled clothes for the fresh ones while the wagon moved out of the swamp.

In the small hand mirror, Kenna gazed at herself in the gypsy outfit with the red scarf hiding her pale tresses. The mirror held other images, other times, when an excited teen-aged girl had stood on a street corner and watched the horse traders ride through the streets of Atlanta—arrogant men on their finest stallions—and inside the covered wagons, their women, hidden from public view, as she was at this very moment. A strange sense of excitement seized her.

They traveled on while Kenna remained concealed in the back of the wagon. Almost an hour later, she heard laughter and greetings and the neigh of horses. She didn't look out. But Kenna knew they had now joined the gypsy caravan. It didn't matter that Irish was the driver of the wagon in which she rode. She was safe from him and his lovemaking as long as they traveled with the group.

All afternoon, Kenna, determined to give the man no trouble, sat inside the wagon. But by the time they finally stopped for the night, her patience had worn thin and her sense of adventure dulled. She felt as if she had been jolted apart, piece by piece.

Eagerly she waited for Irish to come and put the wooden block in place so she could climb to the ground. But instead, he went to join the others, leaving her alone and stranded.

It wasn't fair. She'd been riding in the vehicle all day. She'd had no exercise and little to eat.

The aroma of food cooking, the laughter of the women pierced the early twilight. Then the music started—a slow, rhythmic tune, haunting and strangely poignant, gathering in speed with the sound of clapping filling the air. They were probably dancing, too.

Seething at his cavalier treatment of her, Kenna recounted to herself all of Irish's shortcomings. And she added another one. If he had deserted her, then she would climb out of the wagon by herself, despite her injured hand and foot. Just as she pushed back the curtains to assess the distance to the ground, the man that she was inwardly railing against appeared before her with a plate of food in his hand.

"Here, Kenna. I've brought you something to eat."

Like a petulant child, she spurned his offer. "I don't want it."

Sensing her anger, Irish stared closely at the girl and asked, "What *do* you want, Kenna?"

"To get out of this wagon," she replied instantly. "I want to feel the grass under my feet and listen to the music."

"Do you think that's wise—to be seen by so many other people?"

"Gypsies aren't *other people*," she replied. "I mean— they . . . you . . . well, they're different," she finished lamely.

"You mean—you think your secret is safe with us?"

"I don't know what I mean. I only know I'm tired of being

49

cramped all day, like a chicken in a coop. Couldn't I just go to the edge of the campfire and watch?''

As if he were debating with himself, Irish remained quiet, while the anxious gray eyes stared at him.

"I suppose there'd be no harm in it," he conceded, "if you wore something to cover your face."

She lifted her head. "Like an Eastern woman in a harem?" she said, her voice tinged with sarcasm.

"If you wish to think of it that way," he replied. "You'd be far safer if no other man saw your face."

"Well, what shall I use? The scarf from my hair?"

"That won't be necessary, Kenna. If you're determined to get out of the wagon, there's a lace mantilla in the small chest. Put it on and I'll come back for you when I dispose of this plate."

He disappeared and Kenna turned toward the chest. If she could leave the wagon only by wearing the mantilla, then she was reconciled. She rummaged through the drawers in the small chest and found it in the last one, where it lay carefully wrapped in white tissue. Kenna shook the wrinkles from the lace and surveyed the material. It was quite pretty, actually, and appeared to have been handmade. She placed it over her hair and let it fall in concealing folds about her face.

The lace hid the bruise and softened the scratches made in her flight from Fritz. Yet there was something about the mantilla that bothered her. It seemed to be an heirloom—old lace beautifully mellowed with age—something to be used for a special religious occasion.

The Irish horse traders were Catholic, that much she knew. Kenna, brought up in the Presbyterian faith, fleetingly wondered if the horse traders' saints would be upset at her for using the headpiece, not to light a candle in a church, but to listen to the music coming from a gypsy campfire.

"You're ready?" Irish's voice cut through her reverie. How long had he been standing there, watching her? Hastily, she nodded, and he reached up to help her to the ground. His hands lingered for a moment about her waist before he released her. Slowly, she made her way toward the campfire and, stopping just outside the circle, she watched in awe.

Her response to the slow, rhythmic music was immediate.

Her body, unconsciously, began to sway. As if in hypnotic response to some dormant past, she was caught up in the circle of the campfire, her mind, her eyes feeling and seeing beyond the colorful skirts, the gold coins, the long, dark tresses of the women as they moved in sensuous time to the pagan music.

The tune grew softer and the gypsy circle opened toward Kenna and Irish where they waited at the edge of the campfire. An old man, evidently head of the clan, moved forward and said something that Kenna couldn't understand. He looked at her with keen eyes, almost as if he could see beyond the veil, and Kenna stepped closer to Irish as the man motioned for them to come.

"Would you like to dance in the circle, Kenna?" Irish's voice, next to her ear, held a tenderness she'd never heard before.

Forgotten were the sore foot, the injured hand. "Yes," Kenna whispered, a wistfulness hidden by the delicate lace shadowing her face.

Irish laughed and, sweeping Kenna off her feet, carried her to the circle that had opened for them. Again, using words that the silver-haired girl found incomprehensible, the old man laid his hands, first on Kenna and then on Irish. She looked toward Irish to find out what was happening, but his expression gave her no clue.

Slowly the music began again, and Kenna became a part of the circle, her arms grasped gingerly on her right by Irish, and on the left by a gypsy woman. Round and round the fire, the circle moved.

The melody stopped and Irish led Kenna to the edge of the campfire, where their plates, filled with wild delicacies from the surrounding area, were waiting for them. The gypsies left them alone now, to let them eat their meal together. The aroma of rabbit, roasted on spits over an open fire; the tender green shoots of the pokeweed, blanched and flavored with a strange spicy herb; blackberries mixed with honey, and loaves of fresh bread tantalized and teased the palate with an awareness sharpened by the evening air.

Kenna tore apart a small piece of bread and popped the morsels into her mouth. Next came the blackberries, juicy

51

and sweet. Then Kenna, looking down at her plate, recognized the poisonous pokeweed plant and her appetite vanished. True, only the root was harmful, not the leaves, but the realization of where she was and what she had done punctured the magic of the evening. Her hand began to throb and she became conscious of the ache in her foot.

Irish ate heartily, stopping every few bites to glance quizzically at Kenna, who nervously fingered the lace mantilla, which she had pushed back from her face.

"I thought you were hungry," Irish scolded, seeing her plate still heaped with food.

"Not any more," she replied. "I'm tired." And standing up, Kenna added, "I think I'll go to the wagon now."

"Wait a minute and I'll get a lantern to light the way."

Kenna glanced behind her, in the area where the wagon rested for the night. Pitch black. She'd never be able to find her way by herself. She sat down again—and waited. Her impatience didn't seem to register with Irish, for he took his time in finishing eating.

Finally he stood, and with the plates in his hand, he went back toward the fire site. When he returned, he carried a lantern with him. Kenna's limp seemed magnified in the stillness of the wooded area, and to keep from stumbling, she clung to Irish's arm. They reached the wagon and Irish hung the lantern on a peg jutting from the side of the vehicle.

"Good night, Irish," Kenna said and waited for the man to help her.

"Good night, Kenna," he replied. "Sleep well." He leaned over and kissed the top of her head, as if she were a sleepy child being tucked into bed, before lifting her into the back of the wagon.

With the curtains pushed back, Kenna watched the man disappear into the darkness. The lantern, giving a soft glow, still hung on the side of the wagon. When she removed the lace mantilla from her head, it caught the soft glimmer of light.

Now she was Kenna Chalmers again—no longer a pagan gypsy girl caught in the haunting music of the past.

What had possessed her to behave in such a manner, joining in the ritualistic dance? It must have been the lace—from the moment she'd put it on, it had cast a spell over her.

She shook her hair to rid herself of the feel of the mantilla. But it remained, as if it had become a living part of her. That was silly, Kenna thought. It was a mere bit of lace, used to hide her face, and then put back into the chest. Nothing more.

Kenna curled up on the feather mattress. She was content—for she had the wagon to herself. Irish wouldn't dare bother her, with his people surrounding them. And with that thought, Kenna went to sleep.

The next morning, they started out early. The horses, allowed to pasture during the night, were once again hitched to the wagon. Powerful work animals, they pulled the wagon along with seemingly little effort. But several times during the morning, they stopped to rest. Today, Irish's wagon was at the head of the procession, with the others following a short distance away.

The constant swaying of the vehicle made Kenna drowsy. When Irish pushed back the curtains, he saw the sleeping girl curled up on the mattress. With a smile he returned his attention to the horses and the journey ahead.

Reaching a fork in the road, Irish pulled to the right and waited for the other wagons to pass to the left. In silent salute, he bade good-bye and then turned the wagon, holding the sleeping girl, toward Atlanta.

By the time Irish stopped to make camp, it was getting dark. He looked again into the back of the wagon, and saw that Kenna was still asleep. Not disturbing her, he unhitched the horses and led them to a grassy knoll.

Slowly, the inside of the wagon came into focus as Kenna awoke. But the wagon was still and all around her was silence. Disoriented and not certain of the time of day, she sat up and crawled to the brightly colored curtains. Pushing them aside, she looked out at the sun sinking to the west. Where were the rest of the wagons? And why was it so silent?

"Irish," she called. "Irish." Her voice rose in the stillness and was answered by the moanful call of a bird in the distance.

Had Irish played some trick on her—abandoning her while she slept? "Irish," she called, a touch of fear in her voice.

"I'm here, Kenna," the man answered, and with a relieved cry, she jumped from the wagon and fell into his arms.

"I thought you'd left me," she cried.

He didn't answer but held her closely, giving her time to get over her fright. Finally she lifted her head to look at him and inquired, "Where are the others?"

"On their way to the summer pastures."

"They're not going with us?"

"No."

"We're alone?"

"It looks that way," he said, his brown eyes showing amusement.

Kenna's face mirrored her disappointment but she said nothing. It was her own surmise that the gypsy wagons were going all the way to Atlanta. Irish had made no such promise.

The smell of food cooking in the open air reminded Kenna of how little she'd eaten. She sniffed the air, breathing in the aroma. And her wariness at being alone with Irish was temporarily forgotten.

She sat on a rock and sipped the hot cocoa while Irish finished cooking. She made no offer to help, for it looked as if he wanted no interference.

Later, when Irish handed her the plate of eggs and beans, he suddenly inquired, "Did Fritz cook—or did you?"

Setting down the mug of cocoa to take the plate, she answered, "Fritz cooked. *I* drove the car."

Irish laughed at her answer. "How did you get so far off course?"

"To Savannah, you mean?"

The man nodded.

"It was deliberate. I knew that was where he wanted to go, so I stayed inland just to thwart him. And I thought someone would stop us before we got far."

"And Fritz didn't suspect you were going the wrong way, until you landed in the swamp?"

"It was hard to tell *what* Fritz thought. We had a . . . a language barrier. *Ja*—a language barrier," she repeated, speaking the last in a guttural tone.

Irish laughed at her mimicking. Then his tone sobered. "But you took a terrible chance landing in such a desolate place as the Okefenokee."

"I didn't mean to," Kenna admitted. "I got lost." She looked down at her hand and her soberness matched his.

"Is there a chance that Neal is still alive?"

Irish's abrupt change of subject startled her. She gazed at him a moment before answering. "He *has* to be. And that's why I'm going to France—to look for him."

"You must love him very much."

"Yes—very much," she whispered, the pain and loss apparent in her large gray eyes.

Irish stood up and busied himself with the fire, banking the embers. The camaraderie was shattered. And his actions puzzled her. First, his interrogation concerning Fritz. And then his questions about Neal. She could understand his reaction to Fritz—but not to Neal. It was as if he resented her love for her brother.

Irish picked up the lantern and went to check on the horses while Kenna sat alone. She followed the movement of light until Irish disappeared. Then she listened to the sounds around her in the dark. The supper was over. And the old wariness returned. This was the moment she'd dreaded—the time for bed. Would Irish sleep beside the campfire and let her have the wagon? He'd given no indication where he would sleep, and until she knew, Kenna made up her mind to sit by the campfire.

The pinpoint of light grew brighter. Irish had finished with the horses.

"Come, Kenna. It's time for bed."

"I'm—not sleepy."

"That doesn't matter. You need to get out of the night air."

"Are you going to sleep in the wagon?" she blurted out.

"Yes."

"Then I'll sleep here by the fire."

"The fire's out," Irish reminded her.

"Can't we light it again?"

"No. It's too dangerous."

"Then I'll stay here without a fire," Kenna said.

"Why are you afraid? Do you think I'll make love to you again, now that we're alone?"

"Yes."

"If I wanted you," Irish said, "you couldn't stop me. It wouldn't matter whether you slept in one corner of the wagon or here on the ground."

"Leave me alone, Irish Fitzpatrick." Kenna's voice pierced the night air. "And you can have your filthy gypsy wagon to yourself."

He turned without a word and left a dejected Kenna hiding her face in her hands.

"Here—you'll need this." Irish was back, thrusting the familiar blanket toward her. "And I suggest that you get a stick to ward off the wolves during the night."

Kenna raised her head. "You're just trying to scare me."

"Am I?" Irish sauntered back to the wagon. And Kenna, drawing the blanket around her shoulders, became alert to every noise in the night.

The only light came from the stars overhead and the small crescent of moon. For Irish had blown out the lantern. And no embers glowed at her feet.

Dimly, Kenna traced the outline of the wagon in the darkness. It stood against the sky on higher ground, while Kenna remained below, with the wind flapping at her back and pulling at the blanket draped around her.

With longing, Kenna remembered the soft feather mattress inside the gypsy wagon. But she could do without it. She wasn't about to share it with Irish Fitzpatrick. He'd done enough to her already.

Kenna frowned and tried to remember those days in the cabin. She had no recollection of his making love to her. Wouldn't she remember? Wouldn't her body feel different?

She knew he'd removed her wet clothes and hung them by the fire to dry. But she didn't remember that either—only her humiliation when she first awoke and realized she had on nothing underneath the blanket. Yet, deep down in her heart, she knew he'd had to do it. He'd been a nurse—just as she was—tending to a sick body. Nothing more.

Kenna jumped as a crackling noise sounded near her. Her eyes narrowed and she strained to see what had made the noise. She gripped the large stick at her side and waited. Gradually, though, she loosened her hold on the stick when the noise subsided.

Too nervous to go to sleep, the girl moved and tried to find a more comfortable position on the large rock. But a lizard slid past her and Kenna quickly got to her feet. There was no telling how many other creatures had also chosen the shelter of the rock for the night.

Undecided where to go, she stood in the middle of the campsite and looked around her. Eyes—yellow and gleaming—were watching her. How long had they been there? Kenna's heart began beating so rapidly that she could hear her pulse in her ears. She stood, mesmerized by the eyes. And when a howl came from the same direction, Kenna threw down the stick and ran for safety.

The block was still in place—and so, into the back of the wagon she climbed trying not to awaken Irish. She couldn't stay outside with wild animals surrounding her. And Irish had no right to expect it of her . . . to choose the safety of the wagon and leave her to mortal danger.

Kenna congratulated herself on her stealth in climbing into the vehicle without awakening Irish. But as she settled down in a corner with the blanket around her, a voice shattered her illusions.

"You stayed out longer than I thought you would."

Furious, Kenna ignored his remark. For a long time she sat upright, poised for flight in case Irish should make some move toward her. But he remained where he was and only when Kenna heard his slow, steady breathing did she relax and go to sleep also.

Seven

THEY TRAVELED NORTH ALL DAY, STOPPING AT INTERVALS TO
let the horses rest. Occasionally, when no one was about,
Kenna sat up front with Irish in the open seat.

The man puzzled her. Kenna found it hard to reconcile the
severe military captain on his white horse with the gypsy
around the campfire. Once when his attention was on the
horses, she turned her head and openly stared at him.

His patrician profile resembled the head on a Bellini me-
dallion—a Roman conqueror, with coloring to match—dark,
lustrous hair cut in military fashion, his skin a pale bronze
from the southern sun.

But today, he was dressed as a gypsy in a white shirt, open
at the neck, with a gold chain visible when he leaned over,
and black pants, cut differently from the ones she was accustomed to seeing.

He caught her staring, but Kenna wasn't dismayed. "Why
aren't you in uniform?" she asked.

"I'm on leave," Irish replied.

Kenna frowned. That meant only one thing. Pershing's regulars were scheduled to move out.

"How much longer do you have?"

"Four more days."

So he'd wasted almost all his leave on her.

"I'm sorry," she murmured in a dejected voice.

Irish's golden brown eyes studied her face. "Sorry? Why?
That I have a few more days of freedom?"

"No. You know what I mean. That you've wasted so much
time on me."

"Oh, I don't call the time a complete waste," he said, a
sudden harshness to his voice. "It's had its benefits. And the

58

trip isn't over yet. There're still some compensations to claim.''

It sounded like a warning and Kenna became uneasy. She disliked being so close to Irish, but then, she disliked riding alone in the back of the wagon even more.

Trying to take her mind off the dwindling day and the night to come, Kenna turned her eyes to the landscape. The lush green of the trees and grass along the roadside was in stark contrast with the mud and dirt of the road. But she had other things to worry about.

Scarcely noting the beauty of the mimosa trees with their pink blossoms scattered like exquisite carpets woven of finest crushed velvet, and the wild purple larkspur raising their tall heads from the clumps of grass, Kenna decided to climb back inside the wagon.

On and on the horses plodded and it grew dark. Baffled that they had not already camped for the night, Kenna looked out from behind the curtains. ''Irish, when are we going to stop?'' Her head ached from the rough pace and she longed to get something to eat.

''Get back inside, Kenna, and stay,'' Irish ordered.

She did as she was told, for a carriage was approaching from the opposite direction. With nothing else to do, she closed her eyes and listened. The carriage passed by. She could hear the horses' hoofs on the road—and then, a hypnotic quietness.

The clock in the tower struck eight as Irish guided the horses through city streets. To the left, past a gilded opera house he went, and proceeded down an avenue lined with oaks. In the distance, a brown brick mansion sat—majestic and seemingly deserted, its two-storied cupola towering into the sky.

The horses, as if aware that their day's journey was ending, snorted with impatience when Irish jumped down to open the large double gates. No lights greeted the gypsy wagon as it slowly drove past the house and on toward the back. Irish looked around in the blackness and, satisfied that no one had seen him enter the private grounds, he brought the horses to a stop before the barn.

He frowned at the squeaking barn door that sounded far louder than it should have in the evening quiet. With his hand on the lead horse, he guided the animals into the barn, and only when he'd shut the door behind him did he light the lantern.

"You can get out now." Irish's voice alerted Kenna that they had stopped. She sat up and rubbed her eyes.

His strong hand reached out to help her from the wagon and Kenna, looking around the enclosed barn, asked, "Where are we?"

"In Macon," Irish replied.

"Is this where we're going to spend the night?" Kenna asked.

"Not here in the barn," Irish said, a glint of amusement in his eyes. "We'll have the comfort of a good bed tonight. Come, Kenna, but please keep quiet when I open the door."

With unsteady steps like a sailor long at sea, she followed him from the barn, down a path grown up with weeds and wild Cherokee roses, and toward the back entrance of a house.

She had no idea what time it was. They had traveled much longer than usual, and judging from the darkness surrounding them, the people in the house had already gone to bed. Even in the blackness of the night, Kenna could tell that it was an elegant house—a mansion. Her thoughts turned toward a nice warm bath, food, and the rest of the night spent in luxurious comfort instead of the back of the gypsy wagon.

Kenna's reverie was sharply interrupted as Irish forced the lock on the door. "You can't *do* this," Kenna protested.

"Don't make so much noise," Irish admonished. In a matter of seconds, he pushed Kenna inside. "I'll be back in a few minutes—after I've tended to the horses. Find a place to sit down and wait for me."

He took the lantern with him and Kenna, watching him disappear toward the barn, peered out the glass of the back door until the light was swallowed up. Perturbed by his behavior and being left alone in the dark, Kenna fumed and with her good hand held out to keep from bumping into the wall, she edged her way along the hallway that ran the length of the house. She stumbled into an object that overturned and made a terrible clatter in the emptiness—an umbrella stand, judging by the feel of it. Leaning over, Kenna righted it and continued her search for a place to sit and wait for Irish. In an open doorway she finally stopped and strained to see inside the room. All around her loomed pieces of furniture shrouded like the dead—in white sheets.

Something was wrong. The house was deserted and had been closed for a long time. She could tell by the air, the feeling that pervaded her senses.

Knowledge, filed away in the back of her brain, flooded Kenna's mind. She remembered stories she'd heard from childhood about the gypsies—how they'd spend the night in fine, elegant houses when the owners were away. She'd thought that Irish was different. But now, she realized he was no more civilized than any of the others. He had broken into the house. And he expected her to be an accomplice in his crime.

Well, she wouldn't do it. As much as she longed for a bath, a real bed, she wouldn't spend the night in the house. And she'd tell him so when he returned. Kenna found a divan and sat down to wait for Irish. Too agitated to remain still for long, she jumped up and retraced her steps to the back door. Down the overgrown path toward the barn she went, careful of thorns that tugged at her skirt. She'd make Irish understand that she couldn't possibly stay in someone's house—uninvited.

A tinge of guilt reminded her that she'd done just that in the swamp cabin. But that was different. No one cared. No one claimed the cabin, and it had held nothing of value, except shelter from the wind and rain.

But here. There was no telling when the owners might come back. If they did, they certainly wouldn't find her camped inside, like a gypsy.

Her breath was jarred from her body as she bumped into Irish in the dark. "What are you doing out here? Didn't I tell you to stay inside?" His voice, low and irritable, lashed out at Kenna.

"I'm not staying in that house," Kenna replied when her breath returned. "No matter what you say."

"You prefer the filthy gypsy wagon?" he asked.

61

So he'd remembered her disparaging remark the night before.

"Yes, it's preferable to being an uninvited guest elsewhere."

Irish's hand on her arm stopped Kenna's flight.

"Does a formal invitation mean that much to you?"

Kenna shook his hand from her arm. She took only one step before the iron grip closed around her arm again.

"Then you'll have to wait a long time before you're given permission to stay in the wagon."

"What do you mean? Are you saying I can't sleep there?"

"Exactly."

"Then I'll sleep in the barn with the horses."

"I've gone to a great deal of trouble to get to this place by nighttime, Kenna. And if you don't hush and come into the house quietly, I won't be responsible for anything that happens. As for myself, I don't care how many people know what's going on. *You're* the one who's anxious to keep your escapade a secret."

She had nowhere else to go—no one else to rely on except Irish Fitzpatrick. Dejectedly, she went along with him back into the brown brick mansion.

Later by candlelight, the blond-haired girl stripped off the gypsy skirt and blouse and climbed into the claw-footed tub filled with warm water. It was glorious to smell the softly perfumed soap, to feel the soothing water against her skin. She forgot her trepidation as she squeezed the giant sponge and dribbled water over her shoulder.

Her solitude was soon interrupted by a knock at the door. "Do you need any help?" a male voice inquired.

"No. Go away," Kenna replied, and froze until she heard his footsteps diminish. Awkwardly, with her bandaged hand held in the air to escape the water, Kenna climbed out of the tub and grabbed the towel to dry herself.

The old-fashioned nightgown draped across the chair reminded Kenna that she had no clothes of her own. From the time she'd left Atlanta with Fritz, she'd been forced to accept every stitch of clothing from either the German or Irish Fitzpatrick. First the skirt and blouse purloined from the clothesline, then the gypsy skirt and now this nightgown. And for some strange reason, Kenna felt guilty in donning the delicate white lawn gown with its panel of blue ribbon about the neck. She glanced at the soiled, unkempt clothes at her feet. Then she shrugged and struggled into the gown.

Her hair was still damp and it curled in tiny tendrils about her face. Impatiently, Kenna pushed a wayward lock behind her ears and sank her teeth into the bread and ham before her.

Trying not to feel self-conscious, she quickly laid the sandwich on the Wedgwood plate and grabbed at the gown as it slipped off one shoulder.

Irish, sitting across the table, smiled at her actions. She resembled a small, hungry urchin, with her large gray eyes taking up a major part of her well-scrubbed face. Lost in the gown that dragged at her feet, she sat with her toes curled against the chair rung, hungrily devouring the food he'd managed for their evening meal.

He hadn't intended getting involved with her, but her disappearance had worried him. And finding her nursing cape in the rubble of the fire along Boulevard had prodded him into action. He couldn't accept the possibility that she might have died in the fire. Luckily, he had launched an investigation of his own.

Kenna felt Irish's disturbing, penetrating eyes on her and she looked up. "Why did you go back to the house on Boulevard?" he demanded.

"To save Neal's letters from the fire," she replied, unaware of the effect her answer had on the man.

His eyes narrowed, but his voice casually inquired, "Were you successful?"

"I managed to save one, but even that one was lost," she answered.

Irish nodded. "On Ponce de Leon."

"What?"

"I found an envelope addressed to you—on Ponce de Leon Avenue. It must have been one of your precious letters."

Kenna's face became animated and her eyes showed her delight. "Do you still have it?"

"Yes."

"Then you'll give it to me of course."

Her eagerness for the other man's letter rankled him. "For a price," he said.

His eyes raked over her, and Kenna became more self-conscious than ever in the gown. "How . . . much?" she asked, a wariness now apparent in her voice.

"How much is it worth to you?"

"That's not fair, Irish," Kenna retorted. "You *know* how much it's worth to me, but I could never afford that amount of money."

"I wasn't speaking of money."

His meaning was clear, and embarrassment flooded the girl's delicate, fine-boned features. Determined to have the letter at any cost, Kenna clenched her teeth together and said, "Name your price."

"You know what it is. There's no need to spell it out for you."

Kenna stared at Irish and tried not to show her dismay. Forcing herself to speak calmly she said, "You have the envelope with you?"

"It's in the wagon. I'll get it now."

Irish, with his jaw set in anger, left the kitchen and walked to the barn to retrieve the envelope.

Did this Neal Wexford mean so much to Kenna Chalmers that she would sacrifice herself for the return of a few words written by him? Irish had hoped that he was wrong, but Kenna's reaction had made it far too clear. She was willing to do anything to gain possession of the letter.

If that were the case, then he would make sure that she paid for its return.

Kenna, waiting in the kitchen, had no inkling of Irish's thoughts or his misunderstanding concerning her half brother's name. She was far too busy deciding what to do when Irish returned. Plans darted in and out of her mind, were examined and then discarded. She was in a bad situation, she knew, but before she had latched upon a plan, Irish was back with the envelope in his hand.

Kenna stood and reached out for it, but Irish blocked her efforts to retrieve it. "Not so fast," he said, holding it high. "You haven't bought it yet."

"You expect payment first? You're going to make me . . . ?" Kenna swallowed and stopped.

64

Irish watched her. "Finish the sentence, Kenna."

In a small voice, Kenna said, "You expect me to . . . sleep with you?"

Irish's wicked smile reinforced her opinion of the man. "Is that what you're willing to pay—to get the letter back?" Irish countered.

"I'd rather sleep with a . . . a *pig*," she said heatedly. "But you're the one who named the price; I had nothing to do with it."

"Didn't you?"

He took her by the arm and propelled her toward the stairs that led to the bedroom on the second foor. Reluctantly, Kenna walked with him.

The crystal knob on the newel post captured the light as they passed by, with the facets reflecting the prism colors of yellow and blue. Paid for— The house was free from debt and the crystal knob stood as a symbol to proclaim it to all who understood its meaning.

But her letter, unlike the house, still demanded payment. Kenna glanced toward the man at her side and she grew angry. Irish should have given her the letter freely. But he hadn't. And there was no way she could snatch it from him as they climbed the stairs. She was much too busy trying to stop the long gown from tripping her and sending her headlong down the stairs.

Irish pushed open the dark mahogany door to the first bedroom beyond the stairs, and set the brass candleholder on the nightstand. Massive posts of burled walnut trimmed in black ebony gave boundary to the bed, its white silk cover cascading to the floor on each side.

"May I see the letter now?" Kenna asked. "To . . . to make sure it's Neal's."

Irish held the remains of the envelope out to her. Mud-stained and faded, it nevertheless showed the familiar handwriting. With Neal lost somewhere in Europe, and their house reduced to a pile of ash and rubble, this was her last link to her half brother—her last connection to her own past. Eagerly, Kenna seized the envelope and opened it, but it was empty. In alarm she turned to Irish.

"Where is the letter?" she demanded.

"You have it in your hands," he replied.

"No. It's just the envelope. There's nothing inside."

"That's all I found," Irish said with a shrug.

Realizing that the letter had been lost and she had sold herself for an empty envelope, Kenna ran from the room and raced down the hallway toward the bathroom.

"Kenna," his voice called behind her, but she kept going until she had gained entrance to the white marbled bath. Breathlessly, she pushed the door closed and, letting the envelope drop to her feet, Kenna groped for the key and locked the door.

In the darkness she leaned her head against the door and listened for an angry Irish Fitzpatrick.

His footsteps, loud, floor-shaking, proclaimed his anger. And the wood of the door between them absorbed his rage. She jumped back until her flight was stopped by the large claw-footed tub. There she hovered while she listened to the destruction of the lock that held the door closed. The splintering wood became a deafening roar in her ears and Kenna trembled.

"No," she screamed and kicked as his large, possessive hands found her, lifted her and carried her down the hall toward the bedroom, where the candle from the brass holder flickered its small flame over the white silk cover of the burled walnut bed.

"I hate you, Irish Fitzpatrick," she snarled. "You tricked me."

"I only promised you an envelope," he answered as he lowered her onto the coverlet. Kenna cried out and struggled harder against the man who imprisoned her in his arms.

"You bartered for it, Kenna Chalmers," Irish reminded her. "One night of lovemaking for the return of the envelope. And you're going to pay for it."

Kenna, turning her head from side to side, avoided his lips for a moment, until his hands caught her face.

"Be still," he ordered, and his lips captured hers.

Kenna kept her teeth clenched, her lips taut. But Irish appeared not to notice or be in any hurry. In a teasing manner, he brushed his lips against her cheek, and kissed her eyelids—softly, tenderly—his movements belying his harsh words, his steel strength that immobilized her body underneath his.

Kenna remained rigid while his hands sought the shape of her body. The nightgown, far too large, slipped from her shoulder as it had at the supper table. But this time, Irish pushed the material farther downward until his hand came in contact with her breast.

The feel of his hand against the soft round flesh began a tantalizing exploration that brought a moan from Kenna's lips. As new sensations poured through her body, her struggles slowed. And when Irish's lips brushed against hers again, she parted her once rigid lips, now soft and sensual, to meet his.

"Kenna," he whispered against her mouth.

Her hand moved toward his face, and her fingers traced the outline of his ear before moving to the nape of his neck. He shuddered at her touch, and she found herself trembling in response.

Kenna's gray eyes flew open and met his—deep, dark pools of desire—infectious—encompassing. The envelope lay on the floor unnoticed, the cause of their struggle forgotten in the heat of their desire. Kenna forgot her injured hand, until she pressed it against the white shirt above her. Sudden pain caused her to wince. And Irish, now attuned to the least movement of the girl's body, reacted.

He sat up on the side of the bed, his hand running distractedly through his dark hair. Her cry of pain had brought him to his senses. She had already suffered enough. Kenna, unexpectedly free from his imprisonment, hastily drew up the gown to cover her shoulders.

Irish's eyes found the envelope on the floor and, reaching down, he picked it up. Breathing rapidly, he handed it to Kenna.

"Consider your debt paid," he announced and stormed from the room.

In the hours that followed, the lone candle beside the burled walnut bed burned low, sputtered, and then went out. Kenna, exhausted and troubled, murmured in her sleep, her good hand still holding onto the empty envelope, while in the adjoining bedroom, Irish Fitzpatrick slept—in the bed made especially for the master of the house.

Eight

THE SUNLIGHT, COMING THROUGH THE SAME WINDOW THAT
had framed the silver of the moon the evening before,
touched Kenna's face. She brushed her hand across her eyes
in protest. But her body came painfully awake.

Her hand was stiff, aching, and hot. Not wishing to face
her discomfort too soon, Kenna remained still for another
minute. Then she sat up.

The envelope—or what was left of it— lay on the floor
beside her, a reminder of what had occurred during the night.

Kenna's heart began to beat rapidly as she thought of Irish.
How could she face him? Making sure he was nowhere in
sight, she tiptoed down the hallway to the bathroom. She
pushed a small chair against the broken door to keep it
closed.

As she began to wash her face, she looked in the mirror
and saw the two bright spots of color on her cheeks. And she
was conscious of the throb in her hand. Again, she gazed into
the mirror. Her eyes—unusually bright, feverish—stared
back at her.

Still dressed in the long white nightgown, Kenna left the
bathroom and walked down the hallway to the room where
she had spent the night. She quietly removed the gown and
once again put on the gypsy skirt and blouse and placed the
envelope in the skirt pocket.

Curiosity now beckoned her. Down the steps Kenna went,
her eyes taking in her elegant surroundings—the family por-
traits scattered along the length of the picture gallery—the
deep, red velvet draperies blocking out the sun from the fan-
shaped window at the head of the stairs.

In the sitting room, Kenna lifted a dust sheet to survey the furniture underneath. Dulled from a lack of wax and polish, the wood nevertheless showed its aristocratic heritage. And the upholstered pieces of damask and silk were remarkably well preserved, despite the harshness of the southern sun. Such a beautiful elegant house. Yet there was an air of sadness about it, as if, at one time, a great loss had occurred and the pain still not healed.

Kenna thought of the loss of her own house, the furniture now gone, ruined by the fire; the walls crumbling before her eyes. She had wanted to keep everything perfect for Neal's return. How would he react when she told him their home had been destroyed?

A bittersweet smile passed her lips as she thought of the owners of the house where she now stood. Would they be upset to find traces of its having been occupied in their absence? And what would they say about the smashed lock?

Deep in thought, Kenna was not aware that she was being observed.

"You've finished in the bath?" Irish inquired.

Startled, Kenna stepped back and put her hand over the pocket where the envelope rested.

"Yes, thank you," she replied.

Not knowing whether he had changed his mind from the night before, Kenna, poised for flight, began to edge back from the doorway.

Her action caused him to scowl. "Don't be so skittish, Kenna. I'm not interested in you this morning—only in shaving and taking a bath."

He whirled from the doorway and left Kenna staring after him. A guilty feeling came over her for monopolizing the bath. But her hand had slowed her down in getting dressed. To make amends, she went to the kitchen and began to prepare breakfast.

The black iron stove was already hot, its heating coils having provided the hot water for her bath. Fresh milk and five hen's eggs sat on the small table. Kenna didn't question their presence, or think too much as to how they got there. She found a skillet and cracked the eggs in them, placed in the oven the leftover bread brought from the wagon the past evening, and poured two glasses of fresh milk and set them at each place at the table. When she heard footsteps coming down the stairs, Kenna scrambled the eggs and put them in a large plate.

Surprised to see her, Irish sat down and began to eat. He didn't bother to make conversation. His concentration seemed to be centered on the food, which he ate wordlessly. The silence stretched from the beginning to the end of the meal and Kenna was hesitant to break it.

Finally Irish said, "We have a long day ahead of us, and I'd like to leave as soon as possible. You have everything together?"

"There isn't much to put together," Kenna replied. "I'll be ready as soon as I wash the dishes."

He stood up. "Take your things to the wagon. I'll clean the kitchen." When she hesitated, he went on, "Your hand has given enough trouble already. Do as I say, so you won't slow us down any further."

"All right, Irish," she managed to reply. Taking a few steps toward the door, she turned. "How long do you think it will be before we get to Atlanta?"

"By tomorrow afternoon, if all goes well. That will make you happy, will it not?"

"Yes." Kenna disappeared, leaving Irish alone in the kitchen.

The girl reached up and touched her flushed cheeks. She realized that the infection from her hand was spreading. But she also realized that there was little she could do about it, beyond keeping it clean and bandaged. Even if she saw a doctor, he would tell her the same; for there were no miracle cures to stop the infection. With the change of clothes in her hand, Kenna limped to the barn and deposited the articles in the small chest inside the wagon.

For the rest of the day, Kenna stayed in the back of the wagon and dozed fitfully between the times Irish stopped to let the horses rest and graze. She gave him no trouble. When they stopped for the night in a small grove next to the road, she made no protest.

As she faced Irish over the banked campfire that night, Kenna was still worried about whether she would succeed in getting back to Atlanta unobserved. "You think it's going to work?" she finally asked.

Irish laid his fork on the plate and his attention turned to the girl. "I won't stop at the fort," he explained. "And I'll see to it that no one notices you, including Miss Dacus." He took up the fork and began eating again.

Irish Fitzpatrick was distant, formal, and he acted as if he would be glad to get rid of her. And Kenna, lethargic from the fever, was content to be ignored. When she'd finished eating, Kenna climbed into the wagon and settled in one corner for the night. Now that she was to leave it soon, the gypsy wagon assumed a strangely familiar feel—almost as if she belonged in it.

All the next day they traveled, from early morning into the middle of the afternoon. A rumbling of thunder and a sheet of gray streaks proclaimed rain to the east of them. But in traveling north, they avoided it, and by the middle of the afternoon, the gypsy wagon finally reached the edge of the city.

It was time now for Kenna to change clothes. She struggled out of the gypsy skirt and blouse provided by Irish, and in their place, she put on the more subdued and civilized portion of her meager wardrobe—the white blouse and the dark blue skirt.

From the south the wagon rolled into a wounded Atlanta. The air still carried a lingering remnant of acrid, smoldering, cottonlike odor, combined with wisps of smoke hovering over black holes where houses had once stood—open hells fed by the supplies of coal left over from the winter.

Irish was aware of the devastation of the city by the fire; for in his search for Kenna, he had personally examined the swath the fire had made, sweeping clear houses and churches along an area five blocks wide and several miles long. It had been a terrible sight, out of control, until its flames finally had been subdued at the old Civil War trenches dug to withstand Sherman's fiery advance—the trenches an appropriate epitaph, Irish thought, for a second holocaust almost as damaging to Atlanta as the first. On that day of his inspection, over a week ago, Irish had been aware of the irony. Little more than fifty years had passed and once again, North and South

71

would be fighting—not against each other, but side by side in the rainy, rat-infested trenches dug in French soil, to withstand the onslaught of an imperial German army.

In a matter of hours, he was due to move out, leaving the girl he'd gone to such great lengths to find.

Irish pulled into a deserted alleyway not far from the trolley. With his deep brown eyes, he surveyed his surroundings. A pedestrian curiously glanced at the gypsy wagon and the sweating horses, and then walked on.

Inside the wagon, away from prying eyes, Kenna, with an unsteady hand, held the small mirror and brushed at her silver-blond hair now free of the confining scarf.

It was time to leave the wagon and the man who had rescued her from the swamp and brought her this far. Kenna's feelings at that moment were ambivalent toward him. She didn't know whether to think of him as her savior or her seducer. Yet she had no memory of being loved by Irish Fitzpatrick.

The curtain was pulled aside widely enough for Irish to enter the wagon. Unable to stand, he doubled his large frame into a sitting position and waited for Kenna to finish brushing her hair. She had tucked the left sleeve of her blouse into the top of the bandage to hide the ugly streaks already spreading up her arm. The dark skirt, dull and wrinkled, concealed her slender limbs. Self-conscious at his gaze, Kenna reached up to the top button of the blouse to make sure it was fastened. And with her action she remembered the touch of Irish's hands the day she had come out of her delirium.

"Don't forget your trolley fare," Irish said, lifting some coins from the top of the small chest and giving them to Kenna. His hand closed on hers, and then, slowly relinquishing it, he broke the physical contact between them.

Her large, feverish eyes stared at him. She tried to keep her lips from trembling as she finally managed to say, "Thank you, Irish."

He acknowledged her thanks with a brusque nod, then left his position in the back of the wagon to stand guard until the way was clear in the street.

"You can come out now." He held his hand for her.

Kenna climbed out of the wagon and, resisting an urge to glance back, limped down the alleyway.

Irish watched her go until she had disappeared into the street beyond. She was brave—reckless—stubborn—and all those qualities made him angry. She was ill and had tried to keep it from him. But it was impossible, with the spots on her cheeks, the large, limpid gray eyes broadcasting her battle with infection.

He should have driven straight into the fort and delivered her to the post hospital. But that would have called too much attention to her. No, it was better for her if she could manage to get there by herself. Then no one would ever suspect where she'd been or with whom.

Oblivious to everything around her, Kenna walked down the street toward the trolley barn. Her mind was absorbed with the problem of how to get back to the fort and explain her disappearance from class with a minimum of words that would indict her. She was not worried about the past few days, but about what was to happen in the next hour when she met Miss Dacus face to face.

She walked another block, avoiding the dirt piled high on either side of the street. Then she was in sight of the trolley barn.

The car for Fort McPherson sat idle on the tracks at the end of the line along with two others. Kenna glanced toward the building and then climbed into the empty trolley to wait for the driver. She knew fifteen minutes was the usual length of time to wait. As the moments ticked away, Kenna's heart kept time, each heartbeat, each movement of the pulse in her throat exaggerated in the stillness of the empty car.

Kenna laid her head against the seat and closed her eyes. She had no excuse for her long absence, except the truth. But if she told the truth to Miss Dacus, that would mean her secret trip from the swamp would have been for naught.

The squeal of the car on the tracks and the sudden jolt of her neck startled Kenna. Her eyes flew open and she saw that the driver had taken his place at the wheel. With the clack of metal against metal, the trolley rounded the loop and gathered speed as it began its route toward Fort McPherson and beyond.

Once again the trolley stopped two blocks from the gates to the fort. And once again, Kenna climbed down and stood on the street.

She was not in uniform; she looked disreputable. She knew the guard wouldn't let her pass through the gates without identification. But she could get through the same way as before, and not have to worry about Irish stopping her either.

Close to the hedge she went and squeezed between it and the spiked fence. This time it would be harder to climb over because of her injuries. But she could do it. She'd just have to take more care.

The small opening was no longer there. Blocking her way was a fresh portion of fence—higher, insurmountable—and Kenna, seeing it, backed away. The only thing she could do now was to walk the extra two blocks, identify herself to the guard, and hope for someone to come to the gates to vouch for her.

Nine

THE GUARD WATCHED KENNA CHALMERS COMING TOWARD
him. Still covered with scratches, a bruise on her temple disappearing into her silvery hair, and the bandage hiding her
right hand, she walked the distance to the gates with a slight
limp.

Impassive at first, the guard's face registered contempt for
the shabbily dressed girl as she drew nearer. A she-cat, he
thought, probably injured in a fight and now trying to cause
some man a lot of trouble.

"You can't come onto the grounds without a pass," he
informed her, blocking her way.

The hostility in his voice struck her and she stepped back,
as if she had received a blow.

"I wish to see Captain Davin Grant of the post hospital,"
she said. "Will you please send a runner for him?"

The guard's head turned in surprise at the mention of
Davin's name. "Is he expecting you?"

Kenna shook her head. "Just . . . just tell him that Kenna
wants to see him."

Still wary, he examined her afresh and then reluctantly
went inside the guard box, while Kenna was left standing
outside.

Now that she was back at the fort, she was nervous—for
she knew she faced another type of danger. Would she be
accepted, or would she be sent on her way—in disgrace?

While she waited, Kenna's mind turned to the prison compound across the street. Was Fritz even now watching her
return? Unable to resist looking, she searched for some sign
of the white-clad man. But the exercise yard was deserted.
Seeing the barren soil behind the barbed wire fence, she felt a

certain relief. Naturally at this time of day, Fritz would be with the work detail in the boiler room. Or would he? Perhaps they had reassigned him, now that he had already made one bid for freedom. She hoped she would never have to face him again.

Thirsty now, with the afternoon sun beating down on her unprotected head, Kenna searched for some respite from the heat. But there was no shade, and so Kenna shifted her weight from one foot to the other and wiped the perspiration from her forehead.

After what seemed an interminable time, she heard the motor of a vehicle. The sound grew louder, and with vast relief, Kenna saw a car stop. The familiar figure of Davin Grant climbed out and walked toward the guard.

Suddenly shy, Kenna watched as the guard pointed his finger at her. "Davin?" The name slipped from her lips and the sound hung over the still air while Davin stared at the girl before him.

Incredulity marked his blue eyes at the sight of Kenna. Recognizing the voice more than the shabby figure, he strode quickly to her side.

"Kenna," he said, "Kenna— Thank God you're alive."

His look changed like lightning, as he assumed the studied awareness of a doctor assessing a patient. "You've been hurt," he said, drawing her toward him. He rushed her past the guard and helped her into the military car.

"It's all right," he said to the guard. "She's our missing student nurse."

The guard's eyebrows rose in surprise. "But they're having a mem . . ."

With a flick of his hand, Davin shut off the rest of the man's protest. Realizing he'd said something the captain wished to keep quiet, the guard saluted and went back to his post.

The car started up and Kenna, turning to David, asked, "What was the guard saying to you?"

Davin took his time in replying. He stammered and groped for words. Finally he answered, "From the evidence, Kenna, the authorities assumed . . ." Once more he paused. And

76

then in a rush, the words tumbled out. "They assumed you had died in the blast that destroyed your house."

The delicate flush on Kenna's face grew even deeper as she absorbed the words.

"What happened, Kenna? Where have you been for the last ten days?" Davin demanded.

"I . . . I went to the house. You were right about that. But I got out just in time."

"Then . . ."

"A German prisoner was in the house, Davin, and he forced me to drive him toward the coast in Neal's car."

Davin groaned at her confession. "You know, Kenna, if that story gets out, there's absolutely nothing I can do to help you remain a nurse. How many people know this?"

"The man who brought me back to Atlanta—and Fritz, of course."

"Do you think he'll talk?"

"Fritz, you mean?"

"No. The man who helped you."

"I don't think so."

Davin brought the vehicle to a stop in front of the post chapel. Suddenly he leaned toward her. "You don't remember what happened, Kenna. You've wandered about in a daze ever since the fire. Say nothing about the other," he warned.

He climbed out of the car and walked to the passenger side to help Kenna.

"Where are we going?" she asked, taking his hand.

"To your memorial service."

"What?"

"They're having a memorial service for you at this very moment. I was summoned to the gate right in the middle of the eulogy."

"But I'm not dead. Davin, you see, I'm alive." Kenna began to laugh, hysterically and shrilly.

"Stop it, Kenna—at once." Davin's voice, usually so kind and gentle, now held a cold, firm demand, as his hand tightened on her arm.

She clamped her hand over her mouth to stop the laughter.

Quickly Davin led her inside the chapel, where Miss Dacus stood behind the lectern. Her words floated over the hushed assembly.

"She was a fine girl, talented in the ways of healing, with a feeling of empathy for her suffering fellow man." The matronly voice went on. "We will sorely miss Kenna Chalmers."

There was a sob in the audience and the delicate use of a handkerchief as one mourner blew her nose.

At that moment, Davin urged Kenna down the aisle, his hand under her elbow for support. Kenna shook her head at his actions and whispered, "No, Davin," but he forced her toward the altar.

Miss Dacus's voice in the nave of the chapel halted in midsentence; eyes turned from every pew to see what had caused her to stop speaking.

Davin spoke loudly. "As you can see, Kenna Chalmers is alive. By a miracle, she survived the blast and the ensuing fire. There seems to be no need to continue the memorial to her."

As the nurses recognized Kenna in the aisle, an excited murmur arose and grew to an uproar. And the memorial service for Kenna Chalmers disintegrated before Miss Dacus's eyes. She closed the book on her notes and took her seat in the tall, ministerial chair in stunned silence while the celebration of Kenna's return commenced.

Scarcely heard in the excited murmur filling the chapel was the chaplain's voice. "Praise the Lord. She that was lost is found again . . ."

Steppie pushed her way to Kenna's side. With tears streaming down her cheeks, the dark-haired girl reached out and touched her arm. "Oh, Kenna, I'm so happy. I prayed and prayed that you'd show up . . ."

Steppie was jostled aside by another, who impertinently inquired, "Where have you been all this time, Kenna?"

She was given no time to answer one question before another was asked. But the closeness and heat compounded Kenna's exhaustion. She swayed and Davin, seeing it, separated the girl from her well-wishers. He half-carried her to his waiting car and hurried toward the hospital.

The emotional encounter, coming on top of everything else, was too much for the girl. All her energy had been directed toward reaching the fort. Now the deed was done. And her body, with its raging infection, refused to be subjected any longer to her will. The past ten days were now exacting their toll.

No one but Davin Grant and the nurse on duty went in and out of the infirmary room in which Kenna had been placed. And standing guard outside her room so no one would disturb her was Miss Dacus, who had suddenly assumed the role of protector for one of her own.

"If that girl can survive a dynamite blast, then she has the mettle to be a nurse. Captain Grant, you'll just have to pull her through. I can't afford to lose such a good student."

The septicemia from the wound had taken hold, and it was apparent that Kenna Chalmers was extremely ill. The painful Dakin-Carrel method of irrigating wounds with the chlorine solution became the treatment of choice for her hand, and the blood poisoning threatening to damage her entire system was combated by transfusions of fresh, whole blood, diluting the effects of the bacteria.

Kenna became the main topic of conversation throughout the fort—the girl who had defied death in the dynamite blast and subsequent fire, and had wandered about, injured and dazed, before finally finding her way back to the fort. She became an object of intense interest, and soldiers who'd never seen her before took up a vigil in front of the nurses' infirmary to hear some word of her condition.

News of the girl and her illness filtered to the stockade, where Fritz, his freedom curtailed, was making plans for another escape. Yet he was uneasy. If the girl should die, he would be held responsible by the giant of a man who'd threatened to shoot him at the cabin in the swamp.

But unknown to either Fritz or Kenna, Irish Fitzpatrick had moved out and even now was on his way with the first wave of American officers across the ocean to France.

On June 28, 1917, Captain Irish Fitzpatrick stood on the dock at Saint-Nazaire with his fellow officers and watched the raw American recruits file from the British transports.

Some of the men still carried the rounds of cheese and bread rationed to them by the British army. On and on they came—fourteen thousand in all—filling the dock area, spilling over into the adjoining streets and threatening to burst the town at its boundaries like some overripe persimmon.

Sprinkled with only an occasional regular, the majority of the soldiers resembled schoolboys on their way to a Saturday afternoon picnic.

"Let me at one o' them Heinies," a baby-faced rookie drawled as he swaggered onto land.

"Just one?" a young voice rasped behind him. "Hell, I hear there're more'n a hundred apiece out in them trenches."

A laugh echoed down the line. "Just so's I get a crack at 'em," the first soldier replied.

Then, seeing the military delegation waiting, the soldiers quieted and proceeded in a more orderly fashion.

Irish, overhearing their juvenile banter, knew that the rookies would get their wish all too soon—for on that very day, the British army had lost three thousand of its best men.

That night the hillsides were covered with tents. Every available inch of land was used; thousands of French chickens were purchased to feed the throngs of rookies who waited to be shipped to Soulacourt for lessons in trench warfare.

General Pershing was adamant. His doughboys would not be fed into the fighting lines until they were ready.

While the recruits concerned themselves with filling their stomachs and finding a place to sleep, a group of officers sat in a briefing room and listened to their commander.

"Gentlemen, this morning our destination was Soulacourt," Pershing began. "Tonight, it's been changed to Paris."

The officer sitting next to Irish Fitzpatrick leaned forward as the general spoke. There was no murmur of surprise throughout the group. They waited quietly for the slow, painful, punctuated speech to continue.

"You're aware, I'm sure, that the French have fought this war for thirty-two long and bloody months—and their morale is at a low ebb.

"The doughboys are their salvation. But while you and I

know that it will be some time before they're ready to fight, we *must* make them visible to the French people.

"By direct request from President Poincaré, our soldiers will parade down the Place des Invalides on July 4.

"Gentlemen, please see that our men, at least, know how to march well."

The officers stood as the general left the room. And at his disappearance, the noise began.

Aghast at the change, the captain next to Irish complained, "What will the French do when they see this 'great American army' straggling through their streets? They're such rookies, most of them don't even know how to *hold* a gun—much less use one."

Irish, knowing his fellow officer spoke the truth, replied, "They'll probably weep, Reuben—for they'll be remembering their own sons marching off to war." Irish's somber tones gave way to a lighter note. "But at least the general has given us six days to whip them into shape."

"Six days," Reuben repeated. "What can be done in six days?"

"Ask the Lord, Reuben. That's all the time he had to make the world," Irish reminded him.

"But *he* didn't have the army red tape to contend with," Reuben Gresham answered and stalked out of the briefing room.

For eight hours a day, the soldiers marched, holding the Springfield rifles that few knew how to fire. The men had enlisted in the regular army the moment war was declared and were shipped overseas immediately as the first small segment of the million troops Pershing had requested from the Secretary of War.

"All right, you sorry sons of a Missouri mule," Sergeant Natt Bowen barked, aware of Captain Irish Fitzpatrick's critical supervision a few yards away. "If one of you starts off on the wrong foot this time, I'll personally boot you out of the parade all the way to Berlin."

His voice rose in a crescendo, and the two rookies, Privates Eb Jordan and Seton Campbell, trembled at the vibration.

With eyes straight ahead, and their minds on their feet, they began their drill anew.

Everywhere they turned, Irish Fitzpatrick seemed to have his eye on them. Singled out because of their awkwardness, Eb and Seton drilled even longer than the other rookies.

"Damn gypsy," the freckle-faced Seton muttered to Eb as they wearily trudged to the mess line on the second evening. "He's got more eyes on him than a potato."

"Yeah, and half of 'em are in the back of his head," Eb agreed.

"Something else eerie about him, too," Seton continued. "You notice how he makes that big white horse come to him without uttering a word?"

"The horse, you mean?" Eb asked, suddenly grinning.

"No, idiot. I don't expect the *horse* to talk. I meant Captain Fitzpatrick."

"Oh."

The days passed and on July 4, the battalion of young Americans stood in the courtyard of the Invalides and waited for the parade to begin.

Irish Fitzpatrick, realizing the importance of the day, rode his horse up and down the line, searching for anything that might mar the looks or precision of his company. And he wasn't long in finding it. He rode back to the sergeant and, pointing to the soldier directly in front of Seton Campbell, he said, "See to that soldier, Sergeant," and then rode on.

The sergeant's critical gaze landed on the culprit that had aroused the captain's ire. He walked directly in front of him and began in his Sunday-best voice, "Suck in your stomach, Private." Then his voice began to grow in strength. "We're gonna pay a little visit to Lafayette. AND WE AIN'T GOIN' TO HAVE NO BEER BARREL SPOILIN' THE VISIT."

The man self-consciously pulled in his stomach as his face turned red to match his ears. But no one looked in his direction.

When the sergeant had passed by, Eb, relieved not to have been singled out himself, whispered, "Who's Lafayette?"

Seton, pretending shock, passed the question to the man on his right. "Hey, Professor, tell this ignoramus who Lafayette is."

The tall, thin man answered softly, "He was a French marquis who came to the aid of George Washington and the Continental army during the Revolution. And because of this, all of his lineal descendants are American citizens, by act of Congress."

The blare of the French trumpeters cut off the explanation and signaled the beginning of the parade. They moved out, company by company, with General Pershing at its head.

And behind him, at the head of one of the hastily formed companies, rode Irish Fitzpatrick on his white horse, Godrin.

"Damn gypsy," Eb repeated, still smarting from the captain's harsh criticism of their platoon for the past six days.

Wave after wave of sturdy young men, dressed in campaign hats and form-fitting khaki uniforms, marched forth, some to the martial music of their own brass bands. All along the way, they were greeted with the words "*Vive les sammis.*" Long live the sons of Uncle Sam.

Somehow it didn't seem to matter that the troops didn't keep perfect step, or that the French generals regarded with horror their lack of preparedness, their lack of ships and war materials and even rifles to arm themselves against the enemy. All that was momentarily forgotten in the mounting enthusiasm of the crowd.

To the French people, the tall, long-boned Americans were an answer to the prayers and candles lit in every church and cathedral. And Irish, on his magnificent white stallion, could have been St. George coming to do battle with the dragon.

A woman, dressed in black, stepped out from the crowd and in the brief time when the parade had slowed, hung a garland of flowers on Irish's horse. That was the beginning. Soon, each rider, each foot soldier, including Eb and Seton and the Professor, was covered with flowers and garlands. Cries of hope and tears engulfed the moving army before the five-mile hike through the streets of Paris came to an end at Picpus cemetery.

French President Poincaré, and Marshals Joffre and Foch stood with Pershing in the cemetery on that memorable day of July 4, 1917, and faced the silent tomb of the Marquis de Lafayette. Farther back, in front of his company, stood Captain Irish Fitzpatrick.

On that afternoon that marked the one hundred and forty-first year of America's freedom, the very air demanded a voice—something to break the silence of the years—something to seal the reciprocal bond between Lafayette and America. For now, the French soil, drenched with the blood of its own sons, cried out in need.

The American general—more soldier than orator—realized what was expected. Just as Moses spoke to the children of Israel through his brother Aaron, General Pershing turned to his fellow officer, Captain Stanton, to pronounce the words that would make the deed immortal.

Eb and Seton, far back in the crowd, strained to see and hear as the subordinate stepped forward.

"*Nous voilà, Lafayette.*"

"What did he say, Professor?"

The tall, thin soldier once again became the translator. "He said, 'Lafayette, we are here.'"

Irish, with the other officers, turned and frowned at the slight disturbance in the ranks, but the men could not be contained. The simple words Stanton uttered echoed and re-echoed through the lines of troops. And they became the battle cry, the call to arms for young men from every hamlet, every town in America who heard them.

The ceremony ended. The men—fourteen thousand strong—marched back to the Caserne de Reuilly. That night, with few sights of Paris seen, Eb and Seton and the others under Irish's command were packed into trains headed for Lorraine, the training ground for trench warfare. And Paris, left behind, waited expectantly for these *sammis* to help turn the tide against the enemy.

Ten

"HEY, SWEETHEART, HOW 'BOUT A LITTLE *TÊTE À TÊTE*?" A wounded soldier called from one of the ward beds as Kenna passed by.

"She don't have none of that," another voice cut in. "Only calomel and castor oil."

His comment was greeted with guffaws up and down the ward. Kenna, dressed in her starched uniform, concealed a smile at the banter and proceeded to the next bed, where she handed the medicine cup to a redheaded boy.

"Thank you, ma'am," the boy said shyly. He picked up the glass of water and with a shaky hand held it to his lips and gulped down the tablets.

Throughout the ward at Fort McPherson, Kenna moved, her gray eyes showing a concern for the wounded and sick soldiers recently shipped home from Europe.

She was well. The bruise at her temple had long since disappeared and she no longer limped. If it were not for the small scar on her hand to remind her, Kenna would have denied that anything unusual had happened. Even now, she wasn't too sure of what had actually taken place and what Irish Fitzpatrick had fabricated. But whatever had happened, she considered it a small miracle that Miss Dacus's attitude had changed so dramatically toward her.

The girl glanced down at her watch. She was due to go off duty in fifteen minutes. That would give her barely enough time to dress before the party. Kenna began to tidy the trays on the trolley, and when that was done, she went back into the ward to check on Corporal Hunt.

Walking behind the screen that separated his bed from the others, Kenna saw that he was asleep. Rapid, shallow breathing and a bluish tinge to his lips made the girl uneasy. She placed her hand on his wrist and felt for his pulse. It was fast and weak. Alarmed, Kenna left his bedside to call for help.

"Captain Grant," she called urgently to the man bent over a chart at the desk. When he looked up, the wrinkles across his brow gave way to a more pleasant demeanor.

"Yes, Miss Chalmers?"

"Corporal Hunt, sir. I think you'd better see him."

Davin Grant scraped his chair in his haste to rise. With his long legs making short work of the corridor, he reached the ward in a minimum of time. Kenna, hard put to keep up with him, trailed behind.

Kenna watched as Grant laid his stethoscope against the boy's chest. Then, frowning, he lifted the boy's eyelid. The pupil of his eye did not react to the light. With a sudden mild blow to his chest, Davin Grant began to pummel and massage, the rhythm steadily paced, even.

"Get the oxygen."

Davin's order contained a quiet insistence and Kenna flew to obey him. She'd seen it before—the fibrillation of a heart muscle gone awry—the erratic flutter of a heart unable to supply oxygen to the body's tissues.

Seeing her frantic sprint to the oxygen machine hanging on the wall, the head nurse came to Kenna's aid. "Corporal Hunt," Kenna managed to say, indicating the bed at the end of the ward.

Together the two women carried the tank containing the lifegiving oxygen, and within seconds, had the mask in place over the boy's face.

While the machine fed oxygen to the soldier, Davin Grant continued the slow, methodical heart massage. And then the doctor stopped. Kenna saw the soldier's chest begin to rise and fall of its own volition. He was alive—and breathing.

Unable to hide the relief she felt, Kenna gave a sigh and her smile encompassed Davin Grant and the head nurse. A few minutes later, when an oxygen tent had been put over the bed and the head nurse had returned to her other duties, Davin spoke.

"Aren't you off duty now, Miss Chalmers?"

"Off duty?" she repeated, all time having ceased to matter

with the soldier's life at stake. Kenna glanced down at her watch and in surprise, she answered, "Yes. I was supposed to go off duty half an hour ago."

"Then you'd better be on your way."

At her uncertainty, Davin continued, "I think we have everything under control. And we'll see that Corporal Hunt doesn't get into further trouble." His light teasing tone relieved the tense atmosphere surrounding the screened-off bed.

Kenna relaxed. "Good night, Captain Grant."

"Have a good time at the party," he answered.

"Aren't you coming too?" she asked, turning back to him.

"A little later, perhaps. You'll save a dance for me?"

"Of course."

Kenna rushed from the hospital, and in the darkness, she found her way to the nurses' quarters, a short distance away. When she walked inside, the lobby was empty except for a tall, slender officer pacing up and down, his impatience showing in the slapping of his gloves against his thigh as he moved. Kenna's shoes made no noise when she crossed the floor to him.

"I'm sorry I'm late," she apologized.

He turned and his hazel eyes took in the less than perfect uniform, the slightly windblown look of her hair. She wasn't even dressed for the party.

His annoyance at being kept waiting was evident in his voice. "You're not ready, I see. Perhaps I should come back for you later."

Kenna bristled. The man acted as if she had done an unpardonable thing in keeping him waiting. "Perhaps you'd rather go on to the party without me." The mildly rebuking tone caused the man to narrow his eyes and look closer at the girl before him.

She was acting as if she didn't really care whether she went with him or not—something no other girl had ever done. Suddenly, Kenna Chalmers interested him more than ever.

His imperious manner melted immediately. "No, Kenna. I'll wait."

"If you like," she answered and swept past him.

Carlton Torey sat in the high-backed chair, his military bearing apparent. What would his mother say if she knew he was waiting to take a nurse to a party? Well, what she didn't know . . . The girl was the most beautiful female he'd ever seen—far outstripping any of the others. A pity that she wasn't of the same social class as he; nurses never were. He might even marry her, otherwise.

He remembered the day he'd first seen her—when the infantry had moved out and the fort had become a base hospital, with command of the post transferred to Colonel Bratton, the ranking medical officer. She had sat on that hot, dry day with the other nurses, her face shaded by leaves of the trees, her silvery blond hair half hidden under the nurse's cap. But he would never forget the chameleon quality of her eyes, reflecting the emerald tones of the grassy knoll, and then changing to mirror the blue of the sky as she watched a bird fly overhead.

Carlton picked at a piece of lint on his breeches and then lifted his right boot to check the shine. It was not entirely to his satisfaction. But he'd have the boy trained before long to polish them to his standards.

"I'm ready, Major Torey."

He jumped to his feet. The girl stood before him, transformed from the nurse coming off duty to an immaculately dressed, ethereal creature. His critical eyes leisurely assessed her. The dress, a favorite from her season as a debutante, had an oriental effect, with delicate pink beaded material catching the sheen of the overhanging light. On the sleeves and hem, a myriad of oriental flowers—white, pink, and black, were embroidered in place. And surrounding her waist, two deep pink ribbons, trimmed with minute oriental bells, hung. They flowed down the length of her skirt to end in a flower basket of gold, from which the lush ribbons cascaded.

Carlton looked at the slim, swanlike throat. It, too, was perfection, enhanced by a gold ribbon collar with the same small oriental bells attached at intervals.

Masking his satisfaction—for it wouldn't do to compliment her too much—he held out his arm for her and they departed for the party.

But on the way, Carlton's mind was busy. If he actually married the girl, his mother would have to accept her as his wife. It might be a shock to her, at first, but she'd soon get over it. And she might even find it amusing to take the girl and mold her, in his absence, into the kind of wife that he required.

The first thing he'd make certain Kenna learned—to glance down in a more demure manner rather than meet his gaze as if she were a man's equal.

They walked into the officers' mess and the party to honor the post commander seemed suspended at their arrival—almost as if a wand had been waved over the crowd, making it impossible for anyone to move. Then, with a break in the magic, people returned to their conversations, their dancing. But Carlton Torey, observing the electric effect that Kenna had upon others, made up his mind. She would become his wife.

Later, as Kenna waited for Carlton to bring refreshments to her, a girl's voice whispered happily in her ear. "You look so beautiful tonight, Kenna. What did Major Torey say about your dress?"

Kenna looked at her friend Steppie. "He didn't say a word."

"What? Why, everybody else at the party is absolutely raving about it. What's the matter with him?"

Kenna made a face. "He was miffed to be kept waiting. I was late getting back from the hospital."

"Well, surely *he*, of all people, should understand."

"He's . . . different," Kenna commented. "Haven't you noticed it, Steppie? He's a fine surgeon, no doubt, but so impersonal with the patients. He doesn't seem to have the same heart that Davin has."

"Maybe it hurts too much to show what he feels. I know there're some men like that. At least, that's what Cousin Cricket told me once."

Kenna laughed at Steppie's attempt to placate her. "Maybe he just doesn't find me attractive. Have you thought of that?"

"No—never that. Every man who sees you falls in love with you."

"You're exaggerating, Steppie."

"I'm not," she defended. "Just name one man who hasn't fallen at your feet."

"Irish Fitzpatrick."

The name came too quickly and surprise registered in Kenna's eyes at her blunder. She'd tried to forget him. But here she was, bringing his name into their conversation.

"Well, he doesn't count, Kenna."

"And why not?"

Her attitude puzzled Steppie. "I'd think after he did such a terrible thing to you . . ."

Kenna didn't wait for Steppie to finish. "What are you talking about?" she demanded.

"Blocking your way with his horse. He certainly was no gentleman. Or had you forgotten?"

Intense relief flooded Kenna. For a moment, she had wondered if she had talked while she was ill.

"Gossiping?" Carlton Torey's smooth voice inquired as he handed Kenna the cup of punch.

"Of course," Kenna replied sweetly. "Weren't your ears burning?"

Vaguely pleased at her retort, Carlton Torey took the chair beside her, but hastened to stand when Steppie Hannon was claimed by a fellow officer.

Kenna and Carlton danced, but the girl's mind was on Irish Fitzpatrick. In fact, her mind had never been able to erase the memory of those days spent with him in the swamp cabin and later in the gypsy wagon. Even the reluctant night spent in the mansion in Macon refused to budge from her memory. And regardless of all her efforts, she could not dislodge from her mind his wicked grin, his demand for payment in return for the ragged, faded envelope from Neal—nor the unceremonious way he had dumped her from the gypsy wagon, like some unwanted cargo that he'd been glad to get rid of in a back alley.

As far as she knew, he hadn't even bothered to inquire whether she'd gotten back to the fort safely or not. He'd moved out with the rest of his military company and forgotten her very existence. But whether she wanted to admit it or not, she couldn't rid her mind of him. That was why she'd accepted Major Carlton Torey's attentions—in an effort to forget Irish Fitzpatrick.

Caught off guard by the major's eyes staring at her, Kenna quickly smiled at him. And Carlton, misreading her action, tightened his hand against her back in a possessive manner. He'd speak to her soon—but in a better setting than the officers' mess with other people around them.

His attention was diverted when he saw Captain Davin Grant walking into the mess. He'd taken a dislike to the fellow almost from the moment he'd met him, for the man pampered his patients far too much. Carlton felt that it was better for a doctor not to become too involved with the personal problems of his patients. It wasn't medically necessary.

Oblivious to the slightly hostile demeanor of Major Torey, Davin Grant claimed Kenna for the next dance. "You look lovely, Kenna."

"Thank you, Dr. Grant." Kenna broke into a smile. "You recognize the dress, of course?"

"Of course. You wore it the night I escorted you to Grace's coming-out party."

The easy flowing conversation between the two rankled Carlton Torey as he stood on the sidelines and watched. Let the man enjoy his dance with the girl. For it would be the last one he'd ever have with Kenna Chalmers.

The Sunday afternoon began pleasantly, the sky punctuated by an occasional white floating cloud, lazily skimming by to disappear into an expanse of blue. Dressed in a white lawn afternoon dress with an umbrella to match, Kenna waited for Carlton outside the nurses' quarters.

The letter from the Red Cross had not been encouraging. Neal's name graced no new list of war prisoners or convalescent hospitals or sanitoriums. There was no record of him anywhere. Kenna had now exhausted all sources of locating him. All except one—looking for him herself among the small villages sprinkled throughout the war area. She chafed at having to bide her time until her nurse's training was completed and she was assigned to duty overseas.

That afternoon, with Steppie and Davin both on duty, she had elected to leave the fort, even if it meant having to suffer the attentions of Major Carlton Torey, who somehow always managed to have the weekends off.

His car appeared and Kenna, with the picnic basket on her

arm, climbed in so they could begin the trip that would take them to Piedmont Park.

Up and down the streets Kenna saw other cars carrying other soldiers—convalescent patients out for a Sunday afternoon ride, being chauffeured by townspeople who wanted to show their patriotism and high regard for the young men fighting for their country.

Kenna sat preoccupied while Carlton drove through the deserted business section, past the water tower, and then into the residential area.

The path of the fire was still apparent. Charred remains and chimneys jutted from the landscape, miserable reminders of the devastation that had come to the city from a few small sparks. And it was ironic, thought Kenna, that those sparks had ignited and destroyed every church in their path, while leaving each school intact.

Kenna had no wish to revisit the scene of destruction along Boulevard. For three months now, she had avoided the area. It was better to remember the house as it was—better to remember that portion of her happy childhood, rather than to face the corpse of a once-proud neighborhood, openly exposed to the curiosity of spectators.

Even now, she shuddered as she realized that Carlton had chosen that very route to get to Piedmont Park. As the car began to get dangerously near the section of Boulevard where her house had once stood, Kenna closed her eyes. And yet, in spite of her determination to avoid looking, she couldn't help it. Compelled by some unseen force that had imprinted its mark on her, Kenna's gray eyes flew open and, with a horrible fascination, she saw the remnants of her home.

"Stop!" Kenna's voice rang out, and the man, puzzled at the girl's urgent command, immediately pulled to the side of the road.

"What is it, Kenna?"

She ignored his voice. Jumping from the car to the curb, she ran back down the street and through the wrought-iron gates that separated the pile of rubble from the sidewalk.

"Have you gone mad?" Carlton's voice demanded behind her.

Kenna's white lawn dress swept the dusty path, but she

paid no attention either to Carlton's question or to the uneven, dirty ground.

One, two, three steps—like some ruin from an ancient past, they projected into space—unanchored by verandah or columns of wood. Kenna climbed them and stared down into the hole where the house had once stood.

The memories rose before her and the house took shape again, with its verandah filled with red geraniums, the fan-shaped glass on each side of the door revealing the welcomed light inside—the same as it had been before Neal had gone, before her encounter with Fritz. Her eyes widened and all at once the mirage was gone. And she saw the ruins for what they were—the monument of a past that she could never re-capture. Reaching down, Kenna picked up a fragment of brick—one that had been fired in the kilns along the Chat-tahoochee River and selected for the house by her own father.

She stood, her face lifted toward the heavens, and for a moment, Carlton hesitated to interrupt. He watched while the girl crumbled the piece of porous brick into dust, the action resembling some pagan sacrifice with the blood-red dust fall-ing upon the unsupported stones of the steps.

"You're getting dirty, Kenna. Stop this nonsense and come to the car."

His irritated voice brought her eyes into focus. Carlton took his white linen handkerchief and wiped her hands. And then, treating her like a wayward child, he led her down the steps, back through the wrought-iron gates, and onto the street.

Seated once more in the car, Carlton looked at Kenna. He was unaware that she was seeing her house, or the remains, for the first time since the fire. He only knew she was behav-ing as if she had suddenly seen a ghost. But he didn't dare question her or scold her any further, for that would mar the rest of an important afternoon.

The man cranked the car and drove on in silence, while the girl beside him struggled to put the finishing touches to the past. Her childhood had been buried as surely as the house itself. Now she realized she had no need to cling to fragile letters or bricks or other symbols to give substance to her love for Neal. For love lived in the heart—not in some physical structure that could be destroyed by the vagaries of nature. A great relief pervaded her and Kenna's spirit lightened. She would find Neal. She was sure of that.

Kenna lifted her head and around her she noticed—not the charred remains of the fire, scattered here and there—but new timber, new walls—where people had begun to rebuild. She would have Mr. Ainslay sell the property. She had made up her mind.

With no breeze stirring, the automobile swept past the land shriven of its trees, and came into an oasis of green a few blocks from Piedmont Park.

Eleven

UNDER THE CURVED GRAY STONE ARCHWAY, MAJOR CARLton Torey guided the small car. Already, the tree-shaded lanes of the park were cluttered with carriages drawn by sleek, high-stepping horses.

That had been the original purpose of the park—to give a safe place to drive and show off the tallyhos and the matched teams. Even now, the carriages far outnumbered the motor vehicles.

Carlton edged slowly past the nervous horses and came to a stop in an area marked off for automobiles. He reached into the back of the car to retrieve the picnic basket, and with Kenna beside him, he began to walk toward the lake.

On the turfs of grass, children played, and the sound of their laughter echoed over the water where lazy ducks paddled and waited expectantly for bread to be thrown to them.

Kenna came alive at the sight of the fat, water-bound creatures vying for position at the water's edge. "Oh, Carlton, let's stop for a moment." She dug into the picnic basket for bread and, crumbling several pieces into bits, she flung the bread onto the surface of the water.

Excited quacks and a mad scramble greeted her. Kenna laughed when one duck clumsily tipped its white-feathered body upside down in its search for the food along the mud bottom.

"We mustn't be late, Kenna," Carlton warned. "I've reserved a boat for five o'clock."

"All right," she said and cast one last lingering look toward the ducks before following the man on the trail.

For a moment she had forgotten his preoccupation with promptness and following a rigid schedule. Feeding the ducks was probably not scheduled until after six o'clock. Kenna stifled a giggle. In fairness to the man, she had to admit that the boat might be given to someone else if they weren't on time to claim it.

Soon they reached the dock where the boats were anchored. Placing the basket of food into the boat, Carlton helped the girl down the wooden steps. The boat swayed at her entry and he tightened his hold on her.

"Thank you. I'm fine," she assured him and moved toward the slatted seat in the stern.

He slid onto the seat opposite her and, taking up the oars, began to row away from the dock.

Willow trees, dipping their supple leaf-filled limbs into the water, swayed in the sudden surge of an afternoon breeze. The boat glided past the Japanese teahouse that had been built earlier for the cotton exposition in the park. Kenna, now relaxed, closed her eyes and lazily trailed her fingers in the water.

With a sudden start, her eyes opened and she jerked her hand inside the boat. "What's the matter, my dear?" Carlton asked, seeing her staring down at her hand.

"Nothing," she assured him quickly. "I was . . . remembering something." Making no effort to reveal her thoughts, she became busy with the parasol, adjusting it to cover her face once more.

"They say hundreds of homeless people spent the night here in the park when the city caught fire," Carlton commented, looking over the land in the distance. "I'm glad you weren't one of them, Kenna."

"Why?" she asked.

"It wouldn't have done at all—your spending the night with riffraff."

Kenna's defensive spirit rose at the man's derogatory choice of words.

"I would hardly call children apart from their mothers and schoolboys—and fathers searching frantically for the other members of their family—riffraff."

The man smiled and in a placating manner said, "You know what I mean, Kenna. It isn't good for a young woman to be in such a questionable situation—to have any hint of

96

scandal about her. That's all I meant. And I'm glad you weren't among them.''

Kenna stared at the man. A questionable situation—a hint of scandal. What would Carlton say if he knew that she'd been in a questionable situation for the entire ten days after the fire? What would he say if he found out about Fritz or Irish Fitzpatrick—especially Irish Fitzpatrick? He'd never speak to her again—much less take her on a picnic to the park.

Impatient now to come to an understanding with Kenna, Carlton picked up the oars and rowed vigorously toward the deserted area at the farthest end of the lake. With the slowly lapping waters pushing the boat toward the sandy beach, Carlton stepped out and dragged the craft the rest of the way.

When the boat was stilled, he helped Kenna onto the sand. As she walked, bits of mica catching the reflection of the sun caused her to shade her eyes from the glare. The low-spreading willow looked inviting, and so Kenna, already hungry, took the red plaid blanket from the basket and draped it on the grass underneath the tree.

Fried chicken, potato salad, lemon tarts—all the food was taken from the basket and the aroma filled the air. Plates and cutlery came next from the basket, and then the bottles of Coca-Cola, with an opener attached by a rubber band to one of the bottles.

"I'm starved," Kenna commented, handing a plate to the man sitting rather stiffly beside her.

The girl's shoes, slightly wet from walking in the sand, were discarded at the edge of the blanket. Unaffectedly, Kenna curled up with her feet tucked under her. As she moved, the tips of her breasts jutted provocatively.

Carlton Torey, watching her, reacted immediately to the sensuous movement. Half-hoyden, half-puritan, in her virginal white lawn dress she had the power to affect him more than any other woman. Yet she didn't seem to realize it.

Feeling hot in his uniform with the uncomfortable collar clinging too tightly to his neck, Carlton traced the rim of the collar with his finger before he spoke.

"Kenna," he said, "you know the high regard I have for you."

The girl's large gray eyes stared at him while she held a drumstick poised in midair. Warily, she waited for him to continue.

"We haven't known each other long. And ordinarily, I wouldn't speak to you on such short acquaintance, but the war has caused me to be . . . precipitate. I want you to be my wife, Kenna."

"You do?"

He hardly noticed the incredulous look on Kenna's face. Undaunted by her reaction, he continued, "My mother will be quite upset, at first. But I'm sure when she gets to know you, she'll forgive any of your shortcomings."

Kenna dropped the half-finished drumstick onto her plate and wiped her fingers on the napkin—all the time staring at the man who had just proposed.

"I thought we might be married in the post chapel, about a month from now." Carlton smiled tenderly at Kenna and confided, "I took the liberty of speaking to the chaplain yesterday."

"But . . ." Kenna's hand was lifted, almost as if she needed permission to interrupt.

"Although our family is quite old and wealthy, you needn't be afraid, Kenna. My mother will see to it that you're groomed for society before we present you. And perhaps she'll even invent an illustrious ancestor for you for some of the more formidable grande dames."

"Carlton, I can't marry you."

The man smiled at her words. "I expected you to say that, Kenna, dear. I've taken you by surprise. I know that. But you'll get used to the idea in a few days."

Kenna shook her head. "You don't understand, Carlton. Nurses are not allowed to get married."

"That's no obstacle. You'll drop out of the nursing program," he declared, as if it were already an accomplished fact.

How could she tell this man that she had no intention of marrying him? She didn't want to hurt his feelings, despite what he'd said. "I feel honored that you want me to be your wife, but I can't marry you, Carlton. I *want* to go overseas just as soon as my training is completed," she emphasized.

For the first time his glance narrowed and his lips thinned. "You don't know what you're saying, Kenna." Then a softness crept into his voice. "Just give yourself a few days to think about it, my dear."

The girl looked miserable. When she tried to speak, the major stopped her. "It's almost time to return the boat. We'd better finish eating."

That put an end to their conversation. In silence they ate, and when the lemon tarts were gone, Kenna helped to gather the picnic things and carry them to the boat. With her shoes on her feet, Kenna waded through the water and crawled into the craft before Carlton could lift her into the boat.

He rowed the boat past the drooping willow trees, the Japanese teahouse, and finally to the dock from which they had started out. And then, silently, they walked along the dirt trail at the edge of the water. At Kenna's appearance, the ducks made a polyphony of noise and swam in her direction. But Carlton, with the picnic basket over his arm, hurried on his way and Kenna knew better than to stop and ask him for the leftover bread.

Her wet shoes made a sloshing sound with each step, providing a counterpoint to the squeak of the swing under a nearby tree. First one and then the other—complete in their own rhythmic sequences—interrupted the silence between the man and the slim small girl.

When they reached the car, Major Torey helped Kenna into the automobile, his disapproving eyes noting the limp wet hem of the once elegant dress.

On the way back to the fort, the small car crept. But this time, Major Carlton Torey avoided that area of Boulevard that had affected Kenna so strangely.

Seeing the charred remains of the fire must have had something to do with her hasty refusal of his proposal. He should have realized she was upset at seeing the reminder of her recent injury. But nothing was actually lost. She'd come to her senses soon enough. He had no qualms that she'd refuse him a second time. Still, he'd let her stew for a while before he brought up the subject again. And then she'd be certain to acquiesce immediately.

Twelve

KENNA AND STEPPIE SAT IN THE CLASSROOM WITH THE REST of the student nurses. Kenna, impatient for the test to end, stared at the clock on the wall, and then back at the paper before her.

She'd finished all the test questions, had gone over each one again—and was satisfied that she could do no better. So now she waited for the class to end.

Soon a voice said, "Your time is up. Please turn in your papers."

A sudden rustle, an exasperated sigh, a frantic writing of a few more words underscored the tenseness of the session. Kenna folded her paper, wrote her name on the outside, and placed it on the instructor's desk before she walked out.

In the corridor she waited for Steppie. They had three days of vacation now. That knowledge had kept them going when they'd had to juggle schedules and study time with working shifts at the hospital and attending classes—all this without enough sleep. But now they could relax for three whole days.

As she approached Kenna in the corridor, Steppie shook her head. A worried look was engraved upon her face, and seeing it, Kenna walked toward her. "What's the matter, Steppie?" she asked. "Was there something on the test you actually didn't know?"

Her voice was light, teasing, for Steppie always scored the highest marks in the class.

"I think I missed a question," Steppie moaned.

"Surely not," Kenna replied in mock horror. "Which one?"

"Number three—about the gastrointestinal effects of mustard gas. I knew about the lungs, Kenna—and the skin. But it was all so gruesome when Major Wardlaw spoke to us about it that I think I *tried* to forget.''

Kenna sobered. "Do you remember my telling you about Corporal Jenkins when he was brought in? How he couldn't eat anything except a bland diet—eggs and milk shakes—and very little of that at the time?''

"Of course,'' Steppie answered. "I should have remembered.''

"Not necessarily. He wasn't in your ward.''

The two remained silent as they walked to the nurses' quarters. For Kenna was reliving that day when she'd first seen the corporal. It was heartbreaking to know that he was going to die and that there was so little she could do to make him comfortable.

Kenna brushed her hair from her cheek. She mustn't think of that now. She wanted to forget the sadness, the miles of isolation tents spread upon the grounds at Fort McPherson where sick men were housed—those too infectious to be allowed into the wards.

But how could she forget with the constant stream of khaki on the streets of Atlanta? With the military cantonment only a few miles to the north receiving thousands of men from the surrounding states? Everywhere she looked, she saw soldiers.

How many more of the million men General Pershing had requested for overseas were destined to meet the same fate as Corporal Jenkins, with his lungs burned out by the enemy's poisonous fumes?

Maybe even Irish . . .

No. She had to get it out of her mind. She had three lovely, lazy days of vacation, with no raspy harsh alarm to make her get up before the sun rose. And Steppie's cousin Cricket had invited them to spend a relaxing weekend with another relative—a country cousin who lived in the shade of Kennesaw Mountain outside of Atlanta.

Grateful to be included in the plans, Kenna asked, "Do you think Cricket will mind if we're late?''

"A little,'' Steppie admitted. "She likes to get an early start when we visit Johnsie on the mountain. When Cricket drives, something usually happens to the car,'' Steppie added, suddenly giggling.

"Then let's hurry," Kenna replied.

Major Carlton Torey waited in the automobile outside the nurses' quarters. Soon an orderly came out with two suitcases and, under Carlton's supervision, strapped them to the car. Carlton glanced at the cases and was amused. Kenna was going to be away for only three days—but just like a woman, she'd evidently packed everything she possessed.

While he waited for Kenna to appear, he took out a package of cigarettes, lit one, and paced up and down the sidewalk. When he saw her he threw the half-smoked cigarette to the ground, mashed it with his polished boot, and walked back to the car to open the door.

She hadn't wanted him to take her but he'd insisted. He had waited long enough to speak to her again concerning their marriage plans. Because she was studying for her exam, he had seen her only fleetingly this past week. But today was different.

He'd find a quiet place to have coffee—just the two of them—away from the post before delivering her and her luggage to the friend's house.

"You remember Steppie?" Kenna asked, smiling as she looked up at the major.

"How do you do, Major Torey?" the girl beside Kenna responded. In a self-conscious tone, she asked, "Shall I sit in the back?" Before he could reply, Kenna answered, "There's enough room for all three of us in front. Don't you think so, Carlton?"

His eyes narrowed at the realization that he would not be alone with Kenna as he thought. But his innate politeness forced him to mask his displeasure.

"There's plenty of room," he agreed. With the car door open, he helped Kenna first and then Steppie. When they were settled, Carlton closed the door and walked around to the driver's side of the car.

Frustration lined his brow and gave a tenseness to his driving. The longer he drove, not really listening to the chatter between Kenna and Steppie, the more frustrated he became.

He didn't know why he felt the surging need to speak to Kenna—it was as though if he didn't settle the matter between them that very day, something untoward might occur.

102

Yet how could he speak, with her friend in the car beside her? Damn! Kenna Chalmers had given him no peace since that afternoon in Piedmont Park. Everytime he closed his eyes, he saw the shape of her breasts—the silvery gold hair—the sensuous mouth biting into the drumstick. And a wave of desire shot through him each time the picture intruded into his brain. Even now, he felt the stirring within him. Somehow, he had to be alone with Kenna.

"Shall we stop for coffee?" Carlton asked, his hazel eyes leaving the road for a moment to glance at the girl beside him.

"Thank you, Carlton. But I don't believe we'll have time," Kenna replied. "Cricket is probably standing at the door, looking for us this very minute."

The man's lips pressed together at her refusal. He continued driving, in silence.

As they approached the townhouse on Baltimore Place where Cricket Soames waited for them, Steppie, seated beside the quiet Kenna, let her mind wander to the invincible little woman who weighed only ninety pounds and stood less than five feet tall. For several years now, Cricket had been the bane of the city officials, especially when she was waving her woman's suffrage banner.

"Emmeline Pankhurst," she'd said to Steppie one day, "is the bravest woman alive. And I do so admire her for chaining herself to the iron fence. It's women like that who will get us the vote. Mark my words.

"Of course, I admire you also, Steppie," she'd said, continuing her discourse. "Going into nurse's training. If I were twenty years younger, I'd do it too."

Steppie remembered the frown on Cricket's face when she'd added, "I hope your father won't be upset with me for allowing it."

"I doubt that he'll mind at all, Cricket. He . . . he has other interests now, with a new diplomatic post and a new wife, too."

Cricket made a consoling sound. "If he'd only married someone from Atlanta, instead of that foreign woman."

"She's probably quite helpful to him, since she speaks Spanish," Steppie said halfheartedly.

103

"How are you coming with your French?" Cricket asked, changing the subject.

Steppie smiled as she recalled that earlier conversation with the woman who'd given her a home two years previously when her father had gone to South America. Now that welcome included her best friend, Kenna, who had no place to go on weekends and holidays since her own house had been burned.

The vehicle slowed and Steppie, aware of the cobblestoned street, said, "It's number seven, where the flivver is parked."

Carlton came to a stop directly behind the parked car, with its rumble seat at the back and spare tire attached to the side. Just as Kenna had predicted, Cricket Soames stood at the door, her small body completely engulfed by a driving coat and large hat with veil.

She hurried down the steps to the sidewalk. "Oh, my dears, I thought something dreadful had happened to you. With those awful prisoners just across the street from you, I never have a moment's peace of mind."

Kenna flushed and quickly introduced the major to Cricket Soames. Immediately the little woman preened and changed her manner, becoming the hostess.

"You must be thirsty, Major," Cricket commented, and not waiting for him to answer, she turned to Steppie. "Honey, run in and tell Verbena to fix us all something to drink. And tell her to bring it to the parlor."

Kenna stood on the sidewalk, while Carlton Torey removed the luggage and began to transfer it to Cricket's car. Cricket, glancing toward the townhouse and back to the car, seemed torn—as if she needed to be in two places at once.

"Kenna, bring your young man inside when you've finished. I'd better go and check on Verbena. She'll probably use the everyday china if I don't stop her."

With her coat flapping around her, Cricket hurried into the house—leaving Kenna and Carlton alone on the sidewalk.

Carlton took his time putting the luggage in place. Finally, he was alone with Kenna. It wasn't a proper setting in which to declare his love again. But that couldn't be helped. He had to get it settled, once and for all time.

"Wait, Kenna."

His hand stopped her from turning away. "This is neither the time nor the place," he began. "Yet I can't let you go away for three days without coming to an understanding."

She gazed warily at the man beside her entrapping her hand.

"Your nurse's training has gone far enough," he said. "When you come back I want you to stop classes. And if you'd like, I'll speak to Miss Dacus about it."

"No, Carlton," Kenna protested, removing her hand from his. "I told you—I'm going to finish my training."

"It's not necessary, now that you have me," he countered. "I'll take care of you. You'll never have to worry about money again, or depend on friends for a roof over your head."

His hand indicated the townhouse before them. "I'll speak to the chaplain again," he went on, as if it were settled between them. "And we can have at least six months together before I go overseas and send you to my mother."

Kenna sighed in exasperation. "I can't marry you, Carlton."

"I've heard that before. Now, be sensible, Kenna Chalmers, and say yes."

His smile gave a certain charm to his face. It wiped away the austerity, the formality, and she had to be careful not to succumb.

"I'm sorry," she said, her gray eyes gazing at his with regret. "But the answer is still the same."

The smile disappeared and his arms came to his sides stiffly, as if at attention.

"I won't ask you again, you realize," he warned, all warmth removed from his voice.

"Yes, I know," Kenna said, her voice barely audible.

Hating the awkwardness of the moment, she said, "Cricket should have the refreshments ready. Shall we go inside?"

Carlton was angry, and he didn't feel like engaging in small talk. "If you'll give Miss Soames my apologies, I think I won't stay. I'm in a hurry to get back to the fort."

Kenna nodded. "Thank you for bringing us."

Standing on the steps, she watched the automobile drive

down the cobblestoned street, turn into West Peachtree, and then disappear.

The parlor on the second floor of the townhouse gleamed in pristine splendor. Cut glass vases, their facets reflecting the sun, sparkled on the table by the window. Everywhere, dark mahogany furniture, carefully polished and smelling of beeswax, greeted Kenna as she joined Steppie and Cricket. On the tea table, spread with a fine white linen cloth, stood the chocolate pot and the fine cups of Meissen china, with their turquoise and gold decorations. A small silver tray, with a dent still proclaiming its near disaster with a Yankee bullet, held delectable little pastries filled with melted cinnamon, butter, and sugar. Kenna, as a child, had christened them "stickies" because of their adherence to her fingers. They were Verbena's specialty. And seeing them, a wave of nostalgia swept over the girl.

Seeing Kenna alone, Cricket inquired, "Where is the major?"

"He asked me to apologize to you," Kenna explained, "for not coming in, but he had to leave."

Cricket lifted the spectacles from her nose to peer at the girl. "You didn't have a falling-out with your young man, did you?"

"Not exactly," Kenna replied, uncomfortable at the scrutiny.

"Well, come and have some chocolate," she sniffed. "And then we'll be off."

When they had finished, Steppie asked, "Shall I take the tray to the kitchen?"

"Oh, let me do it," Kenna said. "I want to see Verbena."

Steppie deferred to Kenna and sat down again.

With the little house in the back yard on Boulevard demolished along with the main house, Verbena had been without a home. At the same time Cricket Soames, hearing that one of the German prisoners was still at large, had been afraid to stay in her townhouse alone. It had proved a perfect situation for Cricket to hire Verbena as a live-in servant.

As Kenna walked into the kitchen, the black woman stood at the sink, her back to the door.

"Verbena," Kenna called, setting the tray on the table. The woman, recognizing the voice, turned around. Grabbing a cloth to dry her hands, she laughed and gave the girl a giant hug.

"My, you sho' are pretty today, Miss Kenna. Uh-huh! Turn around and let me see your pretty blue dress."

Kenna pirouetted around the tiled floor and came back to face the woman. Verbena, looking closely at the girl, said, "They treatin' you better out at the hospital?"

"Oh, yes, Verbena. I'm getting along fine. What about *you*?"

"Gettin' along fine, too," she replied, "with Miss Cricket. Course, I miss my little house and Willie. You know, he's been drafted."

Kenna wasn't likely to forget. She remembered how scared Verbena's son had been, with all the German propaganda.

"You don't think they'll cut my Willie's ears off, do you?" Verbena asked.

"No, Verbena. All of those rumors were meant to scare him—and the others—to keep them from signing up."

"That's what I told Willie. I said, 'Well, if Miss Kenna ain't afraid to go all the way across the ocean, what's a big overgrown boy like you shakin' in his boots for?'"

Conscious of the two waiting for her upstairs, Kenna said, "I've got to go, Verbena. They're waiting for me."

"Have yourself a good time," she told the girl. "And watch out for Miss Cricket's drivin'."

Kenna laughed and left the kitchen. Up the steps she went to join Steppie and her cousin. She could still hear Verbena chuckling to herself in the kitchen below.

With the luggage strapped to the car and the picnic basket stashed in the rumble seat, Cricket Soames, with Kenna and Steppie beside her, started on the journey. The gears scraped together as the woman shot out of the side street. The two girls, looking at each other, dared not show their amusement in front of their small, fiery, independent companion.

Cricket was again dressed in the driving coat. The ends of the long scarf attached to her hat caught in the slight breeze and wafted across Kenna's face as they drove along.

At noon, they stopped along the roadside to get water for their car and to eat their picnic lunch under the trees. It was so much more enjoyable for Kenna, being with Steppie, than that day in the park with Carlton.

Kenna twitched her nose as she remembered the unexpected proposal and Carlton's disbelief when she'd refused him. But at least he had been a gentleman—the type of man a girl should marry. She knew that. Not a bit like Irish Fitzpatrick, who'd taken advantage of her when she was too weak to protest.

"You seem so far away, Kenna," Steppie said. With a start, Kenna became aware of her surroundings. She smiled at her friend.

"Just daydreaming, Steppie. Isn't it marvelous to have some time to ourselves?"

"Yes. Thinking of it was the only thing that kept me going this past week," Steppie agreed.

"Speaking of going," Cricket broke in, "I think it's time we were on our way."

They gathered up their things and packed them into the car. And after Kenna and Steppie had climbed into the car, Cricket took her place behind the steering wheel and began the second lap of their trip to the farm.

A mile beyond the stop-off where they had eaten lunch, they saw a small military convoy—trucks and caissons. It had pulled to the side of the road, and as the small car carrying the three women crept slowly past the vehicles, soldiers resting beside the convoy looked up and waved.

They would soon be on their way overseas, Kenna thought, to fill the empty places in the trenches that were being decimated by the enemy.

Thirteen

TOUCHED BY THE AFTERNOON RAINS, SO FREQUENT AT THE end of summer, when flowers remembered their brief existence and flourished in a frenzied blossoming like one last cry of beauty, the red Georgia earth wallowed in softness and color.

Pockets of green moss provided the foreground for Queen Anne's lace in giant bouquets of feathered white. And interspersed in the midst of white were equally tall clumps of black-eyed Susans. Every so often, beneath the shelter of strong limbs and sturdy leaves, sat little patches of squat purple violets, protected from the sun.

All these Kenna saw as the car climbed to a higher elevation. In the distance, purple and green, rose Kennesaw Mountain. Not much of a mountain, as peaks are measured, but a mountain, nevertheless, in contrast to the plateau of the city.

A flash of lightning flame-stitched its way across the sky as Kenna watched. A growl of thunder gave sound to the flash of light. Then large drops of rain pelted the earth. A few at first—and then, gaining momentum, they crashed against the wind, slashing and slanting to bombard the leather curtains of the little car hovering uncertainly on the road.

Steppie closed her eyes and clung to the side strap while the car slipped and slid in the muddy ruts. Kenna said nothing, but her hands revealed her tenseness, the white knuckles of her fingers pressed tightly against each other.

"Don't worry," Cricket said. "I'm used to this. I guess I've driven on more muddy roads than anybody I know."

Peering through the rain-soaked windshield, the woman added, "We're almost there. If you watch, you'll be able to see the house soon."

Through the steady downpour, the car continued. Blood-red spouts of water poured over the crested hills and plopped along the roadside, eroding the indented troughs to reveal small patches of kaolin and lustrous rock underneath the red surface, with the precision of a Chinese knife cutting into the brilliant layers of a coromandel screen.

"There it is. See, I told you we were close." Cricket's voice held a measure of glee as they rounded the curve. Before them appeared the muddy lane, the only entrance to the farmyard. On a slight rise above the weathered barn stood the white farmhouse. Its twelve stone steps leading to the ban-istered porch and front door served as a deterrent for its ever being used for entry.

There was no way the car could make it to the road leading to the back door. With its wheels spinning deeper and deeper into the mud, Cricket shifted into reverse and back again to forward. But she was stuck—as surely as Kenna had been with Fritz at her side.

Finally she sat and fumed. "Looks like we'll just have to make a run for the house. Do you girls mind?"

"What about the luggage?" Steppie asked.

"We'll leave that for now. Bert can come and get it later."

The three climbed out of the car and at the sight of them fleeing in the rain, a woman in the farmhouse held open the back door. Rushing inside the screened porch, they were hailed by the woman's hearty voice.

"Well, Cricket, as soon as I heard the thunder and the rain, I knew you were coming. You haven't missed a time yet, have you?"

"Someday I'll beat that hex, Johnsie. But it's not every-body who can summon a piece of thunder to do their door knocking for them."

She reached up and gave the other woman a peck on her cheek—the small, fragile form of Cricket Soames at odds with the buxom figure wrapped in a large white apron over a cotton print dress.

"Steppie you know. But I'd like you to meet her friend, Kenna Chalmers. I told you about her, you remember."

"How do you do, Mrs. . . . ."

"Call me Johnsie," the woman interrupted. "Everybody

110

else does. Well, I've got the foot tub ready in the kitchen. Just take off your muddy shoes and follow me.''

They did as they were told.

As Johnsie handed the towels to them, she said, ''I'll get Bert to bring your things from the car.''

The woman left the kitchen while Cricket, Kenna, and Steppie became busy, removing the traces of mud.

The storm disappeared quickly—spontaneously, like a guest suddenly changing her mind and deciding not to stay, after all. By nightfall, with the lamps lit, Kenna and Steppie sat in the swing on the porch, while in the front parlor, Cricket and Johnsie talked, the sound of their voices occasionally drifting through the open window.

''The last time I was here,'' Steppie confided above the creak of the swing, ''I found an old horseshoe. I like to think it belonged to one of General Johnston's cavalry officers, charging around the mountain to meet the Yankees.''

''It could have been from a plow horse, Steppie,'' Kenna teased.

''Don't be such a spoilsport, Kenna. It's *my* horseshoe— and if I want it to be from the Civil War, then that's that.''

Kenna laughed. ''You're such a romantic, Steppie.''

''I know,'' the dark-haired girl admitted. ''Sometimes, I think I even see the ghost of Sherman riding over the slopes . . .

''But it's nice to picture him as the redheaded lieutenant when he was sent the first time by the government to reimburse Georgians for their horses lost in the Seminole War— not as the general who burned Atlanta twenty years later.

''It's frightening, isn't it?'' she continued. ''To think that someone like that could see and appreciate all this beauty, and at the same time, be storing up the knowledge to destroy it later on.''

''They say there's a town in France that has been destroyed ten times because of its location,'' Kenna mused. ''So I guess we were lucky that it's happened to us only once.''

''I guess so,'' Steppie agreed.

The swing on the porch creaked in comfortable cadence while the girls were pensive. The air was now cool—and no mosquitoes bothered them. Soon it would be fall, and already

111

the leaves were beginning to turn. In the distance, the trees rose like bulky monoliths to the sky, their hues and colors stolen by the darkness.

Steppie broke the silence. "What would you like to do tomorrow, Kenna?"

She thought for a moment. "I'd like to see the Indian mounds at Etowah," she replied, "if the weather's nice. Or just take a long walk along the mountainside. Anything's fine with me, Steppie. Whatever *you'd* like to do."

"Maybe we can do both," Steppie replied. "That is, if Bert gets the car out of the mud." And then she laughed. "We might even find a horseshoe or a silver bullet for you, Kenna, on the old battlefield."

"No thanks," Kenna said, wrinkling her nose. "I'd rather find some gold at the Indian mounds."

"Not much of a chance there," Steppie assured her. "The gypsies are the ones with all the gold."

"I know. Can you imagine how much noise gold necklaces make when gypsies dance?"

"Have you ever seen them dance, Kenna?" Steppie asked, suddenly interested. "I didn't think they allowed anybody to watch them."

Kenna's speech faltered. "I . . . I just imagine they'd make a lot of noise."

A voice came through the window. "Girls, we're going to turn the lamps down. I think you'd better come inside now."

Relieved to have the conversation interrupted, Kenna left the swing, followed by her friend Steppie.

Taking one of the lamps with them, the two walked past the parlor with its bulky mohair sofa and chairs protected by handmade lace antimacassars—on past the drapery that separated the front hall from the back, and finally to the bedroom at the rear of the house. The marble washstand, the high-backed beds inside the room attested to country comfort—solid, comfortable, the room making no pretensions to be anything other than it was.

Long after the lights were out, Kenna remained awake. She couldn't get the gypsies out of her mind. The music by the campfire, the clink of the gold coins, and the haunting, hypnotic music were still as vivid in her mind as the events of that very day. Her hand brushed across her face as she remembered the feel of the lace mantilla that Irish had provided for her. The circle of friendship. At the thought of it and Irish Fitzpatrick, the invisible bond between them tightened.

A rooster crowed and at its raucous sound, Kenna's eyes flew open. It was early, the sun scarcely up. Kenna frowned. The one day in weeks when she could sleep late and she had to be awakened by the farm's alarm clock. Again the rooster crowed and the sounds of daytime began, while Kenna, sharing the bedroom with Steppie, tried to ignore it all.

The girl's silver-blond hair spread across the soft down pillow as she stretched and then lay quietly with her eyes closed. But the desire to stay in bed had disappeared. Oh well, she'd gone to bed earlier than usual the evening before, so she'd probably gotten as much sleep as she needed.

With her feet dangling over the bed railing, Kenna sat up and reached for her bedroom slippers with her toes.

The dark-haired girl in the other bed turned, her face now in full view, and opened her eyes.

"What time is it?" Steppie's sleepy voice inquired.

Kenna looked at the watch on her wrist. "Six o'clock."

Steppie moaned in protest. "We don't have to get up so early—not today."

"But Johnsie didn't give the rooster new instructions," Kenna lamented.

A giggle came from the other bed as Steppie pushed herself up on one elbow. "Is that what woke you?"

"Yes."

Just then, large guns in the distance began firing a barrage, and Kenna glanced toward the window. "Just listen to that. I thought farms were supposed to be quiet places."

"It must be the military convoy we saw yesterday," Steppie commented. And then she too got out of bed.

By breakfast time, the guns had stopped and the military maneuvers were forgotten as the girls planned their day. Away from the stress of too much work and too little time for themselves, Kenna and Steppie reveled in the slow pace of the day.

They walked along the edge of the split rail fence that sepa-

113

rated the farm from the dense woods beyond. The last of the scuppernongs hung from wild vines circling the overhanging limbs of sweet gum trees, and they stood on tiptoe to retrieve the fruit and pop it into their mouths.

Then they collected wild daisies and sat down on a grassy knoll to weave chains for their heads and wrists. Like two daughters of Diana they emerged from the woods and started back to the farmyard as their stomachs told them it was time for more sustaining food.

The little white goat stared at them through the railing as they passed the barnyard. They stopped to watch a hen with her chicks in their scramble to eat a treasured delicacy, unearthed by the rain of the previous day.

"Do you think the farms in France are like this one?" Steppie asked.

"I don't really know. I guess we'll find out soon, though."

Bert, the farm hand, waved to them before disappearing into the old weathered barn, and Steppie, observing Kenna's interest, confided, "He's good help for Johnsie, you know, even if he isn't too bright. The sad thing is—he wasn't always like this. He fell off a wagon when he was a little boy and hit his head on a rock."

Kenna's gray eyes met the dark, limpid, sympathetic eyes belonging to Steppie. Neal could have been hurt too—in the plane crash. He could be performing the same chores that Bert performed—at this very moment—on a farm half a world away.

A sense of urgency gripped Kenna, and the restlessness that had disappeared for a few hours returned in full measure.

"Let's go to the Indian mounds," she suggested, "just as soon as we finish lunch."

"All right," Steppie agreed.

But that afternoon the shelling against the mountain began in earnest, and the artillery guns of the officers' training camp reverberated throughout the countryside. The mountain, quiet for fifty years, smoked and shuddered under the barrage. Cricket, fearful of their safety, persuaded Kenna and Steppie to remain on the farm.

By late afternoon, Steppie and Kenna had given up any hope of leaving the farm that day. The barrage had pinned them to the spot just as surely as General Johnston's guns had temporarily pinned Sherman and his troops in one of the last Confederate stands to defend Atlanta.

"Wouldn't you hate to hear this for months on end?" Kenna commented.

"It *would* be rather nerve-racking," Steppie agreed. "But I guess people would eventually get used to it, like the sound of a train or a cotton mill whistle. They say if you get used to a certain sound, then you miss it when it's gone."

The guns suddenly became silent on the other side of the mountain. Kenna and Steppie left the safety of the porch swing and began their walk, pausing now and then to examine the yellow chrysanthemums growing against small rock formations at the edge of the road.

Aware of the crash of silence after the steady bombardment, Kenna lifted her head to gaze in the distance. But a sudden whistle—screaming, roaring, deafening—snatched back the silence and in horror, she saw a shell in all its lethal splendor projecting overhead.

With no time to ponder what had happened, Kenna shouted above the noise, "Get down, Steppie." Not waiting for the girl to obey, Kenna pushed Steppie to the ground, and followed just as the earth shook, sickening in its intensity. Fragments of steel flew in every direction, and craters dug earth from earth, like a malevolent banshee unchained from another time.

Fourteen

Major Carlton Torey was still furious. The girl had done it again—refused his offer of marriage without so much as a blink of the eyelid.

He stormed into the officers' mess at Fort McPherson, where Davin Grant sat alone, drinking his coffee and reading a medical journal. Somehow, Carlton knew that the captain was behind Kenna's refusal. He'd encouraged her far too much in her nurse's training.

The major took his cup of cocoa and walked toward Davin. Forcing himself to be civil, he spoke. "Grant, may I join you, old man?"

Davin, surprised at Torey's request, lowered his journal. "By all means," he replied, indicating the chair opposite him.

Carlton sat down and stirred his cocoa. He removed the white residue from the top with his spoon and took a sip of the hot liquid. As usual, it was not made to his liking. But so much of the army was not to his liking.

As he sat in the cavernous mess hall, Carlton debated whether to broach the subject of Kenna Chalmers. He just couldn't understand why she had refused him. Nothing like that had ever happened to him. In truth, she was the only girl he'd asked to marry—a fact that she didn't seem to appreciate.

Skipping any pretext of a casual conversation, Carlton immediately plunged into the subject.

"You've known Kenna Chalmers a long time, haven't you?" he started.

Davin nodded. "Yes—since she was eight years old."

"Then perhaps you can explain to me why a common

116

nurse would refuse an offer of marriage from a doctor with unimpeachable social credentials and wealth?''

"You're speaking of Kenna?''

"Of course.''

"And yourself?''

His chin jerked upward, but Carlton didn't deny it.

Davin laughed aloud. "You evidently don't know much about Kenna.''

"What makes you say that?''

"In the first place, Kenna Chalmers is no common nurse. She was Atlanta's leading debutante two years ago.''

Carlton, surprised, set down his mug of cocoa. "So she's from one of those genteel but impoverished Southern families I keep hearing about.''

"Not at all. She's quite wealthy, especially now that her grandmother is dead,'' Davin answered.

"Then why in heaven's name is she wasting her time in nurse's training?''

"She wants to go overseas.''

"I know that,'' Carlton snapped. "She's told me over and over. But for the life of me, I can't understand why.''

"Has she talked with you about her half brother?''

"No. All I know is that she's an orphan.''

Davin leaned back in his chair and pressed the tips of his fingers together in a pensive pose.

"Kenna's an enigma—you're aware of that. If she had wanted an easier life, she would have married me.''

Carlton's eyes narrowed at the revelation. Davin laughed and said, "I'm no competition for you, Torey. She thinks of me as a friend, nothing else.''

Carlton's hands reached for the cup while he continued to listen to Davin Grant. "Kenna's father was a doctor and Kenna always had the idea she was going to become a nurse to work in his clinic. But he and her mother died together on the *Titanic*. And her grandmother who came to live with her took a firm hand with her. When Kenna was of age to be presented to society, Mrs. Chalmers launched her with all the care of a royal princess.

"That was in 1915,'' Davin recalled, "the same year that Nurse Edith Cavell was hanged by the Germans.''

"I vaguely remember the event," Carlton commented. "The nurse was smuggling wounded Allies out of Belgium under the Germans' noses."

"Yes. And you can imagine what an impression it made on Kenna, who was partying every night. When her grandmother died, Kenna wasted no time in going into nurses' tr—"

"But you mentioned her brother, or half brother," Carlton interrupted.

"Neal." Davin stopped and a sad expression crossed his face. Carlton waited for the man to resume speaking. "You would think that a brother two years older would be the strong one. But that wasn't so. Kenna had the family strength—and by the time they were in their teens, their roles were reversed. She idolized him and watched after him. But he was already in France studying when the war with the Germans broke out. And he immediately joined the French air force, or rather, the Lafayette Escadrille."

By this time, Carlton had pushed his cup aside, making no pretense to drink the liquid. He leaned forward to make sure he didn't miss a word spoken by Davin Grant.

"He was shot down over Verdun a year later. But since his body was never recovered, Kenna has this obsessive idea that he's still alive—somewhere in a small village in France."

Carlton's eyes sparked with understanding. "And so she's doing all of this so that she can find her brother."

"Or his grave, more than likely," Davin said, "although she refuses to admit it. I don't think she'll ever be happy, until she's put his specter to rest."

Carlton was pensive. Why hadn't Kenna told this to him? Did she think he wouldn't understand? It was a pilgrimage of sorts for the girl—to go to France. He smiled. He'd let her go, making certain she was stationed at the same field hospital where he could keep an eye on her. It shouldn't take long for her to realize that finding her brother was a lost cause. Then he'd marry her and send her back to his mother.

Carlton stood up, impatient to seek out the girl. "Thank you, Grant. Now I understand Kenna's behavior."

Another officer walked into the officers' mess and, seeing the two men together, joined them. "Have you heard what

118

happened this afternoon at Kennesaw Mountain?'' he inquired.

At the mention of the name, Carlton immediately became interested. "No," he answered. "What?"

"An artillery shell ricocheted, went over the mountain, and exploded in a farmyard.''

"Was anybody hurt?" Davin asked.

"Four people were killed—and at least one was a woman," the officer replied.

"Which farm?" Carlton demanded.

"I don't know the name. But it was on Burnt Hickory Road.''

"My God—Kenna and Steppie went to Kennesaw yesterday. And if I'm not mistaken, the farm was on that same road,'' Carlton said.

Davin and Carlton, with alarm written in their eyes, immediately left the mess hall, and hoping for more information, they hurried back to the hospital.

But no one knew any more than the initial report. And so Davin and Carlton, in league for once, commandeered a military vehicle and started toward the townhouse on Baltimore Place.

When they arrived, it was already dark and lights blazed from the windows. Both men climbed out of the vehicle and taking the steps two at a time, they stopped before the wide-arched door and rang the doorbell.

No one came to the door.

A second time, Davin twisted the bell, letting it sound for a long, impatient time. At last the sound of footsteps responded to his vigorous signal.

A black woman peered through the beveled glass, and recognizing Davin Grant, she immediately opened the door.

"Nobody's home, Mr. Davin," she advised him. "Miss Cricket and the girls took themselves off to the mountain yesterday. Won't be back till tomorrow sometime.''

"Have you heard from them?" Carlton asked, "since they left?''

"No, sir," Verbena replied. "But then I wouldn't 'spect to—Miss Johnsie don't have a telephone.''

Verbena, acting as if she didn't know whether to invite them inside or not, looked at one man and then the other. "What's wrong?" she asked.

Trying to phrase the information in a way not to alarm the woman, Davin waited too long in his reply. Carlton Torey, stepping into the breach, announced, "One of the farms was hit by a runaway shell this afternoon, and several people were killed."

The woman's eyes grew wide in horror. She began wringing her hands. "Lordy, are you tryin' to tell me something's happened to . . ."

"No, Verbena. We just thought they might have decided to come home earlier than they planned, because of the accident," Davin replied.

Verbena didn't believe him. A low moan came from the woman's throat and Davin, looking at Carlton, let him know he disapproved of his frightening the woman unnecessarily.

"You'd better come in and wait," Verbena finally said, opening the door wider.

They walked into the front parlor, and Verbena, uncertain as to what to do next, went back to the kitchen below. Her low, mournful singing filled the townhouse.

"What's she doing?" Carlton demanded.

"Working out her anxiety."

"Well, she doesn't have to be so *vocal* about it. It's getting on my nerves."

"She has a double stake in this, Torey. Verbena has never worked for anybody but Kenna's family—that is, until after the house on Boulevard was destroyed. So you see, she has three people to worry about."

With Davin's explanation, Carlton remembered Kenna amid the rubble on Boulevard that day of the picnic. So that had evidently been *her* home. No wonder she had acted so strangely for the rest of the afternoon. But why hadn't she told him?

Carlton stood up and paced from one end of the parlor to the other, while Davin sat on the sofa, with his ears alert to the sounds around him. "You think we can call someone to find out? General Swift, perhaps?" Carlton asked Davin.

The sound of an automobile pulling into the street stopped

the conversation. Both Davin and Carlton rushed toward the front door, and when they saw Cricket's car, they were visibly relieved.

Pushing open the door, they walked outside to meet the women. Cricket Soames and a red-eyed Steppie emerged from the car. The two men looked for Kenna but there was no sign of her.

"Where's Kenna?" Davin asked, his voice sounding alarmed.

"She's at the hospital," Steppie replied. "There was a terrible accident and . . ."

Davin caught Cricket as she stumbled.

"Which hospital?" Carlton demanded.

"St. Joseph's," Steppie's trembling voice replied.

Leaving Davin to help Cricket into the house, Carlton jumped into the military vehicle. "I'll be back for you, Grant," he shouted, before starting the motor and taking off. And Davin, with the older woman in his arms, was helpless to stop him, or go with him.

Kenna sat at the bedside with Johnsie. The older woman's color was better, and her breathing had returned to normal after her angina attack.

Still numbed by the events of that afternoon, Kenna realized that they'd been awfully lucky. The damage to Johnsie's farm was minor—not like the devastation on the adjacent one. The woman driving out of the yard in her buggy—the three men removing a tree stump—they hadn't had a chance. Kenna was still sick at the sight of the carnage. She couldn't forget the looks on the young officers' faces, either—the shocked realization of what their war maneuvers had cost in civilian lives.

A slight knock at the door caused Kenna to take her eyes from the hospital bed. In surprise, she saw Major Carlton Torey standing before her. But Kenna's surprise was nothing in comparison to his. Incredulous hazel eyes stared at the girl seated in the chair.

"You're not hurt?" the man's voice questioned.

Kenna, looking back toward the sleeping woman to make sure she hadn't awakened, stood up. With a sweep of her hand, Kenna motioned for Carlton to follow her into the hallway, and only when she had closed the door to the room did she speak.

"What are you doing here?" she asked, remembering the tense parting only the day before.

"I was led to believe you'd been hurt," Carlton replied.

Kenna shook her head. "We were lucky, except for Johnsie. But she should be all right soon."

"Was she hit?"

"No—but her heart couldn't stand all the excitement. It was . . . rather awful," the girl confided.

"How long are you going to stay with her?"

"Until morning."

Carlton frowned. "Other nurses are on duty. Do you think it's necessary for you to remain? It's not as if you were a member of the family."

Defensively, Kenna replied, "That's precisely why I'm staying tonight. Cricket and Steppie are too upset. And Johnsie needs a familiar face near her when she wakes up. She's afraid of hospitals."

He knew better than to argue with her when her chin took on that stubborn tilt. "I'll come for you first thing in the morning."

"You're not on duty tomorrow?"

"No. I've arranged to have the weekend free."

He leaned over and brushed her hair with his lips. Embarrassed, Kenna looked down the hall to make sure she wasn't observed.

"I'll see you in the morning," he reiterated, and Kenna stood watching him until he disappeared down the hospital corridor.

The next morning, Carlton Torey appeared at the hospital at eight o'clock. Impatient to whisk Kenna away from the hospital atmosphere, he walked along the corridor, not waiting for the nurse on duty to announce his arrival.

Johnsie, smiling at the girl beside the bed, said, "Thank you, Kenna. I don't think I could have stayed alone in this place. You know how I feel away from my own bed."

"I know," the girl answered sympathetically. "But everything's better now, isn't it?"

"Well, I missed my big country breakfast," Johnsie joked, looking at the remains of the bland breakfast tray.

Kenna made ready to remove the tray from the room when a tap at the door sounded. And Carlton Torey, with his ramrod military bearing, walked into the room.

"Good morning," the major exclaimed, nodding to Johnsie and then to Kenna. He frowned at the girl's tired face, the pale blue smudges under her gray eyes.

"Are you ready to leave?" he asked.

Kenna turned back to the woman in the bed. "Johnsie, may I present Major Carlton Torey. He's come to take me back to Cricket's."

Again, Carlton gave a curt nod in the direction of the bed. He had no interest in the sick woman—only in the slim, tired girl at her side.

"You're sure you'll be all right until Steppie comes to sit with you?" Kenna asked.

The large buxom woman, sitting up, with several pillows at her back, commented, "I'm not afraid now, Kenna. Thank you, child, for staying with a silly old woman."

"I didn't stay with a silly old woman," she refuted with a smile. "I stayed with *you*, Johnsie."

Carlton made an impatient noise at the exchange, and so Kenna, still holding the tray in her hands, bade the woman good-bye.

Outside the door, she placed the empty breakfast tray on the rolling cart, and began the trek to the waiting vehicle.

"I'm taking you back to the post," Carlton announced when they started off in the car.

"But my suitcase is at Cricket's," she protested.

"Steppie can bring it when she returns tonight."

"Why, Carlton? Why are you doing this?"

Kenna remembered their parting. She had thought that she'd seen the last of him, since he'd left in such a huff. But he had come to the hospital the night before, and now was acting as if that conversation had never taken place.

"You need some rest," he answered, "away from those hysterical women. It's not good for you to be subjected to them."

"Who's hysterical?"

123

"That Johnsie woman, for one," he replied. "There was nothing wrong with her heart—just a matter of hysteria."

"Did you see her chart?" Kenna asked quickly, a certain wariness in her voice.

"No, I didn't have to."

"Then how do you know?"

"Are you questioning a doctor?" he asked, irritated at her bombardment.

"I'm sorry. I thought I was asking a friend. Please pardon me, Major Torey." Her contrite voice held a trace of tiredness.

He leaned over and touched her hand. "I'm sorry too, Kenna. I didn't mean it that way. Of course I'm your friend. And it's because I care for you that I resent anyone's taking advantage of you.

"I want to see those blue smudges under your eyes disappear," he continued. "I want to protect you from anything unpleasant."

How different from Irish Fitzpatrick, who'd taken advantage of her at every turn, not caring that he'd left her to the mercy of the wolves by the campfire. At that moment, Kenna, comparing the two men, was touched by Carlton's tenderness and sincerity.

". . . And I hope you'll give me the right to protect you, Kenna."

The words were not what she expected to hear. "Carlton, I haven't changed my mind. I can't marry you."

He smiled benevolently at her. "I know, my dear. You have to go to France to look for your brother." And with a sheepish look, he confessed, "I had a long talk with Davin Grant. And I think you're quite brave to do what you're doing."

"I love Neal very much . . ."

"Of course you do. He's the only family you have."

The man's reaction took her by surprise. So different from the malicious baiting—the words Irish had spat at her about her brother—"And what will Neal say when he finds out I made love to you?" So different.

". . . And that's why I think it best if we're engaged before you go overseas. That way, you'll enjoy a measure of protection. Anyone trying to take advantage of you would have to answer to me.''

She hadn't heard everything that Carlton had said. She'd been too busy, recalling the conversation with Irish. Her eyes, looking up into the man's face, saw Carlton's handsome features—cleancut, a little aesthetic—a patrician face, actually, free of the sensuality that was so immutably etched on the face of—

She was so tired. What could she say?

''I'll write my mother and tell her you're following the example of the aristocracy in Europe. Princess Sonia, you know, has become a nurse, also—and has opened her château as a hospital.''

Kenna's head dropped forward, and Carlton, seeing the girl fall asleep, tenderly supported her against his shoulder.

Thus by default, Kenna Chalmers became engaged to Major Carlton Torey.

Fifteen

ALONG A SECTOR OF THE FRENCH FRONT, STEMMING FROM the Vosges Mountains to Switzerland, lay rolling hills where clumps of poplars and larches separated small villages from the long-quiet trenches.

Inside the trenches, the French soldiers, or *poilus,* had settled down to a caretaker's duty, merely watching the Boche across the barbed wire no-man's-land, and occasionally firing a round of shrapnel from the French 75s to be answered in turn by the German 77s, but carefully aimed away from the trenches themselves.

Like a sudden explosion, the Americans marred the quiet October serenity of the countryside as they moved into the trenches. Their mock training was over. Now they were ready to do battle with the enemy.

Backed by artillery and a field hospital to take care of their casualties, they waited to engage the Germans. And the *poilus* in their blue uniforms became resigned to the upheaval created by these *Américains.*

Captain Irish Fitzpatrick walked along the line with Sergeant Bowen. With his binoculars he looked beyond the stretch of barbed wire to the German trenches, where he could see the enemy soldiers hanging out their laundry.

"You think our men are ready to fight, Sergeant?" Irish inquired.

"Some of them. Others—I just don't know what they'll do."

Irish nodded. "The first battle will tell."

"They don't seem to be in any hurry," the sergeant said, watching the housekeeping activity across the line. "Have any idea when it'll be?"

"Any day now. They know we're here, but I don't expect them to give us any prior warning."

Over the quiet trench, a youthful voice complained, "I believe they're sewed in for the winter, like a farmer in his long johns."

A deeper, masculine voice with a French accent replied, "You wish to fight Germans in the winter, *mon ami?* Better to nurse our wounds and rest for the spring offensive."

The sergeant chuckled at the exchange. Turning to Irish, he said, "At least that one is impatient to fight, Captain."

The weather changed for the worse while the men waited. It became cold, rainy, the exposure capable of chilling a man's bones. Deep within the trenches, Eb and Seton, wearing the overcoats of the peacetime army, dragged the long, dripping hems through the mud as they stirred and blew on their hands to keep them warm. The two were anxious to avenge themselves against Irish Fitzpatrick, for he had continually kept after them, making them belly through the mud with heads down, pointing out their shortcomings with the wirecutters and shovels, and making life generally miserable for them.

Their antipathy for their commanding officer had mushroomed during training, yet the Professor, who had borne the brunt of Irish's wrath, seemed to have no dislike for either Captain Fitzpatrick or Sergeant Bowen.

"I *should* have kept my head down," the Professor had defended. "Only the mud got on my glasses."

"We'll show 'im when the time comes," Eb bragged. "He's not the only one who knows how to fight."

But the Germans, willing to take their time to engage the Americans, only teased them, firing overhead at mealtimes, with just enough activity to make the soldiers dive into the waterlogged trenches and stay there until their soup was cold.

Late one afternoon, when the smell of food from the cooking wagons told the men it was time to line up with their mess kits, the Americans left the safety of the trenches and stood on the hillside while the cooks began dishing their indigestible fare to the soldiers.

As usual, a barrage of shells exploded overhead. The cooks

127

took cover first, followed by everyone else in the chow lines, officers and enlisted men alike.

Privates Eb Jordan and Seton Campbell were halfway to safety when Eb stopped. He turned back toward the soup wagon, and then the aroma of stew, with real meat, assailed him from the officers' mess.

"Wait, Seton," he called. And his friend, only a few steps ahead, turned to see what had happened.

"What is it, Eb? We'd better hurry before we get our heads blown off."

Eb crouched low as a shell sped overhead and landed in the open field, exploding as it hit the ground.

"Look at that. They're not going to hit us," Eb said. "Why should we let them spoil our dinner? Come on, let's eat."

Undecided, Seton gazed toward the trench where the Professor had disappeared, and then back to Eb.

"Well, I *am* just about to starve to death," Seton admitted, and keeping low to the ground, he edged toward Eb and the chow wagon.

"What're you doing, Eb?" Seton called out, horrified. "That's the officers' food, not ours."

"You think I'd risk my neck for *that* food?" Eb inquired, pointing to the enlisted men's wagon. "Here, hold your plate." He dipped the ladle into the officers' stew and filled Seton's mess kit.

They sat behind the cooking wagons and ate to their hearts' content. When he could eat no more, Eb sighed and wiped his mouth with his sleeve.

The shelling stopped and in twos and threes the soldiers returned to the chow lines and waited for the cooks to reappear.

"Why aren't you in line, Private?" Irish Fitzpatrick asked, as if he already knew the answer.

Eb, flushing guiltily at the close scrutiny, replied, "I ain't hungry, sir. The Boche musta taken away my appetite."

"Me, too," Seton added nervously, and began to walk away.

"Just a minute," Irish said. "I haven't dismissed you

yet." The two halted in their tracks. "You've forgotten to wash your mess kits."

"We'll do that right away, sir," Eb replied, and obeying orders, he rushed to swish his plate and eating utensils in the large drum filled with warm, soapy water.

That night, Irish, sleeping in an officer's tent farther back from the trenches, awoke. It was still dark. The moon had finally won its game of hide and seek with the clouds and was nowhere in sight.

In the makeshift corral behind the tents, the horses began to neigh. Irish listened. They were uneasy. And Irish, suddenly uneasy too, got up from his cot, put on his overcoat, and left the tent. He passed by the sentries on duty and walked toward the front line trenches where his men were asleep.

Immediately the sky lit up with eight-inch mortar shells, machine gun fire, and bangalore torpedoes ripping through the barbed wire. The *Stosstruppen* had moved up to the front during the night, and decided to strike, at three o'clock in the morning.

Irish hit the ground, and in a zigzag manner crawled to the front trench and rolled downward where his men, just awakening, grabbed their guns and ammunition for their initiation with the Germans.

One entire platoon was now enclosed in a box barrage, with no hope of aid from behind, while the *Stosstruppen* sped through the openings in the barbed wire. The upstart Americans were going to be taught a lesson by the special assault teams whose very name brought fear to the citizens in the villages along the Rhine-Marne canal.

Irish pulled his gun from the Sam Browne belt and fired at a German a short distance away. The German fell, but was replaced by another and still another.

Farther down in line, Eb, Seton, and the Professor hurriedly unwrapped their bayonets from the protective newspaper and attached them to their rifles. "Watch out, Seton," Eb called. Seton turned just in time to thrust his bayonet through the middle of a *feldgrau* uniform lunging toward him. A surprised grunt filled the air, a helmet landed in the mud as the German went down.

Then the main wave of crack German troops descended. In the darkness, the uninitiated Americans and seasoned Frenchmen fought with the enemy—some successfully; others not so victoriously. The water standing in the trenches turned a sickly shade of pink and then ripened to dark red.

The battle lasted for a mere three minutes, measured in time. Then it was over. The *Stosstruppen*, taking their dead and wounded with them, dissolved into the darkness toward the torn barbed wire no-man's-land. They had done what they had set out to do; to show the American recruits the superiority of the German troops and the impossible task ahead of them.

Captain Irish Fitzpatrick, flicking the blood from a slight cut on his face, started down the line to assess the damage done to his men. The sickly acid fumes from the shells still lingered over the trenches.

"He's dead. The Professor's dead," a voice cried out. It was Seton Campbell calling to Eb.

"He turned his back, *mon ami*," another voice responded in the darkness.

Irish, saddened, walked on, checking for those who were still alive and needed help.

On a hillside near the village of Bathelémont, the Professor was buried with thirty-five other soldiers who had been killed in the brief battle. Captain Irish Fitzpatrick, Sergeant Bowen, Eb, and Seton stood at attention as the fusillades fired a respectful salute into the air.

Nous voilà, Lafayette.

As the doughboys were fed into the trenches, hospital ships, with the wounded aboard, began arriving in the ports along the Atlantic. Trains marked with a cross, with bunks lining each boxcar, sped from the seaports and distributed the gassed, the lame, those able to walk, and the stretcher cases to the fourteen military hospitals in America. Base Hospital No. 6 at Fort McPherson received its share of the wounded.

That winter in Atlanta, Kenna, Steppie, and the other nurses had little time for anything but the care of these patients. Hungrily they sought news of the war—the firsthand information not found in newspapers—as well as events capturing the imagination of the correspondents overseas. Foremost in the news was the account of a Russian peasant woman who had taken her dead husband's place in battle.

"Madame Botchkerava," Steppie said, stumbling over the name one day when she and Kenna had a few minutes to themselves. "They say she's fighting alongside the other soldiers, as if she were a man herself."

"Not any more," Kenna replied. "Haven't you heard?"

"Heard what? She hasn't been killed, has she?" Steppie asked in alarm.

"No, not that," Kenna answered. "She's commanding a whole battalion of women now. Kerenski asked her to form it—the Women's Battalion of Death."

Steppie shuddered at the name. "Do you think the Russian women are any different from us? I don't see how I could pull a trigger to shoot a man—even if he *were* the enemy."

Thinking of Fritz, Kenna said, "That wouldn't bother me. In fact, I would have taken great pleasure in shooting a certain man several months ago—if I'd had a gun," she added.

Steppie laughed. "Irish Fitzpatrick is out of your life for good, Kenna. You can forget him." Then her expression became serious. "But you actually wouldn't want to see him dead, would you?"

"No," Kenna replied. "Not Irish."

That Christmas, when the homesick doughboys, including Irish, sat and shivered in the trenches and listened to the familiar carols wafting across enemy lines, their destruction was being planned by the German General Ludendorff.

Despite the bravery of Madame Botchkerava and all the others, Russia had been reduced to ashes; the plan now was to drive a wedge between the British and French armies. When the Tommies had been chased to the North Sea and the French had fallen back to defend Paris, total destruction would be accomplished. And the pitifully small American army, caught in the archaic siege warfare practiced by the British and French, would serve as mere cannon fodder for the hungry German artillery guns.

131

In March, Ludendorff began his offensive. He broke through the Picardy line, marching westward toward Cantigny, the village fifty-five miles in a northeasterly direction from Paris itself.

And General Black Jack Pershing, the Iron Commander, left his headquarters at Chaumont to seek out Foch, Chief of Staff of the French Army. He finally located him in a farmhouse outside of Clermont-sur-Oise—in conference with Pétain and Clemenceau, Premier of France, for whom Pershing had no liking. For ten months he had resisted having his doughboys piecemealed to the French and British armies. Pershing was prepared to fight—but on no less than a division front. And in his atrocious French, he told Foch he would take on the crack German troops with all that he had—four divisions that might have a half chance—but they would fight as an American army, not as an appendage to a foreign one.

In April, Foch, now named Supreme Allied Commander, pulled the American divisions from the quiet trenches in the Toul sector. And at Seicheprey and Cantigny, the doughboys began to be forged into seasoned troops, as Ludendorff hammered and fired the anvil against the upstart Americans. The German commander had given orders that each time General Pershing sent an American division into the active line, it was to be subjected to every form of hell the Germans could manage—on land as well as in the sky, with Fokker pilots strafing and bombing their positions.

Eb and Seton, used to being crowded into uncomfortable French boxcars and camions, marched on foot this time—toward Cantigny. Down a road shaded by tall thin poplars on each side they went. In the distance, innumerable small woods sprinkled the countryside with their spring foliage new and light green—against the darker green of the conifers that had survived the previous fighting.

On their backs they carried their packs, their gas masks, their shovels, and their rations of canned tomatoes and salmon. And some, acting as coolies, pulled the Chauchat guns alongside them.

Pointing to one of the guns, Seton commented, "They say these Chauchats are made from battlefield scrap."

"Sure enough?" Eb answered in a surprised voice. "I'd a sworn they were made from rusty sardine cans."

"Well, if they can shoot a Heinie, guess it doesn't matter."

Behind the men came the mule-drawn wagons, the larger guns, the cooks with their field kitchens. Yellow dust, like chalk, spread over the land, and through it all the men sang "Mademoiselle from Armentières" to the rumble of the French tanks making their way across the fields.

On a summery day in Atlanta, when the victory gardens and the corn planted in the city parks were a mass of green and proclaimed a lush plenty, and the meatless and wheatless lunch she'd just eaten proclaimed want, Kenna Chalmers packed her trunk to be stored in the attic of Cricket's townhouse.

The day of graduation had come and gone. The goal was at hand—Europe.

Kenna closed her valise which held the uniforms that would accompany her to France. But at the last minute, she opened it again. Unwilling to relegate the pink beaded party dress to the trunk, she retrieved it and hurriedly stuffed it under her military uniforms.

"Are you ready, Steppie?" she called out.

"Almost," the dark-haired girl replied.

They moved out in convoy to Union Station—the retinue of doctors and nurses on their way to the field and evacuation hospitals. As the truck passed the corner of Utoy and Campbellton roads, Fritz gazed from the barbed wire enclosure of the prisoners' compound. He didn't see the blond-haired girl, but he'd heard that she was in the group. Somehow, he felt relieved to have her gone. And that night, he promised himself to work exceptionally long in the second tunnel he had started digging.

At the station, band trumpets blared, flags billowed, and the mayor and other town officials stood at attention. Above, on the Nelson Street bridge, women and children held aloft their tiny American flags.

For months they'd watched the hospital trains arrive with

the sick and wounded. But now the mountain was going to the prophet—doctors and nurses trained at the base hospital at Fort McPherson were ready to do battle in the front lines, where pain and suffering were the adversaries.

The people stood on the same spot where an enthusiastic crowd had waved good-bye forty-four years before to army regulars leaving to join General Custer in his fight at Little Big Horn. Only four weeks earlier, another enthusiastic group had waved farewell to draftees—the 82nd Division out of Camp Gordon—their own boys from Georgia, Alabama, and Tennessee, with a conscientious objector by the name of Alvin York in their ranks.

Cricket and Johnsie, with their handkerchiefs waving, watched the two girls—one so fair, the other so dark—until they stepped up to the railcar, where they were quickly obscured by the steam rising from underneath the wheels of the iron monster.

The military train pulled out amid cheers and shouts. And on the bridge above, a forlorn Cricket, still waving her handkerchief, turned to the woman beside her. "Our girls have gone, Johnsie," she said, and the two women comforted each other.

Kenna couldn't believe it. She was actually on her way. She gazed excitedly at Steppie by her side and down the long rows of seats filled with nurses in identical uniforms.

In other cars of the train were Red Cross girls, Signal Corps girls, canteen workers—teachers and secretaries paying their own expenses to help out overseas. And in still other cars was a conglomeration of male volunteers and draftees, segregated carefully from the opposite sex. Carlton and Davin, of course, were in the car with the other medical officers.

Kenna looked down at her bare left finger. Carlton had wanted to give her an engagement ring, but she had protested. She had no place to keep it and she couldn't wear it while on duty.

She had wanted to keep her engagement quiet because of the military regulations concerning a nurse. Being unofficially engaged to Carlton hadn't made much difference in her life—

134

except for Davin's change in attitude toward her. He had said nothing, of course, but she could tell he disapproved.

Kenna smiled. Davin was so much like her brother, Neal, and she loved him for it. He had the same kindness and concern—the same exasperating stubbornness. He would make someone a good husband.

If Steppie were not already in love with Neal—but she was. That was why she was on the train with her, on the way to France—to help her find him. She'd just have to be on the lookout for someone suitable for Davin.

"Do you think the ocean voyage will be rough?" Steppie asked, looking away from the window. "I'd hate to be seasick."

"It will probably be a very smooth crossing," Kenna assured her. "I'm told there are few storms this time of year."

"But lots of U-boats," Steppie ventured. "I guess they're more dangerous than the storms."

"We'll be traveling in a convoy," Kenna said. "That should make it safer." She didn't mention the ships that had already been sunk by the U-boats or sabotaged by enemy agents. And she hoped that Steppie had not kept count.

All day and into the night they traveled, the clack of the wheels a monotonous sound occasionally interrupted by the cheers of the people standing on the side of the tracks. As the train slowed, soldiers leaned out of windows to receive kisses offered by fresh-faced young girls with laughing eyes. And each time the train pulled into a station, the Red Cross women, the Knights of Columbus, and the Jewish Welfare Board were there with food, cigarettes, and chocolate.

On the second day, when the train had stopped to take on water in a sparsely inhabited area, a male voice floated through the open window by Kenna's seat.

"Nurse, I have a terrible pain. Will you come outside and hold my hand?"

Kenna looked up into teasing brown eyes and then, ignoring the young soldier, she returned her attention to the book she was reading. But Carlton Torey had chosen that moment to check on her. His angry voice sent the soldier scurrying from the window.

"How long has he been bothering you?" the major demanded. "I'll report him to his commanding officer."

"He wasn't bothering me, Carlton," she said in a quiet voice. "He's probably bored with the long trip. He meant no harm."

"Don't find an excuse for him, Kenna. He should have known better. And you should have known better than to encourage him."

Her surprised gray eyes met his stare. "You have a way of looking at a man, Kenna," he accused, "that makes him forget all propriety. I hope you'll do something to curb it before we reach Toul."

He stalked out of the car and the other nurses gazed curiously at Kenna. Steppie, coming back to her seat, recognized her friend's angry glint, the stubborn tilt to her chin.

"What was that about?" Steppie asked.

"Major Torey thinks I'm flirting with every soldier on the train."

"Surely not."

"Well, not all of them." The angry look subsided as Kenna laughed. "Just one. The poor fellow was so frightened when he saw an officer standing over me that he couldn't get away fast enough. I doubt that he'll come to my window again."

By late afternoon of the third day, the train arrived in New York. And then the confusion began—baggage, food, transportation, a place to sleep. Nothing had been arranged except for a giant warehouse at the dock—as if the nurses and the other women could be stored like canned goods for three more days until the ship was scheduled to leave port.

Kenna balked. Knowing that they would never be missed, she announced to Steppie, "Come on. We're going to the Waldorf instead."

"What about Davin and Carlton?" Steppie inquired. "They'll be looking for us."

"We'll be lucky to see them aboard ship," Kenna replied, searching the unfamiliar faces of the immense crowd. "We're on our own, Steppie—for the next three days—whether we like it or not."

And Steppie, afraid she'd be separated from Kenna also, stayed at her side and fought her way to the exit while dragging the valise behind her.

Loudspeakers announced the comings and goings of trains and passengers, and sought to find the owners of one small, five-year-old boy.

Finally the two girls emerged onto a busy street where no vehicles for hire waited. Kenna managed to catch the eye of a driver just pulling into his place down the street. When he stopped at the curb before her, Kenna said, "To the Waldorf, please."

The man got out to help them with their luggage, securing it in the front seat beside him. Steppie and Kenna climbed into the back.

"I don't know *why* you're doing this, Kenna. We'll never get a room," Steppie complained.

"Oh, yes, we will," Kenna assured her. "We'll stay in the Junior League suite. I brought my membership card—just in case."

"But Kenna, we resigned. Don't you remember?"

"The Waldorf doesn't know it. Would you rather stay in the suite or the warehouse at the dock?"

"The suite, of course. I feel so dirty with all the train soot in my hair. And I do so want a nice long soak in a real tub."

When they reached the Waldorf and the doorman had helped with their luggage, Kenna swept into the hotel as if she were royalty with an immense traveling entourage, instead of one small frightened friend and two bags.

Leaving Steppie to stand guard over their luggage, she approached the crowded registration desk. In her long, slender fingers she held the card—the entree to a reasonably priced room for the night. And she prayed that no one had beaten her to it.

Sixteen

"NO RESERVATION WAS RECEIVED BY TELEGRAM, MISS Chalmers."

Kenna's innocent gray eyes stared helplessly at the man. "What a pity," she said. "And I had so counted on staying here."

She continued staring at the registration clerk. With a flushed face, he said, "I'll check to see if the suite is still available."

The smile hurried him on and Kenna waited, her fingers crossed.

"You're in luck, Miss Chalmers," he said, returning. "No one has reserved it until tomorrow night."

Kenna brightened. At least they'd have a room for one night. As for the next two, she would worry about that later.

In fifteen minutes, Steppie and Kenna were ensconced in the suite, and they laughingly drew straws to see who would be first in the bath.

Steppie won, and as Kenna waited her turn, she could hear a soft lilting voice from behind the bathroom door. Kenna chuckled when she recognized what Steppie was singing. She must have picked up the words in the wards at Fort McPherson. "Mademoiselle from Armentières—parley-voo?" Cricket would have a fit if she could hear her cousin now.

In the elegance of the suite, Kenna performed a few dance steps to the music as she pulled a fresh uniform from her valise. In a few minutes, Steppie appeared at the door, with a towel draped around her, her long dark hair still damp.

"It's all yours," Steppie announced, waving her hand in the direction of the bath, and then quickly clutched at the towel threatening to come loose.

"I've learned something about you tonight, Steppie Hannon," Kenna said, not disguising her mirth.

"What?" the girl asked.

"That you enjoy singing naughty songs in the bath."

The brown eyes widened in consternation. "Was that a naughty song?" she asked.

"As naughty as they come," Kenna answered with a burst of laughter.

"Oh dear," was all Steppie managed to say.

They had their dinner sent to the suite. Exhausted from their days on the train, Kenna and Steppie, as soon as they finished eating, crawled between clean white sheets and closed their eyes.

The doorman's face remained in Kenna's thoughts. Where had she seen him? The last time she was in New York—with her parents? But no—she'd been a child then—and the man wasn't much older than she. He would have been a child too. But where could she have seen him? The face finally faded as the girl went to sleep.

That night, there were no dreams. Peaceful—quiet—the night passed and dawn came—and the two girls slept through part of the morning until a knock at the door summoned them from deep sleep.

The maid had come to clean the suite and change the linens and towels. Kenna let her in. When the woman saw the nurse's uniforms hanging in the closet, she immediately showed her interest in the two occupants of the suite.

"Where are you from?" she asked.

"Atlanta," Steppie replied, now clothed in her lounging robe.

"Then you must be part of the group waiting to go overseas."

The two girls neither confirmed nor denied it. The maid went on as if she were not aware of the silence.

"I have a brother overseas," she confided. "Private Jackson Romero. You might run across him sometime. If you do, I'd appreciate it if you'd say hello for me."

"Which sector is he in?" Kenna inquired.

"He's a hostler, working on a railroad near Toul."

"Why, that's where . . ."

Kenna's quick frown stopped Steppie. And Steppie, remembering the orders not to divulge their destination to anyone, flushed.

"That's where Joan of Arc lived," Kenna said, finishing Steppie's sentence for her. "The bishop of Toul gave her a special dispensation, if I remember, from family obligations, so she could leave to help the king save France."

The hotel maid, acting impressed with the information, said, "You must be awfully smart—to know things like that."

"Oh, I read a lot," Kenna replied.

When the maid had finished and gone, Steppie apologized. "Thank you, Kenna, for rescuing me. I knew better than to mention where we were going. But she seemed so friendly and interested—and when she mentioned her brother—"

"Most spies and sympathizers act friendly and innocent," Kenna answered. "But they're smart. You never know where they might crop up—on a train—in a hotel . . ." she suddenly stopped.

The doorman downstairs—his familiar face—No, it couldn't possibly be—and yet—

She turned excitedly to her friend. "Steppie, do you remember when the four German prisoners escaped from camp?"

"Of course. It was the same day as the fire."

"And one was never caught."

"I know. That's why Cricket was so happy for Verbena to move into the room off the kitchen. She was too frightened to stay in the house alone, after that."

"Steppie, did you see the doorman last night when we checked into the hotel?"

Steppie nodded.

"Did he look familiar to you?"

"I didn't notice him that much. Kenna, are you suggesting . . ."

"Yes. I think he might be the escaped prisoner."

"But New York is so far from Atlanta."

"He's had months to get here—and what better place for a German sailor than the busiest port in the United States, where he can watch the comings and goings of ships? Let's get dressed," Kenna suddenly suggested, "and go downstairs to take another look at him."

"He wouldn't be on duty this soon, would he?"

Kenna hit her forehead in disgust at herself. "You're right. He probably won't come on duty again until late afternoon."

"And by that time, we'll be out of the hotel," Steppie said.

"Why do you say that?"

"We'll have to give up the suite to the people with reservations."

"Maybe not," Kenna replied.

But Steppie was right. There were no other rooms available in the hotel. And with a group of women waiting downstairs for the girls' luggage to be removed, Kenna and Steppie had no recourse but to vacate the suite by noon.

"Where will we go?" Steppie asked.

"Nowhere—until I get another look at the doorman."

Their luggage remained with the bell captain. But after sitting in the lobby for an hour on the round seat that encircled a column rising to the ceiling, Kenna and Steppie decided to leave the hotel. To help pass the time, they began to walk with no particular destination in mind. Finally, in late afternoon, when they had grown tired of peering into shops and trying on clothes and hats they would never wear, they returned to the hotel.

Kenna saw the man on duty. He was the same one that she had noticed the evening before. Mentally clothing him in the white garb of a prisoner, instead of the doorman's uniform with gold epaulets on his shoulders and the hat partially shading his broad face, she was almost certain in her identification.

Kenna walked on, and when the man couldn't overhear, Steppie burst out, "Well, is he the one?"

"I'm almost certain he is," Kenna replied. "He's the same height and build as the prisoner who walked behind Fritz each morning. Don't you remember seeing him when they filed along to the boiler room?"

"I never looked in their direction," Steppie said. "So I'm afraid I'm no help at all in identifying him."

141

Kenna bit her lip and Steppie, watching her, asked, "What are you going to do now?"

"See the manager."

"I think I'll just sit in the lobby and wait for you. You know how I hate any unpleasantness."

"Well then, watch him for me while I'm gone."

The acting assistant manager was quite polite to Kenna Chalmers—but he didn't believe her.

"My dear Miss Chalmers, there is a certain hysteria in New York because of the sabotage of the ship in the harbor last week. You don't know how many potential spies have been reported by the citizens—one 'spy' was actually the president of a bank." His smile confided his humor. "But let me assure you, our doorman doesn't happen to be an escaped prisoner from Georgia. I appreciate your concern, but . . ."

"Was the doorman hired before or *after* May 1917?"

"Miss Chalmers," he reprimanded gently, "our personnel records are closed."

He stood up, dismissing her. And then, attempting to soften the blow, he said, "I think you're quite patriotic—and I'm sure all of America appreciates what you and other women like you are doing."

When Kenna returned to the lobby, Steppie brightened. "What did he say?"

"I didn't see the manager," Kenna replied in a disappointed voice. "Only one of his underlings. And he didn't believe me."

"Kenna, maybe he's right. Maybe you *are* mistaken."

"No, Steppie. The more I think about it, the surer I am."

An idea suddenly occurred to Kenna. Impatiently she motioned for Steppie to get to her feet. "Just pretend you understand what I'm saying, Steppie. That's all I ask."

Puzzled, Steppie followed her friend through the lobby and the man in question opened the door for them to the street.

"A taxi, please," she requested. And his whistle sounded to bring the desired transportation.

As if it were the most natural thing in the world, Kenna, still within earshot of the doorman, began to speak softly in German. Steppie's mouth dropped open. She'd known Kenna had been studying the language along with her French for some time, because of Neal . . . but to burst into the foreign, guttural tongue on a street in New York—that was dangerous. Anyone could overhear.

The taxi door opened, and the doorman, waiting for them to enter the vehicle, said, "You want to go to Forty-second Street, miss, not Madison Avenue."

So he *had* heard her. He *had* understood her, even if Steppie hadn't.

"Thank you," she said, tipping the doorman, who immediately closed the door after them.

When they had made their way down the street, out of sight of the hotel, Kenna tapped at the glass partition. "I've changed my mind," she informed the taxi driver. "I want to go to Pier No. 12, where the British transport is berthed."

"We left our luggage, Kenna—with the bell captain. We'll have to turn around to get it," Steppie said.

"We're going back to the hotel," Kenna replied, "as soon as we report to Colonel Bledsoe at the dock. Then maybe we'll see some action concerning the doorman. They'll listen to a man," Kenna complained bitterly. "I'm so tired of being considered silly and hysterical—just because I'm a woman."

But action came sooner than expected, and in a far different manner than Kenna had visualized.

Unfamiliar with the route, she didn't know that the taxi driver had another destination in mind.

It was getting late and Steppie was hungry. On a side street where the buildings looked more disreputable than the ones in the previous block, the taxi slowed and pulled to the curb.

At Kenna's questioning look, the driver turned to her and said, "I have to pick up something in one of the offices, miss, to take with me. I won't be long."

He seemed nervous, his hand tugging at his red striped tie, as if it had suddenly become too tight for his neck.

Irritated at the stop in such a seedy-looking section, but unable to do anything about it since the driver had already disappeared through the entrance of a low red-brick building, Kenna sat drumming her fingers impatiently against the armrest.

"I don't like this, Kenna," Steppie complained. "I'm almost sorry we ever decided to go to the Waldorf overnight."

Steppie, watching the white porticoed entrance with its paint peeling in spots, saw the entrance door open. "Thank heavens," she said. "I was beginning to think he'd never come back."

But Steppie was wrong. Instead of the driver, two strange men walked out of the building and eyed the yellow taxi. At their scrutiny, Kenna became furious. She watched as they approached the taxi and looked as if they might open the door.

Leaning near the open window, Kenna informed the two men in her haughtiest voice, "This taxi is occupied. It's not for hire."

"You two ladies will please be so kind as to come with us," one man said, flashing an identification badge in front of Kenna's eyes. She recognized it immediately as the sign of the citizens' committee—that vigilante group of private citizens concerned with the welfare of the public.

"Kenna," Steppie wailed, thoroughly frightened.

"It's all right," she assured the girl beside her. "They're not kidnappers."

As they were shepherded inside the building, Kenna saw the taxi driver sneak down the corridor, and she heard the sound when the taxi pulled into the traffic, leaving Kenna and Steppie stranded with the two burly strange men who suddenly looked very dangerous.

"Spies?" Kenna repeated. "Of course we're not German spies. I've told you time and again where you can find an actual spy, if you want him."

The man seated behind the desk seemed oblivious to her denial. "He's being picked up," the man affirmed. "The doorman at the Waldorf."

A measure of satisfaction caused Kenna to smile. "Then you'll let us go now?"

The man didn't answer directly. "You were heard to converse in German together," the man accused. "By the taxi driver."

"I told you all about that. I did it to prove that the man

144

understood German.'' Kenna was so tired of having to explain over and over to someone who didn't believe a word she said.

He stared at their identifications for a while longer. ''Where are the real nurses?'' he questioned. ''Chalmers and Hannon?''

Kenna straightened in indignation. ''You see them—before you.''

The man gave a derisive laugh. ''You should have found a better disguise. No one with a grain of sense would believe either one of you was a nurse.''

''Why?''

''You look much too delicate and you speak out of character for a nurse. But I'll admit whoever trained you did a superb job in coaching you to imitate that soft Southern accent. If I didn't know better—''

Kenna was getting madder by the minute.

''Too bad someone as smart as you evidently had to make two such glaring mistakes.'' He didn't wait for Kenna to ask what they were. Seeming pleased with himself, he recited them. ''First—staying at the Waldorf. Nurses don't have that kind of money. That was a giveaway immediately. But the most glaring mistake was in conversing with your fellow spy in German in front of someone else.''

Kenna sighed in frustration, while Steppie, slumped in the chair next to hers, looked as if she wished the floor would open to swallow them both.

''I'll give you the name of American military officers who can vouch for us,'' Kenna announced.

''You do that, miss. I hope for your own sake we've made a mistake, but somehow, I don't think so.''

He stood up and the two men standing guard in the room—the same men who had hauled them unceremoniously from the taxi—came forward. ''We'll sort it out tomorrow,'' the man at the desk said. ''It's late and my wife expected me for dinner over an hour ago.''

''Tomorrow?'' Steppie repeated, finding her voice again. ''What's going to happen to us until then?''

''You'll be detained here in the building. The cots are actually very comfortable.''

"No," the dark-haired girl protested, shaking her head in disbelief. But the man behind the desk adjusted the black bands on his shirt sleeves, put on his coat, and left the room.

Kenna and Steppie, placed in the custody of the two burly men, were hurried along the dark, musty-smelling corridor to a shabby room where a lone light bulb, covered with a layer of dust, gave out a desolate, meager illumination—like a corpse candle presiding over the pall of two dingy gray cots in the corner.

Seventeen

"WE'RE IN TROUBLE, KENNA. DEEP TROUBLE."

"I know," Kenna agreed.

"What are we going to do?" Steppie asked.

"There doesn't seem to be anything we *can* do until tomorrow when the man comes back—except hope and pray we'll get something to eat."

They heard a commotion in the hallway. And by the sound, they knew that the doorman had been picked up. But the noise didn't last long. Dragging footsteps—a door slamming—and then silence.

Under the dim light of the hanging bulb the two girls sat and listened and waited for food that never came. Across the room, the one small barred window opened onto an alleyway, but it was too small and too well protected by the iron bars for them even to think of trying to escape through it.

Outside, a trash can overturned; a cat yowled. Frightened at the night sounds outside the window, Kenna and Steppie held on to each other. Gradually the noise subsided. The two finally dozed until another disturbance caused them to sit straight up in bed, their uneasy minds attuned to the least change around them.

The clop of a horse and the rattling of glass bottles served to magnify the loneliness of early morning hours. The milkman on his route, thought Kenna, sleepily. Soon now, the sun would be up—and she and Steppie would have the nightmare behind them. Her mind drifted again into slumber.

The gnawing of wood near her penetrated Kenna's consciousness. Sitting up, she rubbed her eyes and glanced at her watch. Seven o'clock. She looked over at Steppie, who was hunched uncomfortably on the other cot, as if she had fought each moment of sleep.

The gnawing sound returned and Kenna returned to listening. Where were the men who'd locked them up for the night and then abandoned them to hunger? Were they still in the building, or had they too gone home to wives and children?

The German was in the building—along the same hall. Probably in the next room, where the sound was coming from.

Suddenly Kenna was certain he was trying to escape. The forcing of wood attested to it. She continued to listen while the sound grew. A sudden crash ripped the hallway and Steppie sat straight up in bed.

"What was that?"

"It sounded like a door bashed in," Kenna replied. "I think our German has just gotten free."

Before Kenna had finished speaking, a voice sounded at their closed door. "*Fräulein?*" the voice called.

Steppie cowered in her cot and moaned. "He'll kill us, Kenna."

"No. He thinks we're spies, too," Kenna whispered.

"*Fräulein,* are you inside?" the voice came again.

"*Ja,*" Kenna replied, trying to put the same inflection in her voice as Fritz had done.

Again, Steppie moaned in fright, but Kenna motioned for her to be silent. The door bulged against the force from outside. Kenna watched while it groaned and creaked. The wood split, and then the door came apart, revealing the doorman from the Waldorf still in uniform, standing on the other side.

The splintered panel was just large enough for the girls to squeeze through. And when they had wriggled past the opening, they began to run down the hall behind the German.

"Our purses," Kenna whispered, stopping. "They're in a cabinet in the office."

The two men who had served as jailers were nowhere in sight. Kenna, Steppie, and the German retraced their steps and went inside the office. With a kick from the doorman's shoe, the small lock on the cabinet came loose. And Kenna quickly reached inside the cabinet for their purses.

Following the man now to the alleyway behind the building, they continued running. Just past the alleyway, on the dingy gray street they saw the empty milk wagon rolling past them.

The German pointed to the wagon—and they ran to catch up with it.

The driver, already asleep, with his day's work behind him, didn't hear a sound when the German helped the girls into the back. The horse plodded on, as he had done every morning for the past ten years—back to the dairy barn where his bucket of oats waited.

Unaware of the two girls hidden in the back or of the man running in the opposite direction, the team rolled on through the city. For horse and driver the day was the same as the one before—the same as the one to come. They had no reason to be suspicious, for nothing out of the ordinary ever happened. They delivered fresh milk; they picked up the empty bottles. It was as simple as that.

Kenna had no idea where she and Steppie were. But it didn't matter. They were free. And with luck, they wouldn't be missed for a while.

But what about the doorman? She had done her patriotic duty in reporting him. But her feelings were now ambivalent. He wasn't at all like Fritz, for Fritz would have thought only of himself—no one else. He wouldn't have risked a moment of precious time to rescue *anyone*. True, the doorman had thought they were German sympathizers. That made a difference. But for the first time, the idea hit Kenna that maybe all Germans weren't monsters as they'd been pictured. Her hatred of them had been so strong because of Neal—and because of Fritz.

Now she didn't know what to think. It was all so confusing. She'd just have to sort it out when she had time. They were at war with Germany. The man was an enemy. She had reported him, but now it was up to the citizens' committee. And at the moment, she was madder at them than at the doorman.

As the milk wagon proceeded down the street, Kenna reached up to smooth her hair, adjusting the large tortoiseshell hairpins to catch the escaping silver-blond strands.

Steppie did the same, wincing slightly at the splinter caught in her hand.

When Kenna deemed they were far enough away from the low red-brick building with its white portico, she jumped down and held out her hand for her dark-haired friend. Afraid to be separated even for a moment from Kenna, Steppie reached out as she, too, jumped.

A curious housewife, sweeping the stoop of a brownstone, smiled at the two who had evidently hitched a ride with the milk wagon.

Self-consciously, Kenna and Steppie walked down the street, away from the brownstone. Their capes disguised the wrinkles of their uniforms, but they were both conscious of a less than immaculate appearance.

Now they must make decisions—how to get to the pier—whether to risk a taxi again, if they could find one—what to do about their luggage, left behind at the hotel.

The smell of sausages wafted over the sidewalk and the two girls wrinkled their noses in pleasure. They had eaten nothing for almost twenty hours. As if by common consent, their priorities changed. They followed the aroma down the street and to its source—a corner cafe, where the sign, pointing to the basement steps, told them that Angelo's was open for breakfast.

Without hesitation, they descended the steps, pushed open the glass door framed in brass, and entered the cafe, where red-checkered tablecloths and a plump, smiling dark-haired woman greeted them.

In an unobtrusive alcove, Kenna and Steppie appeased their hunger with succulent sausages, potatoes shredded and cooked in spicy oil, and long loaves of brown bread, fresh from the oven, with real butter melted between the slices. What a feast for the two, who hadn't eaten for such a long time.

"Have another piece of bread, Steppie."

"You're talking with your mouth full, Kenna."

Swallowing her food, Kenna replied, "The rules of etiquette don't seem to matter that much when you're starving." Her smile lit up her eyes. "And if it offends you, Steppie, please look the other way—because I'm not going to leave

Angelo's cat one single morsel from my plate." At her comment, the orange-striped cat sunning himself on the windowsill meowed and jumped down to rub against Kenna's skirt. Steppie laughed for the first time that day.

They finished eating; they paid their bill. The smiling plump woman allowed Kenna and Steppie to use the washroom just on the other side of the lace curtains that divided the family's living quarters from the public cafe.

Now that they were ready to venture upon the street again, they became nervous. A yellow taxi, cruising slowly down the street, caused Kenna to jump back into the stairwell. She continued to watch until the vehicle stopped a few feet from the cafe entrance. But a man in a dark business suit, with wing-tipped collar, emerged from the taxi. No one was looking for them. The driver was for hire and not the same man as the one who had gotten them into trouble the day before.

Quickly Kenna moved out of the shadow of the basement steps and hailed him. Steppie followed her toward the vehicle.

"To Pier 12, please," Kenna said.

The quicker they reached the pier, the safer they would be. They would just have to send for their luggage later.

Tension mounted as the driver looked the two up and down. But he finally slammed the door shut behind them, and walked around to his side of the car. As he took his vehicle into a stream of traffic—watching out for the carriages and horses, the pushcarts crossing from one side of the street to the other—Kenna and Steppie, sitting in an uneasy posture on the back seat, breathed easier.

By the time they arrived at the pier, it was teeming with sailors, longshoremen, military men, and a carload of officers' horses with their grooms—black casuals—assigned to take care of them on the ocean voyage.

The pier resembled a city itself and for a while Steppie wondered if they would ever find their way to the barracks where the others were waiting.

"Steppie," a familiar voice rang out, and at its sound she turned to search the mass of faces.

"Davin?" she called. And in a louder voice, the name

151

reached over the humanity that separated them. "Davin," she called again, and she saw him weaving his way toward her.

She was never so happy to see anyone. Kenna, hearing the exchange, retraced her steps and braved the crowd, until she and Steppie were reunited with Captain Davin Grant.

"Where have you been?" he demanded fiercely. "We've been out of our minds with worry."

Steppie deferred to Kenna. And with an almost imperceptible break in her voice, she replied, "Oh, we've been staying at the—at a hotel."

He frowned at her answer. "You should have let Carlton know, Kenna. He's had no sleep for the past two days—because of you."

Guiltily, Kenna inquired, "Where is he now?"

"At the morgue—to try to identify a girl fished out of the harbor last night. He thought it might be you."

"Oh, Kenna." Steppie's distressed voice caused Davin to look again at the small, dark-haired girl.

"I knew Kenna might do something rash and foolish," he said, "but I'm surprised, Steppie, that you were a party to it too."

Two large tears swam dangerously near the edge of Steppie's brown eyes, and her look of hurt caused Davin to swear under his breath.

"It's not as if we were AWOL, Davin," Kenna protested, angry now that he'd upset Steppie. "We were free to stay anyplace we could find a bed—and we did."

Carlton Torey returned to the pier. Although he'd been unable to identify the body of the dead girl, he *had* given positive identification to the two pieces of luggage that the police had picked up at the Waldorf. They belonged to Kenna and Steppie. There was no doubt. But nothing inside the valises had given any hint or clue as to the girls' current whereabouts.

He should have made sure that they stayed together when they got off the military train. But each group had been directed through a different gate. And it had been impossible to find them in the mob.

"Hello, Carlton," she said, looking up into his hazel eyes.

152

Alternating between wanting to hug Kenna and shake her for giving him such a scare over the past two days, he did neither. Instead, he sat down in a chair next to hers, and ran his hand through his short, sandy brown hair.

Kenna's appearance gave no hint that she'd been through any unpleasantness. A change of clothes, a bath, and something to eat had given her a refreshed look. But inwardly, she was still shaken. And she would not be entirely at ease until she was aboard the transport headed for France.

Kenna waited for Carlton to speak. Cigarette smoke swirled in layers around the lights. The cavernous canteen hall set up by the Red Cross with counters, tables, and chairs furnished by donations had been divided—one section for the enlisted men, one section for the officers. And the women scheduled for overseas had been divided also—by personal choice—as if wearing different colors of rival football teams and cheering each team for the win. Carlton noticed as he looked around him that it seemed the majority of girls had selected the enlisted men.

"Davin told me you were safe."

"Yes."

A few seconds of silence wedged them apart again. The canteen worker came to take their order and when she was gone, a nervous Kenna began to speak the same instant as Carlton.

"We . . ."

"You . . ."

"I'm sorry. What were you going to say?"

"You got your luggage all right?"

"Yes. Steppie too. It was . . . such a big mixup."

"Davin tells me you stayed at the Waldorf."

"Yes."

He frowned. "But I was told at the desk that you weren't registered."

"We stayed in the Junior League suite."

"Aha," he said. "That accounts for it then. You weren't in the public part of the hotel."

"No."

The hot chocolate was delivered to the table and Carlton began to sip his. There was still something about the episode

153

that bothered him. But his relief at being reunited with Kenna took precedence over the nagging doubt in his mind.

He looked at his watch and quickly drained the hot chocolate.

"It won't be long now before we board the ship. You have your assignment?"

"Yes."

"I don't relish sharing the ship with a load of horses," Carlton commented, "because of the odor. But I suppose the infantry officers must have their mounts when they arrive."

A picture suddenly flashed in Kenna's memory—a giant white horse blocking her way, and the arrogant man astride the animal. A strange feeling came over her as she thought of Irish and his horse. She wondered where they were—which village—which hill. And she wondered if Irish were still alive.

The ship's hold was full—with horses, bales of hay, locomotives, trucks, automobiles, gasoline—and ammunition. Now it remained to fill the topside of the ship with human cargo—soldiers, medical units of doctors and nurses, and volunteer workers paying their own way.

The time finally arrived and the exodus began. Like Noah's ark, two by two, they climbed up the gangplank of the transport, paused to show their credentials, and then, picking up their baggage, hurried past the guards.

Kenna and Steppie stood at the base of the gangplank and waited their turn. The moon, bright overhead, played upon the water, and the twinkling stars fretted the midnight blue of the sky. Military police strolled up and down the pier. Then, as Kenna glanced behind her, they were joined by civilian police. A quick conference ensued, and they immediately spread out, as if in search of someone.

"Kenna, look!" Steppie cried in agitation; for she had spied the man with the black band around his sleeves. With him were the two burly dark men—all members of the citizen's committee. And they seemed to be heading straight toward the group of nurses in scarlet and blue capes.

Kenna glanced upward to the railing where Davin and Carlton waited.

They waved and Kenna, wanting no attention called to her, pretended she didn't see them. She moved quickly between two larger nurses, who glared at her for trying to break in line.

Steppie glanced again at the men gaining on them. "What will we do if they see us?" she croaked, directly behind Kenna.

"Don't look back. Just keep going," Kenna urged.

The line stopped. Kenna and Steppie, feeling trapped, looked downward and shielded their faces from view.

The line moved again. Kenna, still looking at her feet, squeezed closer to the cape in front of her. And once again, the nurse turned to frown at her.

With a sudden surge, the wave of scarlet and blue gained momentum. The men now stood at the gangplank and scrutinized each nurse as she stepped forward. Kenna and Steppie completed the sagging gangplank, showed their identifications quickly, and, dragging their baggage, disappeared on deck where the two doctors waited for them.

Eighteen

NOT LONG AFTER THE PICTURE OF IRISH AND HIS HORSE HAD flashed into Kenna's mind and she had wondered where he was, Irish Fitzpatrick was wondering the same thing.

The mist of the river rose out of the blackness of the night and spread through the forest like suffocating, musty velvet. The front line trenches were now nothing but cratered holes. In rock nests hidden in the woods sat birds of prey—the Huns with their hands still on their clips, waiting to claim the meager number of Americans that had survived.

Telephone lines, stretched from tree to tree and trench to trench, had been blasted apart. There was no way to reach headquarters—no way to find out where the remnants of battalions remained.

The injured lay where they had fallen, for the field medics had been wounded also. There were not enough ablebodied men left to carry the casualties to the collecting stations, even if they could find their way out.

That night, no one knew who had won the battle. Certainly not Irish. He only knew that his own platoons were cut off, his men killed or lost in the mist that wrapped around their bones but gave no protection. The French command had changed the battle plan three times. And they had advanced according to the third plan. Now the Germans were at their backs and fresh troops were filling the trenches ahead.

A noise alerted Irish that someone was near. Taking his pistol from his Sam Browne belt, he advanced cautiously, still holding the reins of the horse.

Seton Campbell, in the darkness, with no food or water, with no ammunition for his rifle, raised his shovel to strike. Irish saw him, and recognizing the khaki uniform of his own division, he quickly identified himself.

"God, Captain, I thought you was either a ghost or a stinkin' Hun," Seton uttered and lowered his shovel.

"Where are the others?" Irish whispered.

"Not many of us left," Seton answered. "We ran out of ammunition yesterday."

Through the darkness, Seton followed and Irish, with an uncanny nose for ferreting out his own, gathered them up one by one from the forest—the wounded, the shell-shocked, the scared—the few remaining from the platoons that had been decimated by enemy guns.

The white horse went forward with Irish allowing the reins to hang almost to the ground. Seeing no better than other horses, Godrin sniffed the earth and felt along the curves and holes of the terrain with his nostrils. Irish was content to allow him his head, for their escape through the woods to safety was dependent upon the horse.

In the crags and boulders, the straggle of men robbed quiet enemy nests of their ammunition, and Seton, searching for food, finally found a piece of black bread stashed away in the pocket of a *feldgrau* uniform.

As they circled behind the enemy, Seton looked for Eb. With the addition of each soldier to the line, Seton searched the new face for familiar freckles and red hair—and was disappointed.

Rain began again, a steady drizzle that quickly turned the ground to a pulpy marsh. A whimper edged through the mist and cut to the heart of each man. They'd heard the sound time and again—that of a wounded man. The small retinue stopped and listened.

From the sound below, Irish knew they were near the river. Yet the mist obscured it from view. Again, the slight whimper carried up to the bluff where they stood.

"It might be a trick," a voice cautioned in Irish's ear. "The Heinies may be down there just waiting for someone to come."

The whimper came again and Seton whispered urgently, "That sounds like Eb. I'd recognize his voice anywhere. I've got to go to him." But then Seton began coughing from the miserable aftermath of gas fumes that had lingered in his lungs, made worse by the penetrating dampness of the night.

"No, Corporal," Irish said. "I order you to stay here. I'll go instead." And he added, "If I'm not back in half an hour, you're to find a shallow place and lead the men across the river." He handed the reins of his giant white war horse to Seton, who had no recourse but to follow Irish's order.

Down the chalky bluff Irish edged, gripping bare roots to keep from plunging headlong to the bottom. He stopped and listened. The sound came again—low, whimpering, like a puppy caught in a trap, yet with no hope of rescue.

Fog, still rising from the river and blanketing the bluff in layers, suddenly drifted above, leaving the dim outline of the river and the reeds at its edge. Large guns in the distance began shelling again, lighting up the sky with an orange glow.

Caught in the brief flash of light, a man's boot—bloody and wet—rose from the earth. Irish crouched and watched for some sign of movement. He looked from left to right to make sure the man hadn't been staked out, as the Indians were wont to do, to attract another visitor.

Now on his stomach, with his gun in his hand, Irish crawled the few remaining feet to the man—a *poilu*, his blue uniform covered by the white chalk of the bluff.

The man was dead. Irish's descent had been in vain. But as he still crouched over the body, he heard a click behind him. Quickly he rolled, landing on his belly in the marsh at the water's edge. He raised his pistol to fire and then lowered it. The boy crawled toward him, his eyes dazed, while his finger snapped the trigger of an empty rifle.

"It's all right, Private," Irish called, advancing toward him. Then he saw the shattered leg that the freckle-faced soldier, Eb Jordan, was dragging behind him.

While the rain descended in torrents, the exhausted soldier rested in the tall cover of marsh growth. Irish, still whispering to him now and again, gathered reedy shoots and whittled them to be used for splints to encase the injured leg.

The *poilu* had no need of cloth to keep him dry, and so Irish, with silent apology, stripped the dead Frenchman of part of his uniform. This he used to wrap the young soldier's leg, cushioning the injury first before applying the long, straight shoots and then tying all together with strips of cloth shredded from the *poilu*'s jacket.

Now came the task of how to get Eb to safety. The wagon bridge had been blown up. The rubble of concrete on either side attested to the span that had connected the banks of the river only a few days previously. The river, a mere trickle in the dry season, had now become treacherous with the rain. And the return trip up the bluff was an impossibility.

Anyway, too much time had elapsed—over half an hour. By now, no one would be waiting at the top of the bluff, if the corporal had followed orders. He would have to keep going along the river and hope to find a place where the water was not so formidable.

Along the shore, through the marshy, soggy ground, Irish and the freckle-faced boy continued, stopping every few feet to rest. Irish had contemplated using the boy's rifle as a splint, but he was loath to give it up. So Irish had allowed him to keep it, and now he was glad, for it served as a crutch.

Off and on the sky lit up, the sound of big guns in the distance a reminder of the past nights and a forewarning of the nights to come. Along the path of the river the two soldiers went, and Irish kept searching for a place to cross during the intermittent flashes of light. But the river, responding to the rain, grew more swollen and treacherous as time passed. And the thunder and lightning merged with the sound of guns.

An abandoned French railroad spur whose tracks had been following the riverbank suddenly changed direction. A trestle loomed in the distance where the current took a meandering curve to the right, and that was where the river and rails parted company.

Irish smiled. If the trestle were intact and unguarded, they could use it for their escape.

"Private, have you ever crossed a railroad trestle on foot?" Irish asked.

Eb's eyes responded. "Once," he answered. "My pa nearly skinned me alive for it."

Then the light in his eyes dimmed and he went back to his own world of silence.

The wooden pilings jutted from the water straight into the air—tall, rickety. Irish realized the hard task of getting the boy hoisted to the top.

"Let's go, Private," Irish encouraged. He went first and, finding a position on the x-shaped support, leaned down to pull the soldier toward him. Eb's useless leg dangled behind him as Irish pulled him up.

Letting Eb rest for a minute, Irish edged along the support. "Hold onto my waist," he urged, knowing that if he slipped they would both land in the water below.

Inch by inch they worked their way up the wooden structure. It creaked and groaned with the weight of the two men. And each time the support protested, Irish stopped and held his breath. One final support remained to be scaled. Once again, Irish climbed ahead, and then leaned down to help the boy. But Eb, like a trapeze artist whose timing was off, missed the strong hand waiting for him. He lost his balance, and as he frantically grabbed the railing to hold on, the rifle that he had hugged to him fell with a great splash. The sound magnified in the night and reverberated over the water. Irish cursed under his breath. Anyone within a hundred yards could have heard the sound. He sat and waited to see if someone would investigate. When there was no immediate response, he reached down again to help Eb to the next x-shaped support. Then at last, Irish gripped the iron rails themselves.

Now began the most dangerous maneuver. Completely vulnerable to anyone lurking nearby, they could be picked off as easily as a clay pigeon hurled into the air for target practice.

Before he had a chance to bring Eb to the top, a sudden ping hit the metal rail near Irish's head. A sniper—and Irish knew they were in trouble. He moved and another shot hit even closer as he dived below to the support under the trestle. He and Eb were pinned down with no possibility to get across unless Irish could locate the sniper and silence him.

They had only one gun and the trench knife—and Irish knew he couldn't leave the boy trapped on the trestle without some means to defend himself. He removed his Sam Browne belt.

"Here, Private," he said. "Take the gun. Use as few bullets as you can get by with, and stay put until I get back."

"Where are you going?" Eb asked.

"After the sniper," Irish replied.

Slowly and with a minimum of noise for such a large man, Irish Fitzpatrick swung down the wooden supports and landed in the reeds near the water.

Another shot echoed over the water and this time, Eb returned the fire. Irish frowned. He hoped the boy wouldn't waste all the bullets before he actually needed them.

At the second exchange, Irish lifted his head and tried to pinpoint the direction from which the sniper had fired. The shot had come from the same distance away, so Irish knew that the sniper had dug in—somewhere.

Carefully, Irish began stalking. He took the trench knife from his belt and held it downward, so that the occasional bursts of light wouldn't pick up the gleam of steel. What he wouldn't give for a couple of hand grenades. They had been denied him—as well as the needed tanks. Otherwise, the outcome of the battle would have been far different and his men would not have been cut down.

The shots had angled upward, so that meant that the sniper was not on a level with the trestle, but on lower ground, somewhere along the path of the river. And if there was one, then others could be nearby.

Irish crouched in a duck blind among the reeds, and waited for the sound of another shot. But there was no further sound except the rain.

Had the German heard Irish, and was he conserving his ammunition? There was one way to find out. Irish reached for a pebble and, skimming it across the water, waited for a reaction. It took only a second. A rifle went off, aimed at the river noise, and Irish saw the brief flash of the explosion.

Now he knew the sniper's position. The rain continued its steady drizzle. And Irish, soaking wet, began his flanking of the enemy. He threw another pebble into the water, and when the sniper responded, he fanned out from his position.

Irish could see the German's helmet now, not the *Pickelhaube* with its spike jutting from the top, but a wide, deep helmet designed to give protection to the back of the neck.

The sky lit up again, and a gleam of light haloed the old rail trestle. There on the support, directly beneath the rails,

Eb was outlined as a perfect sitting target. Irish drew in his breath when the German moved. Getting on his knees, the German raised his rifle and took slow, careful aim at Eb. It was then that Irish lunged with the trench knife.

A surprised grunt anticipated the firing of the rifle by a split second. But the attack had achieved its purpose, diverting the aim of the enemy rifle. Irish remained only long enough to make sure the sniper was dead. Then he took the German's rifle and ammunition and raced back toward the trestle.

The firing would have drawn others and Irish realized he had less time than ever to complete the negotiation of the trestle with the wounded man. A low whistle, like the towhee bird's, warbled through the air and Irish waited for the private to respond to this call. The imitation came—the boy had recognized him. Good. Now he could show himself without fear of being shot by his own gun in the private's hands.

Up the support he swung, while the soldier above watched. And in a minimum of time, Irish had reached the last support.

"Did you get him?" Eb whispered.

"Yes."

Irish climbed up to the rails themselves, and then at the top he laid the enemy rifle down and pulled Eb up until he was on the same level. He couldn't afford to rest. They had to get across as quickly as possible. Now came the painstaking movement—cross tie to cross tie, with wide spaces in between, exposing the treacherous water beneath.

They crawled slowly, with Eb dragging his injured leg. They reached the halfway mark with nothing to mar their progress. Then it happened—a painful grunt alerted Irish that something had happened to Eb.

"What's the matter?" Irish demanded.

"My leg," Eb groaned. "It's caught—between the cross ties."

Irish reversed direction and crawled back to the man. But just as he reached down to help him, a barrage of fire flattened Irish. A shot ricocheted against the rail and Eb too fell back.

"Private?" Irish called, denying the sudden sting in his side.

"Go on, Captain," Eb said. "No need for you to get killed too. As for me, I think I'm too tired to struggle any more."

"Damn it, man, you're going to *try*. Pull that leg up. That's an order."

The sound of fire at closer range opposite them answered the barrage from the other end. Thinking at first that they were caught in a cross fire of enemy guns, Irish's heart sank. They were trapped from both ends of the trestle.

Yet the closer fire had not touched them. It had gone over their heads. Irish looked down at the enemy rifle he had confiscated from the sniper. In that instant Irish realized that they had been given protective cover by enemy rifles—but in more friendly hands.

He wasted no more time. "Your platoon's at the end of the trestle, Private," he said. "Let's get the hell out of here—and fast."

Irish forced Eb's leg through the vacant space. At the twisting the man's shoe fell off into the water with a splash. But Eb was free. With a sudden spurt of energy, the two soldiers crawled over the remaining cross ties to the waiting soldiers, while Godrin, the white war horse, remained hidden behind them.

Hands reached out to drag them to safety, while guns echoed and reechoed across the river. Taking cover in the clump of trees, Irish saw Seton, his mouth wide open in a grin.

"I thought I gave you orders to go on, Corporal," Irish admonished.

"That you did, sir. And I obeyed." With a sly look, he added, "But after I was in charge, sir, I decided to come back and wait for you."

An ironic smile twisted the square jaw of Captain Irish Fitzpatrick as he headed toward his horse, Godrin. He removed his hand from underneath his jacket and stared down at the sticky red mass of blood that had oozed from the wound in his side.

Nineteen

THE CONVOY SET SAIL FROM NEW YORK—THE HARBOR BE-
reft of lights. Deep inside the transport, Kenna and Steppie
hid from sight. They passed Bedloe's Island, where the Statue
of Liberty loomed against the black sky.

At the feet of the copper statue lay a broken shackle that
symbolized the overthrow of tyranny. In her right hand rose
Liberty's torch, now dimmed by war. A fitting gift, symbolic
of the tie between America and France.

But the two girls were not concerned with the landscape.
From the moment they had rushed aboard the transport, with
the citizens' committee directly behind them, they had longed
for the open sea.

Now they were free from the channel—free from the committee that had mistaken them for spies—and despite their
entry into submarine-infested waters, Kenna and Steppie felt
safe for the first time in several days.

Reveille—breakfast—sick call. The days on the transport
began the same. And they ended the same, with lights out at
nine—with the constant sway and creak of the ship, the odor
of horses drifting upward from the hold of the ship.

During each day, the ship's crew constantly watched for
periscopes. Occasionally a depth charge was dropped, searching out the metal monsters lurking underneath the ships—
ready to do harm.

The *City of Memphis* and the *Carpathia* had already been
sunk. But as the days passed, the nurses who could maintain
their equilibrium and keep from turning green reported to sick
bay for duty. That was where Kenna saw Davin on the fourth
day out.

"How is Steppie?" he asked.

"She's a little better today. But you know how it is—can't lift her head from the pillow for any length of time."

Davin nodded. "Just like Carlton. She'll be all right as soon as we reach port."

"How long do you think that will be?" Kenna inquired.

"Nine days is the shortest time out. Anywhere up to thirteen. Don't expect we'll break any records, though."

Kenna continued on her rounds—checking on each soldier, each sailor. Looking down into one white face, she recognized the same young soldier who had gazed at her outside the train window on their journey from Fort McPherson to New York.

"Where is the pain?" she inquired softly.

The soldier's eyelids fluttered open at the sound of her voice. "In my . . ." He stopped as he recognized her, groaned, and turned his face to the bulkhead. And Kenna, smiling sympathetically, walked on.

By afternoon, a deadly calm pervaded the sea. Whispers, as quiet as the waves, rippled up and down the decks. A U-boat was tracking them. Anxious glances spread out from the decks and took in the distant waters.

"It's probably a whale," a cynical young soldier commented, seeing nothing.

"Whales don't have antennae," another disagreed. "Besides, whoever heard of a ship following a zigzag pattern to avoid a whale?"

"Maybe it's a large whale," the first soldier quipped.

The movement of the ship became more pronounced as the engines gathered speed. A floating city, the transport was a prime target now, for the convoy had entered the most dangerous part of the voyage.

Kenna went belowdecks to see about Steppie. The dark-haired girl moaned with renewed anguish at the increased rolling of the ship. Her pale face stared at the overhead, while her tongue ran over her parched lips.

"Have you had anything to drink this afternoon, Steppie?" Kenna asked.

Steppie merely turned her head from side to side. Before she knew it, Kenna lifted her head and held a cup to her lips.

165

"No, Kenna. Just let me be," Steppie moaned.

"Drink it," Kenna insisted.

"It will only come up again."

"Maybe not."

Steppie sipped the water, then fell back against her pillow. Kenna walked on from bunk to bunk, pouring water for the nurses with severe cases of *mal de mer,* and seeing that they drank some.

The sudden blast of sirens took them by surprise. Loud—wailing. A cry rose up from the bunks as the women sat up to put on their life jackets.

Kenna rushed to Steppie's side to help her.

"Have we been hit?" Steppie asked.

"It doesn't feel like it," Kenna replied. "Maybe it's just a drill."

"But I'm not dressed," Steppie protested. "I can't go on deck in my nightgown."

Kenna thrust Steppie's right hand through the preserver. "You don't have *time* to get dressed," she scolded.

With her arm around Steppie's waist, Kenna propelled her along the companionway and topside to the lifeboat station assigned them, while others made their way around them to their own stations.

The whine and whir and sound of bells cut through the running of feet, the nervous, quick breathing of spectators, watching and waiting. A U-boat had been sighted. It was no drill.

The destroyers patterned themselves into a protective formation around the ships carrying the cargoes of troops, nurses, and war goods. Seeming to sense the danger, the horses in the hold, without the restraining hands of the black casuals to calm them, kicked and neighed in terror.

"Just listen. The horses are as frightened as we are," one of the nurses commented.

"We don't stand a chance, with all that ammunition. We'll be blown to bits."

A girl began to cry softly. But no one paid attention to her. All eyes watched the sea.

Depth charges, seeking out the enemy, rushed through the deep blue waters, but to no avail. For when the explosion came, it was not a German U-boat, but a cruiser—one of their own—off the starboard bow.

The girl cried louder. But all the others were silent—white-faced.

The enemy had been successful. And Kenna, sick at the sight, watched the cruiser's disintegration before her very eyes. Flames spread rapidly over the waters, hungrily licking at the oil and fanning into the air. Then a second explosion followed the first as the boilers came in contact with the cold ocean water.

With the salt spray whipping over her uniform and bathing her silvery hair, Kenna remained at her station with Steppie for over an hour more—until the bells sounded again, giving them the signal to go belowdecks.

By late afternoon, no survivors had been picked up. The remaining ships of the convoy proceeded on course, while sober-faced Americans—men and women—engraved upon their memories the destruction of one of their own by the enemy.

On the twelfth day they landed in Brest, the busiest and liveliest seaport along the French coast. A large sausage balloon, tied to a tug in the harbor, monitored the comings and goings of ships from its vantage point in the sky.

Almost as soon as they docked, Steppie and Carlton and all the others who had been seasick for the entire voyage began to feel better. They gathered their belongings, and when it was time, they marched with unsteady gait down the gangplank to the concrete dock on French soil.

At the sight of the women pouring from the transport, a great roar of approval went up from the seamen of the U.S. destroyers in port. But the streetwalkers from the Rue de Siam were not so enthusiastic. Their painted faces turned downward in a pout until they spied the soldiers also waiting to disembark.

"'Allo, *sammis*," they called out, waving their handkerchiefs at the soldiers, until the shore patrol, swinging their clubs above them, quickly dispersed them.

"Kenna, look," Steppie whispered, her brown eyes wide

at the provocatively dressed girls fleeing from the shore patrol.

"I see," Kenna whispered back. Not since the days of the Barbary pirates had there been such a fascinating port, Kenna was sure. Her gray eyes took in the swarm of humanity, the stevedores unloading the cargo from the hold of the ship, the horses, skittish from the long voyage, rearing and neighing as they were led onto land.

Kenna watched as the streetwalkers regrouped farther down the street—and waited for the soldiers to stream out of the ship. But the soldiers never got close. In military formation, they were marched straight to Pontenezan Barracks, for shipment the next day to the front. The action was greeted with sneers and hisses from the streetwalkers deprived of new clients.

The nurses, in their voluminous uniforms, starched and clean, were loaded into cars to be taken to the local convent for the night. As they passed the street corner where the scantily clad women stood, staring boldly and curiously at them, many diverted their eyes and pretended not to see them.

"They're not very . . . very nice, are they?" Steppie said in Kenna's ear. Kenna laughed at the dark-haired girl's reaction.

A great excitement pulsed through Kenna's veins. At last, she was on the same continent as Neal—in the same country. And she would find him, even if it took the rest of the war—and afterward, too.

"I'm hungry," Steppie announced. "For the first time since . . . since Angelo's, I'm starving. Do you think the French food will be any better than the English?"

"I hope so," Kenna commented. "I don't think I could take dried billy beef a day longer."

Kenna did not see Carlton until the next day when they boarded the train that would take them to Toul. Only one man—a priest—was in evidence at the convent. The rest were nuns. The boarding school attached to the convent was no longer in operation because of the danger along the coast. But the fine linens and silverware were all intact in the quiet cloistered walls—and the appetites that had suffered so during the ocean voyage were assuaged by the food.

Apricot trees espaliered against the stone walls gave a perfume to the air and the quiet evening bells provided a serenity out of all time and place. The busy port and the cloistered sanctuary were but a few minutes apart. Yet as Kenna and Steppie walked along the archways, trying to get their land legs back, they found it hard to reconcile one with the other.

That night, they slept in narrow, virginal cots, side by side. Kenna closed her eyes and was lulled to sleep by the gentle breeze coming through the window.

Early the next morning, after they had been awakened and fed, the nurses gathered their belongings and climbed into the camions that took them to the trains. All roads led to Paris. At least, that's what Kenna had read. But if she expected to see the living heart of that romantic Gallic city—to savor the streets where Neal had walked, to eat in the little cafes where artists and writers congregated—she was doomed to disappointment: for she stayed in Paris only long enough to change trains.

Chaumont was the center of activities for the Americans—the headquarters of the American Expeditionary Force. Around it, the network of railroads shuttled men and supplies to the front.

Chaumont—Neufchâteau—and finally Toul. Their destination was the base hospital directly below the Saint-Mihiel salient that had been held for four years by the Germans.

Again Kenna caught a brief glimpse of Captain Davin Grant and Major Carlton Torey. It was in Neufchâteau, when they stopped for the night. A regretful wave of the hand and then the two were gone.

"I'll bet they're going to have dinner at the Lafayette Club tonight," Kenna commented. "*We'll* be lucky to have a bowl of thin onion soup."

"Isn't it strange how *food* has assumed such an importance in our lives," Steppie said. "I never thought much about it until the past few days. Now I watch to make sure no one gets a *teaspoon* more than I do."

Kenna laughed. "I know. Neal and I used to fight over the number of peach slices. I can see Verbena in the kitchen now counting them as she put them in our bowls—'one for Kenna, one for Neal.' We haven't changed much, have we, Steppie?"

Her question was never answered, for a man swaggering down the street caught their immediate attention. Their mouths dropped open at the great overcoat with its heavy fur collar, which was a little shaggy from the delousing vats to which all military clothes were subject. He was wearing it proudly, even in the heat of the summer day.

"Look, Steppie," Kenna whispered. "He's a flier, just like Neal."

The man was conscious of being watched. For he was a member of the privileged class of fighter—a pampered romantic god of the skies—with his silver wings proclaiming his spectacular courage in the air, his boots and spurs a contrast to the hobnailed brogans of his land-grounded brothers in the trenches.

"Do you think he's stationed near here?" Kenna asked, watching while the man disappeared.

"Probably. There's an airfield at Colombey-les-Belles, between Neufchâteau and Toul—or so I heard."

"I hear a plane now," Kenna replied. "Listen."

The drone in the distance brought their attention skyward. And fascinated, Kenna, in her nurse's uniform, stood and watched while a plane came into view near the treetops and began its descent over the street in which she was standing.

An iron cross—the *Balkankreuze*—painted upon its wings indicated its nationality.

"Get off the street. Take cover," a male voice shouted behind her. Kenna and the small group of nurses she was with scattered in every direction, just as the strafing down the center of the street sent the dirt flying. An enemy Fokker—in broad daylight—at Neufchâteau.

There were no casualties except for the bruised ego of the fur clad aviator, who stood shaking his fist at the Fokker pilot as he climbed back into the clouds—and a few dirtied uniforms of nurses forced to find cover from the sudden afternoon attack.

Twenty

IN WHAT HAD ONCE BEEN CALLED THE *BON SECTEUR* WITH ITS quiet trenches, lay the medieval city of Toul, with its double walls of stone, lichened green from centuries past, and an old drawbridge calling attention to the tall green grass in the double moat surrounding it.

Now, this ancient town of Lorraine, second only to Verdun as a fortress city, was not so formidable as it had once been. For the strong gates that pierced the rough-hewn stone wall no longer protected. They framed the roadways leading into the park—*porte de Nancy*—*porte Jeanne d'Arc*—where the branches of the linden trees provided a green respite from the rest of the city with its dingy, winding streets and drab gray buildings.

The town appeared to have two seasons at the same time. One, emerald spring—the other, winter gray. And overshadowing the entire city hovered the cathedral of St. Etienne where the skull of St. Mansuy remained the holiest of relics.

On that late summer morning, Kenna didn't come into Toul by way of the park, green with beauty. She saw only the gray of the railroad station and the square surrounding it—the small Goutte de Café, and the Hôtel de la Gare, where thousands of enlisted men on their way back and forth to the Rhine stopped for coffee, showers, and fresh clothes.

The train slowed; the brakes wheezed and steam rose to meet the humidity of the misty landscape. Kenna's eyes, dismissing the dinginess of her surroundings, swept over the hills as she thought of Saint-Mihiel, Montfaucon, and the tiny German-held villages and valleys lying between Toul and Verdun—where her brother, Neal, had been shot down.

Abri 23; Abri 12. The numbers on the houses indicated the

171

number of people who, in the event of an enemy attack, could take refuge from the bombs and the artillery guns in the strong, high-vaulted wine cellars of the stone houses. And beside each sign was painted the dual cross of Lorraine.

The camion, roaring away from the railway station, held both Kenna and Steppie and their luggage. Soon they would be billeted with a French family, and they would be assigned to one of the eight military hospitals on the outskirts of Toul.

"Can you believe it? That we're actually here?" Steppie inquired happily atop the bouncing seat of the camion. "Two whole weeks it's taken us . . . and now we're here."

But Steppie was wrong. Not two weeks—but two *years*—filled with determination, untold obstacles, and near death.

In one of the hospitals three miles away, a nurse stood by an officer's cot and wiped the perspiration from his brow. He had evidently been reliving the nightmare he'd been lucky enough to survive.

They had brought him in from one of the collecting stations at the front, his large body carried on a blanket stretched between two enemy rifles. The surgeon on duty had removed the steel-jacketed bullet to find a wound that was not deep, but uncomfortable—and dangerous, because of the risk of infection.

They said he was due a medal for bravery—and a promotion too—this Captain Irish Fitzpatrick. He had saved the rest of his battalion from certain death.

A name formed on his lips, while the nurse straightened the blanket. She glanced down at the wrinkled, mud-spattered newspaper picture he held in his hand. It was evidently something he treasured—a picture of his girl, perhaps—the one he kept calling for. The nurse smiled and placed the clipping on the nearby table. Then she moved on to the next cot to check another patient.

"You've been assigned to my hospital," Carlton Torey informed Kenna as they ate together that night. "I made sure of that this afternoon."

"Hmmmm," Kenna murmured, her mind on the crepe that slid in its sauce from one side of the plate to the other.

"You haven't heard a word I've said all evening," he complained. "Stop chasing your food, Kenna Chalmers, and look at me."

She put her fork down, and gazed up at him innocently.

"The advice I've been giving you is for your own good. I've seen how all the soldiers watch you. You're not safe at all. And I should have had my head examined for allowing you to come."

She opened her mouth to protest, but he continued. "But now that you are here, there are certain rules you must abide by."

"I have the nurses' code, Carlton. No dancing with enlisted men, no . . ."

"I don't mean the official ones." He began a recital of regulations that he had made up himself, and Kenna sighed as she listened.

"It's all right for you to dine out—if I'm with you. But you're not to go with Steppie. You should have your meals quietly with the Juvin family at times when I can't watch over you or be with you. And you're not to hitch a ride from the military warehouse either, even if the trucks are going right past the hospital. That doesn't look nice."

"The other nurses do it—all the time."

"That doesn't matter. You're different from the others. And you're to stay away from the Rue Pierre Hardie, where the airmen hang out. That's asking for trouble."

The proprietor came with the wine bottle. As he made to replenish Kenna's glass, Carlton stopped him. She'd had enough. It wasn't good for a woman to drink too much wine, even if it were watered down.

"Why did you wave him away?" Kenna asked. "I'm still thirsty."

"You can get some water later—at Madame Juvin's. But you must make sure to put your purification tablets in it."

After they had finished their meal, Carlton paid the bill in francs, carefully counting them out.

"*Bon soir, m'sieu. Bon soir, madame.*"

"*Bon soir, m'sieu—et merci,*" Kenna returned politely in her schoolgirl French. The old man's eyes softened.

Away from the busy little cafe Carlton and Kenna walked,

173

searching for the route through the narrow, winding maze until they finally reached the Juvin house not far from the military warehouse and commissary.

"I won't come in, Kenna. It's already late," Carlton said. He leaned down and kissed her on the cheek.

"Good night, Carlton. I'll see you in the morning."

Madame Juvin, who was watching at the window, opened the door. Like a mother hen gathering her chicks in for the night, she looked at Kenna to make sure she was all right. And once she had assessed that the girl had come to no harm, she locked the door behind her, the sound of the heavy, oversized key in the lock putting a finishing touch to the evening.

Kenna climbed the stairs to the small bedroom that she had been assigned to share with Steppie. Sitting up in bed, with a plump pillow at her back, the dark-haired girl was busy, studying.

"How was the dinner with Carlton?" she asked, putting her book on the bed cover before her.

"The food was all right, but the advice was a little too much."

"He's merely trying to protect you, Kenna," Steppie responded.

"I know." Kenna sighed. "But sometimes I wish . . ." She stopped—and started again. "Sometimes I wish that Carlton—Oh, I don't know *what* I wish."

Quickly she changed the subject. "How was your meal with the Juvin family?"

"Very nice," Steppie replied. "They're so kind. But they speak so fast, Kenna. I could hardly follow the conversation. That's why I'm studying tonight."

"It *is* different from language class, isn't it?" Kenna admitted, removing her uniform and pulling her gown over her head. "But I suppose we'll get better as time goes on. Are you anxious about your first day tomorrow?"

"A little," Steppie admitted. "It's too bad we couldn't be assigned to the same hospital."

"But at least we have the same shifts, so we can leave at the same time and come back here at the same time. And we're only two miles apart." Kenna began brushing her hair, and her eyes reflected concern for Steppie, who never liked

174

going into a new situation alone. "Carlton said that Davin will be at the hospital with you."

At the mention of Davin's name, Steppie smiled. "You know what he told me about the hospital where we'll be?"

"What?"

"That it was an insane asylum only last week. It's complete with bars at the windows—and the only eating utensils are wooden spoons and bowls."

"What happened to the inmates?" Kenna asked.

"Nobody knows. They took them somewhere else. That's all he found out."

That night, Kenna did not sleep well. The shaping up for a giant offensive toward Saint-Mihiel was already in the air. It was no secret to anyone, least of all the taxi drivers in Paris who had been able to pinpoint the movement of troops and name the divisions that would soon be involved. If it was common knowledge to the French people, then the Germans were well aware of the battle plans too. That boded ill for the American army—and for Kenna's success in searching for Neal in the war sector.

Kenna's throat was dry when she awoke the next morning. She'd forgotten to ask for some water. She stirred and stretched, and then glanced at her watch just as the tap on the door sounded.

Madame Juvin opened the door without waiting to be acknowledged. In her hands she carried a tray of fresh croissants, jam, and hot, black coffee. The white ceramic cups were large, to match the white ceramic coffeepot.

"Your breakfast, please," she said, smiling as she laid the tray on the small table by the shuttered window.

"Oh, please—you shouldn't have gone to such trouble. We could have come downstairs," Kenna said.

"*Déjeuner*, yes—you come downstairs for that—but *le petit déjeuner* you have in your room. It is the custom."

Madame Juvin threw back the shutters to allow the early sun in the room.

"*Merci*," Kenna and Steppie chorused as the woman marched out and closed the door behind her. Lured by the

175

aroma of the freshly baked bread, the two girls climbed out of bed.

Large white cabbage roses stared at them from the fading wallpaper above their heads. And red geraniums twisted toward the sun on the open window ledge just outside their room. Only a few feet separated the window of the bedroom from the tiled-roof shed at the back.

It didn't take the two long to eat breakfast and get dressed. With plenty of time to spare, they walked to the warehouse just inside the gates, and Kenna hailed a truck that was heading out in the hospital's direction. She didn't mention Carlton's concern about the propriety of it to Steppie. It was much easier to listen to him and then do as she pleased.

The day was uneventful. Except for a few minor details, Kenna found the service no different from that at the base hospital at Fort McPherson. The wounds were fresher, the breaks more recent—and the gas cases more severe. Those casualties were put into a separate ward, with more privacy, for even a sheet touching the burned flesh caused untold agony.

Several days later, when the routine at the hospital had been established, and her shift had ended, Kenna waited by the roadside with Annette, one of the older nurses on duty with her. The driver of a military vehicle, seeing them in the distance, slowed down at the intersection where the roads crossed.

"Are you going into Toul?" Kenna inquired. "And do you have room for us?"

The driver grinned and nodded twice. Before Kenna climbed in, she looked over her shoulder to make sure her fiancé hadn't seen her. She deliberately climbed into the back, leaving the passenger's seat for Annette, much to the driver's disappointment.

Settled, she looked down at the piece of paper in her hands and the name Brett Lawrence written there. He was in the Balloon and Aviation Service and she was to ask for him at the Red Cross canteen on Rue Pierre Hardie at four. A sense of fear and dread mingled with her excitement. At last, she was going to talk with someone about Neal—not the man

176

Lawrence actually—but a Frenchman, Major Thibault, who might be able to guide her in looking for her brother.

The truck took a long time in spanning the three miles into town. Impatiently, Kenna sat fingering the card, and praying that this meeting would be profitable.

It was almost four o'clock when the truck reached the commissary. Kenna waved good-bye to Annette and the driver, and headed for No. 3 Rue Pierre Hardie.

Promptly at four o'clock each afternoon, the fliers began to drift into their exclusive club maintained by the Red Cross. With a jangle of their spurs, a shake of their fur-collared coats, they lit for the day, their duty done in chasing German Fokkers and harassing ground troops whenever possible.

Carlton Torey didn't like the aviators. And he had made it clear to Kenna. They were a pampered, egotistical lot—and he wanted Kenna to have no truck with them.

But Carlton didn't understand. She wasn't like the railroad canteen girls and some of the other nurses and Red Cross workers who congregated each afternoon to worship at their feet. She needed their help in locating Neal, for she had exhausted all other channels.

Laughter greeted her as she came round the corner on Rue Pierre Hardie. For a moment she stood at the open door of No. 3 and took in the scene before her. French and American and British fliers—exuberant in their greetings to each other—their speech and actions in such contrast to the subdued infantry soldiers coming in from the front each day and frequenting the canteen at the rail station.

"Well, hello, Angel of Mercy," one called out, seeing Kenna hesitate at the door. "Come on in." His long coat with shaggy fur collar dipped to the floor as he executed an exaggerated, courtly bow. Several others joined him and Kenna found herself escorted to a table.

"Looking for someone?"

"Yes. Brett Lawrence," she answered.

The first airman groaned, but the second brightened. "He isn't here. Will I do instead?"

"That's not fair, Ingle," another scolded. "Let the Angel choose."

All three sat down at the small square table with her and proceeded to view her as if she were some rare exotic bird that had just flown into their midst.

Several Red Cross girls eyed Kenna with suspicion.

"Coffee? Chocolate? A doughnut maybe?" one of the men offered.

"Chocolate, please," Kenna requested, and the man got up to go to the counter. His vacant chair was quickly taken over by a boy hovering near the table.

In the corner close to the dingy wall disguised by a bright, amateurish mural, sat two Frenchmen, engaged in a rapid-fire conversation. Now and again, they glanced toward Kenna and then continued talking.

The man returning with the cup of chocolate glowered goodnaturedly at the boy usurping his seat. "Back to your high chair, Junior," he admonished. Embarrassed, the boy got up.

"He's the baby of the bunch. Flew his first mission three days ago."

"How many Fokkers chased you home today, Junior?" one of the men teased.

"Six," the boy promptly answered and grinned.

The men laughed at his obvious exaggeration.

"Hey, didn't I see you in Neufchâteau last week?" The man seated on Kenna's left had been studying her as she sipped her chocolate.

Her gray eyes searched his rugged features. And the memory of Neufchâteau came back—the Fokker strafing the street and an airman in coat and fur collar shaking his fist at the disappearing pilot.

"We stopped in Neufchâteau on our way here," she admitted.

"I remember you. You were in the crowd when the German pilot plowed up the street."

"Yes."

His eyes held a measure of satisfaction when he informed her, "That's the last time he'll ever do that."

"Was he the one you got yesterday, Ace?" the youngest of the group inquired.

The aviator nodded. "The flaming dragon— It took me a week to find him."

"How many does that make for you, Ace?" Junior asked, proud to be included in the conversation.

"Thirteen."

"That's an unlucky number," one of the others stated.

"For the Boche—not for me," replied Ace.

"Miss Chalmers?" The man had come in quietly and now stood beside the table.

"Brett, old boy—pull up a chair."

"Sorry. Some other time, Ace."

Amid the groans of protest, Kenna Chalmers followed Brett Lawrence across the room where they joined the one remaining Frenchman at the corner table.

"Miss Chalmers, I wish to present Major Thibault of the French Flying Service."

The Frenchman stood, snapped his heels together, and, looking straight into Kenna's face, smiled his Gallic smile.

"You knew my brother, Neal?" she asked, sitting down in the chair offered her.

"*Oui.*"

Major Thibault and Brett Lawrence took their seats opposite her. Looking at the Frenchman, Kenna said, "I came to France to find him."

"You believe he is still alive, *mam'selle*?"

"I *know* he's alive, Major. But, more than likely, he's still in enemy territory. That's why I want to get in touch with the underground. Can you help me?"

The man hesitated. "I will make inquiries."

"And you'll let me know?"

"*Oui, mam'selle.*" Major Thibault, with a sudden pain crossing his handsome, weathered face, absentmindedly massaged his left shoulder as he stood. "If you will excuse me, I must leave. *Au revoir, mam'selle,*" he added, clicking his heels together again in old-world politeness.

He nodded to Brett Lawrence and walked toward the door.

"*Au revoir,* Major, and . . . and thank you," Kenna called out, suddenly elated.

Twenty-One

IRISH FITZPATRICK WALKED SLOWLY TOWARD THE WARD where Eb lay with his leg encased in heavy plaster and elevated on a pulley.

The gauze bandage on Irish's wound was small. It was healing well. Another few days and he would be out of the hospital. And within a week or so, he would take command of another unit—this time, under an American general.

Pershing had finally gotten his own command, not subject to either the British or the French. And Irish was pleased with the news. He was tired of elitist generals with their aristocrat's disregard for individual lives. Fury rose in his throat as he thought of the past months of fighting, the lack of food and supplies, the certainty of death, and the archaic French general who couldn't seem to grasp that his textbook methods of warfare were obsolete against the German machine guns.

"Good morning, Captain." Eb's face brightened at the sight of Irish.

"How's the leg this morning, Private?"

"The plaster has finally dried, but it's still as heavy as lead," he quipped. Then his face turned a bright shade of pink. "Captain, I can't thank you enough—"

Irish brushed aside his words. "They tell you how long you'll be here?"

"The doctor talked of sending me back to the States, but I told him I wanted to stay and fight, sir."

Irish nodded and walked on. As he disappeared from the enlisted men's ward, Kenna Chalmers, unaware of his nearness, walked through the other door.

Later, on her way to the officers' ward, she was stopped in the hallway by Annette.

"Kenna, Major Torey wants to see you in his office immediately. Here, I'll take those supplies for you."

Kenna handed the armload of supplies to the older nurse and then crossed the courtyard to the cloistered area where Carlton had requisitioned one of the priests' rooms for an office. She was surprised that he wanted to see her. Usually he ignored her while she was on duty.

She knocked at the door, but there was no answer. She stood outside and waited uneasily. Had one of the nurses at the airmen's canteen mentioned seeing her there? Or had Carlton found out that she wasn't waiting for the service vehicle to take her home in the afternoons? Kenna knocked again. And still there was no answer. The door was unlocked, and so Kenna, hoping he wouldn't mind, walked into the office and sat down to wait.

A crucifix hung on the wall over the desk—probably where the monk's cot had been previously. But that was the only sign of the religious order. Heavy draperies now hung over the windows and an oriental rug—red and beige—covered the tiles of the floor. It was comfortable—in fact, sumptuous—in comparison with the rest of the monastery. Carlton had been busy at the commissary. She could see that.

The ornate gilt frame of the magnificent oil painting caught her eye. This was no commissary art, but old, treasured. She got up from the chair to take a closer look.

"You like my oil painting?"

Kenna whirled. "It's beautiful," she replied. "Where did you find it?"

"It came from the ruins of a château nearby," Carlton said. "I got it at a very good price, since the old gentleman who owned it was rather destitute."

"Is it Flemish?" she inquired.

"Probably, although it's unsigned."

He was in no hurry to enlighten her as to the reason she had been summoned. And that made Kenna uneasy.

"Have a seat, Kenna."

She sat down and smoothed her skirt with the palm of her hand. And she waited for the scolding that seemed inevitable.

"I'm sorry I have to do this to you, Kenna."

181

She gave a start at the seriousness in his voice. Her hand left her skirt and nervously smoothed her hair.

"You're going to have to work an extra shift today. I've just received word that a hospital train is coming in this afternoon. You'll be on ambulance duty until we get the wounded transported and bedded down."

Her relief at his message was short-lived. she was to meet Major Thibault that afternoon at the canteen. Now that was out. The disappointment showed in her face and Carlton saw it.

"You knew when you came, Kenna, that it wasn't going to be easy—that you'd have to work long hours."

"I know," she answered. "I don't mind the hours, it's just that . . ." What could she say? That she had other plans? "How long do you think it will take?"

"I have no idea. Probably into the night."

"Is that all you wanted to see me about?"

"Yes—for now."

"Then, if you'll excuse me, I'll get back to the wards."

He sat behind his desk and tapped his pencil long after Kenna had gone. Yes. This was the only way to handle it. Just keep her on duty longer so she would have no opportunity to get into further trouble at No. 3 Rue Pierre Hardie.

He was grateful to Nurse Brockett for calling her behavior to his attention.

By mid-afternoon, the long row of Tin Lizzies began its trek to the train station. Seated in each vehicle was a driver and one nurse. Empty berths in the back waited to be filled with the wounded.

Kenna sat beside Wells, a gray-haired old man with only one lung and a black patch over his eye. They'd sent him home three times, but each time he'd managed to come back in another capacity. Now he was in the ambulance service. He claimed to be forty-seven, but everyone knew he had shaved at least twenty years off the date of his birth.

Chalky dust rolled over the terrain and sprinkled the golden hillsides of grain interspersed with green patches of turnips as the convoy progressed. A ruined bunker by the side of the road provided a landmark with its rusty tin hat serving as a guard—and an empty artillery shell planted into the earth beside it. Twisted metal rods jutted from the concrete—victim of a hand grenade. The guns in the distance, steady and rumbling, sounded louder than they had the day before. Usually the sound was taken for granted—like a clock chiming on the hour and half hour. But there was a difference today and Kenna felt it.

Overhead, a French Spad flew low. And then two more. And tagging along behind—a fourth plane, sporadic in sound, erratic in flight.

Wells looked up toward the plane. "That fellow's in trouble," he announced to Kenna. "Hope he makes it back to the field."

In alarm, Kenna saw the smoke trailing behind the plane. "It's on fire." Her eyes remained on the plane while Wells was forced to turn his attention back to the road.

As Kenna watched, the engine of the plane sputtered and stopped, and it began to lose altitude. "I think he's going to crash," Kenna announced. But just then, the engine started to sputter again.

Briefly the driver cast another glance toward the sky where flames had now begun to shoot from the fuselage.

"You think he'll bail out?" Kenna asked.

"I don't know. He's close to the field. He just might be daredevil enough to try to ride it in."

The plane, going in a southeasterly direction, was now farther away from the ambulance and Kenna had to turn her head to see it. A great cloud of black smoke obliterated her view, enclosing the plane in fiery fumes. And then a sudden explosion in the air left no doubt as to what had happened.

Kenna bit her lip and tears came to her eyes. "He didn't make it, Wells."

"Most of them don't," he informed her matter-of-factly. "Flying's a dangerous occupation. Me, now—I'd rather be in a foxhole any day."

Kenna continued looking back. The black smoke parted and slowly drifted into the white billowy clouds. But just as she lost sight of the horizon, Kenna saw a small pinpoint of white floating downward.

"He bailed out, Wells. He bailed out."

She touched the man's shoulder in her excitement and he reacted with a start.

"You want to cause a wreck?" his voice rasped. "You got to learn to be more philosophical about this war, miss, or you won't last a month over here."

The ambulances arrived at the train station, and the wait began for the hospital train bringing in the heavy casualties of battle. Most of the nurses went to the officers' canteen on a side street to wait, but Kenna, wishing to see Simone, the worker at the enlisted men's canteen, went to the Hôtel de la Gare on the square.

The girl was busy behind the counter and so Kenna, finding a seat by the window, sipped her cup of chocolate and watched the comings and goings of soldiers, the constant replenishing of coffee, the buying of sandwiches.

She watched as a thin young private walked toward the counter and asked for a cup of coffee, his eyes coveting the tray of sandwiches nearby. Simone, seeing his hungry glance, said, "Have a sandwich, soldier. And some cookies."

"I . . . I don't have enough money."

"That's all right," she assured him. "You can pay the next time you're through."

His eyes lit up. "You're sure it's all right?"

"Sure. Go ahead," she urged.

He quickly took a ham sandwich from the tray and two gingerbread cookies, and with the cup of coffee in his hand, he found an empty table where he began wolfing down the food.

Kenna smiled at Simone behind the counter, and continued drinking her chocolate. When there was a lull, Simone poured herself a cup of coffee and walked over to join Kenna near the window.

"That was nice of you, Simone—to let him have the sandwich," Kenna said.

"Well, I couldn't stand seeing him like a hungry little boy staring in a candy store window. And he'll pay for it another time. They always do." Simone sighed. "If it weren't the rule to charge *something,* I'd let all of them have the sandwiches for free. Heaven knows, they deserve everything we can do for them."

The sound of a troop train down the track caused the girl to jump up from the table. "Here they come—complete with cooties. I'd better tell Marnie to get the vats ready."

Small and plump, Simone treated the thousands of men coming through the hotel in the same manner she treated her third-grade class back in De Kalb County, Georgia.

The troops came—unshaven, dirty. Awaiting each soldier were hot showers, fresh underwear, razors to remove the week's growth of beard from chins and hot coffee in the canteen. But first, the soldiers had to be fumigated.

"Off with your underwear, Corporal," Simone demanded. "You can hand it to me on the stick."

"No thank you, ma'am. I . . . I'll just keep it, if you don't mind."

"But I *do* mind," Simone countered. "Now, hurry up. I don't have all day," she said in her schoolteacher voice.

Thoroughly intimidated, the shy corporal obeyed and hung his dirty linen on the proffered stick. Simone, with her nose turned up, walked over to the steaming caldrons and plunged the underwear into the water.

Back and forth she went, standing outside the shower stalls, holding out the pronged stick to snare the dirty laundry of the soldiers, and then turning it over to the French women hired to help.

"I sort of grew partial to those, ma'am," one soldier argued. "What's going to happen to 'em now?"

"They'll be laundered and given out to somebody on another train," she answered.

The long, low toot of the hospital train, the crosses painted in white on each car, alerted the nurses and ambulance drivers of its arrival. It had a special sound, different from the regular troop trains—a sadness that went before it.

Kenna hurried from the canteen, and with Wells beside her, she waited for the train to stop.

With surprising speed, the stretcher cases were transferred from train to ambulance, as men were stashed into the Tin Lizzies—one above the other on the berths in the back. And Kenna, not sitting with Wells as she had done earlier, remained in the back, her attention on the patients, who looked as if they might not last long enough for the ride from the station to the hospital.

One by one the ambulances left the square. The bumpy road increased the men's discomfort, but they were too ill to complain. Drained—weak—some in shock. The strain of battle seemed etched into their faces, old and knowing before their time—weary of war that destroyed a man's spirit as well as his body.

The procession edged through the town, out into the parkway, and retraced the route of an hour before. By the time they reached the monastery that had been turned into a hospital, the doctors were ready for them.

"He needs to go to surgery immediately."

"This one, too."

"A cigarette, may I have a cigarette?"

One of the orderlies lit a cigarette from his pack and placed it between the wounded man's lips as he was carted off to the operating room.

And one young boy asked for nothing. Kenna sponged his face with water and held his hand.

"Too late for this one," a voice announced and the orderly drew the sheet over the man's face.

The heat—the smell of ether—the sickly steam from the sterilizers—the mutilated bodies. For hours, the atmosphere had held an oppressive pall. And Kenna, working constantly, with only an hour's rest at the canteen while she waited for the hospital train, was exhausted.

Late that night, she was finally relieved of duty. She had eaten nothing. Her uniform was spattered with blood and her heart was sick. For the first time, she had witnessed the horrors of war, had seen men who'd never stood a chance to last through the night, much less be sent home to a hospital in the States.

She thought she was prepared, but she wasn't. Her mind and body were outraged at the senseless waste of lives, the carnage. And in the privacy of the cloistered courtyard, she wept—for all the mothers, for all the wives. And she wept for herself.

186

Irish Fitzpatrick sat in the courtyard and smoked a cigarette. The moans of the newly wounded placed in his ward had driven him outside for a while. He heard the girl crying—great sobs racking her body.

A nurse. He could tell by her uniform. But she wasn't hardened yet. Her tears attested to that.

Curiously, he watched the girl from the shadows. Her face, bent low, was obscured from sight at first. Then she raised her head and the beams of moonlight, filtering through the courtyard, framed the uplifted face, the silver-blond hair. And his heartbeat witnessed his sudden shock.

Kenna.

He couldn't believe it. Quickly, he snuffed out his cigarette and stood. He drank in the classic, small-boned features, stained with tears. Her eyes, shuttered with grief, drew him closer. And her name on his lips broke the spell of silence between them.

"Kenna."

She gave a start at the sound of her name spoken so softly. But she saw no one.

The man moved from the shadows and again her name formed on his lips.

This time, Kenna saw him.

She watched the giant of a man slowly approach, and from the first moment she saw his frame outlined in the darkness, she knew who he was. The proud tilt of his head, the massive shoulders, and his overpowering physical aura broadcast his identity.

"Irish," she whispered, brushing a tear from her eyes.

Twenty-Two

HE TOWERED OVER HER, DRINKING IN THE SIGHT OF HER, AND he was shocked at the exhaustion that haunted her face. Even in the moonlight, he could see the dark smudges under her eyes, and it was clear that she had lost weight. His anger, uncontained, burst from his lips.

"So you found out what war is really like," he said. "Not very pretty, is it, when a man screams in agony and begs to die."

"Don't," she whispered, cringing from his harsh words. "Please—don't talk like that."

"How do you expect me to talk? To make polite conversation about the weather? To inquire about your ocean voyage? And to ignore the very thing that's tearing you apart?"

His voice, intense and strained, continued. "Tonight is only the beginning. And you're a little idiot, Kenna Chalmers, if you think you can stand up to the kind of hell that's coming."

Her hand went to her forehead and she swayed, as if she had been dealt a physical blow. Irish, seeing it, reached out to steady her.

Before he knew it, his lips had found hers. "Kenna—Kenna," he murmured, his breath mingling with hers.

The comfort and strength he offered were too much for her. Her arms wrapped around his waist and she returned his kiss. For a brief time, everything was as it should be. The world was not in chaos—and the cries of the wounded were erased.

His hands caressed her, drawing her closer to him; her breasts pressed against his chest, while his hands moved downward along the curve of her thigh. She trembled at his touch and the feel of his strong, hard body against hers.

But then, the sound of a closing door broke the spell. And Kenna became aware of the courtyard, draped in shadows, and of the compromising embrace. She was engaged to Carlton Torey. And she had no right to seek comfort in another man's arms—especially Irish Fitzpatrick's.

She drew away from him and as her hands dropped from his waist, Kenna felt the gauze bandage. "You've been hurt," she said in a stunned voice.

"Only a small wound," he replied.

She should have known that something was wrong when he wasn't in uniform. Yet Kenna was so used to seeing the patients in their hospital robes that she had not questioned it.

"When did it happen?" she asked, suddenly sitting on the bench in the shelter of the linden tree.

Her question was not answered. For at that moment, a voice behind her said, "Oh, there you are, Kenna my dear. I've been looking for you."

She turned to face Major Carlton Torey. "I've come to take you home," he said. And then, acknowledging a fellow officer, Carlton said, "I see, Captain Fitzpatrick, that you've already met my fiancée."

Irish stared at Kenna and back at the major. "My congratulations, Major."

He departed abruptly, leaving a devastated Kenna alone with Carlton.

"A strange chap," Carlton mused, as Irish disappeared in the darkness. "But it's rumored that he saved over fifty men from a German trap."

Safe in the little attic room with the faded roses, Kenna fell into bed. Steppie was already asleep. Kenna suspected that Madame Juvin had been also when she finally arrived and had to ring the bell to be let in.

But the woman had been kind. Seeing Kenna's exhaustion and the state of her dress, she had insisted on fixing her a cup of hot tea with jam and bread while Kenna cleaned up.

Now, in between clean linen sheets, a well-scrubbed Kenna closed her eyes. The torment of the day and the shock of seeing Irish were mercifully pushed aside as her body demanded sleep.

The following morning, Steppie, unaware of Kenna's trauma at seeing Irish Fitzpatrick the night before, climbed down from the military vehicle and began to walk along the entrance road to the dismal buildings of the hospital that had once been an insane asylum.

The hospital, different from the others, was a long-term facility, where severely injured men stayed for long periods of time—some waiting to die, others waiting for reconstructive surgery and rehabilitation.

Davin had worked hard, attempting to make the place brighter for the patients, but it was a losing venture. Nothing could effectively mask the oppressive atmosphere of the wards with their prison cell structure.

The only salvation came from the recreation room maintained by the Red Cross, where games and an old Victrola player provided some respite from the long hours of tedium.

But so many of the patients were bedridden, with no hope of getting to the recreation room. And so, Steppie, with an eye to helping brighten the wards, had begun to bring in flowers from the garden she had stumbled upon at the rear of one of the buildings.

This she did each afternoon when she had gone off duty, for she was in no hurry to return to Toul, especially now that she hardly ever saw Kenna because of her friend's erratic working hours.

That day she worked hard, tending to the patients on her ward, and when late afternoon came and she was relieved of duty, Steppie walked down the path to the garden.

The weeds had grown quickly, fed by the afternoon rains, and now they vied for space with the blossoms. A half hour each afternoon, Steppie had struggled with the weeds, but that was not enough time to do much good.

She heard the methodic chop of a hoe as she rounded the path. There, in the middle of the flower beds, she came upon an old man in a chasseur's faded uniform. His back was to her and she saw that he was busy putting the garden into order again. Steppie was glad to see someone had been hired to take care of the flowers.

"*Bonjour,*" she said.

The old man, startled at her voice, straightened and took several steps back, as if afraid of her.

The dark-haired girl smiled at the man to reassure him. "I've come to cut some flowers," she said, "for the wards. Will you help me select some?"

He acted as if he didn't understand her. But of course—she was speaking in English. And so Steppie, in her careful French, began talking to the old man in his language.

When there was no response, she finally resorted to sign language—pointing to the flowers and then to the basket in her arms. He nodded.

Steppie sighed. Almost no one understood her French, and she had worked so hard.

The old man took the shears from her and, carefully selecting the best blossoms, he cut them and laid them in the basket until it was filled.

"*Merci*," she said, and taking the shears with her, she walked back along the path toward the hospital, while the old man began again to chop weeds.

There was now no need for Steppie to stay late that afternoon to work in the flower garden. And so, after arranging the flowers, she caught a ride back to Toul.

On her way, she passed the hospital where Kenna worked. She looked carefully at the nurses standing by the side of the road, but Kenna was not among them. Disappointed, Steppie rode on, to spend the next several hours alone, until Carlton Torey had dismissed Kenna for the day.

Unable to face the officers' ward where Irish Fitzpatrick was a patient, Kenna had swapped duties that morning with Annette. As Steppie passed by, she was still on duty in the enlisted men's ward.

She had had double duty serving all three meals to the patients. That morning she had shaved the soldiers unable to hold a razor in their hands, had changed their bandage dressings, administered morphine to those still showing the effects of surgery hours before, and checked the painful Dakin-Carrel solutions irrigating their wounds.

Her anxious eyes searched for the four who had ridden in

Wells's ambulance. Three of them she found. But the fourth bed was empty. The boy had already become a statistic—a casualty of war.

Now she made her late afternoon rounds, picking up the empty supper trays to take back to the kitchen. When that was done, Carlton let her leave.

She arrived at Madame Juvin's house just in time for the evening meal. She was quiet, subdued. Steppie, thinking it was because of her arduous schedule, was sympathetic but said nothing.

Early the next day, Kenna, unable to avoid the officers' ward any longer, squared her shoulders and carried fresh supplies past the door. Down the rows she went from patient to patient, her eyes trying not to search out the bed where Irish Fitzpatrick lay. But it was inevitable that she would eventually come to it.

He sat in a chair and watched her approach—saw the long elegant fingers at work smoothing the corners of the cot blankets, saw her smile returned by each man on his row. And then she stood at the foot of his own bed.

"Good morning," she said in a low tone toward the chair where he sat. All life had gone out of her voice.

There was no returned pleasantry. "Your loyalty didn't last long, did it?" he asked sardonically.

Kenna's face flushed in embarrassment and she looked up to see if the other patients had heard Irish's accusing voice. But she kept her silence and began to change the linen on Irish's bed.

"If I were Major Torey, I wouldn't trust you out of my sight."

Kenna had no defense. Her behavior in the courtyard two nights before had been inexcusable. She finished with the bed, smoothed the pillow in place, and put a clean towel by the washbasin.

"Is there anything else you would like, Captain Fitzpatrick?" she inquired.

"Yes. Another nurse," he informed her. "The one I had yesterday."

The gray eyes masked the hurt and sting from his words,

but the telltale tremble of her lips told Irish that his words had hit the mark. Even then, he felt no satisfaction.

Steppie, coming down the path of the garden, saw the old man again. It was miraculous the progress he had made with the garden in only one day. He helped her again with the flowers, but this time, he refused to give up the basket. Instead, he followed her and carried it to the pantry room just off the kitchen where the vases were waiting.

The old man, gazing toward the kitchen, looked hungry. And Steppie felt sorry for him. The cooks always had food left over. Surely, it wouldn't hurt to fix him a plate.

She went to the kitchen door and, seeing one of the cooks, asked for food for the old man. She motioned for the man to take a seat at the table while she began arranging the flowers—purple and yellow dahlias—in the vases.

A great noise erupted behind her as the cook brought out the food for the old man. "Gigot," he exclaimed, amazement apparent in his voice.

At the sound of his name, the man grinned happily. With a barrage of words the other cook was summoned from the kitchen and the two hovered over the old man, laughed, and patted him on the shoulder.

He took up his wooden spoon and greedily ate from the wooden bowl, as if he had eaten nothing for days.

"Gigot—old Gigot has come home."

The cooks laughed, shook their heads. "It is marvelous, *non,* that he found his way back?"

"I wonder how far he walked?"

Steppie looked toward the cooks and back to the man at the table. "What do you mean?" Steppie asked. "That he has come home?"

"For Gigot—this is his home. He has outfoxed them." The cook laughed again while Gigot attended to his bowl of food.

Steppie's face lost all color. If this had been Gigot's home, that could mean only one thing. He had been an inmate in the insane asylum. And wherever they had taken him, he had escaped and returned to familiar surroundings.

Her hands, holding the shears, trembled as she stared at

them. Large—pointed—dangerous. And without a qualm, she had handed them over to Gigot to use earlier.

Steppie slipped from the room adjacent to the kitchen and hurried to seek out Davin. He would know what to do.

His office door stood ajar, the sun coming through the barred window. Steppie knocked and at the sound, Davin looked up from the pile of reports on his desk.

He smiled when he recognized her, and then frowned at the frightened look on her face. "What is it, Miss Hannon?" he inquired.

Her hands still held the shears and she had not bothered to remove the apron that protected her uniform.

"Captain Grant, I . . . I think you'd better come to the kitchen," she said. "Gigot has come back."

"Gigot? Who's that?" he asked, racking his brain for some clue.

"One of the former inmates."

He stood up immediately and accompanied her to the other building.

"He was in the flower garden yesterday—chopping down weeds. He was there again today."

"How do you know he was here in the asylum?"

"The cooks recognized him," Steppie answered. "Do you think he might be dangerous?"

"It's hard to tell."

Davin peered through the window and for a time watched the old man seated at the table. One of the cooks brought out a *pâtisserie* that had just come from the oven. He said something to the old man and Gigot smiled happily.

The cook, laughing, ambled back into the kitchen. The old man stared at the sweet for a while. Then he lifted it, held it to his nose for a moment in appreciation before putting it on the table again.

One bite he tasted, closing his eyes and rolling the fragment on his tongue before swallowing—like a connoisseur determined to make the sweet last as long as possible.

"The cook didn't seem to be afraid of him," Davin commented to Steppie at his side.

"What are you going to do?" she asked. "Call the French authorities?"

"Not yet."

Davin walked into the kitchen and the cooks, thinking it was an unannounced inspection, stopped their chatter and stood at attention.

"The old man in the pantry—you know him?"

One cook cast an alarmed look at the other. Would they get into trouble for feeding Gigot?

"For over two years, monsieur," one admitted.

"He was an inmate here in the asylum?"

"*Oui.*"

"He is harmless, monsieur," the other cook ventured in Gigot's defense. "Like a baby. I will pay for the food he has eaten," the man offered.

"That isn't necessary," Davin replied. "I only want to make sure he's not dangerous."

"Oh no, monsieur. Gigot is harmless, as I have told you."

"He was beaten by the enemy," the other added. "That is why he was sent here. He had nowhere else to go."

"He missed his flowers—and the garden."

The first cook nodded. "Gigot has come home," he announced.

And so Davin allowed the old man to stay. He slept in the toolshed at the back and each day he came to the kitchen door for food. Happily, he worked in his garden. Gigot was home again.

Twenty-Three

IRISH FITZPATRICK DRESSED IN HIS NEW UNIFORM. THE OLD one had been burned because of its contact with the mustard gas. And on his shoulder, the bars had been replaced with a cluster. He was now officially Major John Ireland Fitzpatrick.

He packed his few possessions and looked around the cot to make sure he had left nothing—except the mud-spattered picture of Kenna. He crumpled it and dropped it in the wastebasket by his bed. Not looking back, he walked down the corridor, out into the cloistered courtyard, toward the other building where the orthopedic patients were lodged.

He intended saying good-bye to Eb, and by that time the car would be waiting to take him to the officers' club off the square. He had another week to recuperate, but there was no need to stay in the hospital any longer. They needed the bed.

As he passed through the courtyard, he paused to smoke a cigarette. And his mind went to that night when he had heard Kenna sobbing her heart out. He had been touched—fierce in his anger—until Carlton Torey had come to claim her.

Faithless! She had vowed her undying love for the man Neal. And yet, here she was—engaged to another man, the first one forgotten.

He reached for the picture he had carried for well over a year. But his pocket was empty. He had thrown the clipping away. A great loss suddenly invaded his heart, and despite his anger with the girl, he knew he'd made a mistake. He set his satchel on the bench and retraced his steps. If he hurried, he could retrieve the picture before someone came to empty the trash from the basket.

*   *   *

196

Kenna stayed at the empty bed. Irish Fitzpatrick had gone. She stripped the linen from the bed, rolled it into a ball, and tied the ends in a knot. As she removed the washbasin from the stand to replace it with a sterilized one, she noticed the full wastebasket beside the cot.

Curious at the wrinkled newspaper clipping lying on top, she stopped to look at it. Her face and Steppie's stared up at her. PATRIOTIC DEBUTANTES JOIN ARMY NURSE CORPS . . . the headline read. It was torn at the edges, worn—and now, crumpled in disgust and thrown away.

She hadn't even known that Irish had cut it out or saved it, until now. She left the ball of dirty linen on the floor, as well as the washbasin. With her breath coming in gasps, she hurried down the corridor.

In both arms she carried the offending wastebasket. Seeing the metal drum smoldering in the service yard, she rushed to it and dumped the contents of the wastebasket into the flames. The sudden spurt of fire caused her to jump back, as the flames were fed, relegating her picture to a residue of ashes. And Kenna, by her action, destroyed the one remaining link with Irish Fitzpatrick. But in doing so, she had destroyed part of herself.

Irish stared at the ball of linen on the floor—and the empty space where the wastebasket had stood only moments before.

Someone had come and taken it. He was too late.

He saw her coming toward him, a small piece of soot smudging her chin. Without speaking, she reached for the dirty linen. With the washbasin in one hand, she held onto the dirty linen with the other and dragged it beside her.

"Kenna," he called.

She continued walking, not looking back, not hearing his voice—for the roar in her ears, the beat of her heart spoke of a betrayal that she could not understand.

"Kenna, what's the matter?"

Carlton, taking one look at the girl, was alarmed. She was exhausted, ready to drop. All at once, he felt guilty for making her work such long hours. He hadn't intended it this way—merely to keep her out of trouble. But it had backfired. If something happened to her, he was responsible.

"Kenna my dear. Are you ill?"

"Yes, Carlton," she admitted, and sank into the chair.

He rushed toward her, lowering her head and pressing between her eyes with his fingers to keep her from fainting.

"I'm all right now," she said, lifting her head moments later.

"No, you're not. You've worked much too hard. And I'm taking you home."

She didn't protest.

As he drove the military vehicle into Toul, Carlton said, "I'm giving you leave for three days, Kenna. Don't even attempt to come back to the hospital before then. And if you still feel sick, you can have more time off."

"Thank you."

The vehicle came to a stop in front of Madame Juvin's house. Carlton gazed anxiously at Kenna. "You think you'll be all right?"

She nodded. "I just need some rest. That's all."

She climbed out, holding the official pass in her hands, while he hurried to get back to his duties at the hospital.

For twelve hours straight, Kenna slept. She had no idea when Steppie came in. The house was quiet. No one disturbed her. But sometime during the night she woke to the sound of rain on the tiled roof. It was still dark outside.

After a few minutes, Kenna turned over and went to sleep again.

Kenna yawned and stretched and then opened her eyes. She was alone in the bedroom. Sunlight poured through the window across the room and its rays slanted toward the light blue coverlet at the foot of her bed.

She felt refreshed. But for another minute, she was content to stay where she was. A sense of freedom pervaded her being. And what had seemed so dark and dismal the day before now assumed a proper significance.

So what if Irish *had* thrown away her picture? And what if he *had* thought her disloyal to Carlton? That wasn't the end of the world.

Anyway, what had happened in the courtyard was as much his fault as hers. Her dismay turned to anger. Always like a man to put the entire blame on someone else. She couldn't change his dislike for her or what had happened. But she could forget it and not let it bother her.

Kenna smiled and relaxed. Amazing what a good night's sleep could do for a person.

Her glance rested on the pass that Carlton had issued her. Now *that* was what really mattered. Three days of freedom. The weather was beautiful, and if she was lucky, Major Thibault would be at No. 3 Rue Pierre Hardie that afternoon with information from the French underground.

Kenna's long blond hair hung down her shoulders as she got out of bed. She twisted a strand as she planned her day.

Soon a tap on the door brought Madame Juvin with a breakfast tray. "You slept well, mam'selle?" the woman asked.

"Yes, thank you."

"Mam'selle Steppie said you were very tired and not to wake you. But I heard your footsteps and knew you were up."

Kenna was apologetic for having slept such a long time. "I could have gotten something to eat later on, madame. You should not have gone to such trouble."

"No trouble," the woman assured her. And then she pointed to the note on the tray. "Mam'selle Steppie left this for you."

When she was alone, Kenna sipped her cup of hot black coffee and read Steppie's message. Judging from the scrawl, it had been written hurriedly.

"Saw your pass, so didn't wake you. I'm staying at the hospital tonight. Party in the Red Cross recreation room. If you aren't going anywhere, you and Carlton come if you can. Seven-thirty. Steppie."

Later, she sat on the stone steps at the back of the house and dried her hair in the sun. Madame Juvin, gazing out the window, drew in her breath as the sun's rays struck full force. Regretfully, she touched her own dark hair, and then looked back to the lustrous, sparkling strands that caught fire in the sun.

A wonder that the girl had not already been kidnapped—

for she knew her countrymen's weakness for blond-haired women. She must remember to warn the girl to be careful.

Jacques Thibault was not surprised to see Kenna that afternoon in the canteen. His eyes lit up appreciatively as she walked across the room toward him. He didn't want to get her hopes too high, for the information he had might lead to a dead end. But at least, it was more than she had managed on her own.

"Mam'selle," he acknowledged, standing and smiling at her.

"It's good to see you, Major Thibault. I . . . I hope you have some news for me."

They talked in low tones, away from the others, and Kenna, interested in what the Frenchman had to say, was not aware of anyone else in the canteen. But Nurse Edna Brockett was very much aware of Kenna. She edged closer to the table, watched Kenna's animated face, and tried to read her lips.

The girl finally stood up. "Yes. I can be ready in an hour," Kenna said.

"I'll come for you at Madame Juvin's."

"No. I'd rather keep it a secret. Let me meet you under the clock at the rail station."

"If you insist," Jacques Thibault reluctantly replied.

When Kenna walked out of No. 3 Rue Pierre Hardie, Nurse Brockett followed at a discreet distance.

Kenna's mind was busy. She'd have to dress in something besides her uniform—and she'd need an evening wrap instead of the nurse's cape. She glanced at her watch and hurried toward one of the little seamstress shops on a side street, and when she went inside, Edna Brockett remained down the street, in sight of the door.

There were only two to choose from—and so Kenna took the dark blue cape that fit her, paid the required number of francs, and then hurried toward Madame Juvin's.

Edna Brockett did not follow Kenna any farther. She had already surmised what was going to happen. Edna, keeping a finger on everything that went on at the hospital, knew that the girl had been given a three-day pass. Now she knew more than that. Kenna Chalmers was going away with the French flier. They were meeting at the railway station. And that could mean only one thing. The blond hussy was going to spend the weekend in Paris with the Frenchman. And she was engaged to that nice Major Torey. Well, she wouldn't get away with such shenanigans. Edna would see to that.

Kenna, her hands trembling with excitement, pulled out the pink beaded dress from the chest in the attic bedroom. The accessories to match were wrapped in tissue beside the dress—the collared choker with the miniature bells, the small purse, and the pale pink satin shoes with the oriental heels.

She stared at her hair in the mirror. It had grown longer. She had debated about getting it cut in a wavy movie-star bob. But it was so much easier to twist into a knot under her nurse's cap. Now she was sorry that she had not had it cut short.

Kenna frowned. What could she do with her hair to make it look chic and elegant? Her eyes went to the ribbon of bells lying on the bed. If she could take one of the ribbons, she could weave it in and out of her hair.

Quickly, she took her scissors from the sewing box and snipped one of the ribbons from her dress. It would never be missed. Carefully she worked, pulling and twisting her hair into ropes—weaving the ribbon and bells throughout, until, at last, she was satisfied. When she shook her head to make sure the strands would stay in place, she smiled at the sound of the miniature bells.

"Ah—very beautiful," Madame Juvin exclaimed when she came downstairs. "Your fiancé will be very proud of you, *non*?"

Kenna, with an anemic smile, acknowledged her appraisal. "I'll be quite late tonight, madame," she apologized.

"No matter. I let you in."

Kenna put on the navy cape, and pulling the hood over her hair to conceal it, she walked down the sidewalk and hurried toward the clock at the entrance to the rail station.

Edna Brockett and Jacques Thibault both kept vigil at the railway station for Kenna—Edna in the enlisted men's canteen across the street, and Jacques at the curbing beside the square.

He paced up and down, and Edna watched him. The clock visible through the windows of the canteen told her that Kenna had better hurry if she wanted to catch the train to Paris.

The figure in the dark cape walked up the slight hill to the square, and Edna, watching, saw Jacques Thibault throw down his cigarette. Furtively, Edna slipped out the side door nearest the train tracks.

Simone, at the counter, wasn't sorry to see her go. The woman was a troublemaker. Simone had seen her kind before. The nurse rarely came here, preferring the officers' canteen instead. But it had suited her tonight, judging from her actions. And Simone felt sorry for whomever the woman was after.

"Mam'selle?"

"Yes?"

"I have the car ready."

Kenna followed him to the street and in the darkness, she climbed in. With no headlights, the vehicle ambled down the street and disappeared toward the *porte de Nancy*—to the town twelve miles away, where the assignation with the underground had been set up by Jacques Thibault.

Edna Brockett remained by the baggage wagon. She watched the couples boarding the train, each man, each woman. But there was no sign of either Kenna or the Frenchman. She waited a while longer, but the train pulled out.

An irritated Edna marched inside to the ticket counter. But the man behind was no help to her. Finally, she had to admit defeat. They had gone somewhere together, but Edna had no proof of *where*.

Feeling thwarted, she walked across the square, down a side street, and entered the officers' canteen. The pout of her full lips changed to a smile when she recognized one of her recent patients from the hospital. And he was sitting alone.

"Good evening," she said. "May I join you?"

The man stood politely, helped the woman into the opposite chair, and then sat down again. "Would you like something to drink?" he inquired.

"A coffee, please. And a little sandwich. I missed my supper," she admitted.

While she stirred the sugar in her coffee, her mind nagged at her defeat. "The strangest thing happened," she said aloud to the man.

"What is that?" he asked, not particularly interested.

"There's this blond nurse at our hospital," she said. "She's supposed to be engaged to the surgeon in charge."

Immediately, Irish Fitzpatrick looked up from the table.

"Yes, I know."

Edna gave a quick little laugh and said, "Oh then, if you know who I'm talking about, maybe I'd better not say anything."

"Why?"

"Because—well, because I don't really like to malign people."

"What's the matter? Did the surgeon abscond with a wagonload of bandages?"

"Oh, Captain—I mean, Major," she twittered. "You *are* a major now, aren't you?"

"Yes."

Edna lowered her voice. "It's not what *he's* done. It's what his fiancée has done."

He waited, for he saw that the woman was going to inform him, whether he wanted to hear or not.

She looked from one table to the other and in a low voice, she announced, "She's run away for the weekend with a *French* flier."

Twenty-Four

JACQUES THIBAULT'S EYES REMAINED ON THE NARROW RIBbon of road. But his mind was on the girl beside him. She'd kept the dark hood about her head, yet the tantalizing moonlight occasionally fell upon the silk sheen of her hair—like tassels of corn in the sun. He remembered the same coloring in her brother.

"Your last name is different from your brother's," he commented.

"Yes. Actually, he's my half brother," Kenna admitted. "My mother was married twice."

"And yet you have a great love for this half brother."

"Of course. Love doesn't come from having the same last name," she explained. "Love comes from caring—from nurturing—from sharing other things."

"Yet you're very similar in looks."

Kenna nodded. "The hair, mainly. And the eyes. I remember before Neal began to grow so tall, we were often mistaken for twins."

The sound of a gun in the distance cut off their conversation. Anxiously, Kenna lifted her head and strained to see along the roadside. It was dangerous to be traveling, especially at night when a sniper or advance patrol could be lying in wait.

The hour passed slowly and in the quietness, Kenna's mind began to wander. In Atlanta, it would be early afternoon. She wondered what Cricket and Verbena were doing.

A sudden longing for Verbena's "stickies" hit her . . . and the country breakfast that Johnsie liked so well, eggs and bacon and stone-ground grits, and fresh, popping hot biscuits with melted butter.

Everything was so different in France. The food—the lack of water—even the smell of the earth was different, with the piles of manure a hundred years old, in each farmyard and on the cobbled stone squares of the towns, bombarding the nose. The lack of sanitation appalled her. But at least around Toul, the sanitation officer had begun to make some progress.

Atlanta seemed so far away that night—more than a continent apart. And Kenna suddenly became homesick. But she'd forgotten. She had no home. Only a feeling was left of belonging to red clay hills and wide rivers. And yes—even to the trembling earth of the Okefenokee, with its moss-covered, dangerous world.

The road widened, and the car passed over the long bridge. Down below sat the city of Nancy, covered during the day with belching black smoke from the factories and munition plants—and covered at that moment by the blackness of night, permeated by the odor of smoke and soot.

Jacques Thibault slowed the car and pulled to the curb a block away from the restaurant Chez Garonne.

"I wish I could come in with you," he said to Kenna. "But there are too many spies, and a military uniform does not blend. It would not be good for you to be seen with me."

"I understand."

"His name is Shecki—the headwaiter. You give him this, and he will put you at the proper table. And when the man he's expecting comes in, he will bring him to you."

"I don't know how I can thank you, Major Thibault."

"Perhaps you will not wish to thank me at all, if nothing comes of it. Remember, I'll be waiting here for you at eleven."

As Kenna walked away from the car, he whispered, "Be careful, mam'selle."

From the outside, Chez Garonne didn't look as if it were open for business. And there was still doubt in Kenna's mind after the doorman had opened the massive door for her. For it was still dark inside.

But once she had walked down the short corridor and pushed open the heavy draperies, Kenna saw the restaurant come to life. Chez Garonne's elegance had not been dimmed by the war. The sparkling crystal, the pristine whiteness of starched tablecloths, the dark suits of the waiters, and the aromas of food and wine all seemed to be of another era—sumptuous, baroque—far beyond the pocketbooks of any of the factory or munitions workers. Kenna was surprised that such a place was still in existence.

Jacques had said that it was frequented by both friends and enemies, some slipping over the lines to enjoy a good meal in the anonymity of civilian dress.

"Madame?" the black-suited waiter said, with a question in his voice. "You are alone?"

Nervously, she handed him the blue cockade that Jacques had given her.

"I'm expected," she replied.

"But *certainement,* mam'selle," he agreed, quickly stuffing the cockade into his pocket. "This way, if you please."

His quick change of greeting—from madame to mam'selle—amused her. She had noticed that often among the French—the politeness of giving the woman the benefit of the doubt, and calling her madame, for it was no compliment to be thought unmarried after a certain age.

He placed her at an unobtrusive table, partially concealed by a large palm. "Your cape, mam'selle?" he asked. "You wish me to take it?"

"No thank you," Kenna replied. She had no desire to remove it at the moment in the alien environment.

"As you please," the waiter replied. "A glass of *vin blanc,* perhaps, while you are waiting?"

"Yes. That would be nice."

The wine warmed her blood and Kenna, feeling a little more at ease, removed the cape that had concealed her hair and the pink beaded party dress.

She was glad she'd worn the dress, for all the other women in the room were clothed in their best. Kenna smiled as she mentally counted the francs in her purse. She hoped she brought along enough to pay for the meal.

Five miles away from the city of Nancy, André duBois, the man Kenna was to meet, swore under his breath. His vehicle lay on its side in the ditch. He climbed from the wreckage

206

and stumbled toward the overturned cart in the middle of the road.

"Old fool," he said. "Don't you know better than to hog the middle of the road when a car is coming?"

"I did not see you, monsieur. A thousand pardons. My eyes are not what they used to be."

Crates of chickens lay across the road and in the ditch. The raucous squawk invaded the quietness of the countryside, as the chickens struggled for freedom. Still swearing under his breath, André began to help the old farmer set his cart aright. One by one he retrieved the crates and stacked them on the cart. And while he did that, Kenna Chalmers waited.

In the opposite direction, the Vicomte d'Arcy left his hunting lodge in the hills. Down the mountainous road he flew, his matched team of blooded horses exhilarated by the unexpected journey.

All day he had waited for his boredom to be relieved. Everything was ready. And his exuberance was transferred to the horses as they spanned the two miles to Chez Garonne.

A fresh-faced farm girl—unwise to the ways of the city— and preferably a virgin. He didn't want to be infected, like so many of his fellow officers, by the little tarts that hung around the waterfronts and military garrisons. Surely, in all the factory workers, Shecki could find a girl that suited him.

He passed the tall trees, the old part of the city with its ancient walls no protection against its enemies. Then the horses began their climb to the more modern section of the city, and in the square that bordered Chez Garonne, he brought them to a stop, climbed out of the carriage, and walked a few feet until he stood before the restaurant.

He'd been glad to get out of uniform for a few days, to make acquaintance again with his dogs and hunting jacket. And even the dark evening attire he was wearing felt like an old friend. The vicomte looked down to make sure the suit was impeccable. Smoothing his hair and mustache, he parted the heavy dark draperies inside the restaurant.

The waiter saw him immediately and rushed across the room to greet him.

"*Bonsoir, monsieur,*" Shecki said.

"You were successful in your procurement?"

"*Oui.* She will suit you well, monsieur." He lowered his voice. "A virgin, too. That calls for an added bonus, does it not?"

"Which one is she?"

"In the corner, monsieur, behind the palm." Shecki pointed toward the left, where a small, nervous, dark-haired girl sat, her brown eyes large with uncertainty.

The vicomte looked at the girl partially hidden by the palm and a smile spread across his face. "You have outdone yourself, Shecki. She's ravishing."

Overcome at his good fortune, the vicomte crushed large numbers of bills into Shecki's hand. In amazement, the headwaiter looked down at the money—more than he'd ever made before. Then he looked back toward the girl. Maybe he'd done better than he thought.

He too began to smile, but as the vicomte started walking in the wrong direction, Shecki's smile froze. There'd been a terrible mistake.

"Monsieur," he called. But Vicomte d'Arcy didn't hear. Shecki looked toward the blond-haired girl in the other corner and again at the money in his hand.

"*C'est la vie,*" he said to himself with a shrug and pushed the bills into his pocket.

"Mam'selle?"

"Yes?"

"May I join you?"

Kenna glanced uncertainly toward the disappearing Shecki. "It's all right. I'm the one you're waiting for."

At his assurance, Kenna smiled. And the vicomte, dazzled by her loveliness, congratulated himself on his great stroke of luck.

He ordered a bottle of wine and a tray of cheese and bread. Although supper was waiting for them at the lodge, he was content to sit for a while to savor the beauty of the girl before starting on his way.

Kenna, looking eager, waited for the man to tell her what he'd discovered. Ever since Jacques had told her about some prisoners' escape over the mountains—an American with them—she'd been filled with hope. And even if Neal weren't the man, the American might have news of him.

"Shecki said that you—"

The man put his finger to his lips. "Not now," he cautioned. "Too many people are ready to eavesdrop."

Kenna stopped speaking and looked warily around her. She suddenly felt exposed, for people were openly watching them from the nearby tables. The man was right. It was too dangerous to talk where they could be overheard.

"You are anxious to leave?" he asked.

"Yes," Kenna agreed, playing with the stem of her wineglass.

Shecki grew more nervous by the minute. If they didn't leave soon, the whole thing would blow up in his face. Already, the brown-eyed girl was getting impatient. And each time a customer parted the draperies, Shecki held his breath.

At last, the vicomte picked up the girl's cape and draped it over her shoulders. With a possessive hand on her elbow, he guided her toward the exit. A man coming through the parted draperies quickly stepped aside. "*Pardon,*" he exclaimed and waited for Kenna and the other man to pass.

André duBois handed the matching blue cockade to Shecki. "The girl—she is still here?"

The headwaiter hesitated. And suddenly feeling sorry for the small, brown-eyed girl in the corner, he nodded and pointed in her direction. With narrowed eyes Shecki watched the drama unfold. The girl's eyes lit up—the man sat down. And Shecki, making the sign of the cross, hurried toward the kitchen to check on an order of snails.

He led her to the square where the horses were tethered. "Your name, mam'selle?"

"Kenna," she replied. "And yours?"

He hesitated. "Bernay."

Kenna noticed his hesitation and wondered if he had given her a false name because of his underground work. But that didn't matter. She only needed something to call him. And Bernay suited as well as any other name.

When they reached the carriage, he helped her into it and then climbed in beside her.

"Where are we going?" Kenna asked.

"To the lodge in the hills."

"I have to be back by eleven o'clock," she informed him. Bernay frowned but made no comment.

The horses' hoofs clattered over the stone bridge and then made a dull thud on the hard dirt road. Steadily they climbed and Kenna, conscious of the chill in the air, hugged the dark cape to her body.

The man did not appear to want to talk. And so Kenna remained silent beside him and waited to get to the lodge before bombarding him with questions. It had been so hard not to ask him about the escaped prisoners—where they were and how they'd gotten back over the mountains—and where the blond-haired American had been taken.

The hunting lodge rose in the darkness amid the hills—rustic timber and steep-pitched roof. Everything was in darkness. But all at once, Kenna's hopes soared. Perhaps Neal was inside, waiting for her.

Eagerly she scrambled from the carriage. Bernay, helping her, felt her slim warm body against his for a moment and his masculinity responded to the brief encounter.

Out of the darkness a servant appeared and led the horses toward the rear of the lodge. An old woman, appearing at the same time, held an oil lamp at the opened door.

"You may go to bed, Zita. I won't need you again tonight," Vicomte d'Arcy said gruffly.

But the old woman was in no hurry to disappear. She held her lamp toward Kenna's face and her knowing eyes examined every facet of Kenna's features—gray eyes, sparkling with excitement and promise, small, sensual lips, natural pink to match the color of her dress that peeked from underneath the dark cape.

The hood fell from Kenna's head and set off the tiny bells woven through the strands of silver-blond hair, and the woman jumped, with the sudden flare of the lamp licking at the oil in its base.

Kenna's hand flew up to quiet the bells and the glow from the lamp pinpointed the small scar still visible on her hand.

The old woman noticed it and triumphantly she began to speak to Bernay in a dialect foreign to Kenna.

Bernay silenced her and taking Kenna by the arm, he impatiently led her past the old woman and into the main room of the lodge, where a fire had been laid in the hearth of the giant fieldstone wall that stretched to the ceiling.

The woman, Zita, remained a moment longer in the hallway and trembled. The girl would cause her Bernay much trouble. She was the handiwork of the devil—far too beautiful to be real flesh and blood. And the two-pronged scar on her hand claimed her for Satan's own.

Gazing at the girl standing by the fire, Bernay suddenly lost all appetite for food. All he wanted was to bed the creature before him—to take down her long blond hair and wrap it in his arms.

The food in the dining hall could wait until later. He knew they had the entire night, for he wasn't about to let her go at eleven o'clock. She would stay with him for the rest of his leave. And she wouldn't have to worry about her job at the factory. He would make her his mistress, and even when he rejoined his regiment, she wouldn't have to return to work.

"Well, how much longer are you going to make me wait?"

Her candid question startled him at first. With a smile, he asked, "Are you not hungry?"

"Eating is furthest from my mind right now," she admitted.

"And mine, also," Bernay answered. "Come, we'll go upstairs."

Twenty-Five

At ten minutes past eleven o'clock, Jacques Thibault began to get worried. He paced up and down and waited for Kenna to appear. Finally, at a quarter past the hour, he decided to go inside Chez Garonne.

Avoiding the front entrance, Jacques slipped into the back door where the scullery boy was stacking garbage. The messy corridor inside contained the droppings of lettuce and rutabagas. And a small cat sat patiently by a mousehole.

Into the kitchen Jacques went, pushing open the swinging door. The chef, cleaning the butcher block with salt, looked up at Jacques's entrance.

"I want to see Shecki."

The chef motioned for him to go through the other door, but Jacques shook his head.

"No. Send someone for him."

Sensing the airman's anger, the chef looked around for the scullery boy. "Petitmouche, go and tell Shecki to come here."

The small boy hastened to obey the chef, who silently went back to his work.

The door swung open and the headwaiter stopped short when he recognized Jacques Thibault. His profusive greeting was cut off.

"Where is the girl?"

"Which one?" Shecki inquired with a studied innocence.

"The one who gave you the cockade."

Shecki's face turned pale. "She is a friend of yours?"

"Yes. What happened to her?"

Shecki looked toward the chef and drew Jacques Thibault aside. In a low, nervous voice he began to explain. "The

212

vicomte mistook her for the young girl I procured for him, and before I could . . ."

The chef across the room hung his pots and pans on the hooks above him while Shecki's excited hands moved in rhythm to his words and Jacques Thibault's face turned a thunderous red.

As the chef removed his hat and apron for the night, Shecki and the major left Chez Garonne by the back door. An unwilling Shecki walked toward the car at the curb and climbed inside.

"Go over the stone bridge at the left. The lodge is in the hills beyond," he directed.

Through the blackness, with the mist rising, the car crept slowly, with Shecki gazing anxiously at the encircling mist. The sounds that he had waited for came in all their fireworks splendor. The road between Nancy and Toul was being bombarded. He knew that Jacques Thibault would stand no chance of going in that direction anytime soon.

Up into the hills they went, their progress impeded by the mist that grew thicker with each centimeter of elevation. Shecki was in no hurry to disturb Vicomte d'Arcy. He peered at his watch, straining to see the dial in the darkness, and he smiled when he caught sight of the time. At least, he wouldn't have to return the money. It was already too late. The girl would have been in his bed long ago.

The faint glow of artillery fire penetrated the mist. "You could not have gotten back to Toul tonight anyway, monsieur," Shecki confided. "You should thank me for the mix-up. It has saved your life."

"And the girl? You were concerned for her safety also?"

"Better to lose one's virginity than one's life," he said, shrugging philosophically.

Inside the lodge, Zita listened to the storm taking place in the bedroom upstairs. As the noise floated downward, Kenna's voice sounded like that of a Valkyrie awakened. The occasional thud emphasized her anger.

Zita shook her head. The vicomte should have listened to her. The girl was trouble. She knew it from the moment she first saw the gold of her hair and the scar on her hand.

"She is a wild one, *non*?" the man beside her ventured.

"The devil's own. I tried to warn him, but he wouldn't listen."

"Come, it's none of our business, Zita. Let's go to bed."

He held out his hand for the lamp and together they walked past the dining table filled with food and on into the kitchen.

"You think we should do something about the food?" she asked.

The old man shook his head. "I expect they will be hungry later." And looking at Zita, he smiled a regretful smile for his own lost youth—and hers.

"What's the matter with you?" Bernay, his face still stinging from Kenna's slap, reached out tentatively to calm her.

"There's nothing the matter with me," Kenna snapped, backing away from him. "*You're* the one who's gone berserk."

Puzzled, Bernay said, "You were quite willing to come to the lodge with me."

Kenna nodded. "But I didn't expect you to try to make love to me."

"Come now, mam'selle. You can't be that naive, especially after Shecki procured you for me."

Kenna wasn't sure she had heard him correctly. "Procured? What are you talking about?"

"I paid Shecki for you. Far more than you're worth, I'm afraid," he answered.

The Vicomte d'Arcy ducked as a small wooden carving left the table, sailed by his head, and struck the wall behind him.

"I came to find my brother," Kenna shouted. "You're supposed to be from the underground. And if you don't let me out of your bedroom, I'll . . ."

Meanwhile outside the château, the old vicomtesse, waiting in the touring car for the driver to alert the servants, leaned her head out the window and listened.

Her driver tugged at the brass bell at the side of the door. When its doleful dirge reverberated, the noise above subsided. But no one came to answer the summons.

The driver looked hesitantly back to the vicomtesse. "Keep

ringing," she ordered. "Someone is bound to come, eventually."

Footsteps and a flickering light inside gave truth to the woman's words. "Who is it?" the irritable male voice demanded from the inside.

"The vicomtesse, monsieur," the driver replied.

Immediately, the sound of scraping wood indicated the bar was being removed. And Bernay, Vicomte d'Arcy, opened the door.

"*Maman*?" he called out.

The driver went back to the car to help the woman alight and Bernay, standing at the door, shielded the lamplight with his hand.

"There is much noise in your house tonight, Bernay," the vicomtesse said, allowing him to kiss her on the cheek as she swept into the entrance hall. She stood back and, seeing the scratch on his chin, laughed.

"At last you have found a wench that's unwilling?"

"A terrible mistake, *Maman*," he answered with a worried look.

"Well, invite me to sit down and then tell me about it." The white-haired woman turned to the driver. "Pierre, put up the car and go on to bed."

"*Oui, madame.*"

She settled herself on the divan before the fire and dropped her dark coat from her shoulders. "I hope I haven't complicated things for you, my son, but the road to the château is being bombarded. It was impossible to get home tonight."

"Actually, I'm happy to see you," he replied in subdued tones. And he began to enlighten her with his dilemma—from the time he first saw Kenna at Chez Garonne, up to the moment Pierre rang the bell.

"She's not even French, *Maman*," he finished. "She's an American nurse—and she's threatened to charge me with kidnapping."

"Is she still upstairs?" the vicomtesse asked.

"Yes. She refused to come down for supper, even though I have apologized."

The vicomtesse looked at her youngest son—the only one left alive from her four strong boys—and her heart softened.

"Let me talk with her," she said, standing up.

"She's very beautiful, *Maman*. And I would not mind marrying the girl—if I have to."

She raised her eyebrow in surprise. Her Bernay—offering to marry someone he tried to seduce? The girl had to be unusual to invoke such a rash offer.

"That probably won't be necessary, son," she replied, and climbed the dark narrow stairs to the master bedroom.

Kenna, frightened and tired, jumped when the knock came. "Go away," she called.

"Mam'selle Chalmers? May I come in?"

The woman's voice surprised Kenna. "Who—who are you?" she inquired, her words filled with uncertainty.

"Bernay's *maman*," the vicomtesse responded. "May I come in?"

Kenna walked to the bedroom door and turned the large key. She opened the door only a few inches, and seeing the woman alone, opened it wider.

The bedroom was a shambles, and the girl, in a state of disarray. Her long silver-blond hair hung down her shoulders, the careful weaving of strands and ribbon no longer visible.

The vicomtesse, seeing Kenna tremble, inwardly castigated her son for making the exquisite little beauty afraid. But she smiled and walked inside.

"My son tells me he has made a grave mistake."

"Yes."

"Would you like to tell me about it?"

The woman was soothing, comforting, and Kenna, relieved to have a sympathetic ear, poured out the evening's trouble, as Bernay had done, but with little sobs between the words. Her large gray eyes misted with tears.

"I'm sure Jacques doesn't know what has happened. He's probably still in the square, waiting for me."

"That is regrettable," the woman commiserated. "If the mist were not so dangerous, I would have Pierre drive you into the city. But it's impossible until morning. Shall we go downstairs for something to eat? Then we can decide what to do."

"I can't," Kenna replied.

"Because of Bernay?"

"Yes—and . . . and my appearance."

"Your appearance can easily be remedied. Just pull your hair back and tie it with the ribbon. And as for Bernay—leave him to me."

A few minutes later, Kenna followed the vicomtesse down the stairs, and when the vicomte saw them together, he rose. As he glanced toward Kenna, he resembled a chastened little boy.

"Shall we go into the dining hall, Bernay?" the vicomtesse asked.

The baronial room contained a large Gobelin tapestry. Just under the exposed rafters hung a deer head, its antlers large and overwhelming. The deep red velvet of the chairs matched the deep red of the Venetian goblets filled with wine.

Kenna was seated and all at once she felt hungry. No wonder—it was almost midnight. Looking at the girl who had caused such consternation only moments earlier, Bernay commented, "*Maman* is a nurse also."

"But you're a vicomtesse. Is that not unusual?" Kenna asked the woman.

"Not in Europe, especially during a time of war," the white-haired woman replied. "The tradition of the lord's lady caring for the sick is as old as the feudal system itself."

Kenna smiled. "That was the custom among the plantations of the South also. But now that tradition is gone. Girls of the better families are not encouraged to care for the sick. That's why it caused such a furor when my friend Steppie and I became nurses."

The vicomtesse nodded in understanding. "Your country is still young. And you have had little experience with war fought on your own soil. Attitudes are quite different when war is a constant companion and your sons are dying. If I can help save one life, I count it an honor."

"After my eldest brother was killed, *Maman* turned our château into a hospital," Bernay confided.

Admiration for the woman was apparent in Kenna's face, and seeing it, Bernay was glad. For he was still uneasy about the girl.

217

When they had almost finished eating the sound of the brass bell at the entrance carried into the dining hall. Kenna lifted her head and Bernay scowled. He continued drinking his wine and made no effort to get up from the table.

Finally, the vicomtesse looked at her son. "Where is Zita?" she inquired.

"I sent her to bed long ago."

"Then don't you think you should see to the door?"

"No one has any business knocking on the doors this time of night."

"Perhaps someone is stranded in the mist—as I was."

With obvious reluctance Bernay arose and left Kenna and the vicomtesse alone. Kenna, with her face freshly scrubbed and her hair pulled back and tied with ribbon, resembled a young schoolgirl. She laid her fork on the plate and listened to the voices emanating from the entrance hall.

"Where is she?" It was Jacques's voice, demanding and angry.

"He's here," Kenna whispered.

Bernay, Vicomte d'Arcy, looked at his friend Jacques Thibault. And Jacques, recognizing the man before him, showed his surprise.

"Bernay?"

The vicomte glanced toward Shecki, who hovered nervously in the shadows, and then back to Jacques Thibault. All at once, Shecki saw both pairs of eyes staring at him—hostile, full of blame. He should never have come. He should never have taken the money.

"There's been a terrible mistake," Shecki said, removing the bills from his coat and thrusting them toward the vicomte. "I've come to give your money back."

Bernay's laugh was ironic. "It's a little too late for that, Shecki."

The headwaiter moaned as Jacques Thibault thundered, "Just what do you mean by that, Bernay? If you've treated Kenna like one of your *amies*, I'll . . ."

"You don't have to worry, Jacques," Bernay hastily assured him. "The little hellcat is perfectly capable of taking

218

care of herself." He touched the scratch on his chin. "Would you like to see for yourself that the girl is unharmed?"

"Yes. I don't trust you, Bernay."

Shecki, uninvited, remained in the entrance hall. Quickly, he put the money back into his pocket.

Jacques followed Bernay to the dining hall. Standing in the doorway, the airman saw the two women seated at the table—Kenna and the old Vicomtesse d'Arcy.

"My dear boy," the vicomtesse exclaimed in delight as she recognized Jacques. "How nice to see you."

Jacques's surprised eyes acknowledged the older woman and then immediately turned toward Kenna to make certain she was unharmed. He took in the difference in the girl's appearance—her hair no longer in the carefully designed coiffure, her dress slightly awry. Accusingly, he looked toward Bernay.

"How is your *maman*?" the vicomtesse asked, seemingly oblivious to the undercurrents in the room.

"Very well, thank you."

Acting as if Jacques Thibault had dropped into the lodge on a purely friendly visit and not to confront the man who had abducted Kenna, she turned to her son. "Bernay, you must offer Jacques a glass of wine."

And then in a confidential, friendly tone, she announced to Kenna, "I've known Major Thibault since he was a little boy. His *maman* and I were good friends."

Bernay motioned Jacques to one of the red velvet chairs and, walking to the wine cabinet, brought out another goblet of Venetian glass.

"You'll have to spend the night with us, Jacques. There's no hope of leaving—with the mist and the bombardment getting worse by the hour."

"It's kind of you," he replied. In wide-eyed amazement, Kenna listened to the polite, constrained conversation.

She'd been abducted. Bernay d'Arcy had tried to make her his mistress. And yet, here she was, sitting at the dining table with the man, his mother, and Jacques. She was totally ignored, as if she didn't even exist. And worst of all, she had

219

wasted an entire day of her pass, and still knew nothing of Neal.

Bernay, as if he suddenly remembered some unfinished business, rose from the table. Excusing himself, he went into the hallway where Shecki still waited.

Shecki jumped to his feet and still feeling guilty, he again pulled the bills from his pocket to offer them to Bernay. But the man again shook his head.

"You'd better hold on to the money, Shecki. You may need it one day—to pay the surgeon—when someone finally breaks your neck."

"But monsieur—"

His fright at Bernay's words spread from his eyes to his knees.

"There's food in the kitchen, if you're hungry, and an empty cot in the butler's pantry. I suggest you stay out of sight until morning."

"Thank you, monsieur. You're very kind, monsieur," he said to Bernay's back, for the vicomte had already left the entrance hall.

Kenna, so tired that she could hardly keep her eyes open, was happy when the vicomtesse rose and left the two men at the table. Kenna followed and climbed the stairs behind her to the second floor.

Twenty-Six

THE GUNS IN THE DISTANCE FINALLY STOPPED. BUT THE MIST, thick and rising rapidly, continued to envelop the hillside. The tiny light burning in the bedroom mattered little, for it would be impossible for the enemy to see it through the thick white mist. Only by chance could a shell find its way to the rustic hunting lodge hidden in the hills.

Zita, careful to wait several hours, carried a breakfast tray up the narrow staircase to the master bedroom. With a discreet tap at the door, she sailed into the room and placed the tray in the usual place by the window.

As she opened the heavy draperies, she saw that the mist was entirely gone. Through the tall conifers, the sun held a promise of a better day. The old woman couldn't resist a quick glance about the room. The girl's beaded party dress lay across the chair. One pink satin slipper protruded from underneath the stepping stool to the high bed. A strand of silver-blond hair lay outside the comforter.

So—the girl had quieted down. It was as her husband had said.

"Oh, good morning, Zita," a voice murmured sleepily from the other pillow. And Zita gave a start.

"Madame?"

"Is my son up yet?"

"I don't know, madame. I thought he was . . ." She stopped, not knowing how to continue.

"You thought he was here?" The vicomtesse laughed. "I'm afraid he was pushed out of his own bedroom—to make way for his old *maman*. But you have brought breakfast for us, *non*?"

"*Oui, madame.*"

"Then bring it to the bed, Zita. You know how I hate to get up in the mornings until I've had my chocolate. Kenna dear, are you awake?"

"Yes, madame." Quickly she sat up, pushing her long hair from her eyes. Kenna and the vicomtesse were clothed in identical gowns of white batiste with tatted lace made by the nuns at the convent.

Zita brought the tray to the bed and set it down between them. Shaking her head at the strange events, she quietly closed the door.

Kenna began to eat her buttered croissant and in deep thought, she unconsciously twisted a strand of hair around her finger. Madame Juvin and Steppie. What were they thinking?

"You are worried about something this morning?" the vicomtesse inquired.

Kenna stopped twisting the curl around her finger. "Yes, madame. The woman I stay with will be worried about me. She usually stays up to let me in the house."

"And if you return in full daylight with Jacques, she will think the worst."

"I'm afraid so."

"Then, of course, you must let me help."

"How, madame?"

"You will ride back to Toul with me."

"But that's out of your way."

The woman dismissed Kenna's objection with a wave of her hand. "I will tour one of your hospitals, to see your methods of surgery. That will make a good excuse."

"Thank you, madame." Reassured, Kenna broke the remainder of her croissant in half and spread the tart strawberry jam on one end before taking a bite.

Later, with the pink dress hidden under her dark cape, Kenna followed the vicomtesse downstairs. Bernay and Jacques, already informed of the plans, stood by the car as Pierre cranked the engine.

"*Au revoir*. I'll see you in Toul later on," Major Thibault said to Kenna.

"Good-bye, Jacques."

Bernay, with a regretful look toward the girl, kissed the vicomtesse good-bye. "Try to behave yourself this time, Bernay," the woman said, her face revealing no amusement. "And God go with you."

Kenna, for a split second, saw the pain etched into the vicomtesse's face. Her last remaining son— And because of this awareness, Kenna's animosity toward Bernay melted. She smiled at him.

"Good-bye, monsieur," she said, her spirit forgiving. The sun struck her silver-blond hair in full force and the Vicomte d'Arcy drew in his breath.

At that moment, he made up his mind. Kenna Chalmers had not seen the last of him.

Carefully, Pierre, the driver, picked his way along the road from Nancy to Toul. In several places, he left the road to bounce along the edge of the fields, for the shells the previous night had left craters at regular intervals. Kenna and the vicomtesse held on to keep from being thrown from the car.

"Pierre," the vicomtesse admonished. "Do try to stay in the road, if you can."

"*Oui, madame*," he replied, immediately detouring along the ditch to avoid another large hole.

By midday they reached Toul. Kenna directed Pierre to the street where Madame Juvin lived. Glancing nervously toward the house, she climbed out of the car and walked up the steps with the vicomtesse at her side.

Madame Juvin, seeing only Kenna when she opened the door slightly, made a commotion at her appearance. She stood blocking the entrance.

"Well, what do you have to say for yourself, mam'selle?" the woman inquired.

"I'm sorry, Madame Juvin. There was trouble . . ."

The woman drew herself up in righteous indignation. "I waited up half the night for you and you never returned. Do you expect me to let you in now, as if nothing had happened?" She made a noise through her teeth.

At that moment, the vicomtesse moved into her line of vision. Madame Juvin's eyes widened in surprise.

"My good woman, will you please open the door?" the vicomtesse began. "We've traveled quite a long way today."

Her appearance produced an instant reaction. Recognizing

the aristocratic tone of voice, the aura of a woman used to being obeyed, Madame Juvin forgot her anger at Kenna and swiftly stepped aside.

"Come in, madame," she said, taking a hasty glance at the large touring car in the narrow street and the uniformed chauffeur at the wheel.

"*Merci.* Kenna, *petite,* hurry and change, so that you can take me to tour your hospital."

The vicomtesse walked airily into the front parlor and removed one glove as she went. "The roads were so abominable, you wouldn't believe them. And guns bombarding great holes in the middle. We were lucky to find a place to stay for the night. Even then, Pierre had such a time avoiding the craters on the way back today."

"May I get you something to drink, madame?" the woman asked in a nervous voice.

"Not for me," the vicomtesse answered. "But my driver would appreciate a small glass of wine to remove the dust from his throat."

Madame Juvin rushed from the small front parlor to the kitchen. A moment or so later she carried the requested glass of wine out to the surprised Pierre.

Upstairs in the small bedroom, Kenna quickly washed her face and changed her clothes. The vicomtesse, sitting downstairs in the front parlor, seemed pleased. Flustered, Madame Juvin returned and stood in the entrance, as if undecided as to what to do with such a distinguished guest in her house.

Kenna, dressed in her uniform with her official cape about her shoulders, came down the stairs and the decision was taken from Madame Juvin. For at the girl's appearance, the vicomtesse rose from the sofa. Madame Juvin hurriedly opened the door for them and was still standing there when Pierre returned the empty wineglass.

She watched as the chauffeur got back into the car and guided it out of the narrow street in the direction of the hospital.

Kenna relaxed. The vicomtesse had made everything all right.

"Why are you doing this for me, madame?" Kenna asked the woman seated beside her.

The vicomtesse's eyes softened as she looked at the girl. "Because you are so like my Bernay—spirited and impulsive. That makes you vulnerable to people who would destroy you."

Kenna thought of the indignant actions of Madame Juvin. And yet the woman had been so kind, previously.

"And you also have a special beauty—not only your outward appearance, but from within. It's evident in your unselfish love for your brother." Her voice, kind and sympathetic, finished, "And I pray for your success in finding him."

"Thank you, madame."

Down the road toward the hospital Pierre drove the touring car. As they neared the intersection, Kenna thought of Carlton for the first time since she'd left Toul nearly eighteen hours before. She didn't know why but she hesitated to seek him out. She knew, though, that she would have to secure his permission to show the vicomtesse through the hospital. And so, after Pierre had stopped the car, Kenna led the vicomtesse to the nurses' lounge.

As she walked through the cloistered courtyard she passed Edna Brockett. Kenna nodded in greeting and walked on. But Edna stopped for a moment, watching Kenna's progress toward the surgeon's office. And her eyes held a malicious glint.

The door was open—unusual for Carlton. Kenna tapped and waited to be acknowledged. Carlton, looking out the window, turned. An immense relief pulsed through him when he saw Kenna standing in the doorway. But the relief was soon supplanted by an intense anger.

"You deceived me," he accused. "You've been going to Rue Pierre Hardie behind my back."

His sudden attack was not what she expected.

Taken back by the abrupt greeting, Kenna glanced along the walkway of the cloister and then back to her fiancé. "Who told you?"

"That's beside the point." He acted as if he were waiting for an apology which didn't come.

Instead, Kenna said, "I never promised that I wouldn't go,

225

Carlton. I found someone who knows Neal—and he's helping me to look for him.''

His harsh laugh penetrated the room. ''Yes. Jacques Thibault.''

At the mention of the French airman's name, Kenna looked surprised.

''I've just heard about your latest dealings with the man. And although I don't believe for a minute that you ran away for the weekend with him, as someone suggested, you've put me in a very embarrassing position as your fiancé. I've been made to look like a cuckold.''

''I'm sorry, Carlton.''

''Heaven knows I tried to keep you out of trouble—making you work a double shift, once I found out what you were doing.''

His casual admission confounded Kenna and she forgot everything else. ''You mean you weren't shorthanded at all?'' she inquired.

''Of course not.''

Kenna, remembering the long, arduous hours, the bone-wearying strain of each day, and the devastating heartaches, suddenly felt her fury against Carlton take form. She put her hand to her head in an effort to control her emotions.

''I want your promise, Kenna—that you won't ever see Jacques Thibault again.''

Incredulously, Kenna looked at the man before her. What was she doing—engaged to someone who had deliberately made it difficult for her? He wasn't concerned with her welfare, or her search for Neal. He was only concerned with his own image. ''And if I don't give you my promise not to see him again?''

Impatiently, Carlton stepped from behind his desk. ''Then I've made a mistake in asking you to be my wife.''

''I believe you have, Carlton.''

He was startled at her agreement. His eyes narrowed as he peered closely at Kenna. She wasn't the same. There was a new stubbornness—a quality that he didn't like. Had Edna Brockett been right?

In the silence, Kenna remembered her reason for seeking out Carlton Torey. With an impersonal tone she spoke. ''Major Torey, the Vicomtesse d'Arcy is waiting in the nurses' lounge. Do I have your permission to show her through the hospital?''

"The vicomtesse is here, in this hospital?" His anger with Kenna was put aside at the mention of the vicomtesse.

"Yes. She wants to view the Dakin-Carrel method in operation.''

Carlton was clearly impressed to have the woman who was a legend in all of France here in his hospital. He smiled. "I'll take care of it, Kenna. It won't be necessary for you to stay since you're officially off duty. You say she's in the nurses' lounge?''

"Yes."

Already, Carlton was closing the door to his office. And Kenna, having a hard time keeping up with his long strides, retraced her route through the courtyard.

"My mother will be pleased when I write her about this," Carlton said. "It's quite an honor for the vicomtesse to visit *my* hospital."

When they reached the lounge, Kenna walked to the waiting vicomtesse. "Madame, may I present Major Carlton Torey, the chief surgeon. Major Torey, the Vicomtesse d'Arcy."

Carlton took the woman's hand, and making an appropriate response, turned back to Kenna. "Thank you, Miss Chalmers, you may leave now."

At his imperious dismissal, the vicomtesse hid her amusement. "Kenna, *petite*," she said, "wait for me. I shan't be too long."

Carlton, surprised at the intimate endearment, looked from the vicomtesse to the girl before leading the way from the room.

While she waited, Kenna went over in her mind the antagonistic meeting with Carlton. The more she thought about it, the more certain she became. She had never wanted to marry him. Why, then, had she allowed herself to become engaged to him?

Irish Fitzpatrick. The name crept into her thoughts—unsolicited. *He* was the reason for her pairing with Carlton Torey. In an effort to put him out of her mind, she had become

227

engaged to a man who meant nothing to her emotionally. Carlton had never been able to stir her with his polite, chaste kisses. Only Irish Fitzpatrick—but his kisses were neither polite nor chaste.

She thought she had rid herself long ago of the feel of his lips against hers. But she knew that wasn't true. Her encounter with him in the courtyard had proven that. Her emotions, so long relegated to the hidden recesses of her heart, had re-emerged, more powerful than ever. She could no longer deny them, even though Irish hated her.

But her way was now clear. Yes, she had to make a complete break with Carlton—ask for a transfer to another hospital—and forget Irish Fitzpatrick. From now on, she would be concerned only with caring for the wounded and continuing her search for Neal.

Twenty-Seven

STEPPIE, UNAWARE OF THE DRAMA SURROUNDING KENNA, came to a decision. She was no help at all in searching for Neal. Yet the solution seemed so simple.

She had thought of it that day when one of the hospital trains had arrived with the nurses on board. If she became a hospital train nurse also, she would be able to question hundreds of men who had come from behind enemy lines—some of them refugees from prison camps, others familiar with the towns and farms sprinkled all the way from Verdun to Saint-Mihiel. There was a small chance that one of them might remember something that would lead to Neal.

Kind, gentle Neal. Steppie smiled as she remembered their childhood together. Neither she nor Neal alone had been a match for Kenna, and it had taken the two of them to thwart any plans that Kenna made.

The only time they had actually succeeded in doing it was the day of the gypsy weddings in the Church of the Immaculate Conception.

"No, Kenna. Stephanie and I absolutely refuse to go with you," Neal had said. "You'll have to go by yourself this time."

Kenna, disguised as a gypsy, in her red skirt and blouse, with long gold earrings dripping from her ears, had finally persuaded Davin to take her. Steppie would never forget Kenna's face when she returned, or Davin's hearty laughter at the fiasco, for they had been barred from the church.

"You should have seen her, Steppie," Davin had said. "She was the only one dressed as a gypsy." Steppie and Neal had joined in the laughter, much to Kenna's chagrin.

Poor Kenna. She'd been so overworked lately. That both-

229

ered Steppie. Surely Carlton could have distributed the load more evenly. She sighed. There was nothing she could do about that. It was up to Carlton. But the other—yes. Steppie could do something about that. And she knew that Davin Grant would help her.

Kenna's look was unwavering as she faced her former fiancé. "I want to transfer to another hospital, Major Torey."

"That's not necessary, Kenna," he replied.

"Under the circumstances, I think it is."

"So you're still determined to go against my wishes?"

"If that means continuing to see someone who might help me find my brother—yes."

"You're making a mistake, Kenna."

"Perhaps. But I still want the transfer."

Carlton was irritable. Nothing had gone right that day. And now to have Kenna act this way. Well, if she left his hospital, he would see that she didn't work with Davin Grant.

"I'll send your request to headquarters."

"Thank you, Major Torey."

He watched her leave his office and then sat down immediately to draw up the papers. At the end of the document, he recommended her transfer to Paris—as far away as he could get her from both Davin Grant and Jacques Thibault.

Her three-day leave expired and Kenna went back to work while she waited for the transfer to come through. Madame Juvin said nothing further about the night that had caused words between them.

As Steppie rode in the military truck on her way into Toul, she was amazed to see Kenna standing on the side of the road. The truck slowed and Kenna climbed aboard.

"What are you doing off duty so early?" Steppie asked.

"I'm working the same shift you are," Kenna said, smiling. "No longer, no shorter than anyone else."

"That's good." She was relieved that Carlton had finally done something about Kenna's extra hours.

Steppie, anxious to tell Kenna what she had done, waited until the truck came to a stop in front of the warehouse. And as they began their trek to Madame Juvin's house, Steppie

230

confessed, "Kenna, I have something to tell you." Her brown eyes held a measure of excitement.

"You've discovered that Gigot is the long-lost son of Count Thierry."

Steppie giggled. "Be serious, Kenna. I really do have something awfully important to tell you."

Kenna sobered and waited for Steppie to continue.

"I'm going to be a nurse on one of the hospital trains—beginning next week."

Kenna showed her alarm. "But Steppie, you can't do that."

"And why not?"

"Remember how seasick you were, coming over on the transport?"

"That was different. I'll be on land."

"But night and day—the train will be moving all the time. You won't even be able to do your laundry."

"I've already found out about that. The canteen at the railway station takes care of it. Simone said someone collects the nurses' dirty laundry several times a week and brings back the clean."

Steppie, still feeling Kenna's disapproval, rushed on with her explanation. "I thought you'd be pleased. I did it because of Neal."

"You think you'll find him on the hospital train?"

"No. But there are hundreds of soldiers I can talk with. And one just might be able to give us a clue as to where to look."

"Oh, Steppie," Kenna moaned. "It's so dangerous for you."

"No more so than what *you've* been doing."

Kenna's head jerked toward Steppie as she continued. "Don't think I don't know *something* has been going on. I've heard the rumors Edna Brockett has been spreading about you. And . . . and then, Madame Juvin was mad as a hatter at you—You didn't get home that night we had the party, did you?"

"No," Kenna admitted. "But it wasn't Jacques Thibault's fault."

"Did you spend the night with him?"

"Of course not, Steppie," Kenna replied indignantly. And then, with a twinkle in her eye, she said, "I spent the night with the Vicomte d'Arcy. He wanted me to be his mistress."

Steppie choked. Kenna gave the girl a light whack on her back, and waited for her to catch her breath. "What?" she gasped.

While they walked, Kenna regaled Steppie with the entire story. Now she could look back and laugh about it, although it wasn't amusing at the time. "Promise you won't tell a soul?"

"Nobody would believe me," Steppie commented, still overwhelmed.

In the orthopedic section of Carlton's hospital, Eb hobbled across the room. He could get around rather well despite the heavy plaster cast on his leg.

Eb finished packing his belongings in the Dorothy bag, given him for that purpose by the Red Cross and named for the woman who had designed it. On top he placed the two Luger pistols and the pair of Zeiss binoculars he'd won at poker. He was slightly sorry to go, even the two miles down the road to the long-term convalescent hospital. He'd been comfortable here and the food was good.

"You ready to leave, Private?" Wells, the ambulance driver, asked.

"I guess so," Eb answered, taking a last look around him to make sure he hadn't left anything. Fleetingly, he remembered the hayloft that he'd shared with Seton and the Professor when he'd first come to France—and the baked potato they'd shared one night. A momentary sadness hit him. The Professor was dead. Seton, his best friend, was now with Major Fitzpatrick. That's where he longed to be, too. Instead, the redheaded Eb climbed into the Tin Lizzie beside Wells and began his journey to the convalescent hospital.

The large stone building rose out of the landscape, the bars at the windows giving it a prison-like atmosphere. Eb, taking one look at his new home, said, "Christ, what a dismal looking place. I wonder if it's as bad on the inside as it looks on the outside?"

"More than likely," Wells replied. "Used to be an insane asylum, they tell me. But it has a good Red Cross recreation room. That should ease the pain some for you." He grinned at Eb as he said it.

A few minutes later, the dust whirled behind the Tin Lizzie as it disappeared down the road. And Eb, standing on his crutches before the hospital, shook his head in disappointment.

Captain Davin Grant sat in his small, bare office and waited for his call to come through from headquarters. The box telephone rang and Davin quickly picked it up. "Captain Grant speaking."

Over the crackling telephone line the Signal Corps girl called out, "Captain Grant, Colonel Blanton is waiting to talk with you."

"Gerald, how are things with you?" Davin began, and then quickly got down to business.

"I need a favor," Davin said. "You have a nurse, Kenna Chalmers, who's just received a transfer to Paris. I want her here in my hospital, Gerald. Can you fix it?"

"Where is she now?" Colonel Blanton asked.

"Two miles down the road, at another hospital. She's already settled in Toul, and it would be ridiculous to uproot her, when I'm looking for a replacement myself."

"Did she personally request the transfer?"

"Yes. But not to Paris. She only wanted to leave that particular hospital." And he added in a more confidential voice, "She broke her engagement to the C.O., so it's a little sticky for her there."

"Well, there doesn't seem to be much sense in moving her. You're right about that. Let me see what I can do, Davin. And I'll get back in touch with you."

"Thanks, Gerald."

"Are you all right for supplies, Davin?" the man asked.

"I could use some malted milk for the diet kitchen," he replied.

They talked another minute and then a satisfied Davin hung up.

"Captain Grant," a voice at the door called as soon as the

233

click of the telephone told the nurse that the doctor had finished talking. "The orthopedic patient has arrived."

A week later, the sun, coming over the spires of St. Etienne, gave a momentary glitter to the gray dinginess of the town. It spread rapidly along the streets to the railway station, where Kenna, shading her eyes, glanced up at the hands of the giant clock over the entrance.

"You'll be careful, won't you, Steppie?" Kenna asked. "You won't fall off the train or anything?"

"Of course not, Kenna. I can take care of myself. Don't worry about me."

The train whistle signaled its low, mournful sound as the two hurried through the station, already busy in the early morning hours. The double tracks, running alongside the Hôtel de la Gare, vibrated as the light turned red.

"I'll miss you, terribly," Kenna confessed.

"You'll let me know where you'll be, won't you—as soon as you get your transfer?"

Misty-eyed, the two clung to each other. Then they parted and Steppie, holding onto her valise, climbed into the car. Kenna stood on the platform until the train was out of sight. She felt an emptiness with Steppie finally gone. For three years they'd been inseparable. Now Steppie had branched out on her own with a new independence and self-assurance—all because of Neal.

Slowly, Kenna left the empty platform and walked toward the canteen, where Simone was already busy getting ready for the hungry and dirty hordes of soldiers that would pass through Toul that day.

"So she actually went," Simone said, holding out a cup of hot coffee to Kenna.

"Yes." Kenna looked at Simone and said, "You'll watch out for her, won't you, Simone, if I'm not around?"

Simone nodded. "Do you have any idea where you'll be located?"

"Edna Brockett told me I'll be sent to Paris."

"How does *she* know?" Simone said in a disparaging tone.

"She probably steamed open Major Torey's mail when he wasn't looking," Kenna said.

234

"Wouldn't put it past her," Simone snorted. "A pity you couldn't stay in Toul, though, with all the other hospitals around here."

"That would be too much to hope for," Kenna replied.

But later that day when Kenna was summoned to Carlton Torey's office, she discovered that she had not been transferred to Paris after all.

"So you went behind my back again," Carlton accused.

Puzzled, Kenna remained silent and waited for him to enlighten her.

"I should have known he wouldn't allow you out of his sight."

"I'm sorry, Major Torey, but I don't seem to be following the conversation very well. Whom are you discussing?"

"Your friend, Davin Grant."

Still seeing Kenna's puzzled look, Carlton became impatient. "Come, Kenna, don't put on that innocent expression with me. I know better. You and Davin hatched this between you to make me look like a laughingstock at headquarters."

It was now Kenna's turn to be impatient. "Am I not going to Paris?"

"No. My orders have been rescinded—by a subordinate. You're to report to Captain Davin Grant."

A pleased look spread from Kenna's soft gray eyes to the corners of her upturned mouth. "How nice," she murmured.

"Do you mean you didn't know?"

"I had no idea, Major Torey. But it is rather nice, isn't it, not to be moving—especially with Steppie coming back and forth on the hospital train."

For a moment he glared at her, and holding onto the transfer papers, he finally thrust them across his desk toward Kenna. "You're to report to Davin tomorrow."

"Thank you," Kenna said, a great relief showing in her face.

"You won't have long to be with him, you know."

Kenna, already halfway out the door, turned around. "What do you mean?"

"We're all scheduled to move out soon. The offensive toward Verdun has started."

Twenty-Eight

THE NEXT MORNING, KENNA, IN HER FRESHLY STARCHED UNI-
form, walked from Madame Juvin's to the warehouse. Hoping for a ride earlier than the usual supply truck, Kenna
waited for some sign of activity in the barracks behind the
warehouse where many of the chauffeurs, assigned to the
base hospitals, bunked.

Seven francs a day and a subsistence allowance were all the
chauffeurs could hope for in the way of pay. But for most of
them, it didn't seem to matter. They were content with their
lot—playing poker, drinking the cheap mirabelle liqueur, and
gathering each noontime at the Chariot d'Or for their main
meal. From the young, only seventeen years of age, to the
very old like Wells, they came and went independently, and
calmly ignored rules and regulations that didn't suit them.

The sky, threatening with rain, contained no hint of blue as
Kenna waited. Minute wisps of bleached clouds rolled together in centrifugal motion—like cotton candy wound on a
stick—until they became great, billowing, low-hanging
clouds, so near that Kenna felt she could reach up and touch
them.

Uneasily she watched the drops of rain. And she gathered
her cape closer to her body to ward off the dampness.

The door to the barracks opened. The chauffeurs were
ready for the day. And one of the first ones out the door was
Wells. Recognizing the girl, the man with a patch over his
eye walked toward her. As the rain began its descent, he motioned her toward the camion. "Get in," he called.

"I'm going to a different hospital this morning, Wells. It's
two miles farther down the road."

"That's all right," he barked. "I'll take you anyway."

Comfortable in Wells's company, Kenna relaxed. Despite his crotchety manners, she enjoyed being with him. In the silence of the morning, the sound of a plane overhead caused Kenna to look upward.

It was a French Spad; she could tell from the markings on the wings—red, white, and blue in a different combination from the British or American planes. It was bad flying weather. Something important must be happening for it to be aloft.

Only once had she seen Jacques Thibault since their trip to Nancy. And he had brought disappointing news. The blond-haired American escaping from a German prison had been identified. So there was now no need to seek out the man who had helped the prisoners over the mountains.

The face of the Vicomte d'Arcy fleetingly passed through her mind—his boyish face, the clipped mustache. She didn't realize it at the time, but his amorous actions had saved her life. For precisely at eleven o'clock, the shelling of the road to Toul had begun. If it had not been for his abduction, she and Jacques would have been buried alive—like the men in the Trench of Bayonets at Verdun, their blades sticking through the earth in rows, serving as a marker for each man in the trench line.

They reached the dismal stone buildings. Instead of turning around and heading back to Toul, Wells parked the camion. "I think I'll go in and see that Private Eb Jordan."

At Kenna's surprised look, Wells confessed, "He won a German Luger off me in a poker game right before he left the other hospital."

"You're not going to try to win it back this morning, are you?" Kenna asked.

"Don't have time," Wells admitted with a sheepish grin. "But I have my hopes, later."

The rain had stopped, leaving only a fine mist in the air. Kenna, on her way to report to Davin Grant, walked past an old French gardener, busily clipping a wayward hedge along the side of one of the buildings.

"*Bonjour,*" she said as she saw him look up at her approach. He didn't return her greeting. He dropped his clippers and openly stared, his eyes traveling immediately to the silver-blond hair. A strange look came over his face, as if he had seen a ghost.

Kenna shrugged at his behavior and continued walking. Halfway to Davin's office, she looked over her shoulder. The man in the faded trousers was following her. She frowned and began to walk a little faster.

The door to Davin's office was closed—an unusual occurrence. Kenna tapped and Davin's voice called out. "Who is it?"

"Kenna Chalmers, reporting for duty, sir," her saucy voice rang out.

"Come in."

She opened the door and faced a smiling Davin across the desktop. Behind him hung a small banner—"Welcome to Kenna Chalmers" it read. Seeing it and the smug expression on Davin's face, she laughed with delight.

"Oh, Davin, how nice of you."

He smiled. "Sit down, Kenna. We're going to have a private celebration."

Before him a large ceramic pot, chipped and worn, and two tin cups from some discarded mess kits waited. Kenna sat in the chair before the desk and watched her childhood friend pour the chocolate into the two cups.

"I'm glad you're here, Kenna," he said as he handed her a cup.

"So am I," she admitted.

"I shouldn't say it, but I will anyway. I'm glad your engagement to Major Torey has been called off."

Seeing the face peering at her through the window caused a momentary frown. Davin, seeing only the frown, said quickly, "You're not sorry, are you, Kenna?"

Her gray eyes turned back to Davin. "No, of course not, Davin." She smiled again at him. "Don't look now, but there's an old man in faded chasseur's trousers staring at us through the window."

Not heeding Kenna's advice, Davin turned to look. The old man moved out of sight just as Davin caught a glimpse of him. "That's Gigot, our gardener," Davin explained. "Harmless—though he was an inmate here when the place

238

operated as an asylum. I guess he's just curious this morning."

"Does he always follow your nurses?" Kenna asked.

"Why? Is that what happened? He followed you here?"

"Yes. I spoke to him by the hedge and he acted as if he'd seen a ghost. Then he started tracking me."

"He never paid any attention to anybody, except Steppie. Now that she's gone, you've inherited his allegiance."

"What have I done to merit that?"

"He probably thinks you're an angel, flown down from some altar niche," Davin teased.

Kenna smiled and sipped her chocolate. Her eyes sobered and in a low, grateful voice she confided, "Thank you, Davin—for everything."

Kenna settled into the new routine with the other nurses on the wards. And for the rest of the day, she forgot Gigot and his curious interest in her.

Eb, appalled at the dramatic difference in the two hospital facilities, looked down at his wooden bowl and spoon and determined to do something about the situation.

The warehouse, filled to the brim, contained shelf after shelf of things that could make the place comfortable—even luxurious. The trick was to get them out of the warehouse. He didn't know how he was going to do it, but he'd find a way.

Hobbling on his crutches, with a pen and paper stuffed in his pocket, Eb began a methodical tour of the hospital. It took him two days of hard work, but there wasn't anything else to do, except play poker and listen to the warped records of the old Victrola in the recreation room. And somehow, with Wells out of the game, it wasn't the same.

A dreariness set in with constant drizzle and dampness touching the nerves like an aching tooth. The insidious epidemic of Spanish influenza had begun to spread. Mangy mules and influenza—both from Spain. He'd had more than his share of grief, trying to cure the scruffy mange on the caisson mules. Stubborn as their American cousins, they understood neither English nor pidgin French. And their ugly hides had been just as stubborn.

All at once, gazing out the rain-covered window, Eb wished for the weeks before, when he'd trudged the mud-troughed roads alongside Seton and the others. He heard a cough and as he turned toward the noise, he recognized his friend Wells.

Eb's face brightened and his boredom disappeared. "I'll get my deck of cards," he said. But Wells shook his head.

"Can't stay but a minute. Just wanted to check on that plaster leg of yours, since I've got an investment in it."

"You can't stay?" Eb repeated in a disappointed voice.

"Nope. Got to go pick up the supply of malted for Captain Grant."

"I'll ride with you," Eb said, "if you got room."

Wells coughed again. "You'll get wet," he warned.

"I don't mind. I'm going crazy with nothing to do."

Eb put on his coat and the folded paper crackled in his pocket. His head suddenly lifted. "You say you're going to pick up supplies?"

"Yep."

"Signed by the C.O., with the district officer's initials?"

"It's official, all right. You know how that new lieutenant is down at the warehouse. Make you sign your life away for a ditty bag or a pair of drawers."

Eb smiled and fingered the four-page list he had carried around with him for three days. He climbed into the camion, with his leg sticking straight out.

"You better get your leg inside, son," Wells advised. "Some pretty wild young fellows just arrived as drivers. No telling when one might come along, shaving your toenails."

When they reached the warehouse, Wells looked longingly down the street. "You thirsty, Eb?"

"Not much."

Wells looked crestfallen and Eb, noticing the old man's expression, said, "Hand me the requisition, Wells. I'll take care of it while you get something to drink."

"You don't mind?"

"No. I told you I was bored. It'll give me something to do."

As soon as Wells walked away, Eb hastily removed the

papers from his pocket. At the bottom of the last page he signed his name as the official searcher for the base hospital.

That was the trouble. Red Cross headquarters had not bothered to assign a searcher to the long-term convalescent hospital. That's why the others in the vicinity had fared better. No one had been watching out for Captain Grant's hospital. But now, Eb decided, he'd change all that. He took the one official sheet and attached it on top of the other four.

Along the rows of shelves he went, pointing to the sets of dishes, the silverware, the ceramic chocolate pots, wool pajamas in all colors, linens. And he saved the best until last—the food.

Can after can stared at him. And his mouth began to water in anticipation. They'd have a feast that night for sure.

The small boy, monkey-like, climbed to the top shelves as Eb pointed to the items on his list, until a thunderous voice behind filled the great cavern of a warehouse.

"Private, just what do you think you're doing?"

Eb pointed to one more item before he finally turned around. His innocent freckled face stared at the lieutenant in charge.

"I have a requisition to fill, sir."

"But you're stripping my shelves."

"It looks like a lot, sir, but we're in great need," he replied. "The men at Captain Grant's hospital are even eating out of wooden bowls. *Wooden bowls*," he repeated. "Is that any way to treat men who're just waiting to die from their wounds? To make heroes do without because they're too weak to ask for anything?"

"Let me see your requisition papers, Private."

Eb handed them to the lieutenant and held his breath while he scrutinized them. He flipped each page, his eyes traveling down the list of items. "There's only one official page. The rest haven't been initialed."

The boy's earnest eyes looked at the man holding the papers. Eb's crutch slipped and the lieutenant reached out to steady him.

"Where were you, Private, when you were wounded?"

"Outside Château-Thierry, sir. My commanding officer saved my life. But he was wounded too."

"Bad?"

"Yes, sir. He's dying. That's why the hospital needs these things—to make him and the other men more comfortable during their final days."

Touched by Eb's sincerity, the lieutenant handed back the papers.

"You've gotten everything you need?"

"Except for the malted, sir."

By the time Wells returned, the camion was filled to the top and the boxes were hanging over the sides. Amazed, Wells said to the waiting Eb, "What's all this?"

"Supplies for Captain Grant."

"But . . ."

"Shut up, Wells. Just crank the durn camion and get out of here before the lieutenant changes his mind."

On the way back, Eb silently apologized to Major Irish Fitzpatrick for stretching the truth about his condition.

Twenty-Nine

WITH CORPORAL SETON CAMPBELL AT HIS SIDE, MAJOR IRISH Fitzpatrick rode in the slow-moving convoy with the great white horse Godrin tied to the back of the military vehicle. Damage caused by shelling from both sides greeted them everywhere—ruins of villages, blackened tree stumps where trees had once stood in leafy splendor.

They stopped in a village square to water the horses from the trough. Across the street, with the chill of the early fall surrounding it, stood the ruins of a church, its steeple and roof gone. Perched precipitously on a ledge was a statue of the Virgin Mary, miraculously unharmed amid the ruins. An old man, standing in the square, saw Irish's fascination with the strange sight.

"Someday, *soldat,* the blessed Virgin will come down. And on that day, the war will be over."

His prediction stayed with Irish for the rest of the day. Wrapped in his ground sheet and blanket that night, he went to sleep with two images in his mind—one of stone, and the other, living, with hair the color of molten fire.

With less than a week to enjoy the fruits of Eb's foraging of the warehouse, the majority of the base hospital personnel got ready to move out, leaving only a skeleton staff to care for the long-term patients.

The giant offensive toward Saint-Mihiel had started and every available doctor, nurse, ambulance driver, and aide were needed at the front.

On that chill September day, Kenna packed her few things while the guns roared and thundered. Observation balloons, planes overhead, camions and ambulances, trucks holding the hospital tents and supplies—all pointed to the sudden escalation of war, the face-to-face confrontation between the *sammis* and the Boches.

"Kenna, over here," a voice shouted amid the din and sputter of running engines.

Eb sat beside Wells in the ambulance, with his plaster cast sticking straight out.

"You're going too?" Kenna asked, surprised.

"You don't think I'd be left behind, do you?" he countered. "I might not be able to fight yet, but I sure can roll bandages. Come on. Get in."

Kenna climbed in, with Annette, the older nurse, immediately behind her. Wells cranked the engine. Slowly the vehicle took its place in the convoy, moving away from the dismal stone buildings that had served as an asylum toward the long avenue.

Gigot, in his faded chasseur trousers and khaki wool sweater, came running around the corner of one of the buildings. His face contained an unfathomable disappointment.

Seeing him, Eb said, "Did anybody remember to say good-bye to Gigot?"

His question was greeted with silence. Kenna, looking back, commented with a sadness in her voice, "He looks like an abandoned child."

Eb waved and shouted, "Gigot."

The old man looked in the direction of the slow-moving ambulance. He grinned as he recognized the people in it. Down the road he began to run—faster and faster in an attempt to catch up. Kenna and Annette and Eb watched. He'd almost made it when he stumbled. His peasant shoe came off, but Gigot didn't bother to stop. Instead, he scooped up the shoe and held it in his hand while he continued running. Finally, with an extra spurt of energy, he reached the back of the ambulance. With one great heave, he hoisted himself inside. And only then, with a satisfied smile, did he attend to his shoe.

"Guess Gigot can roll bandages as good as anybody else," Eb said.

And so the motley crew of Wells, Eb, Kenna, Annette, and

Gigot traveled toward the salient that had waited for four years for its liberation from the enemy.

Along the trenches, a voice shouted, "Get down, you idiot, before you get your head blown off."

The major turned to see who had spoken to him in such a manner and when the soldier saw the cluster on the man's shoulder, he said, "Beg your pardon, sir. I didn't know you were an officer."

Irish Fitzpatrick smiled at the sergeant. The other men, digging in and waiting for the battle to begin, marveled to see their commander surveying the front lines for himself.

"That Major Fitzpatrick," one soldier whispered, with admiration in his voice. "Doesn't sit on his can like a lot of the other officers way back behind the lines."

Another agreed. "Bet he knows every nook and cranny of the entire sector."

"He's the kind you'd follow to hell and back," another commented.

"And I already know what hell's like," a young soldier complained. "A salty corned beef sandwich and no water to drink. Jeez, I'm thirsty."

"Water wagon," someone yelled, asking for relief from thirst, and the request spread up and down the line.

At one o'clock in the morning, three thousand guns began bombardment. To the Germans, it came as no surprise. From the spies, even from the newspapers, Ludendorff knew about the first all-American offensive. And the French general who had been denied Pershing's troops waited for the big-boned, long-legged Americans to be blasted to kingdom come.

The guns roared for four hours straight, and then promptly at 5 A.M. the *sammis* left the trenches to begin their advance. General Pershing, watching their progress from a nearby hill, knew that this fight would determine his military future—for the entire forty-mile front, including the American and French divisions, was under his command.

The Americans struck the salient on both sides, attacking eastward from the Verdun sector and northward from Nancy in a pincer-like movement. On the southern face the I Corps, with its 82nd Division out of Camp Gordon, hit. At the tip of the salient, three French divisions harassed the enemy.

"Stretcher-bearer," came a shout, and Gigot, doubling over to keep from being hit by enemy bullets, rushed toward the voice. Back and forth he went, bringing the wounded to the field tents just beyond the lines.

Later in the day, Wells gave up his ambulance to Eb. Even though he couldn't walk or run that easily because of his leg, Eb managed to drive. And so Wells gave Gigot a helping hand with the stretchers.

As the wounded were brought in, their gas masks and helmets were thrown in a heap. Not taking time to remove the soldiers' clothing, Kenna and the other nurses marked with an indelible pencil the place where bullets and shell fragments were lodged, so that the surgeons need waste no time in looking for them.

Because of the pathogenic germs from the soil manured for centuries, the wounds were cleaned with gasoline and then iodine. Stretchers were placed directly on the operating tables.

All night, Kenna worked. This time, there were no tears as there had been when she'd first met the hospital train. Only a numbing weariness.

"Someday, we *both* might be in hell." Irish's words that day at Fort McPherson returned to Kenna's memory in full measure. And she knew that his prediction had come true.

Quietly, with no sound coming from the stretcher, a French officer lay in the semidarkness. Kenna took a lantern and walked between the rows of men, pausing to check on each one.

Her lantern shook in her hand as she recognized the boyish face, the clipped mustache and the brow wet with perspiration.

"Bernay," she whispered.

His eyes, glazed with pain, stared up at the girl in uniform and a brief smile twisted his lips. "Kenna."

His paleness, his weak pulse alarmed her. As a corpsman

passed by, Kenna whispered to the medic, "Please go and see how much longer it will be."

"I can tell you now," the corpsman replied. "There're five others waiting before him—just as bad, or worse."

"Don't worry, Kenna," the Frenchman comforted her. "It's already too late." And she saw the telltale trickle of blood seeping from the corner of his mouth.

"No, it *isn't* too late," she protested, her voice quivering with emotion. Putting down the lantern, she sat on the floor beside the stretcher.

"I remember . . ."

His voice was weak and Kenna leaned closer to hear him.

". . . when I first saw you—with your golden hair."

"Don't talk," Kenna urged. "Save your strength."

But he went on as if he hadn't heard her. "An angel—and I wanted you." The regret in his voice touched her.

"You'll . . . tell my *maman?*"

"Yes, Bernay—anything you want."

"Tell her—I don't mind going to my brothers. I'm *not* afraid of death. You were behind the palm—I'll never forget—the bells in your hair. I hear them now, Kenna. Can't you hear them too?"

The tears began to run down Kenna's cheeks. "Yes, Bernay."

His hand found hers and she let it remain in his grasp. "So beautiful," he murmured, and then his hand fell to his side.

A small, choking noise came from Kenna's throat. The Vicomte d'Arcy was dead. And the old vicomtesse was left alone, the blood of her four strong sons now poured upon the altar of war.

Five miles away, a young French woman sat in a woodland park and watched her two-year-old son, Hans, play with his ball. While his sturdy legs chased the red ball amid the excited barks of the large brown dog, her mind was on the rumors that Marie had whispered to her that morning as she'd brought the milk to the kitchen door.

The Americans were coming.

Emil had mentioned nothing to her. But of course, she didn't expect him to talk of the war with her.

For three years now, the château had been Ailly's home. Unwillingly she had come, and heartbreakingly, she had stayed.

It was difficult being the mistress of a high-ranking German officer—to be cut off from one's own family in the village and to know that there was little future for her or her child, with Emil's wife waiting for him in Berlin.

"Very good," she called out to Hans in an encouraging manner as he caught his ball.

"*Gut*," he repeated, laughing, and she cringed at his use of the language. He would not fare well outside his own small world of the high stone wall and woodland park. For the occupation had caused a hatred of everything that smacked of German.

Sadly she assessed her baby's blond hair and blue eyes. He was a small replica of Emil. And although she had saved her family from death by consenting to live with the officer, they would have preferred death—theirs *and* hers—rather than the disgrace. To them, she was already dead. When the war ended, she could never go back home.

She smiled as she saw the tall blond man, just as fair as Hans, carrying the eggs in a basket toward her. But this one had gray eyes instead of blue—like the silver linings of the storm clouds—searching, a little bewildered. He'd never spoken to anyone but her—and that was his salvation. For the few words he'd uttered had given him away. He was English, or perhaps American. But he was recovering. She could tell. And one day he would remember who he was.

She'd never forget the day Gigot hid him in the stone barn—his flier's jacket scorched from fire. Little Hans had been three weeks old. Emil, tired of the forced celibacy, had taken her to his bed—far too soon after the birth of the child. And that was why, in her anger and hurt, she had decided to hide the flier right under Emil's nose when Gigot didn't return for him.

The screech of a vehicle stopping before the château brought Ailly back to the present. It sounded like Emil. She hurried back, for he expected her to be waiting for him when he came home, whatever the time of day.

She was right. Emil's driver was sitting in the vehicle and waiting. Passing him, Ailly went inside the château and over the cold, square tiles.

The door to Emil's office, usually locked, stood open. Seeing him taking papers out of his desk, she stopped and watched from the doorway.

"You're home early," Ailly said.

The German officer turned from the desk when he heard her voice. "Yes," he said, matter-of-factly. "The Americans are coming. We're moving out."

"Moving out?" she repeated. And then she saw his luggage by the door.

"What's going to happen to Hans and me?" Ailly asked, suddenly fearful.

"That, my *Liebchen*, is up to you. You're free to do what you wish."

Sensing his mother's distress, little Hans ran to Emil and his chubby hands encircled the booted leg. *"Vater?"*

Emil removed the child's fingers and, with a stern voice, said, "Go to your mother, Hans."

Ignoring Ailly and Hans, Emil von Freiker folded his papers, stuffed them into his luggage, and walked to the military vehicle waiting in the courtyard. Without looking back, he gave the driver orders to leave.

Outside, the dog ran in circles as the vehicle disappeared, while Ailly, standing at the window, held little Hans in her arms. The vibrations of the guns in the distance rattled the windows. With the sound, a sudden coldness struck her and Ailly tightened her arms round her baby.

Kenna, with eyes red from lack of sleep, continued to minister to the casualties that came in a steady stream.

The toll of battle was high—eight thousand. But Pershing's future was assured. For the attack on the Saint-Mihiel salient was a definite victory.

The quickly constructed railroad tracks carried the wounded from the front lines to the base hospitals around

249

Toul and other nearby sectors. Wells, now back to driving his ambulance, delivered his share of patients to the railroad spur.

On the third trip of the day, Kenna rode with Wells over the slow, bumpy trek from the field hospital to the railroad tracks, where the hospital train waited.

"Be careful of his leg," Kenna admonished while walking beside the stretcher of one of her patients. The bearers heeded her words.

They climbed into the train car that had the great white cross painted on its top. "You'll be fine, Private, once you're at the base hospital in Toul," she assured him.

"Just so the nurses there are pretty as you," he replied with a faint smile disguising his pain.

"Here's a pretty one coming your way right now."

Kenna turned to the nurse on the train. "Steppie," she exclaimed as she recognized her friend.

"Kenna. Oh, I'm so glad to see you," the girl said. "Are you all right? I've been so worried about you."

"I'll be fine, once I get some sleep."

"It was bad, wasn't it?"

Kenna nodded. "They're still out there, Steppie, in no-man's land—fliers shot down, wounded soldiers in the marsh, everywhere. When I get some sleep, I'm going to go out and look for them with the others."

"Be careful, Kenna. It's so dangerous. I heard that the retreating Germans are setting fire to everything and destroying the bridges."

"It's no more dangerous than staying around the hospital tents," she exclaimed. "Three of the nurses were wounded when a shell exploded outside Davin's operating tent yesterday. But luckily, they're going to be fine."

At the mention of Davin's name, Steppie hurriedly asked, "Davin wasn't hurt too, was he?"

"No. But he'll drop from sheer exhaustion if he doesn't get some rest soon."

The train gave a signal that it was ready to pull out. Steppie's attention returned to her patients while Kenna climbed down from the railroad car and rejoined Wells in the ambulance.

Train after train left, taking the wounded away from the battlefield. Kenna knew the nurses who met the trains in Toul must feel the same as she had that first time. She looked toward Wells as he picked his way over the cratered terrain. He didn't look well, either. They were all exhausted from the overwork, the sleeplessness—and still, there was so much to be done.

Kenna could no longer keep up the pace. Without removing her uniform, she crawled onto the cot in the nurses' tent for a few hours' rest. Within seconds, she was sound asleep.

Thirty

FROM THE HEIGHTS IRISH WATCHED THROUGH HIS BINOCU-
lars. Kenna's hair caught the glint of the afternoon sun as she
walked with the old man over the field. For three days he'd
known she was in the hospital unit moving directly behind the
advancing troops, but he had not sought her out. Now he
could wait no longer. She was in actual danger.

Urging his great white war horse Godrin down the hill,
Irish raced after the girl to stop her. The retreating Germans
were still hiding in the cellars. And stray gas shells made the
low places extremely dangerous.

"Kenna, stop," he shouted over the trees, but Kenna, with
Gigot guiding her, continued to walk in a westerly direction.

This section had been caught in a double disaster, bearing
the brunt of the retreating Germans as well as the advancing
Americans, with the French sappers—men armed with liquid-
fire tanks mounted to their backs—using a spew of flames to
flush out the remaining Germans from their hiding places.
Now the villages lay in ruins.

Kenna, aware of Gigot's sudden interest in the landscape,
looked in the direction he pointed his finger.

"What is it, Gigot?" she asked, knowing that he would not
be able to tell her except by signs.

He reached over and touched a strand of her hair and then
eagerly pointed again. From the moment he'd seen her, Gigot
had been mesmerized by her hair—its unusual color, so in
contrast to all the other nurses.

Still puzzled, she asked, "You want to show me something, Gigot? Is that it?"

He bobbed his head up and down, and Kenna began to
follow him across the recently occupied terrain.

She hadn't intended going so far without her gas mask. They had all been cautioned about that. But Gigot's enthusiasm was catching and Kenna pushed aside the thought of danger as she increased her pace to match the old man's steps.

The ever-present sound of guns marred the serenity of the September landscape. The gentle movement of yellow wheat in the fields dotted with red poppies provided a dramatic contrast to the blackened ruins of buildings jutting toward the sky. A remembrance of a winter-weary Georgia country landscape rushed to her senses—the bare, thin branches of woods, emaciated from the cold blasts of winter, and half-hidden in their depths, a blossoming redbud tree, the first spring color amid the gray.

Kenna, seeing the desolate landscape, felt a kinship with the French people. The sweep of the fire that had destroyed her own home now widened to include an entire nation lying in ashes, except for one small bit of struggling color on the horizon.

"Hey, sweetheart, need a ride?" The camion slowed and came to a stop. Kenna, grateful for the offer, immediately accepted for both Gigot and herself.

Up the winding road the camion went, leaving the wheatfields behind. The village with its cobblestoned streets came into view. And rising above it, in the hills, sat an ancient château, with four corner turrets touching the low-hanging clouds and proclaiming ownership of the lands below.

As they entered the narrow, uneven street, Gigot touched Kenna's hand. "You can let us off now," Kenna said to the driver.

He stopped and when they had climbed down, the driver said, "Be careful," and drove away.

A sense of adventure touched Kenna. She hurried up the path with Gigot, until they came to the château's approach—an *allée* of trees. The level land was beautiful and untouched, with a view of the village below, now occupied by American troops. But overhead, a telltale whine suddenly spoiled the sense of beauty.

"Get down, Gigot," she shouted, a split second before the earth shook under the impact of mortar shells.

253

With her face in the dust, Kenna heard the direct hit. Brushing the dirt from her eyes, she raised her head high enough to see what was happening. With a great tiredness—a weight of centuries—the château came apart, a corner turret separating itself from the ancient walls and plunging slowly to the ground.

Pinned by the sudden bombardment, Kenna and Gigot lay on the open earth and covered their heads from the falling debris. They dared not move, for there was nowhere to escape.

Flames began, rapidly overtaking the château. Kenna, watching their fury, saw a man in the distance carrying a basket of eggs. Looking at the spreading fire, he dropped the basket to the grassy meadow and started running toward the château.

Kenna's mouth flew open. The man's hair was the same color as her own. She tried to cry out, but no sound came. It was Neal! He was alive! She watched in horror as he disappeared toward the flames.

No. She hadn't come this far to see him destroyed by fire. "Gigot," she moaned. "We've got to stop him."

Unmindful of the danger, Kenna rose from the ground and she, too, began to run toward the château, with Gigot behind her, pulling at her cape to keep her from entering the inferno. But she tore loose from his grasp and followed her brother inside.

"Ailly," Neal's voice shouted frantically through the dense smoke. "Where are you?"

Kenna heard a woman answer, "*Ici*," and then she heard a baby cry. As she struggled to follow the sounds her eyes filled with tears from the smoke. Because of her blindness, she knocked against a piece of furniture. Her cry of pain went unnoticed.

"Neal," she called. Through the smoke she heard his voice, responding not to hers, but to his own anguish, "Ailly."

A crash of timbers behind her told of the fire's onslaught. Rushing away from the sound, she was stopped by musty damask draperies suddenly bursting into flames before her.

Wood and cloth, dry and rotten from age, made a feast for the flames.

Quickly, Kenna stepped aside. It was madness to stay inside. "Neal," she shouted again. "Where are you? Answer me."

She ran frantically past the leaping flames, from one room to another, until finally there was no time left. Her lungs were filled with smoke. She had to get out. But how?

Kenna was lost inside the burning cavern—separated from Gigot and from Neal. Now the smoke was so thick that she couldn't find the way out. Another crash—flames licking at her cape—a fiery timber—and she cried out at the scorching sear of heat against her hand.

Disoriented, not knowing which way to flee, Kenna coughed and backed away just as another timber crashed beside her, blocking her path in another direction. As she retreated from it, she fell into a man's outstretched arms. Seeing him only dimly through the dense smoke, she croaked, "Neal. Thank God, I've found you."

He dragged her away from the smoke and fire, lifting her over the burning debris, past the flaming draperies until he reached a balcony opening. He dropped to the ground and held out his arms to catch her.

When they faced each other, he removed the handkerchief from the lower portion of his face. Breathing hard, he said, "Little fool." And Kenna looked up into the angry eyes—not of her brother—but of Irish Fitzpatrick.

"Neal?"

"He's already out—safe with the baby."

She looked around and saw her brother standing at the edge of the courtyard, his face blackened, his hands singed by the flames. In his arms he cradled the two-year-old Hans.

"Ailly's dead," Neal cried, ignoring everything but his own grief. Walking toward Gigot, he went past Kenna without acknowledging her.

"He doesn't recognize me," Kenna sobbed.

Irish Fitzpatrick looked at her with a strange, intense anger apparent in his scowling face.

He too walked away from her, toward the hitching post

where Godrin was tied. "Take the horse, old man," Irish commanded Gigot. "And get the boy and baby back to head-quarters."

Gigot looked at Kenna standing alone. He pointed toward her and then to Neal.

"Don't worry," Irish assured him. "I'll take care of her."

Kenna watched while Neal, Gigot, and the baby left down the *allée*. Behind her, the sound of flames from the château roared in her ears, as Irish glowered beside her.

"Are you ready?" he inquired.

"What about the woman inside? Ailly?"

"She's dead." Irish repeated Neal's words. "Buried underneath the stone."

"Are we just going to . . . to leave her?"

"What else can we do until the fire burns itself out?" he demanded. For a moment his voice softened. "We'll come back later, Kenna, to give her a decent burial."

"Yes. Neal will want that."

The military fire brigade arrived from the village below. The men began fighting the flames, while Kenna, retracing her steps down the *allée,* left the château behind.

In silence, they walked down the path to the village. Irish walked briskly, making no allowances for her. Kenna, disheartened, straggled behind. For over two years she had searched for Neal. She had lived for the day when she would see him again. And he had passed her by as if she were a stranger.

"Are you coming?" Irish inquired, pausing from his brisk pace.

"Yes," Kenna replied and hurried to catch up with him.

They stopped in the village square, where the tiny trickle of water from the fountain plopped against the stone and filled the basin. Irish dipped his handkerchief into the water and handed it to Kenna.

"Wash your face," he ordered.

Without a demur, she took the handkerchief and wiped the soot from her forehead and her cheeks. Then she returned the linen to Irish.

"You still have a smudge on your chin," he complained, and holding her face steady in his large hand, he scrubbed the remaining dirt away and remembered the other time when a smudge of soot had marred the whiteness of her skin.

"Thank you," she whispered.

They had passed the canal, walked over the footbridge, and were leaving the village behind when there was the sound of a shrill whine. Kenna and Irish looked toward the sky. Green shells—the color of death—appeared in the air, and then came a deafening roar. Irish, recognizing their casings, knew that within minutes, the acid, mustard-smelling gas fumes would rise from the deep craters and float over the earth.

His hand reached out, nearly jerking her arm from its socket in a sudden assault. Half dragging her, half carrying her, Irish ran to the nearest house for cover with Kenna beside him. Without hesitation he kicked in the tall iron gate from the street and broke open the closed door. When he had shut it behind them, he whirled toward Kenna and surveyed her.

"Damn," he said. "Where is your gas mask, Kenna?"

"I . . . I left it at the field hospital."

Irish quickly removed his own from around his neck. "Put it on."

"No. It's yours. I haven't any right to take it from you."

In anger, he jerked the satchel across her breast. Before she knew it, the gas mask was in place, the charcoal ready to filter the lung-destroying fumes from the air. But Irish was left unprotected.

Quickly he removed his military jacket and stuffed it under the doorway. "What can I do, Irish?" she asked, pushing aside the mask for a moment.

"Find some blankets—old clothes, tablecloths—anything to use—to stuff in the windows."

Kenna ran up the narrow straight stairs toward the bedrooms. She jerked open the lid of a chest. It contained one blanket, that was all. The armoire in the bedroom was bare. She ran to the second bedroom and stripped the bed of its sheet and the old faded quilt lying across the footboard.

Before she could get downstairs again, Kenna heard Irish's voice behind her. "We'll stay upstairs," he said. "We stand a better chance of survival here."

She couldn't converse with the gas mask in place, but

Irish, seeming to sense her thoughts, said, "They had plenty of time to get to safety, Kenna. Even with the extra load, Godrin would make it." Changing the subject, he said, "Give me the blanket."

She watched as he hung the piece of wool over the lone window that faced the back of the house. He secured it against the ledge with a Bible that had been left open on the small table.

When he had completed the task, he turned back to the girl. "Take off your clothes, Kenna."

"What?" she said, her voice muffled by the mask.

"You heard me. Take off your clothes."

In horror she saw that he was already removing his shirt. She backed toward the door.

"No," she answered.

His cynical laugh filled the small room. "Have you forgotten so quickly the effects of poison gas?"

Her face turned red with embarrassment. In every manual, she remembered the admonition. Gas fumes penetrated material, making the burns on the skin much more severe. To cut down on the devastating effects, uniforms needed to be replaced immediately with fresh clothing.

Kenna turned her back to Irish and with the sheet shielding her, she slowly began undressing.

"Don't be so modest, Kenna," Irish's voice teased. "Remember, I've seen your beautiful body before."

The cabin in the swamp. Yes. How could she forget?

Encased in the sheet, she walked toward the bed and with her legs trembling, she sat on the old feathered mattress. Irish, with the faded quilt draped around him like a Roman toga, watched her and smiled.

He came and sat beside her and together they listened to the sounds of war. He coughed and Kenna's heart quickened. The trembling in her legs increased.

She had no right to take his mask, to cause his death by her own carelessness. Suddenly, Kenna snatched the mask from her face and flung it toward Irish.

"It's yours," she screamed hysterically. "I won't take it from you."

Swearing, he picked it up, and grabbing her by the hair, he

tried to force the mask back over her head. But she struggled against him.

"No. I won't be the cause of your death. I won't let you die a martyr."

The sheet slipped and Irish's hand brushed across her breast. "Kenna," he murmured. And his lips found hers—gently at first—touching the corners of her mouth in a teasing caress. He brushed away her tears.

"Put the mask on," she begged.

"No. If you die, then we'll die together." And he threw the life-saving equipment to the other side of the room.

He lowered her against the soft feather mattress. His lips found the hollow between her breasts. And his hands began their seeking—searching.

A man and a woman—alone—with the world in flames around them. They were going to die. They should be kneeling in prayer. And yet, all Kenna could think about was Irish's body close to hers. And his kisses upon her breast.

She had loved him from the moment he had swept her from the ground on his great white horse Godrin. But she had denied it. Now there was no need to deny her love, for by morning, they would both be dead.

"You've always been mine, Kenna. You know that," his voice whispered in her ear.

"Yes. Yours," she admitted, the fever of desire pulsating through her body.

His mouth closed on hers, stopping any other words. But their bodies needed no vocabulary, for the language of love became the ecstasy of flesh upon flesh.

Irish's arms swept Kenna to him. His strong, sensuous body, shuddering in anticipation, entered hers, and the brief stab of pain Kenna felt was vaguely recorded in her mind.

She was a virgin—had been a virgin all along. But the moment she recognized it, it was no longer true. Kenna now belonged to Irish, and his deception in the swamp cabin didn't matter any more.

Thirty-One

SHE OPENED HER EYES, TENTATIVELY AT FIRST. IRISH'S DARK head lay on the pillow beside her, his hand still cupping her breast.

Kenna sat up, conscious of her breathing. Quickly, she looked down at her naked body. It was not even pink, but white, silken, as it had always been. She was alive—a miracle. And she showed no ill effects from the mustard gas. Seeing Irish's chest rise and fall in sleep, she realized he, too, was unharmed.

Disturbed by her movement, he reached out for her, but Kenna moved to the other side of the bed. In shame, she remembered the night of love—passionate, heated—her wanton behavior denying the magnitude of Irish's sins against her.

His brown eyes opened. "Good morning," he said.

Kenna returned no sweet greeting. Instead, her gray eyes blazed. "You deceived me," she accused.

"Oh?" He leaned on one elbow and a curious expression invaded his brown eyes.

"Yes—deceived me," she reiterated. "You pretended that I was no virgin."

"Are you?" he inquired, attempting to keep a serious expression on his face.

Kenna bit her lip in frustration and her cheeks flushed with embarrassment. With a tremor to her voice, she continued. "And last night, you led me to believe that we were going to die."

"Are you disappointed that we're still alive?"

"No, of course not. But if I had known we were going to live, I never would have allowed you to make love to me. Why did you do it, Irish?"

260

His laugh was short, ironic. "What did you expect me to do? Tell you that we weren't in any real danger once we barricaded ourselves in the house? When you were so willing to share my bed during our final hours?"

"You . . . you bastard!" she screamed and flailed her arms toward him, catching him off guard and hitting his chin in a solid wallop.

"Witch," he countered, and grabbed her hands before she could do further damage.

Her body moved to avoid his, but she was imprisoned in his arms, with his angry brown eyes gazing down at her sullen face. "Just remember, Kenna. You'll never belong to another man. You're mine now."

"No," she retorted. "I'll never be yours."

He became angry at her stubbornness. "Neal doesn't want you, Kenna. He made that apparent yesterday."

"He . . . he has trouble with his memory. He'll remember me eventually. He has to."

"And you think he will want you when he discovers we've slept together as man and wife?"

"As soon as he's strong enough, my brother will kill you for what you've done to me."

"Your brother? Who are you talking about?"

"My brother, Neal."

A sudden silence pervaded the room. "Neal is your *brother*?"

Kenna's eyes widened at his obvious surprise. "Didn't you know? Everybody knows he's my half brother."

"Not everyone, Kenna. *I* didn't know."

Kenna, dispirited, climbed out of bed—dragging the sheet. Realizing that her nurse's uniform was not that dangerous, she put it on and began to twist her hair into a knot at the nape of her neck.

She kept her back to Irish. But she heard him when he, too, began to dress. Without speaking, they left the house at the edge of the village and trudged toward the tents in the distance. He delivered her to the field hospital and quickly disappeared.

"Where have you been?" an irate voice demanded, and she looked up into the angry hazel eyes of Major Carlton

Torey. Surprised to see him standing before her, Kenna glanced guiltily back in the direction Irish had gone.

"Finding my brother," she replied.

"He came in yesterday, with his love child. But *you* have over twelve hours to account for, young woman."

"Is this an official interrogation?" she inquired.

Her question angered him further. "You may consider it as such."

"I was caught by the gas shells. I had no mask. I spent the night in a deserted house at the edge of the village."

Her recital was wooden. She gazed down at her muddy shoes and waited for the tirade to come. But his voice, curiously calculating, said, "So you finally found your brother."

She looked up. "Yes. Gigot showed me where he was hiding. I couldn't understand why Gigot followed me around all the time—why my blond hair fascinated him. But then yesterday it became plain. He evidently had seen Neal first, and connected the two of us in his mind.

"If it hadn't been for Gigot—" Kenna stopped, suddenly remembering. "If it hadn't been for *you*, Carlton, in transferring me . . ." She smiled. "Thank you for doing that."

He wasn't sure he wanted her thanks. "But now that you've found him, you can go back to the States."

"Yes—when the war's over."

"Surely you don't intend to remain any longer over here."

"I still have a job to do," Kenna told him.

"As your fiancé, I think you should . . ."

"But you're *not* my fiancé, Carlton," she corrected.

"We had a small misunderstanding, my dear. That's all. You didn't think I actually meant to break off with you, did you?"

She looked at the officer before her. "It's too late for us, Carlton—entirely too late." Not waiting to be dismissed, Kenna Chalmers turned and walked toward her own tent.

"How is he, Davin?" Kenna inquired. She sat across from the medical officer in the hospital tent, her freshly brushed hair and clean uniform denying the harrowing experience of the past hours.

"Better than I might have expected," Davin replied, "after all he's been through."

"He doesn't remember me." The hurt showed in her eyes and her voice.

"No. His memory is quite hazy. But that happens with head injuries, Kenna."

"But it's been *two years* since the crash. Do you think Neal will ever return to normal?"

"Eventually. But we can't rush it, Kenna. Just give him more time."

"And what do we do in the meanwhile?"

"Give him all the support we can. Get him out of the war sector, so he can come to terms with his grief."

"Ailly?"

"Yes. Her death has shaken him considerably."

"Carlton said that the baby is Neal's love child. Do you believe that, Davin?"

"Not unless he knew the girl before he crashed. It's hard to say—one way or the other—until he tells us. Right now, the only thing that's keeping him going is the child. They need each other."

"What about his leg?" she asked. "It evidently was set badly."

"If at all," Davin agreed. "A good orthopedic surgeon can operate and improve his mobility. But not anytime soon. It's better to wait on that."

Kenna nodded. "Until he comes to terms with his grief," she repeated.

"Don't be bitter, Kenna," Davin admonished, his sympathy for the girl showing in his face. "We can't expect him to dismiss what has happened in these last two years. That time period is the only portion of his life that's real to him. The past and everyone in it—you, me—mean nothing to him."

"All right, Davin," she replied with an impatient shake of the head. "So—what do we do now?"

Davin folded his hands together and his brow wrinkled in deep thought. "There's a place right outside Paris where he and the baby can be cared for. I assume you want him to stay in France for the time being?"

"Oh, yes. I wouldn't want him to go back to Atlanta alone."

"Then, I'll make the necessary arrangements. The Red Cross can handle all the paperwork."

Kenna glanced at her watch. "I'd better go." She looked up at Davin and with a gratefulness in her heart, she said, "Thank you, Davin."

Just before she left the tent, she asked, "Should I try to talk with him before he goes?"

"I wouldn't advise it, Kenna. You might upset him."

But at the end, Kenna couldn't stay away. When the time came for Neal Wexford to board the train leaving the war sector, Kenna arranged for Wells to take him, while she herself held the baby all the way to the railroad spur.

Steppie Hannon, inside the hospital train, walked toward the compartment where the light casualties sat. Today the train was less crowded. Fewer berths held severely wounded men. And Steppie was glad. The worst seemed over.

Her face brightened when she saw Kenna climb aboard with a fair-haired baby in her arms. And she rushed to greet her. But then, she stopped where she was. Her face turned pale. Directly behind Kenna came a man with silver-blond hair. There was no doubt. It was Neal—alive—the object of her thoughts, her actions, her reason for coming with Kenna overseas.

"Neal." The name escaped from Steppie's lips. She stood and memorized his face with her limpid brown eyes, hungrily exploring the planes and shadows of light and dark—his angled chin, his gray eyes. Tears spilled and blurred the image before her.

"You found Neal." Steppie's eyes remained on the man even as she spoke. She took a step forward and waited for him to recognize her.

Instead, Kenna rushed to her side. "Oh, Steppie," Kenna whispered. "He doesn't remember anything because of the crash."

Steppie reluctantly turned to Kenna. "What are you saying? He . . . he doesn't remember how it happened?"

264

"He doesn't remember *me*, Steppie," Kenna answered mournfully. "He doesn't remember *anything* from the past."

The baby squirmed in Kenna's arms, but Steppie ignored the child, while she watched Neal select a seat. The joy that Steppie felt in seeing him was still apparent in her voice.

"But you found him, Kenna. That's the important thing. He'll remember. I know he will." She smiled through her tears, as if to give herself reassurance. "Where did you find him?"

"Several miles from Saint-Mihiel," Kenna replied. "The château was bombed and Neal and the baby barely got out alive."

For the first time, Steppie allowed her attention to rest on the child in Kenna's arms. "Is the baby being sent to an orphanage?"

"No. Neal won't allow that. A Red Cross worker will meet them both in Toul and ride with them to Paris."

Steppie's face showed her alarm. "Where is the . . . the mother?" she asked.

"She died in the fire at the château."

"Is the child . . . Neal's?"

"I don't know." Kenna's quiet voice was barely audible over the train whistle. She quickly thrust the little boy into Steppie's arms. "There're some squares of gauze in the satchel. And Neal has some food for him. Take care of them, Steppie," Kenna said, hurrying to leave the train.

She stopped for a moment at the seat where her brother sat and, without saying anything, ran down the aisle toward the exit as the train began to leave the war sector and start its journey to Toul.

Neal watched the nurse walking toward him, carrying the baby in her arms. He saw the darkness of the girl's hair, the soft brown eyes looking at him, and something stirred in the back of his mind.

"Stephanie?" His voice was tentative, low.

All at once, Steppie's hopes soared. He had said her name—not the one Kenna used, but the formal one he had called her in Atlanta.

"Do you recognize me, Neal?" she inquired, her voice unable to disguise the emotion she felt.

He brushed his hand across his eyes. His words were halting. "I . . . I'm not sure. For just a moment . . . No, I guess I don't know you after all."

Steppie struggled not to show how his words affected her. Quickly searching for a change of subject, she looked at the little boy and inquired, "What's the baby's name?"

Neal's face brightened. "His name is . . ." But again, he paused, as if suddenly protective of the child. "He has a French name," he informed her, "but I'll change that. What do *you* think he should be called?"

Before she could answer, Neal said, "I know. I'll call him Daniel—since he was plucked from the jaws of death."

The baby reached out his arms to Neal and he took him. "Daniel," Neal repeated in a satisfied voice. And for a long time, he held the child and said nothing else.

Steppie hated the hospital train, the constant movement. It was almost as bad as the ship, but she had remained because of Neal—had questioned innumerable survivors of the front—and all to no avail. For it had been Kenna who found him.

Steppie gazed toward Neal and the child he had just christened Daniel. She was glad for Kenna's sake—for Neal's sake—for everyone but herself.

Steppie made up her mind. She wanted to leave the train and join Kenna and the other nurses at the front. She would see about it as soon as she reached Toul and made sure that Neal and the baby were in good hands.

While Kenna rode in the ambulance beside Wells, Eb Jordan lay on the operating table in the hospital tent and watched Davin Grant wield the saw.

"Be careful, sir," Eb said uneasily. "I'd hate for that thing to go through my leg, too."

Davin smiled. "You're the fiftieth soldier to have told me that, Eb. I'm only going to remove the cast. And I guess you'll be glad of that."

266

"Yes, sir. I'm anxious to join my new outfit and get into the fighting. I hear we're going to the Argonne Forest next."

"What am I going to do without you, Eb?" Davin asked. "If there's a scrawny French chicken within ten miles, you're the only one who can find it. We'll probably starve to death when you leave us."

"Wells is pretty good at it, too," the freckle-faced boy replied. "Except for that one day—when the rooster turned on him."

Davin laughed. "I know. I was the one who treated him for the spur wound."

They knocked down their tents, packed their hospital supplies, and made ready to move out. The mop-up was nearly over and the first phase of the bloodiest, fiercest battle in American history was ready to begin—the attack of the impenetrable German defense line of Brieulles—Romagne—Montfaucon—Grandpré.

With no transportation offered him, Eb hurried to catch up with the 77th Division. Along the muddy road, with the wind and rain slashing against his face, he tramped, passing by refugees that stared at him with vacant eyes. Their meager possessions were carried in dog carts or wheelbarrows. They had nowhere to go—and after four years of war, they had no more to show for a lifetime than Eb Jordan, with his mess kit and utensils rattling in the rucksack upon his back.

Thirty-Two

"GET THAT MULE OFF THE ROAD," THE SERGEANT'S VOICE shouted above the bedlam surrounding the mass exodus.

Willie Ratchet, out of Atlanta, Georgia, rushed to unharness the dead animal from the supply wagon. These past few days he'd never worked so hard in his life.

"Hey, you, *Kamerad*," he shouted in turn to the German prisoners working on the corduroy road. "Gimme a hand." He pointed toward them and then back to the mule. They put down their shovels and, shoving and pulling, managed to get the animal to the ditch.

Willie smiled as he began to harness another mule in its place. He'd never forget how scared he was to register for the draft. He'd believed every word of the German propaganda—that he'd get his ears cut off if he ever got to France alive. But his mama, Verbena, was right. That was the least of his worries.

The boy looked again at the German prisoners. They were out of the fighting, but there were plenty more ahead who hadn't surrendered.

Under the cover of night they moved—troops, mule-skinners, supplies, and guns—over rain-soaked muddy roads, filled with holes and craters, to give the Boche a surprise. In a diversionary tactic, one division turned toward Metz and disguised the Americans' true intentions of cutting off the railroad lines of supply and breaching the three strong lines of German defense—the *Stellungens* named for the three witches Giselher, Kriemhilde, and Freya.

Overhead, Lieutenant Manfred Schiller, flying in the dark, cut off the engine of his Fokker *Dreidecker* and glided along, listening to the ground sounds beneath him.

His heart had gone out of his flying. With his beloved commander gone, it wasn't the same any more. It had been five months since Baron von Richthofen had been brought down. And his flying circus, with the gaudy triplanes, had been left without a ringmaster.

Manfred, losing too much altitude, throttled his engine again and skimmed over the clump of trees.

The war had lasted too long and the people were tired. It would be a hard winter at home, with little food, little coal to burn in the stoves, and the constant loss of loved ones. The Spanish influenza was still spreading and killing almost as many people at home as on the front.

"Margrit," he said aloud, thinking of his sweetheart, with a poignant remembrance. How he wished for the sight of her sweet face, the thick plaits wound around her head. How he wished that he might be sitting at that very moment before a nice warm fire and listening to her high, clear voice singing *"Mitten im Schimmer der spiegelnden Wellen . . ."*

Manfred cleared his goggles of the mist and left the valley of the Aire. Dawn was just over the hill and the movement of troops beneath him would cease until another night. He hoped that Giselher had the caldrons ready for the enemy forces when they arrived.

Early on the morning of September 26, Jacques Thibault flew his Spad toward Montfaucon. He had a particular reason to be grim, for there was no more hated German observation post than the crown prince's telescope aimed at the surrounding French countryside.

German cannon interlocked every inch of ground. No roads breached the heights where machine gun nests spilled in every direction—catching anyone foolish enough to try in a wicked, hellish cross fire.

Montfaucon—where, a thousand years before, God in the guise of a falcon had shown the way to the monk St. Balderic to found the town and the monastery on the highest hill. Now almost nothing remained of the town and amid the ruins of the monastery rose the godless observation towers of the Boche.

And he, Jacques Thibault, on wings of his freshly painted

Spad, with the head of a falcon on its fuselage, had determinedly stayed alive for this one day. His hand caressed the throttle of his machine gun as his eyes scanned the hills below.

He passed over the thousands of soldiers crawling toward the first line of defense with their wire cutters, and was glad, at least, that he was aloft and not in the infantrymen's hell on earth. For he could see the fire of the cannon, the holes made in the ground that buried whole platoons in one fiery grave.

On he flew, with his squadron in formation behind him in the shape of an arrow, his falcon eyes searching continually for the enemy—the Fokkers and Pfalz D. XII's with their *Balkankreuze* emblazoned on the sides.

He flew between great white bursts of shells, avoiding them at each turn with the expertise of one who had defied them time and again. Then he met the enemy and the dogfight began. Tracer bullets, incendiaries—the constant rat-a-tat in the sky combining with the roaring guns below—and his machine gun bore down upon the Pfalz-Jasta 35, perilously close to his own wing tip.

As the Pfalz burst into flames and began its descent trailed by a cloud of smoke, Jacques Thibault veered off to the side and then, righting his Spad, climbed to a higher altitude. For a Fokker was now on his tail. A tracer bullet smashed into the panel before his eyes; his cheek felt the sting and a piece of his sleeve was ripped away from the heavy jacket he wore. Jacques's hand touched his cheek and a small stain of blood appeared on his fur-lined glove.

Yet he felt no fear. For one day, he had been dipped in Vulcan's fire—protected until his deed was done.

And down below, Giselher the witch had her burning caldron boiling.

From the moment the French 75s stopped their barrage ahead of them, ground troops fought for every inch, every foot of marshland, ridge, bald, pockmarked stretch of land that lay between them and the heights of Montfaucon. Through the slime they crawled, naked to the guns that would destroy them.

In the front line of attack came Patton's 1st Tank Brigade. And then Bullard's corps and Cameron's corps, and the divisions commanded by Liggett—left flank, right flank, frontal attack. They fought, one hundred thousand men strong, in the most crucial battle of the Western front.

During the night, the Germans, realizing the massive strength of the offensive, moved up more infantry and machine gunners, while the Americans struggled over sandbagged roads in the cold, misty blackness, and dug into the sides of the ravines, with one ear listening for the sound of the gas shells, and the other, for the rolling kitchens that never came.

"Gawd, I could do with a hot cuppa coffee," one shivering infantryman whispered.

"You're not the only one," another agreed. "And a blanket," he added, his teeth chattering with cold. "I'm soaked straight through to my liver."

At noon on September 27, with eleven thousand men lying dead, the survivors moved into the shattered main street of Montfaucon, where in concrete walls eight feet thick rose the telescope of Crown Prince Friedrich Wilhelm.

For the first time in four years, friendly eyes peered through its lens. And the first sight they recorded was the French Spad flown by Jacques Thibault, caught in enemy fire to the west.

"Hey, take a look at this," a young American infantryman exclaimed—and let his buddy beside him have a quick glance.

The Spad's wing splintered, the motor sputtered, and the plane became a toy tossed by the wind. Manfred Schiller, in his more maneuverable Fokker *Dreidecker,* bore down for the kill.

"What's happening?"

"The Boche got him, I think."

"Let me see."

The first soldier took over the telescope and, setting his sights on the fight, watched as Jacques Thibault saluted the black knight a split second before he was blinded in a fatal barrage.

"Yeah, he doesn't have a prayer now," he agreed.

As the soldier watched, the tired war bird plummeted from the sky in a glorious burst of flame that grew and spread its sparks over the hallowed ground. Jacques Thibault's mission was finished. The falcon had finally been avenged.

"Wasn't that something?" the boy said. "It was like I was up there beside him."

He reverently touched the telescope of the crown prince and walked away to let others take their turn in looking through its powerful lens.

Kenna Chalmers, with the newly arrived Steppie beside her, trudged slowly over the mud-filled road. Soaked to the skin, she coughed and the hacking sound caused Steppie to glance anxiously at her.

"We've got to get you under shelter, Kenna," Steppie said. "You should be in bed."

"I'm no worse than Annette and some of the others," Kenna replied.

"Oh, why does it have to be so cold and rainy?" Steppie anguished. "All I'd like is one, clear, sunny Atlanta fall day."

An ambulance passed by, going in the opposite direction, overloaded with wounded, while the less severely hurt perched on the top. It swayed as it passed by and an apologetic ambulance driver looked briefly at the nurses when the mud splattered them.

Almost unconsciously, they wiped their faces with their handkerchiefs. The splashing had happened so many times that they accepted it as a natural occurrence.

In a hut by the side of the road the nurses stopped to rest—Kenna, Steppie, Annette, and two others. Ahead of them were the hospital tents, waiting to be set up for the second phase of the offensive.

Giselher had not stopped the advancing Americans. Now it was up to the witch sister Kriemhilde to light the fires under her larger caldron.

During the night, as a cold and sick Kenna rested in the hut by the side of the road, Major Irish Fitzpatrick and the 82nd All-American Division passed by.

Dawn came and Kenna, with every muscle, every bone in her body protesting, sat up and took a small portion of bread and cheese to eat before starting on her way again.

272

"How are you feeling?" Steppie inquired, seeing Kenna's slow, measured movements.

"I'm up. That's all I can say," Kenna responded.

Steppie glanced in Annette's direction. "Well, you're doing better than Annette. She's certainly a sleepyhead this morning. You think we should wake her now?" Steppie asked.

"Yes. We'll have to move out soon," Kenna replied.

Steppie walked over to the corner of the hut where Annette lay wrapped in her scarlet and blue cape.

"Annette, you'd better get up," Steppie called gently. But there was no response. "Annette?" she called a little louder. Again, there was no response.

Frowning, Steppie laid her hand on the woman's shoulder to shake her. She moved, stiffly—with no sign of life. In alarm, Steppie touched her face. Cold—no warmth—no life.

"Kenna," the strangled sound emerged from Steppie's throat.

"What is it?" Kenna asked, moving toward her.

"I think Annette's . . . dead."

Kenna quickly knelt beside Steppie and felt for Annette's pulse. The cold, limp wrist produced no life-throbbing movement. And the heart sounded no beat underneath the nurse's cape. Sometime during the night, Annette had died of influenza. Kenna and Steppie, seeing death over and over but never getting used to it, wept.

"She didn't even complain," Kenna said, with a pathos in her voice.

"But she was sick," Steppie replied. "I noticed yesterday how bad she looked."

The other two nurses joined Kenna and Steppie, and they, too, cried. Brushing away the tears for a moment, Kenna croaked, "Oh, how I hate this awful war!" And her voice was stopped in a fit of coughing.

Outside, the rain drizzled steadily. Kenna, with the still damp wool of her cape around her slender body, hunched her shoulders and left the poor hut by the side of the road.

Doubly alarmed because of Annette's death, Steppie watched Kenna—ready to come to her aid if she should stumble. Behind them, the sounds of mules and mule-drawn supply wagons indicated the supply trains. And once again, Steppie and Kenna stepped aside to let them pass. Rivulets ran down their capes and joined the muddy pools at their feet.

One supply wagon passed by and still another. As a third wagon approached, Kenna watched the vaguely familiar face of the black driver. "There's Willie—from home," she said in a surprised voice to Steppie. "Willie," she shouted and waved, and the boy turned his head in the direction of her voice.

At first, he didn't recognize her. But then his large dark eyes widened. "Miss Kenna, what're you doin' in this god-awful mess?"

He pulled to the side of the road.

"Can you give us a ride, Willie?" Kenna asked, indicating Steppie beside her.

"Hop in," he said, "and put the tarpaulin over you. You got no business bein' out in this weather."

They didn't wait for a second invitation. Willie pulled out into the line of traffic, with the two sheltered under the tarpaulin.

"Have you heard how my mama is?" Willie asked, turning his head.

Steppie, answering, said, "The last letter from Cousin Cricket said she was fine."

"But they haven't been able to get any sugar, so that stopped Verbena from making her stickies," Kenna interposed.

Willie grinned. "You always *did* like those stickies, didn't you, Miss Kenna?"

"Just as much as you did, Willie."

He chuckled and then said, "Wish I had some right now."

"Me too," Kenna replied, homesick not only for the sweets but for Verbena's comforting black arms. As she rode on, in the back of the wagon, she wondered how much longer the war would last.

Thirty-Three

Eb Jordan left Châtel-Chéhéry with the crates of pigeons slung over his back. "Damn pigeons," he muttered, tired of their constant cooing in his ear.

"Hey, Private Pigeon," a voice called from behind. "You received any billet-doux today?"

"Knock off, you cotton-pickin' jerk," he yelled back.

But the men were bored and the song he hated floated down the line, gathering force as it was taken up by the marching men.

He'd never live it down. The wounded pigeon two days before had been done for, and Eb hadn't seen any need to let it go to waste. He tried not to listen, but the last lines grew louder and louder in a chanting rhythm to the tramping of feet.

> ". . . It's better to brave the Boche's shot
> Than land in the Private's cooking pot.
> Oh, yez—Oh, yez—
> Than land in the Private's cooking pot."

The song went on to Eb's chagrin as the 77th Division marched toward the whalebacks of the Romagne Heights and the second great German barrier, the Kriemhilde Stellung.

On October 7, the 82nd Division launched an attack toward Cornay, to divert attention from the buildup east of the Meuse. Irish and Seton remained in foxholes along the road—dodging the barrage of heavy artillery and diving for cover at the sound of gas shells. As automatically as putting one's slippers by the hearth, they covered their faces with their gas masks at the first telltale sound of the shells.

275

They waited for the promised covering barrage, but it never came. And so by six o'clock the next morning, they moved without it.

Deep in the Argonne Forest, split by a fog-filled ravine, the 77th Division rested during the night. All around them was the forbidding German gunfire, hammering steadily. Orders had been given to resume attack by morning and bridge the gap in the line.

In the early hours, beyond the ravine, the commanding officer waited for two of his companies to catch up with him. When they didn't appear, he sent a small force to backtrack to find them. The ground gained behind them had been infiltrated by the Germans during the night. The battalion was trapped—six hundred and fifty men—with fresh German divisions on all sides of the small pocket.

With no food and little ammunition, they were surrounded by a sea of German troops. Against insuperable odds, the battalion began to fight its way out of the trap. Eb, taking one of the few remaining pigeons from the crate, wrapped an SOS message around its leg and sent it aloft.

"Your cough sounds better," Steppie said, listening to Kenna.

"Yes, it helped for the rain to stop," the girl replied, her gray eyes still watering from the cold.

They rested in the marquise tent for a few more minutes. Soon they would be on duty again, while the never-ending stream of wounded would continue to be brought from the heights by Wells and Gigot and others like them.

In the past few days the nurses had dropped like flies. Pneumonia, exhaustion, influenza—the women in their scarlet and blue capes were victims of war just as surely as the soldiers in the field.

"Edna Brockett has pneumonia," Steppie ventured.

"I'm sorry," Kenna replied, unable to feel any animosity toward the woman who had caused trouble for her.

Neither Kenna nor Steppie talked about the people uppermost in their minds—Neal and Irish. It was as if by remaining silent, they could protect them from the attention of the vengeful gods.

Finally Steppie glanced at her watch. "It's time to go back," she said and hastened to smooth the tendrils of dark brown hair from her face.

Twilight gleaned the hills of all color but a hazy blue. Kenna, walking through the tent opening, paused and stared in the direction of the Romagne Heights. The guns didn't sound nearly so fierce as the day before. Kenna hoped with all her heart that the battle was over.

Wells and Gigot, finished for the day, started across the muddy concourse. When they saw the two nurses, they changed direction.

"Have you heard about that Corporal York?" Wells asked, grinning.

"No. Who's he?" Kenna inquired.

"The fella from the 82nd. I heard a few minutes ago that he brought in the largest number of prisoners ever captured."

Wells chuckled in delight. "The officer at headquarters said, 'Well, York, have you captured the whole damn German army?' And you know what he said?"

"What?"

"Cool as a cucumber, he answered, 'No, sir. Just one hundred and thirty-two.'"

Wells slapped his breeches and Gigot grinned. But soon Wells's face sobered as he looked over the hills in the distance. And in a quiet, serious voice, he said, "Eb's out there, somewhere."

The wounded continued to pour in and there was still no sign of Eb Jordan, until late one afternoon, Wells saw the familiar figure walking toward the hospital tent, a bloody, smelly gauze bandage wrapped around his left hand.

Eb was alive. And Wells's heart sang. Then he got mad. Durn the boy for keeping him so worried. He had no business getting into so much trouble and worrying a fella to death. Casually he walked toward Eb. "Well, I heard you were in the lost battalion," Wells barked.

"Hell, no. We knew where we were all the time. But nobody else did."

Wells didn't let him out of his sight. He followed him inside the tent and sat beside him while Eb waited for his wound to be dressed.

"You're lucky, Eb Jordan. You always were," Wells said.

"I wasn't so sure about that, especially when our own guns turned on us," Eb grumbled. "That bastard pigeon nearly gave me heart failure—flying up in the tree, with the Germans shooting at it. Now I know what they mean by sitting pigeon."

"I think it's sitting duck," Wells corrected.

"Or stool pigeon," Kenna said, laughing as she entered and heard the last of the conversation.

Eb grinned and held out his injured hand. "You gonna kiss it and make it well?"

"If you promise not to pop my garters," Kenna said, remembering her first encounter with Eb Jordan.

The odor of the wound assailed Kenna's nose. "Where did you get the bandage?" she asked. "It looks secondhand."

"It is. I got it off one of my buddies who didn't need it any more."

A sad, perceptive glance passed between them, and Kenna lowered her head to attend to his wound.

"You heard anything from Major Fitzpatrick?" Eb asked in a low tone as Kenna completed the dressing.

"No. Not a word."

Kenna, afraid Eb might see her anxiety for Irish, averted her face and became busy straightening the surgical tray.

The freckle-faced Eb left again, his hand freshly bandaged, and a new set of pigeons on his back. This time he headed toward Saint-Juvin, where Irish Fitzpatrick and Seton had been fighting with the 82nd Division for a month without relief.

The ugly mound of fieldwork called Saint-Juvin held the key to the capture of Grandpré. The Germans had no intention of giving it up to the *sammis,* for that would herald the collapse of their right flank.

Irish left Godrin in the relative safety of the copse of trees, and with the binoculars hung around his neck, he crawled toward the winding road to locate the heavy fire that had kept one of his platoons pinned down for the past two hours.

In his hands he gripped his automatic with its five-cartridge clip. As he advanced, yard by yard, he was ready to use it if a

German sniper happened to rear his head. A shell screamed above him and Irish, knowing it was uncomfortably close, fell flat in the brush and covered his head.

After a few minutes, he began again, crawling for a few feet and then stopping to listen.

On a hillside above him, the red-tiled roof of an old stone barn flashed fire. Irish, crouching in the brush along the road, looked through his binoculars. It appeared that some of the red tiles had been removed, and as he watched, he saw a large artillery gun jutting its lethal cylinder out of the roof and pointing in the direction of his unit below. So, he had located it.

The land between the road and the barn had been swept clean of trees and rocks, leaving no place to hide. But Irish knew he would have to put the gun out of commission before his men could advance.

As he tried to figure out his best approach to the barn, a telltale rattle of German tanks below filled the dismal, chilling air. Jerking his binoculars to his eyes, Irish looked behind him. Like great, round-backed turtles coming out of the sea, the enemy tanks were advancing across the field where his men lay hidden.

There was now no time left to ponder. His men were trapped—in front and from behind. Within a few minutes they would all be crushed or captured.

Irish put his fingers to his mouth and the whistle reached the copse where Godrin waited. The white war horse obeyed his master's call and the platoon, having heard the tanks, followed Godrin toward Irish, while all around them snipers opened fire, not on the riderless horse, but on the men following behind.

The horse continued to follow Irish's whistle to the very spot where he suddenly rose from the brush. In one quick movement, Irish was astride Godrin and urging him into a gallop toward the barn that held the lethal gun. The gun fired into the midst of the soldiers still in the field, but Irish was too close for its shells to do him any harm.

A great cloud of smoke obliterated the countryside, so that Irish Fitzpatrick could no longer see what was happening in the field behind him.

Taking a grenade from his saddlebag, he unpinned it and hurled it toward the wooden doors of the barn. The blast brought the doors down, as Godrin raced past. Two times the horse galloped around the stone building, and two times Irish hurled a grenade. The second time, the grenade, the last one in the saddlebag, found its prey. The red-tiled roof crumbled, and a roaring crash signaled the collapse of the gun supports.

A round of smaller-sized shells was directed from the upstairs window toward the man and his horse. As Seton Campbell came running up the road with the others, he was just in time to see Godrin falter and fall to the ground, the blood of Major Irish Fitzpatrick mingling with the death spurt of red from the great war horse.

Reinforced by the 77th, the battle-weary men of the 82nd Division continued fighting. And in four days, Saint-Juvin fell.

Now the 82nd could be relieved. They had fought long and hard with no respite between battles—first Saint-Mihiel, and then the Meuse-Argonne.

With their casualties, they moved out, leaving a fresh 78th Division to finish the job of taking Grandpré and meeting with Gouraud's French army across the Aire River.

Kriemhilde's caldron had not been sufficient to stop them. Now only Freya the witch remained to guard the last bastion of the Hindenburg line.

In the back of one of the hospital tents, scores of stretchers spread in all directions—holding the bodies of men who no longer needed the attention of the doctors or nurses.

Placed out of sight, they were forgotten until the living had been attended to.

Kenna shuddered as she hurried past them, stepping between the stretchers, avoiding looking toward these men killed in battle.

But in her tiredness, she stumbled over a boot jutting from the end of a stretcher that lay slightly apart from the rest. Kenna's eyes fleetingly recorded the size of the man and the bandage wrapped around his head.

She was already past him when she suddenly stopped. No.

She wouldn't look back. She couldn't. She didn't want to risk recognizing him. The months of anguish and fear had been too much of a nightmare already.

But the fleeting impression refused to be denied. Her head turned, and a strange moan escaped from her lips.

Irish. She had known it was he from the moment she had touched the boot, heavy with mud.

So still—so peaceful. She sank to her knees beside the stretcher. Through a blur of tears, she murmured, "Irish—Irish," her voice breaking with her heart.

The October breeze, raw and cold, rippled his hair, as the sun fell, blood red, behind the horizon. No April time for him, Kenna thought, or riding through the streets of Atlanta with his proud, arrogant face staring straight ahead. Irish Fitzpatrick was dead. For him, there would be no more laughter around the campfire—no spring grazing pastures. She cried, but her tears weren't for Irish alone.

Kenna leaned over and pressed her lips against his brow in a final farewell.

"Is this the way you greet all your patients?"

Kenna jerked her head away and made ready to flee, but he reached out and stopped her.

"Irish!" Again his name escaped her lips as she met his intense tobacco-brown eyes.

"You haven't answered my question," he said.

"What are you doing here—on the stretcher?" she asked indignantly, struggling to get away from the man.

"It was the only dry place I could find to lie down."

He sat up, still holding Kenna's wrist. "Are you angry because I'm not dead—like all the others?"

"Of course not. I . . . I just think this is a . . . a sick joke."

"When a man hasn't had any sleep for over forty-eight hours, he doesn't much care *where* he lays his head."

Despite the tiredness and the heavy lines etching his face, Kenna was still irate. "Let me go," she ordered, "you . . . you horse trader."

His hand dropped from her wrist and she scrambled to her feet. As she rushed past him, she hurled a last invective. "I hope they *bury* you, Irish Fitzpatrick.'' And she ran the rest of the way to the marquise tent—her humiliation complete.

On November 1, when the first light of dawn crept through the gray mist, the American army stood before the final caldron of Freya.

The march to Sedan began, with Liggett's First Army ready for this last assault. Fresh troops, eager for battle, pressed forward toward Buzancy and Barricourt. They met fierce resistance all the way in a fight to the death. Yet the Americans broke through the center and joined the French. Germany's time was at hand.

On the night of November 10, in the ruins of a small French village, a statue of the Virgin Mary fell from its sepulchered ledge and smashed into the street—a victim of a stray German shell.

"Someday, *soldat*, the blessed Virgin will come down. And on that day, the war will be over."

Irish Fitzpatrick remembered those words spoken earlier by the old man at the village fountain. Now his prediction had become history. The war was over.

Thirty-Four

Two weeks from the day of the Armistice, Kenna Chalmers, accompanied by her friend Steppie Hannon, said good-bye to Wells and Gigot and boarded the train for Paris.

"The first thing I'm going to do—after seeing Neal—is to get my hair cut short in a fashionable bob," Kenna confided.

"I'd like to get out of this uniform and into a decent dress again," Steppie replied, ". . . that is, if I can find an exclusive little shop I can afford."

"I wonder what the people are wearing in Paris?" Kenna mused. "Do you realize that we've been away from civilization so long that I don't have any idea of even the *length* of a dress?"

Steppie sighed. "Well, one thing for sure—I've seen enough *black* to last a lifetime. Even if it *is* winter, I want something bright." Her dark eyes crinkled in delight. "What about a dashing red coat?"

"Like Gigot's trousers?" Kenna teased.

Steppie's smile suddenly disappeared. "Where do you think he'll go?"

Kenna became pensive. "Probably back to the asylum in Toul, where he can work in his garden again."

"Yes. He was happy there," Steppie agreed.

They rode in silence for a while, with Kenna's mind on the town of Toul and her first encounter there with Irish Fitzpatrick. Then, shaking her head to rid herself of the unwanted thoughts, she pulled out a piece of paper with the address of the pension where Neal was staying. "I wonder if Neal's memory has improved," she said aloud.

"I hope so," Steppie replied. Recalling her first sight of Neal near Saint-Mihiel, she said, "Did I ever tell you that he called me 'Stephanie' after he boarded the hospital train?"

"No, you didn't." Kenna smiled, pleased at the revelation.

An hour later at Gare de l'Est, they signaled for a taxi. But as it moved toward them with an awful rattle and groan, Kenna and Steppie looked at each other.

"You wish a taxi, mam'selle?" the driver inquired over the noise.

"*Oui*. We wish to go to this address," Kenna said, adding dubiously, "if you think your machine can travel that far?"

The man drew himself up in typical Gallic indignation.

"Mam'selle, if my machine could take General Gallieni's troops to the Marne, it is capable of going this small distance."

"Of course, monsieur," Kenna replied apologetically and climbed in.

The man had reason to be proud, Kenna thought, for the Germans had been driven back and Paris saved because of the taxicab army that moved troops to the front in a hurry.

"That was a glorious day, mam'selle," the driver recollected. "Taxicabs filled with troops—as far as the eye could see. Papa Joffre has been maligned by some. But *moi*, I consider him a genius. Who else would have thought of such magnificent strategy?"

"I'm impressed, monsieur," Kenna agreed, thinking of the feat of September 1914. But she was even more impressed when the old rattletrap arrived in one piece at her destination on the road to Saint-Germain.

"*Au revoir, monsieur,*" she said, waving from the road as the driver disappeared in a thunder of sound.

Neal was not at the address that Davin had given her. In alarm she heard the woman at the door say, "Monsieur Wexford doesn't live here any more."

Kenna's heart beat rapidly. "I'm his sister," she said. "Do you have any idea where he might be?"

The plump woman's eyes lit up. "Ah, mam'selle, I have the address. Come in, and I will get it for you."

While the woman looked for the address in another room, Kenna and Steppie waited uneasily in the small front parlor. "Why do you think he left?" Steppie asked when she was alone with Kenna. "It seems to be a very pleasant place. The grounds are quite lovely."

"Maybe it had something to do with the baby," Kenna answered, frowning.

"Here it is, mam'selle," the woman said, coming back into the room. "As you can see, it is an *appartement* in the center of Paris."

"Thank you very much, madame," Kenna replied, taking the paper.

"You wish for a taxi?" the woman asked.

Kenna nodded.

"I will ring one for you. And then you must both have a cup of hot tea while you wait."

"It's very kind of you, madame."

The woman brought the tea tray, set it down, and said, "If you will excuse me, I must see to the preparation of the evening meal. The new cook is not yet used to the stove."

"*Certainement, madame.*"

In quietness, they sipped their tea. Kenna, trying not to show her impatience, kept her eyes on the window until finally the taxicab appeared. In relief, she saw that it was in much better condition than the one in which they arrived.

Back to Paris they rode, with the blustering wind sweeping through the taxi. They shivered despite the afghan robe draped over their laps. Steppie, remembering the wretched trip on the overseas transport, was in no hurry to brave the winter storm upon the ocean. She was glad that she had decided to stay in Paris with Kenna until spring. And perhaps by that time, Neal would be able to travel with them—Neal and the child he called Daniel. Steppie drew the afghan closer to her body as the wind continued to whip against the moving vehicle.

Fine mist sprinkled the air, giving the landscape an impressionist appearance not quite in focus, the lines hazy and indistinct. As they approached the city, a cathedral rose toward the sky, its spire lost in the mist and the rain.

"Look, Steppie," Kenna said suddenly, pointing to it. "Doesn't that remind you of the picture on front of the Debussy music?"

"A little," Steppie admitted. And then she laughed. "Miss Chopes didn't like Debussy, did she?"

"No. He was too avant-garde," Kenna said. "You remember what a terrible time I had convincing her to let me play *Cathédrale engloutie* on the last recital."

Kenna became sad. She would never hear the man who had composed it, for Debussy had died in March while Paris was being bombarded by German shells. And his funeral procession had followed the same route that she and Steppie were now taking.

The streets swarmed with people; gaiety pervaded the air despite the sea of somber black umbrellas. An old man, dressed in a dark suit patinaed with age, leisurely walked along the leafless Champs-Elysées with his two gray poodles.

In the midst of the busyness, the taxi plunged, its driver honking the horn for the right of way that no one wished to concede. "He drives like Wells," Kenna whispered.

Then the taxi stopped. "This is the address, mam'selle."

Digging once again into her purse for the required francs, Kenna paid the fare. The two girls stood on the street and looked up at the architecturally splendid building before them—mansard roof, balconied windows, and large, square blocks of white stone that gave it the authority of centuries past.

"It's very grand," Steppie said, looking at the building and back to Kenna.

The doorman, seeing them, rushed to open the door. Once inside, Kenna glanced at the paper in her hand—*Appartement quatre*.

She smiled at the doorman and walked on as if she knew exactly where she was going. When she reached the proper door, she hesitated before ringing the bell.

"What are you going to say to him, Kenna?" Steppie asked, suddenly fearful of coming face to face with Neal again.

Before Kenna could answer, a uniformed maid opened the door. "Yes?"

"Please, we have come to see Monsieur Neal Wexford," Kenna stated.

"Who is it, Marie?" a woman's voice inquired from inside.

The maid turned in the direction of the voice. "Two young ladies, madame, for Monsieur Neal."

"Have them come in," the familiar voice replied, and the maid stepped aside for Kenna and Steppie to enter.

Footsteps on the tiles of the entrance hall brought the woman immediately. Kenna's gray eyes registered her surprise at seeing the white-haired woman before her. "Madame."

The Vicomtesse d'Arcy smiled. "I thought perhaps you would arrive this week. Come, let's go in to the fire. You are surprised, no?"

"Yes, madame."

"Your brother isn't here at the moment," the vicomtesse explained. "He should be back in an hour's time."

"But I don't understand, madame, how he came to be staying with you," Kenna said.

"It was the least I could do, *petite,* after learning of your care for Bernay." The pain showed in her eyes when she mentioned her dead son's name.

"But I did nothing," Kenna refuted.

"You were with him when he died. That was enough. Your Dr. Grant added to your letter, *petite.* And so I know."

"I wasn't even sure that you would receive my letter."

"It took some time for it to be forwarded. After Bernay died, I left the château and came back to Paris. I could no longer watch other sons dying. But we will speak of this later."

Changing the subject, she inquired, "Where are you staying?"

"For the moment, at the Hôtel de la Gare."

The woman shook her head. "That will never do. We will send Pierre for your luggage immediately."

"But the other hotels are so crowded."

"You will both stay here with me," the woman stated. "It is settled."

Pierre had little luggage to retrieve. Kenna had only the damaged pink party dress and the few uniforms and underwear, dingy from the frequent washings. These were brought with Steppie's things and placed in a luxurious bedroom that bordered the inner courtyard, away from the noisy street.

Back in the salon, Kenna waited for Neal to appear and she grew more nervous as the time drew closer for him to return.

287

"He is much better, *petite*," the vicomtesse confided. "Every day he talks more."

"Has he mentioned . . . me?" Kenna inquired. "He didn't remember me, you know, in Saint-Mihiel."

"I judge that Dr. Grant has been writing to him. Neal knows that you're his sister, although I'm not sure that he remembers you. Nevertheless, he has accepted the idea."

"And little Daniel?"

A strange expression passed over the vicomtesse's face. She looked toward Steppie and back to Kenna.

"You know the child's parentage?" she inquired.

Kenna hesitated. "I know his mother was named Ailly. She was killed in the fire at the château."

The vicomtesse nodded. "The child's father was German."

"Pardon, madame?"

She repeated it. "The child is half German. That accounts for his fairness."

So the baby was not Neal's. Steppie's spirit soared at the news.

"But if that is the case," Kenna pondered, "why then did my brother refuse to let the baby go to an orphanage?"

"He hasn't discussed it with me. Perhaps he loved the mother?"

Steppie's face turned pale, and the old vicomtesse, seeing her reaction, apologized. "I'm sorry, mam'selle. I did not realize . . ."

"You must not apologize, madame, for telling the truth," Steppie replied, her dark brown eyes now bereft of the luster they had acquired at the first bit of news.

The sound at the door indicated that Neal had returned. Daniel came into the room first, followed by his nursemaid. The chubby blond child didn't stop until he stood before the woman's chair. In his hand he held a tiny nosegay of purple pansies.

"For you," he said, stuffing them in her hand.

Disbelieving what she saw, Kenna watched while the Vicomtesse d'Arcy lifted the child to her lap and kissed his chubby cheek. Her own sons lay dead—victims of war—but she was treating the child of the enemy as a treasured loved one.

Perceptive of her interest, the vicomtesse smiled. "Off with Jolie," she said, "for your glass of milk, *petit*."

The child, obeying, climbed down and he passed by the man who stood in the doorway and watched.

Kenna's hungry eyes traced his face, now fuller and not quite so tense as it had been. His impersonal glance passed over Kenna and Steppie, and as the child had done, his face lit in a smile to see the vicomtesse in the high-backed chair before the fire.

"Come in, Neal," she said in a gentle voice. "We have guests. Your sister Kenna and her friend Steppie have arrived."

The occasion which could have been filled with awkwardness was softened by the white-haired woman's behavior. Just as she had soothed Kenna's nerves in the mountain lodge outside Nancy, so here in Paris she did the same.

"Hello, Neal," Kenna said, afraid to stir from her chair.

"Hello, Kenna," he replied with the faint trace of a smile. "I'm glad to see you. And you also, Stephanie."

"Hello, Neal," Steppie replied, her voice low and choked, her nervous fingers twisting the handkerchief in her lap.

"The girls are staying with us in the apartment," the woman mentioned casually to the man. "Will you come and join us before the fire?"

"A little later?" he asked. "I'm wet from the rain. If you'll excuse me, I'll change clothes."

Disappointment mixed with Kenna's other emotions. How different Neal was from the brother she had known. Any other time, he would have lifted her off the floor and planted a kiss on the top of her head. Kenna's lips trembled and she swallowed to remove the lump stuck in her throat.

"You must not be sad, my dear. Give him time," the old vicomtesse advised. "Now, what do you wish to do while you're in Paris?" she asked.

Taking the cue from her, Kenna replied, "First, we want to have our hair cut and then buy some clothes."

"I heard there's a little shop several blocks from here," Steppie ventured.

The woman shook her head. "No, you mustn't go there. The Salon Lumineux is the place for both of you. Tomorrow I will take you."

That night, long after Kenna had gone to bed, her mind remained in a whirl. The evening meal with Neal was better than she had expected. True, he treated her as a stranger, but it was a start. And the vicomtesse, urging her to be patient, had given good advice—if she could only keep it.

Tomorrow would be even better. They were to spend it with Neal and the child—and the Vicomtesse d'Arcy, who had personally undertaken to make Kenna and Steppie fashionable young women of Paris.

Thirty-Five

"I THINK—NOT SO MUCH ON THE SIDES," THE VICOMTESSE said, presiding over the cutting of Kenna's hair. "And we must save the long tresses for a chignon for the evenings."

Kenna sat in the chair while she was discussed almost as if she were an inanimate object. Back and forth the words flew between the vicomtesse and the hairdresser.

The blond hair, carefully saved with each snip, mounted up and Kenna, afraid to look, kept her èyes diverted from the mirror. Then, with a great flourish and a voilà! the man removed the cutting cape from Kenna's shoulders and thrust a hand mirror toward her.

"Kenna," Steppie said, observing the girl. "You look so chic."

Large, solemn gray eyes stared at the soft waves that curved and capped her head. She turned her back and held the hand mirror in place. So different. Yes, she liked her new image—and would like it even more when she was out of uniform.

"Now it's your turn, Steppie," the vicomtesse stated.

But Steppie, taking a faltering step backward, said, "I think I'll wait."

"Oh, no, Steppie," Kenna reprimanded. "It's too late for you to change your mind." With a playful push, Kenna forced Steppie to the chair and the cutting ritual began all over again.

The scissors snipped the first long strand and Steppie, closing her eyes, made an anguished sound.

"You'd think she was going to the guillotine," a laughing Kenna said to the vicomtesse.

"It's only your hair, *petite*, not your neck," the vicomtesse said, reassuring the girl.

291

In a slightly different style, the hairdresser cut Steppie's hair, parting it in a curve instead of a straight line, and placing a wave farther down on her forehead. Beside her left ear, he placed a gold clip. And he murmured in satisfaction at the change.

Kenna picked up the mirror to hand to Steppie, but the girl shook her head. "I'd rather not look," she said.

"But you have to—sometime," Kenna protested.

"No. I'd rather not—at least for now."

"Suit yourself, Steppie," Kenna replied and laid the mirror on the table.

The three walked out of the hairdresser's shop to the street, where Pierre waited with the car. And with Steppie having no idea of the dramatic change in her appearance, they headed for the Salon Lumineux.

The vicomtesse, seeing Kenna take out a huge bundle of francs to count, threw up her hands.

"It is dangerous to carry so much money on your person, *petite*."

"But I wanted to be sure to have enough to pay for my shopping today."

The vicomtesse smiled. "Such independence. I expected you to charge the clothes to my account—and settle later."

"Oh, no, madame, I couldn't do that. You've been more than kind already. But if I see something that I don't have enough money for, I'll remember your offer. Thank you, madame."

"You are lucky, you know," the woman said, "to be able to buy what you want. Most French mothers scrimp and save for one good dress for their daughters. And—oh, such care that one good dress receives."

She looked at Steppie and back to Kenna, and she began to plan aloud. "You both need coats, some day dresses with cloches to match, and, of course, evening wear—the little dresses with the backs out for dancing—and the satin *jupons*."

The vicomtesse's eyes twinkled. "I am excited," she confided, "since I never had a daughter to dress."

Her eyes momentarily lost their twinkle. And Kenna understood. Rushing to fill the gap in the conversation, Kenna said, "Steppie wants a red coat."

The vicomtesse recovered herself. "Yes, that is possible— strong, dramatic color for Steppie—but silver and gold for you, *petite*."

Pierre stopped the car and once again, the three climbed out—this time in front of the Palais des Fils, Tissus et Vêtements, which contained everything that a young woman might wish with the special collections in the Salon Lumineux.

Steppie stood before the floor-length mirror and gazed at herself. Her eyes widened in disbelief—at not only the hair, but the dress. The black velvet with its skirt trimmed in red with a giant red rosette attached to the waist looked as if it might have come from a Spanish dancer's wardrobe.

"I thought I didn't ever want to see a black dress again," Steppie said in amazement.

"But it is good for you, *non*? And it will go well with your red coat."

Steppie turned slowly, seeing the new shape of her hair, the flattering shape of the dress.

"I love it," she said, and finding Kenna staring at her, she asked, "What do you think, Kenna?"

"I think when Neal sees you in that, he'll call you *lovely* Stephanie."

The girl blushed, but was pleased.

First one dress and then another—and the vicomtesse presided over all, shaking her head or giving her approval, as three women rushed back and forth with dresses and accessories to match.

"That one, I think," the vicomtesse said, pointing to a colorless pouf of material with an overlay of satin.

Now it was Kenna's turn to frown. The dress, of the softest, finest wool, embroidered with lilies on the right breast with its small diamond brooch twinkling from the center, was all right from the front. But the dress had no back. It plunged daringly in a V-shape all the way to the waist, where it ended in a matching, colorless satin sash with three small puffs of material, like the curved tail feathers of a cockatoo.

293

Kenna shook her head.

"Just try it on, my dear," the white-haired woman coaxed.

"Yes, Kenna. Try it on," Steppie urged, stifling a giggle.

"Well, it's certainly different from my nurse's uniform," Kenna responded, looking at her reflected image.

"Yes, quite different," the vicomtesse said, in a satisfied voice. Turning to the woman in charge, she said, "We'll take it."

"I . . ." Kenna wasn't allowed to finish.

"Yes, we'll take it," the Vicomtesse d'Arcy reiterated, and then before the girl could protest, the white-haired woman said, "Please see to the packing. I think we've done enough shopping for the day."

"*Oui, madame*. Right away, madame."

Neal was sitting by the fire and staring into its flames when the three returned. When he saw them, he attempted to stand, but the vicomtesse held out her hand to stop him.

"It is not necessary, Neal. The leg must be favored until it is completely healed."

But he stood anyway. "I'm almost well, madame," he said, smiling. "You shouldn't continue to spoil me."

"There was never any possibility of that. You're like my eldest," she said. "Bernay, now—he was different. Was that not true, Kenna?"

The girl, uncertain as to how to answer, asked, "In what respect, madame?"

"The youngest is always a little spoiled. Don't you agree, Neal?" She looked to him for corroboration.

"Of course, madame. Kenna was always the spoiled one in our family."

Without thinking, Kenna countered, "I was not. You were just as spoiled." All at once, it dawned on her what Neal had just said. "Neal?"

"I'm sorry, Kenna," he apologized, with a hooded look over his face. "I have no idea why I said that."

"It's . . . all right," she said. "It's true. I *was* spoiled." She suddenly brightened. "Do you remember, Neal, when we . . ."

"No."

Kenna felt as if he had struck her. She stared at him. His mood had changed completely.

"Why don't you try on a new dress, Kenna dear?" the vicomtesse suggested. "I know how anxious you are to get out of your uniform."

Steppie, standing before the fire, had remained silent during the conversation. Now, still silent, with her cheeks flushed from the heat, she looked toward the stricken Kenna.

And Neal, watching her, said, "I like your hair that way, Stephanie."

"Thank you, Neal," she replied self-consciously, her hand nervously touching her bare neck as she and Kenna went to their room.

"He doesn't even *like* me," Kenna moaned. "What have I done, Steppie, to make him act this way?"

"I don't know, Kenna. Maybe if you don't try to push him into remembering—"

"He seems to relate better to *you*, Steppie."

"I don't know why."

"I suppose I should be grateful, instead of resentful."

Steppie's sympathetic eyes moistened. "I know it's hard for you, Kenna," she said. "But it's just as hard for me, especially with Ailly." The girl's voice trailed away. "I love him too, you know."

"Yes, I know."

Shaking off her despondency, Kenna said, "Well, let's remove our uniforms once and for all. Which dress will you put on, Steppie?"

"The blue one," she promptly replied. "What about you?"

"The yellow one, with the buttons sewn over the skirt."

Suddenly, Kenna swung around and faced Steppie again. Her eyes, strangely aglow, feverish, came alive.

"Why should I be so upset about Neal?" she asked aloud. "He's alive—that's the important thing. It will just take time for him to get well—and we have all the time in the world, Steppie. We're in Paris—with a brand-new beautiful wardrobe. And it's time we all had some fun."

She took the yellow wool dress from the armoire and, holding it in front of her, began to dance a tango through the luxurious bedroom.

Steppie, with her mouth open, was amazed at Kenna's sudden switch in mood, almost as severe as Neal's. She watched while Kenna's slender legs, forming the steps of the tango, slid from the folds of her pink marabou negligee while her head snapped with each completed turn.

A knock at the door stopped the performance immediately. Kenna froze with the dress in her arms and Steppie called out, *"Entrez."*

Marie, the maid, opened the door. In her hand she carried a small silver tray with a white calling card on top.

"For you, mam'selle," she said to the blond-haired girl. "A gentleman left his card for you a few minutes ago."

"Thank you, Marie."

The maid left and a curious Steppie asked, "Who is it, Kenna?"

Kenna draped the yellow dress across her bed and gazed down at the card. "Major Carlton Torey."

"Here in Paris?"

"Evidently so. And he wants to call on me tomorrow at four."

"What are you going to do?"

Kenna shrugged. "Let him come."

Surprised at Kenna, the dark-haired girl inquired. "Have you changed your mind about him?"

"Not really, but I want to see Paris, Steppie. And I need an escort. I'm tired of the war, the ruins, the heartbreak. I want to see Montmartre—and eat at Maxim's—go to the theater and the ballet—and ride in the Bois de Boulogne. They say there's a new restaurant that's just been opened by a Russian prince."

Kenna's gray eyes caught fire and burned ever brighter. "I want to see it all, Steppie—to climb the Eiffel Tower—to watch the cancan girls. And I want to drink champagne from a slipper until dawn—

"This way, it's so easy—with the four of us."

"What about Neal?"

"He'll be your escort, Steppie."

"Do you think he'll come?"

"If you ask him, he will."

But Steppie wasn't so sure. When she finished brushing her hair and pinning the gold clip at the side, she left the room while Kenna sat near the window and stared out into the bare winter garden.

Her gay mood had left her. Kenna looked down at the card in her hands and traced the letters forming Carlton's name. If it had only been Irish—

An explosive noise in the distance caused her to jump. Automatically Kenna moved from the window to seek safety. And then she stopped in the middle of the room. No artillery, no gas shells could mar her afternoon. That nightmare was over—for good.

Kenna smiled. It was probably a fireworks display. Curious, how quickly one got used to running for cover. Yet the noise triggered the memory of another afternoon—of gas shells exploding near the village outside Saint-Mihiel the same day she had found Neal. She could see the deserted house—the gate that Irish had broken down.

Suddenly tired from her shopping expedition, Kenna took the yellow wool dress from the bed and draped it over a nearby chair. She lay down and closed her eyes. Her body ached for the touch of Irish Fitzpatrick, his lips covering her mouth, and his hands caressing her body.

"Kenna, Kenna," a voice whispered in her ear. "You'd better get dressed for dinner."

Her eyes fluttered open and she sat up, completely disoriented. "What time is it?" she asked.

"Seven-thirty," Steppie replied.

Thirty-Six

PARIS, DARK FOR SO LONG, NOW LIT UP LIKE A NEON SIGN from one end to the other. Not since the Exhibition had such a display of lights been seen.

In the midst of the milling crowd, drunk with the relief of victory, Kenna wedged herself, with Carlton, Steppie, and Neal. The vicomtesse had declined the invitation to join them.

"I have promised to read Daniel a bedtime story," she said.

"But we're not going out until nine o'clock, madame. That will give you plenty of time," Kenna argued.

". . . And then I shall go to bed early," the woman continued. "No. You must go out—the four of you—without me."

Kenna drank in all the sights and sounds around her. She gazed frankly and curiously at the prostitutes, while Carlton carefully turned his head to look in the other direction.

They arrived at Maxim's, where they sat on red divans that reflected themselves in the wall mirrors. On dowagers' hands and bosoms the jewels, catching the light of chandeliers, twinkled like stars in a galaxy.

"Isn't it magnificent?" Kenna murmured to Steppie.

The sound of violins came closer. Gypsies, with their dark eyes, gazed boldly at the silver-blond girl with her gray eyes bright and curious.

At a table farther away, another set of admiring eyes gazed at the girl. With the meal almost over, Carlton leaned toward Kenna. "Would you like to go dancing, Kenna?"

"Oh, yes. I'd . . ." Then, thinking of Neal and his leg, she stopped and gazed in his direction.

Steppie also looked at Neal and then she turned toward Carlton and Kenna. "You two go ahead. If you don't mind, I'd like to go home. It's rather late . . ."

Neal nodded. "We'll get a taxi from here."

And so the foursome parted at Maxim's. Kenna watched her brother and Steppie climb into a taxi. Then she and Carlton took the next one. His arm curved possessively over the seat and his eyes showed his satisfaction at the way the evening was progressing. He now had Kenna to himself.

The oriental ballroom, with its striped, canopied ceiling, its cages of birds and Turkish-dressed orchestra, looked as if it might have dropped out of an *Arabian Nights* dream. Waiters with scimitars at sashed waists, red curled toe shoes on their feet, and fezzes on their dark heads moved silently amid the tables that were drawn up to harem couches filled with pillows of every exotic hue.

They were lucky to get a table, for the place was crowded. Men in dark evening suits, others in decorated military uniforms, served as foils for women in lighter-colored dresses, with furs and plumes. No one, seeing the crowd, would ever guess that a war had been waged for over four years and that a large part of the countryside lay in ruins, with no farm animals, no lofts filled with hay. Yet the uniforms and the medals attested to bravery and sacrifice, too.

A tango began and Kenna moved to the dance floor with Carlton. With their faces cheek to cheek, they began the hypnotic dance. Kenna swung out in a fan, but momentarily faltered when she met piercing dark eyes staring at her from a nearby table.

Irish Fitzpatrick was here in Paris—in the same ballroom. He inclined his head toward her but she ignored him completely. With her cheeks flaming in sudden color, Kenna returned her attention to Carlton and the intricate dance steps. She had promised herself never to speak to Irish again.

But back at the table where she and Carlton sipped a glass of champagne, Kenna unobtrusively cast her eyes toward Irish's table. He was no longer there.

Forgetting to be discreet, she searched the dance floor openly until she found him—dancing with a dark-haired girl, young and obviously French. Kenna picked up her champagne glass and smiled at Carlton as she sipped.

From that moment on, Kenna appeared to have a marvelous time. Not looking again toward Irish, she laughed and smiled and talked intimately with a delighted Major Carlton Torey.

By the time they left, the table Irish had been sitting at was empty. Three o'clock in the morning. She had never stayed out so late in her life. But this was Paris, where people danced until dawn.

Still pretending a gaiety she didn't feel, Kenna said goodnight to Carlton at the apartment door and made no objection to his quickly administered kiss upon her cheek.

In the next days Kenna hid her unhappiness in a frenzy of activity. And Carlton, with nothing else planned, served as her willing escort. More and more, Neal and Steppie remained apart, choosing instead to take walks with Daniel when the weather permitted, and pursuing a quieter life with the vicomtesse.

Paris remained crowded, for American troops, transported mainly by British ships to Europe, now had to wait for transportation home while the ships of England saw to the return of their own colonial troops and the Canadians and Australians. A country that helped to turn the tide of war with its massive manpower still did not have sufficient equipment to see those men home.

Early one afternoon in the second week of her stay in Paris, when the cold wind sweeping over the River Seine had changed direction and subsided somewhat, Kenna dressed in her riding habit and boots. She placed the black velvet helmet on her head. Her large gray eyes stared at the picture in the mirror. In the daring new outfit—jodhpurs and coat with white cravat—she looked like a young boy instead of a grown woman.

At the sound of the doorbell, Kenna grabbed up her white gloves and riding crop. Carlton had come.

Steppie and Neal were ready and waiting in the salon. They left the apartment together and climbed into Carlton's taxi and headed for the stables, where horses were selected for their ride through the Bois de Boulogne.

"I think I'll take the reddish-gold mare in the second stall," Kenna said to the groom. "She looks as if she wants the exercise."

"You'll have to be careful with her, mam'selle. She's a little skittish today."

Kenna smiled. She knew how the mare felt. She herself was tired of the staid old mares that never got beyond a trot. She was ready for a run today. And the red one looked as if she would enjoy it, too.

Saddled and ready, the four horses moved out, as other riders returned with their mounts. The mare on which Kenna sat sidled toward the edge of the road before Kenna could control the horse and urge her in the right direction.

Then she was on her way down the carefully manicured avenue, with its clipped hedges and trimmed trees.

A restlessness pervaded Kenna's entire being and she didn't know why. Paris had suddenly palled. Urging the mare forward, Kenna passed Steppie and Neal and Carlton. Hoofs kicking up the dust, the little red mare moved into a gallop, while the chill wind made Kenna's face sting. With gray eyes matching the color of the clouds overhead, she watched the hedges go by, faster and faster. The cold air filled her lungs with an ache, but she kept up the pace, past the lone rider coming from the opposite direction.

A motorcar, sputtering from the road to her right, pulled into the avenue and honked. The little red mare, reacting to the sudden noise, dug her hoofs into the soft earth, whinnied, and then reared into the air.

The car passed by with a group of sightseers, leaving Kenna to deal with the frightened horse. "Easy, Red," she said, but the horse could not be contained.

Thoroughly spooked by the car, the mare began to gallop again with no certain destination in mind, and all that Kenna could do in the sidesaddle was to hold on and pray that she wouldn't be spilled headlong into the ground.

Mixed with the sound of her own mare, another horse trampled the dusty trail and bore swiftly upon her, erasing the distance between them. The large chestnut horse drew up beside Kenna and a long arm reached out to seize the reins. The red mare slowed and Kenna, relieved that someone had seen her distress, glanced gratefully in the direction of the rider.

"Thank you, monsieur. It was the automobile," she explained.

"You had no business galloping in the first place," the gruff voice of Irish Fitzpatrick censured her.

Kenna's body tensed. "I shall gallop when and where I please," she replied, her grateful expression now wiped from her angry face. "Kindly remove your hand from my horse's reins."

His hand dropped at the imperious voice, but just then, the motorcar reappeared. And the mare, still skittish, reacted again. But this time, Kenna felt her body sliding from the saddle. Irish swore at the automobile and grabbed Kenna before she fell.

The red mare, free of restraint, began to gallop headlong down the road into the path of the automobile. The driver slammed on his brakes as the horse grazed its front bumper and the vehicle landed in the ditch.

"You may put me down, Irish Fitzpatrick," Kenna said.

"It's a long way back to the stables," he reminded her.

"That's all right. I'll walk."

But her request was denied. Instead of going in the direction of the stables, Irish wheeled the chestnut horse toward the left, where a *bocage* of trees hid them from view.

"What are you doing?" Kenna's irritated voice lashed out.

"Finding a place where we can talk."

"I'll be missed. Carlton will see the mare and come looking for me."

He ignored her warning.

"Kenna, I've waited long enough for you. I'm ready to go home."

"What has that to do with me?" she snapped. "Your going home?"

"Everything. I want my wife to travel with me."

A choking sound in Kenna's throat kept her from responding immediately. She took a deep breath and with blazing eyes, she said, "I'm not your wife. And don't think the night

302

we spent in the deserted house outside of Saint-Mihiel gives you any power over me."

"I'm not speaking of that night," he replied, "although I've dreamed of it many times since."

"Then don't think you can force me into marriage. I have no interest in you, Irish Fitzpatrick. If you thought to marry me for my money, you should think again. Neal is *alive* and he's the one who'll inherit it."

"Kenna, you don't seem to understand. We're already married."

"That's preposterous," she snorted. "You're just making that up to annoy me."

"Do you remember the ceremony around the campfire, when you wore the white lace mantilla?"

"You mean—the circle of friendship?"

"It was no friendship circle. It was a marriage ceremony performed by the king of my clan. He married us that night, Kenna."

Kenna's head jerked toward Irish. "No. I don't believe it. And anyway, if it were true, a pagan ceremony wouldn't stand up under law."

"How do you know?" he asked. "Even common-law marriages are recognized in Georgia."

"Why, I . . ."

"Once the vows are consummated, there's no turning back. We're wed, Kenna—in the eyes of my people—and in the eyes of God."

"No."

"Yes."

Kenna saw Carlton in the distance. He evidently had discovered the mare with her empty saddle.

"Carlton's coming," she said. "You can let me down now."

"I'll let you go for today, Kenna. But on Thursday afternoon, I'll come to get you."

"You don't even know where I'm staying."

"With the Vicomtesse d'Arcy. I've known every step you've made since you left the Argonne Forest."

Frantic now, with Carlton only a hundred yards away, Kenna said, "But I can't leave Neal. He needs me."

"No, Kenna. You only *think* he needs you."

"But I can't just go off and . . ."

"Steppie would stay, I'm sure. And she'd be a lot better for him in his present state than you."

"And if I refuse to go with you?"

"Then you'll leave me no choice but to tell everything, including the swamp episode."

"That . . . that's blackmail," she accused.

"No, it's a winning poker hand," he said, grinning. "And I'm ready to cash in my chips."

"I hate you for this, Irish Fitzpatrick."

He tightened his hold on her and moved the chestnut horse from the *bocage*. Carlton, seeing them together, frowned. As Irish freed her, he whispered in her ear, "Just remember—Thursday afternoon."

Irish and Carlton saluted, and passing by, Irish put his horse to the gallop.

"I found your mare . . ." Carlton said to Kenna, still frowning.

"Yes. An automobile spooked her," she replied, hardly knowing what she was saying.

"And Major Fitzpatrick was nearby?"

"Yes."

Carlton got down from his horse, and holding the reins, he walked with Kenna back to the stables.

She was subdued the rest of the afternoon. "I'm tired, Carlton," she said. "Do you mind if we don't go out tonight?"

"Not at all, my dear. We'll just spend a quiet evening before the fire."

Kenna hesitated. "Not even that, if you don't mind. I think I'll go to bed early."

"Are you feeling all right, Kenna?"

"Just a little tired—that's all."

He leaned over and kissed her on the cheek. "Have a good night and I'll see you tomorrow."

Kenna watched him—tall and proud—walking down the street. What was he going to say? What were they all going to say if Irish carried through his threat and came for her?

"Steppie, I . . ."

"Yes, Kenna?"

"Oh, nothing."

For the next two days she waited uneasily. And by early Thursday afternoon, she was a total wreck emotionally.

The dismal rain had begun. And with it . . . sleet. It was cold, even inside. Kenna, shivering, left her chair in the salon and went to sit with Daniel on the cushion before the fire.

He smiled at her as she helped him stack his blocks—old wooden ones salvaged from some trunk, with their painted sides wearing from so much usage.

The doorbell rang and Kenna jumped. She slowly relaxed when she recognized Steppie's voice—and Neal's.

Perhaps Irish was right. Her brother seemed to be happier in Steppie's company than in hers. He wasn't the same person she had thought to find. But she wasn't the same either. And she supposed she would have to take that into account. They were both different. It could never be the way it had been between them before the war.

Daniel, also listening to the voices, smiled when he heard Neal's. He dropped a block onto Kenna's lap and, pushing himself up from the floor, started toward the door.

The blond-haired man, seeing him, reached down and swooped him in his arms. "And how's my Daniel?" he asked.

Steppie, walking past them, came toward the fire. "It's so cold outside," she commented to Kenna. She sank to the cushion near the hearth, and rubbing her hands near the flames, she commented, "I wouldn't be surprised to see some snow."

The doorbell rang again and Kenna jumped. Her hand flew up to her cheek as she listened for Marie to open the door. Could it be Irish? Was he coming for her after all?

Carlton's confident voice greeted the maid. "Is Mam'selle Kenna at home?"

No. What was Carlton doing—coming at this hour? Kenna didn't want him in the apartment, especially if— But it was too late.

"Please excuse me for breaking in like this," he apologized, looking toward Kenna and Steppie.

"Come in, Carlton," Neal invited, still holding Daniel in his arms.

Now it only remained for the vicomtesse to join them—to make the circle complete.

Thirty-Seven

KENNA COULD STAND IT NO LONGER. SHE FLED FROM THE salon to her bedroom. Everyone seemed to be waiting for something to occur. The very air contained an electricity that gripped them, and Kenna, feeling it most of all, like some nervous animal waiting for a cataclysm to strike, paced back and forth from the window to her bed.

She realized she couldn't stay long, especially with Carlton waiting for her to reappear. She looked toward the armoire where her dresses still hung. She had made no effort to pack.

The sound that she had dreaded to hear now came from the distance. There was no one else expected—no one but Major Irish Fitzpatrick to ring the doorbell. Kenna pushed open the bedroom door, but somehow, she couldn't force herself to go any farther. And it was Steppie who came and found her hovering at the door but afraid to move.

"Kenna, Irish is here and insists on seeing you," Steppie said.

"I know."

"You knew he was coming?"

"Yes."

"But you didn't say anything about it. It's a little awkward with Carlton in the salon, too. They're glaring at each other like two stallions ready for battle."

"I . . . couldn't do anything about it, Steppie. I didn't know Carlton was going to show up this afternoon, too."

"Well, you'll just have to carry it through as best you can."

"Yes."

Like a sleepwalker, Kenna followed Steppie into the salon. With their entry, three men rose. Kenna looked from Neal to Carlton to Irish.

Before she could alleviate the awful silence, an unsmiling Irish asked, "You're ready to leave?"

Kenna's hand fluttered nervously in the air. "No. I . . ."

"See here, Fitzpatrick," Carlton cut in, seeing Kenna's distress. "Aren't you being a little presumptuous?"

"I've come for my wife. There's nothing presumptuous in that."

Kenna closed her eyes and moaned.

"Your wife? What kind of a joke is this, Fitzpatrick?"

"Is it a joke, Kenna?" Irish asked, and Kenna, opening her eyes, looked at the warning in the dark-haired man's face. In a low voice she said, "No. It's no joke."

"You mean it's the truth? That's impossible. You'd have to have permission from the consulate—and the military. You haven't had time to get married," Carlton concluded triumphantly, while Steppie and Neal looked on in amazement.

"The ceremony took place before I left Fort McPherson," Irish stated.

His answer took Carlton by surprise. "You were at Fort McPherson?"

"Yes. And Kenna and I were secretly married before I left for overseas. Isn't that right, darling?" Irish moved beside Kenna and took her hand in his.

Struggling hard not to snatch her hand from his, she swallowed and in a voice barely audible in the room said, "Yes."

Carlton, his face set and grim, glared at Kenna. "I can't believe you could have done such a thing, Kenna Chalmers. I'm extremely disappointed in you."

"Fitzpatrick," Irish corrected.

"What?"

"Kenna Fitzpatrick."

"If you please, I'll have my coat and cane."

"Of course, Carlton. I'll have Marie get it for you," Steppie replied. "And I'll see you to the door."

"Well, Kenna. You're full of surprises today. Now, introduce me properly to my new brother-in-law," Neal said when they were alone.

While Steppie helped Kenna pack, Irish remained in the salon with Neal. "You'll stay as long as Neal needs you, won't you, Steppie? You'll do it for me?" Kenna asked.

The dark-haired girl hesitated. "I'll stay in Paris," she announced, "as long as Neal doesn't mind. But the vicomtesse is *your* friend. I won't feel right about remaining here in the apartment without you."

"But she invited us both."

"Only because of you. No, I'll find a place of my own. A small pension, perhaps, not far from here."

The trunk was nearly full. Only one dress remained to be packed—the colorless wool dance dress with its daring V-cut in the back. Kenna smoothed the material in place, and as she did so, she thought of that night when she had seen Irish across the ballroom. And now he was waiting for her.

"What are you going to tell the vicomtesse?" Steppie inquired.

Before she could answer, the white-haired woman walked into the bedroom.

"So, I'm losing you, Kenna," she stated.

"Yes, madame. I'm sorry that I didn't . . ."

The wave of a hand cut off Kenna's apology.

"I have met your husband, *petite*. He's a fine young man."

Kenna clamped her teeth together to keep from blurting out the truth—that he wasn't fine at all, but a blackmailer, forcing her to go with him.

The woman looked at her sympathetically. "War is hard on a young marriage," she continued. "And although I am sorry to lose you, I'm happy that your husband has decided to forgive you."

Kenna stared uncomprehendingly. What had Irish told her? Stifling her anger at Irish, Kenna said, "I'll never forget your kindness, madame."

"Nor I yours," the woman replied.

The good-byes were said. The small trunk was strapped to the back of the waiting vehicle and Irish, placing Kenna into the sheltered seat, with her amber-colored fox muff to keep her hands warm, instructed the driver to leave.

"Where are you taking me?" Kenna demanded as soon as the hired car pulled into the traffic.

"To the Hôtel Castille," he replied, "in the Rue Cambon."

The unhappy Kenna asked nothing else. The weather was miserable. Keeping as far away from Irish as possible, she huddled in the corner of the taxi, her cheeks already pink from the blast of wind through the icy streets.

Later, when her trunk was brought upstairs, and the maid and the porter had gone, Kenna whirled toward Irish.

Only one giant bed—she had seen it the moment she had walked into the room. With her eyes blazing, she said, "I want a separate room."

"Kenna, it's impossible," Irish replied. "You know how crowded the city is. I was lucky to find one room."

"I don't consider myself married to you, so don't think I'm going to sleep in the same bed with you."

"That didn't stop you before," he answered unconcernedly.

"You're not a gentleman—to remind me," she countered bitterly.

"I've never professed to be a gentleman—like your Major Torey."

She ignored his barb. "The least you could do is have a cot brought in."

"The situation will be remedied this afternoon," he promised.

"Thank you."

Kenna removed her muff and the matching fur hat. And with her coat still around her, she sat on the edge of the small chintz boudoir chair, as if she might take flight at any moment.

Irish glanced at his watch. "We have an appointment in an hour. I suggest you lie down and get some rest before then."

"I'm all right in the chair."

Shrugging at her answer, Irish began to put on his military topcoat.

"Where are you going?"

"Downstairs—for something to drink."

He walked to the door and closed it behind him. Hearing his footsteps down the hall, Kenna relaxed and removed her coat.

She lay on the bed—sound asleep—when he returned. Irish, standing by her, saw long, golden lashes making curved

309

shadows on her pale skin. The evenness of her breathing caused her breasts to rise and fall. Gently, he pushed a strand of blond hair behind her ear. The touch awoke her.

"Kenna, it's time to get dressed," he said. Her eyes, focusing on the man hovering over her, darkened. Quickly, she moved away from him, and in her stockinged feet she stood on the opposite side of the bed.

The pipes in the basin rattled as she turned on the water to wash her face. When she had finished, she found a dress thrust toward her.

"Here, put this on."

"I don't want to wear that one," she replied.

"Now isn't the time to be so stubborn. You've overslept. And you're going to make us late."

"Then hurry and select something else. It's too cold today for that. I'll freeze in it." She was adamant.

"Do you want me to dress you?"

The threat brought immediate action. Kenna took the dress and stepped behind the screen to change.

With her lower lip in a pout, Kenna followed Irish from the room. "You still won't tell me where we're going?"

"No. You'll see—soon enough."

Once again, Kenna, dressed in fur hat and muff, with the flimsy apricot dress hidden under her coat, climbed into a taxi. It wound its way in and out of the traffic. It honked its horn and impatiently waited for the traffic to move. Finally, the taxi pulled up before a limestone gray building and stopped.

Irish turned to Kenna and informed her, "I'm doing this for *you*, Kenna. If it were left to me, the ceremony around the campfire would have been sufficient."

"What are you talking about?"

"We're getting married, according to French law—to protect you from any further gossip."

"But I . . ."

"I have the necessary documents. The officials are expecting us."

Kenna, caught in his trap, not knowing which way to turn, knew that Irish, with this one step, had closed any escape.

In five minutes, they were married—officially, irrevocably.

But the ceremony, spoken in French and witnessed by two strangers, had been totally impersonal. Kenna, leaving the building, felt no more married to Irish Fitzpatrick than she had when they first walked in.

The gold circlet on her finger felt alien—heavy—like her heart. She had gotten herself into a situation that offered no way out, unless—

They didn't go back to the hotel immediately. The taxi sped out of town, past the Arc de Triomphe, past the Bois de Boulogne. And Kenna, disheartened and miserable, knew better than to ask where Irish was taking her.

The clouds, gathered in a heavy dark shroud enveloping the sky, seemed too heavy to remain aloft for long. Disintegrating, they began to move and shift across the sky, as if some incautious giant had ripped his bedcover while turning over in sleep—losing the stuffing in the process. Large flakes of snow swirled from the midst of the gray and fell upon the earth.

In a small copse of trees not far from the main road, a stone house with red-tiled roof nestled on the side of a hill. Smoke spiraled from the chimney and rose to become a part of the swirling sky.

Without instruction, the taxi driver turned off the main road and drove toward the house. Kenna, chilled to the bone, saw the smoking chimney and was glad.

The taxi stopped. Irish, taking one look at Kenna's flimsy shoes, lifted her from the seat and carried her to the door of the stone house. It was late—not by Parisian standards, but by the setting of the sun, barely visible beyond the trees.

"Ah, *bonjour,* monsieur," the woman at the door said, smiling. "Everything is ready, just as you requested."

No violins—no red divans at Maxim's—merely an intimate little room, with candlelight and the glow of the fire on the hearth. Simple things—in contrast to the gaudy fare that was Paris. And on the table next to the window perched a white ceramic flower bowl filled with green conifer, giving the room a scent of the woods.

The table, with its fresh white tablecloth and crisp linen napkins, was set for supper.

"Why are we doing this?" Kenna asked when they were alone.

"I had no wish to eat our wedding supper in a smoke-filled restaurant with a rowdy crowd. Are you ready to remove your coat?"

Kenna, now warm from the fire, nodded. And Irish, taking the coat, hung it on a peg by his own military topcoat.

"I want to be back in the States by the first of the year," Irish informed Kenna, returning to the seat by the fire.

"Aren't the wagons awfully cold to live in during the winter?" Kenna inquired.

Irish seemed amused at her question. "No more so than tents. You lived in a tent, didn't you?"

"Part of the time," Kenna answered. "But it's not a way of life I would have chosen."

The woman knocked and the food, steaming hot with a delightful aroma, came behind her. Good thick onion soup, followed by fish, beef, little potatoes, and delicacies that Kenna did not know even existed. A different wine was served with each course.

Feeling hungry, Kenna began to eat. Too many times within the past few months she had gone to bed with an empty stomach. She would never behave as an obstinate child refusing food because of the company. Irish, watching her, took note.

The meal was finished; the candle on the table had burned low. And still Irish made no effort to leave. He rose from his chair and placed another log on the fire. The resin in the wood spewed and whistled as it caught fire.

"When is the taxi coming back for us?" Kenna inquired, yawning.

"Tomorrow."

Kenna sat up straight. "You're planning to spend the night here?"

"Yes."

"Well, why didn't you tell me? If I had known, I would have brought a change of clothes."

"You haven't looked in the bedroom, have you?" He indicated the adjoining door, and Kenna, rising abruptly from her chair, went to look.

312

Her pink marabou negligee lay across the old-fashioned bed with its carved headboard reaching toward the ceiling. And on the chair beside it sat her small valise, companion to the trunk left at the Hôtel Castille.

Livid at seeing her things placed so, Kenna rushed back into the other room.

"There's only one bed in there. You promised me this afternoon that we wouldn't share a bed."

"I did nothing of the sort."

"You did. Don't try to get out of it, Irish Fitzpatrick. You promised me—when I asked for a cot."

"If you recall, I said the situation would be remedied. It was. We were married, legally and aboveboard, this afternoon, Kenna. Now you have no reason to refuse sharing my bed."

"I do have a reason, too. I don't want to—and that's reason enough."

"Come, Kenna. Stop acting like some shy virgin who's never been with a man."

"You insufferable—" She picked up a plate from the table and made ready to throw it at him. But with three steps, Irish had reached her. He wrestled the plate from her hand and placed it back on the table.

"There's no need to break the woman's dishes," he scolded.

Now angry at Kenna's behavior, Irish lifted her off the floor, carried her to the bedroom, and with his boot closed the door behind him.

Thirty-Eight

No," SHE PROTESTED AS SHE FELT HIS LIPS BRUSH HERS. SHE squirmed and fussed, refusing to remain still, refusing to let him make love to her. But Irish, on the bed beside her, held her face between his hands and time and again covered her face with kisses—moving sensually to her throat—teasing, caressing—and then tracing her ear with the tip of his tongue.

Kenna moaned. It would be so easy to give in. Her body cried for love, but then she remembered all that Irish had done to her. And she hardened her heart against him.

But he was stronger than she and he ignored her effort to free herself. He kept up the bombardment—moving his hands to the buttons of her dress. She felt the material fall from her body. And knowing that within a few moments she would be utterly lost, she lashed out at him.

"Can't you see that I don't want you to make love to me? That I never want to be your wife, as long as I live?"

Irish lifted his head and stared into her blazing, angry eyes. "But you *are* my wife, Kenna. Make certain that I will eventually claim my rights as a husband."

He let her go abruptly, and feeling vaguely disappointed, Kenna quickly sat up.

She heard the outer door close. Tiptoeing to the sitting room where they had eaten their evening meal, she saw that his topcoat was missing from the peg.

Afraid at first that Irish had left her, Kenna soon realized that he couldn't have done so. The taxi wasn't coming for them until the next day.

She put on her gown and the matching pink marabou negligee. Finding a blanket in the chest at the foot of the bed, she walked to the sitting room, and with the blanket around her, sat in the chair before the fire.

Her eyelids drooped. She glanced down at her watch—a little after ten o'clock. In Paris, the evening would just be getting under way. But Kenna, having slept little the previous night, laid her head against the arm of the chair, and the soothing crackle of the fire lulled her to sleep.

A wintry blast of air swept through the hall, and Irish, returning from his walk in the snow, quickly closed the door. When he entered the sitting room, the fire was almost out. He hung up his coat and hastened to put another log on the fire. Kneeling on the hearth, he looked at the blond-haired girl asleep in the chair—his wife, Kenna.

Being careful not to awaken her, Irish lifted her from her cramped position and placed her on the large bed. She sighed and Irish, with a carefully hidden softness in his eyes, turned and began to undress.

In the middle of the night, Kenna's peaceful sleep was shattered. She began to toss and turn and mumble in her sleep. She cried out, "No— No." And she began to rock her body back and forth in desperation.

Irish awoke. "Kenna," he whispered, "what's the matter?"

"He has no arms," she cried, and great sobs racked her body as her voice grew more hysterical.

"Kenna, wake up. You're having a nightmare."

Her cries filled the room. "It's not fair. He's too young. Oh God!"

"Kenna, wake up."

He reached out and drew her to him, soothing her and wiping the tears from her eyes. "It's all right, Kenna. The war's over. You're not on the battlefield any more."

A great shudder rippled through her body and her teeth began to chatter. Still, he held her close, comforting her.

Kenna's eyes gradually came open. "Irish?"

"Yes?"

"I . . . I woke you, didn't I? I'm sorry."

"That's all right. You had a nightmare."

"Yes . . . I . . . often do, you know," she admitted. "I . . . can't seem to forget the horror."

"That's over, Kenna. We're going home soon." All at once she realized where she was—in Irish's arms—sharing

315

his bed. In alarm she tried to free herself, but Irish refused to release her.

"Go back to sleep, Kenna."

Emotionally drained, with no fight left in her, Kenna did as she was told.

She awoke the next morning warm and relaxed. She stretched and yawned and then opened her eyes.

The other side of the bed was empty, but the pillow's indentation told her that she had not been alone for the night. Frowning, Kenna sat up and tried to remember what had happened.

The nightmare. Yes, it had come again, disturbing her sleep. But someone had soothed her back to sleep. Irish.

As she thought of him, the door opened and he walked in, carrying a breakfast tray of steaming coffee and fresh croissants.

"I've brought our breakfast," he announced.

Kenna, searching for her negligee, pushed the covers back and started to get out of bed, but Irish stopped her.

"The boy is laying the fire now, Kenna. But it won't be going for a while. It will be warmer to have our breakfast in bed."

Her hand reached up to push a stray blond strand from her eyes and she watched Irish set the tray on the nearby table and climb into the bed—as if it were the most natural thing in the world for him to share bed and board with her.

"Cream?" he inquired.

"Yes, please," she answered with a wariness to her voice.

He didn't seem to notice. "You're feeling better this morning?"

"The coffee will help." She paused. "About last night—I'm sorry."

"You're speaking of the nightmare?"

"Yes." She looked at him with her sad gray eyes.

"Would you like to talk about it? Sometimes it helps."

Kenna hesitated. And then she began to recall the horror of the previous weeks. "It wasn't so bad, at first," she said. "But then there was no relief—from Saint-Mihiel to the Argonne. Everywhere I turned, there was destruction—mutila-

316

tion—death. And we were all sick and still trying to care for the wounded.''

Irish nodded sympathetically and listened.

"Annette died in a little hut by the road. She didn't even make a sound, Irish. She just died—quietly. That's when it really began to get bad for me. It was as if the entire world were intent on destroying itself—the phoenix bird consuming itself in its own fire. And every time I closed my eyes, I saw death. It wasn't God's will, Irish, for all those men to die—and women, too.''

Irish, angry that she had seen so much and had been so affected, said gruffly, "Drink your coffee, Kenna, before it gets cold.''

She took a sip and broke off a piece of croissant.

She was still reliving it. He could tell by the marring of her brow.

"The nightmare's over, Kenna,'' Irish continued. "Now you can forget it.''

"But all those villages—all those people, with nothing left. What's going to happen to them?''

"They'll rebuild,'' he assured her. "Your phoenix bird rose from its ashes. And the people will rebuild too.''

"I hate war. No one really wins a war.''

"Then shall we call a truce?'' Irish asked, his eyes twinkling.

"What are you talking about?''

"Or would you rather surrender immediately?''

"Never,'' she answered, spreading the jam on her croissant and taking a large bite.

In mid-morning, they left the stone house nestled in the hillside and returned to Paris. The sun had come out of hiding, searching for the remaining patches of ice and snow to turn them into liquid pools sparkling in the morning light.

Kenna still wore the flimsy apricot dress, the fur muff and hat—her wedding apparel.

"We'll cross the Channel,'' Irish informed her, "day after tomorrow. And then we'll sail for home.''

"On a military transport?''

"No. On the *Windsor*,'' he answered, naming the luxury ship, companion to the *Prince of Wales*.

317

"That's expensive, isn't it?"

"No more so than remaining in Paris for another month, waiting on other transportation." Irish's voice and eyes suddenly betrayed his teasing. "Since you were threatened with a dishonorable discharge, you wouldn't fare well in getting a berth on a transport."

"Isn't that a silly rule," Kenna responded indignantly, "to give a woman a dishonorable discharge for getting married. It seems to me that it would be far wiser for that rule to apply to men. Then there wouldn't be enough left to fight a war. And the world would be better off."

Irish groaned. "The lady has claws, I see. Next you'll be wanting to vote."

"How did you know?"

On the day Kenna and Irish left Paris, Neal, Steppie, and the vicomtesse saw them off at the rail station.

"I'm so glad the vicomtesse has insisted that you stay in the apartment," Kenna whispered to Steppie.

"I'm grateful too. I didn't like the idea of moving to a pension and living alone."

Kenna glanced toward Neal. "Take care of him, Steppie."

"I will."

"Good-bye, *petite*. I'll miss you," the white-haired woman said, kissing the girl on her cheek as the train sounded its whistle.

"Good-bye, madame. And thank you for everything."

With only a second left, Kenna looked toward the fair-haired man who was almost her mirror image, except in size. "Neal?"

"Have a nice voyage home," he said cheerfully. And for the first time since Kenna had found him at the château, he leaned down and gave her a kiss on the top of her head.

Tears blurred her eyes. She didn't want to leave him. He was her brother—her reason for going overseas, for living through the hell of war until she could find him. And now she was being wrenched from him.

"The train has started moving, Kenna," Irish said beside her. She felt his hands encircle her waist and lift her from the platform to the steps of the train.

318

She leaned toward the disappearing platform and waved, with Irish's strong arm protecting her from falling. The station became a small speck in the distance and Kenna, looking up at Irish, said, "I don't want to leave him. Can't you see that?" The tears, unchecked, began to run down her cheeks.

Irish handed her a clean handkerchief and without speaking, led her back to their compartment.

The crossing of the Channel was rough. The wind moaned and blew in great gusts across the water, whipping a froth onto the waves. Kenna, belowdecks, kept her face averted from Irish. At times, when it was necessary to face him, she stared at him accusingly. *He* was the one who had spoiled things for her. She realized it more the farther she got from Paris.

But once she arrived home, she would find out about the gypsy marriage—just how legal it actually was. Yes, she'd go to Mr. Ainslay and he would tell her. She gazed down at the gold ring on her finger. The civil ceremony in France could be annulled—that is, if she could stay out of Irish Fitzpatrick's bed until she got back to Atlanta. Thinking of it made Kenna feel much better.

The short journey to Dover ended. Kenna and Irish, moving overland to Portsmouth on Monday, boarded the *Windsor* and waited to set sail across the Atlantic.

At the same time they were getting settled in their cabin, military officers at the prisoner-of-war camp at Fort Mc-Pherson were discussing the escape of their German prisoner.

"Well, ole Fritz finally did it," the sergeant said. "After all this time, he met with success."

"But the war's over," the lieutenant responded in a puzzled voice. "He was due to be repatriated within the next month. A strange thing for him to do, don't you think—right when the war was over?"

"I guess he just got started digging and it became a way of life for him." The sergeant grinned impishly. "I wonder how

319

many buckets of Georgia clay he disposed of in all that time?"

The lieutenant took up his pencil. "Let's see—almost two years of digging—ten buckets a day— That would make— say seven hundred thirty days— that would make seven thousand three hundred buckets . . ."

Thirty-Nine

KENNA FIRST SAW CARLTON TOREY IN THE SHIP'S DINING room. He gazed at her across the room, his lips pursed in disapproval.

It was an awkward moment. Kenna didn't know whether to acknowledge seeing him or not. He saved her from making a decision by looking the other way.

Irish, sitting opposite Kenna, said, "I see your friend is on board with us."

"I suppose he has as much right as anyone else."

"He doesn't look as if he's enjoying himself."

"Major Torey was quite seasick on the way over. I hope he fares better going home."

"He probably will. The *Windsor* is a much smoother vessel than an army transport."

Kenna finished eating and Irish, waiting for her, said, "Would you like a stroll around the deck before going back to the cabin?"

"I don't think so. It's too windy for me. But you go ahead. I'll find something else to do."

He left her, and Kenna, walking rapidly toward the cabin she shared with Irish, heard her name. She looked up, but saw no one.

"Kenna," the voice repeated. "Over here."

She gazed toward the half-opened door leading into the lounge. And there stood Carlton. He had ignored her in the dining room. Why was he trying to get her attention now?

She walked toward him and he opened the door the rest of the way for her to enter the empty lounge.

"I didn't know you were leaving Paris so soon," she said.

"I hadn't planned to do so—until I discovered something quite interesting."

"You're going to tell me what it is, I presume?"

"As soon as we sit down," he said, leading her to a table with blue benches on either side. "He forced you to marry him, didn't he?"

Kenna's hand flew up to her mouth. "Why—why do you say that?"

"You weren't actually married until four days ago in Paris. I found out. And on that Thursday when he came for you in the apartment, I could tell you were afraid of him. He's holding something over you, isn't he?"

"Yes," she admitted.

"I knew it."

"But it's too late to do anything about it until I get back to Atlanta," she said.

"You haven't slept with him, have you?"

Kenna hesitated. "We've slept in the same bed."

Impatiently, Carlton continued, "But you haven't allowed him to make love to you in these past four days, have you?"

Kenna shook her head.

"We'll have the marriage annulled."

". . . But he's making noises like a husband. I think I won't be safe from him much longer."

Carlton nodded in understanding. "We'll just have to find another room for you—before tonight."

"The ship's crowded."

"That doesn't matter. I'll arrange something. Just be patient, darling. I'll get you out of this as soon as possible."

A woman with a child walked into the lounge. Kenna and Carlton, afraid they would be overheard, stopped talking.

"I'd better go," she said, getting up.

"Yes—but be careful of the man, Kenna."

She hurried toward her cabin, anxious to get there before Irish returned from his walk. When he finally opened the door, Kenna sat in a chair reading a magazine.

"Did you have a nice stroll?" she inquired.

"It was windy, as you said."

Kenna was nervous. It showed in her face, in the constant movement of her hands.

"What's the matter, Kenna? Why are you so restless?"

322

"I don't know," she replied. "I guess it's—well, I guess it's because I don't feel well."

"Would you feel better lying down?"

"Maybe." Kenna moved toward the bunk and, plumping the pillow at her head, she lay down and closed her eyes—anything to get away from Irish's piercing, prying eyes.

He took the chair and picked up the magazine. From time to time, he glanced toward Kenna, and then back to the magazine.

The afternoon passed and finally the time came to prepare for dinner. "Do you feel like eating?" Irish asked.

"Not really," Kenna answered. "You . . . you go ahead. Maybe I can get something in the lounge later."

Kenna heard Irish getting dressed. And still she remained in the bunk. She hadn't thought to ask Carlton when they would meet again. And it was impossible to contact him until Irish had gone to dinner.

"You're sure you'll be all right while I'm in the dining room?"

"Yes, Irish. I'll be fine."

He hesitated at the door, but Kenna's eyes were already closed. And so he softly shut the door. As soon as Kenna heard the door click, she jumped up from the bunk and began to dress. She had slipped her dress over her head when she heard the knock.

In her bare feet, she walked to the door. "Yes?"

"Kenna, let me in," Carlton whispered.

Quickly, she unlatched the door.

"I can't stay," he said. "But here, take this."

He thrust a small vial in her hand and she asked, "What is it?"

"It's ipecac, Kenna. Don't say anything," he whispered, as she started to protest. "There isn't another cabin or bunk available on the entire ship. So we'll just have to put you in the infirmary for tonight. I hate to do this to you, darling. But he'll never let you out of his sight unless you really appear ill."

He stared down the passageway. "Wait a few more minutes, and then drink the dosage. I'd better go now."

323

Kenna closed the door and stared at the vial in distaste. Why couldn't there have been another cabin available?

She was in the bathroom when Irish returned from the dining room. The emetic had taken full effect.

"Kenna?" Irish's voice called from the other side of the door.

She held onto the sides of the basin, and wiped her face with a cold towel when she had finished. But then the retching began all over again.

The bathroom door was wrenched open. "Kenna, darling."

He stayed with her, and then carried her to the bunk and rang for the steward. When the steward appeared, a worried Irish tersely informed him, "My wife is quite ill. Please get the ship's doctor right away."

When the doctor saw the pale, limp Kenna and Irish had informed him of her symptoms, the man frowned uneasily. "It doesn't sound like seasickness. It's more like appendicitis. Major, I expect we'd better get her to sick bay. I'll send a stretcher for her."

"I'll carry her myself," Irish informed him. Wrapping a blanket around her, he lifted her from the bunk and followed the doctor to the ship's infirmary.

All night Kenna remained in sick bay, and despite the doctor's attempt to get Irish to go back to his cabin, he refused to leave. He sat beside her and watched over her until the morning came. Kenna, miserable enough from the emetic, was even more miserable when she realized how deceitful she had been.

"She's much better, Major Fitzpatrick," the ship's doctor informed Irish. "It must have been food poisoning—instead of appendicitis. But we'll keep her in sick bay another day, just to make sure."

Kenna, still weak, saw the relief in Irish's face. Shadowed from a night's growth of beard, tired from a lack of sleep, Irish's face showed the strain.

"Why don't you get some food, Major Fitzpatrick, and a little sleep?" the doctor urged. "I'll call you if there's any change. But I believe your wife is now on the mend."

"Kenna?"

"I'll be all right, Irish," she said. "Do as he says."

The dark-haired man leaned over and kissed her on the forehead. "I won't be long," he promised.

Kenna was sitting up when Carlton walked into sick bay. "Well, it worked, didn't it?" he said.

"Yes, Carlton, it worked. But I'm not happy about it."

"What do you mean?"

"It was a deceitful thing to do. Irish was frantic when he thought I was really ill. Did you know he sat beside me all night?"

Carlton, taken back by her words, replied, "You shouldn't feel sorry for a man who blackmailed you into marrying him, Kenna. And as for the ipecac," he added, "it was the only thing I could think of to get you out of his cabin immediately."

"You said there were no other cabins available. What about yours, Carlton? You could have moved in with someone else and given me yours."

"I didn't think of that. Yes, I suppose I could have." Carlton frowned. "Is the doctor letting you out of the infirmary today?"

"No. He told Irish he wanted to keep me here for observance at least one more day."

"Then I'll think of something."

"No, Carlton. Don't."

"What do you mean?"

"Just that—I've decided I don't want your help. I'll handle it my own way. This was all a . . . a big mistake."

Irish Fitzpatrick stood at the door, watching them, and wondering what they were talking about so secretively. His dark eyes narrowed at the sight of Carlton Torey, but he carefully disguised his feelings as he walked toward Kenna.

Freshly shaved, with clean clothes on, Irish presented a neater appearance than the hour before.

"Oh, hello, Fitzpatrick," Carlton said. Not waiting for Irish to respond, he turned again to Kenna. In a professional voice he said, "Dr. Harrison is correct, my dear. You *should* stay in the infirmary for observation at least another day."

He nodded to Irish and walked rapidly out of sick bay.

"Did you have breakfast?" Kenna inquired.

325

"Yes."

"Irish, thank you for staying with me last night. You didn't have to, you know."

"I wouldn't have slept anyway, knowing how ill you were," he replied. He started to sit down beside her, but Kenna protested.

"Go to the cabin, Irish, and get some sleep now. I'll be fine—I promise," she said.

For the next few hours, Kenna rested and felt like a malingerer. She'd seen soldiers pretending to be ill at the battlefront—cowards who'd vowed they'd been gassed just to get out of fighting. She had felt a contempt for them but she was no better.

Remorse set in. Her muscles were sore. But there was nothing else wrong with her, except she was hungry.

By mid-afternoon, Kenna decided she could stay put no longer. And so she convinced Dr. Harrison to let her leave the infirmary. When Irish appeared, she was already out of bed.

Surprised to see her up, he said, "Kenna, do you think you should be walking around so soon?"

"I'm over my illness, Irish," she informed him. "And Dr. Harrison has given me permission to go back to the cabin. Could you get some clothes for me?" she asked. "The yellow wool dress will be fine."

"Of course. It will take only a few minutes," he said, his tobacco-brown eyes showing his pleasure at Kenna's rapid recuperation.

But when he returned with the clothes a while later, Irish was unusually quiet. Silently, he waited for her to get dressed. And in silence, he walked with her from sick bay, guiding her along the narrow passageway until they had reached the cabin door.

Kenna, recognizing a dramatic change in mood, glanced uneasily as he closed the door.

Then the accusation began. "You don't fight fairly, do you, Kenna?"

Her gray eyes darkened in alarm. "What are you talking about?"

"This," he said, walking over to the drawer and picking

up the small vial that had contained the ipecac. "Who gave it to you?"

Kenna swayed and reached out for the chair. She should have remembered where she'd hidden the empty vial before asking Irish to bring her fresh clothes.

"I'm waiting for your answer, Kenna. Who gave it to you?"

"Carlton," she confessed.

"But why? What purpose did it serve?"

"He didn't want me to spend another night with you."

"Is this what you planned yesterday in the lounge?"

"How did you know?"

"I cut short my walk around the deck. And I saw you leave the lounge together."

Suddenly, Irish came toward her and the look in his eyes made her take a step backward.

"You're my wife, Kenna. There's nothing he can do about that."

"But *I* can," Kenna countered, trying not to show her fear of him. "I'll have the marriage annulled as soon as I get home. You forced me to marry you—but you can't force me to stay with you."

"Can't I?"

With a tear, the yellow wool dress with buttons covering the skirt disintegrated in Irish's hands.

"Irish," Kenna protested. But he was in no mood for mercy.

With the yellow dress at her feet, she stood and waited for his wrath to descend upon her. Closing her eyes, she braced herself for the blow she felt certain would come. Yet, when his hand touched her, it was curiously gentle, loosening the silken chemise about her breasts.

His finger began its tantalizing motion around the pink-tipped nipple, and then she knew the form of punishment he had chosen.

"No," she cried, opening her eyes, pleading for him to stop. "Please don't."

With a sadness to his voice, Irish said, "I have no other choice, Kenna. You and Carlton Torey have seen to that."

327

Her tears meant nothing to him. He tortured her with his kisses, his caresses, and then took her casually, with no display of love or emotion beyond that of a man seeking his own satisfaction.

Irish had exacted his revenge. Kenna's punishment was complete.

Forty

HER EYES, LARGE AND LIMPID WITH TEARS, STARED AT HIM accusingly.

Ignoring her wounded look, Irish said, "It's almost time for dinner. I presume you won't be foolish enough to do without it tonight."

She didn't answer him. Instead, she turned her face to the bulkhead. He had totally devastated her with his kisses—his caresses. Now there was no avenue left her. The marriage could no longer be annulled. He had seen to that.

Her lip quivered. Still feeling the imprint of his flesh upon hers, her body trembled. He was a man experienced in the ways of bringing a woman to the very edge of ecstasy. How different it would have been if he had not forced her into marriage. She could have loved him, totally, ecstatically, if things had been different.

"Are you all right?" the voice inquired, with a caress in its tone.

"I'll never be all right," she responded, brushing the moisture from her eyes.

"Kenna, Kenna," he said, sitting beside her. "You brought this on yourself. I was prepared to let you get used to me before I claimed any further rights. But you must have known that I wouldn't tolerate any schemes between you and Carlton Torey."

Carlton— Where was he? Kenna suddenly sat up. Her fury extended to the man who had made the past twenty-four hours even more difficult for her.

Irish, continuing to dress for dinner, kept his eye on Kenna.

"What time is it?" she asked.

"A few minutes before seven," he answered.

She stood up and headed for the bath. "You go on, Irish. I . . . I'll meet you in the dining room."

Realizing she would feel better left alone, he put on his coat. "I'll see you in a few minutes," he called. "Be sure to wear something warm. It's quite windy." Glad that she had decided not to remain in the room and sulk, Irish departed.

She heard the door close. Kenna looked in the mirror and began to brush her hair vigorously.

The wind blew in great gusts, the ship coming alive in protest. Rocking and listing, the vessel's movement increased so rapidly that Kenna was forced to hold onto the railing as she hurried toward the dining room.

A figure coming in the opposite direction also held to the railing. They met, and Kenna, looking up, saw that it was Carlton.

"I thought you were still in the infirmary," he said, recognizing her.

"I left this afternoon."

"Well, I've arranged for another cabin for you, Kenna, but it won't be available until tomorrow night."

The wind howled, and Kenna lurched away from the man. "Don't bother, Carlton." The wind muffled her voice.

"What did you say?" he shouted.

"I said—don't bother. It's too late."

Carlton, already queasy from the sudden action of the storm, looked even sicker at Kenna's words. "What do you mean, Kenna?"

"I'm Irish's wife. There's no chance for annulment now."

She watched as he rushed toward his cabin without another word. Poor Carlton and his *mal de mer*.

In the dining room, the crystal clattered against the dinnerware. Kenna grabbed a fork that threatened to leap from the table.

Irish, with his eyes on the rain now slashing against the glass, turned back to Kenna and said, "It looks as if we'll have to batten down everything for the night. The wind seems to be getting worse."

"I've never been in a storm on the ocean before."

"Are you frightened?"

330

"A little," Kenna admitted.

"I'm glad you're beginning to be truthful with me, Kenna," he said.

"Irish, about last night . . ."

"That's in the past. We won't ever speak of it again."

With the meal over, Irish and Kenna hurried back to their cabin, with Irish protecting her from the rain.

"I didn't ask if you wanted to stay for the moving picture," Irish commented politely as they reached the passageway.

"Not really," Kenna responded. "I don't think I could keep my mind on it—with the storm going on."

She paused and listened to the sound of rain coming down in great sheets. "It would be ironic, wouldn't it, Irish—if we both survived the war and then went down with the *Windsor*."

Irish unlocked the cabin door and waited for Kenna to enter. "That's not likely to happen, Kenna."

She turned toward him. "The *Titanic* went down."

"But it hit an iceberg—and that was six years ago. Besides, there weren't enough lifeboats. That's why so many people were lost."

"Did you check on the *Windsor*'s lifeboats?"

"Yes. There are more than enough, if we should need them."

Kenna, still unable to dismiss the subject, said, "I heard that some of the passageways of the *Titanic* were intentionally blocked, and that's why some didn't get to the lifeboats."

"Stop worrying unnecessarily, Kenna," Irish growled. "We're on the *Windsor*. What happened on the *Titanic* doesn't concern us."

"My mother and father were on the *Titanic*," she shouted, suddenly angry with Irish.

His brown eyes softened. "I'm sorry, Kenna. I didn't know." He held out his arms for her and she took a step toward him. Then she stopped. Refusing the comfort of his arms, Kenna walked past him into the small bath cubicle to remove her wet clothes.

The ship rode out the winds and gales and within two days,

331

the sea had calmed and the sun shone again. But it remained bitterly cold.

Occasionally, Kenna saw Carlton from a distance, but he avoided her. Their estrangement was complete. Irish had seen to that.

Once Irish had taken her to his bed, he seemed to have no further interest in her—except to keep her by his side, reminding her that she belonged to him and no one else. She still blamed him for forcing her into marriage and for forcing her to leave Neal in France. But he ignored her silences, her efforts to remain apart from him. And there were no more love-filled days.

The *Windsor* arrived in New York harbor on schedule and Kenna rushed to the deck to wait for the Statue of Liberty to come into view.

Six months before, when she had left for France, the harbor had been in darkness. That June night seemed so long ago. The Waldorf—the citizens' committee—the milk wagon—the German prisoner of war and her fear for Neal. So long ago.

A cheer arose from the crowd on deck as the magnificent giant of a statue appeared. Liberty held her torch high, to light the way for the tired and the homeless.

She couldn't see it, but she knew the broken shackle was there at Liberty's feet—tyranny destroyed.

She should have been happy. Neal was alive, the war was over, and she was home again. But the homecoming was all wrong. She hadn't pictured it like this. In her dreams, Steppie and Neal were the ones at her side—not Irish Fitzpatrick.

Kenna wiped a tear from her eyes and hastily glanced toward Irish to make sure he hadn't seen her action. His face showed no joy at being home.

But of course, he wasn't home yet. He wouldn't be until he was riding over grassy southern meadows and woodlands—free as the wind, free as the blooded stallions that were a part of his heritage. Godrin—she had forgotten.

"What happened to your white stallion, Godrin?" Kenna suddenly asked.

A flicker of pain passed over Irish's face. "He was killed by a volley of shells at Saint-Juvin."

"I'm sorry, Irish. He was a beautiful horse."

"Yes—the greatest companion a man could ever ask for. He saved my life," he confessed, a great sadness in his voice.

They disembarked, they spent the night in New York. And the next morning, without recuperating from the sea voyage, Kenna and Irish, with their luggage, boarded a train that would take them south.

It was a quiet trip, in contrast to the noisy, boisterous sounds of the troop train that had been greeted with cheers and flags and music all along the way. Davin—and Carlton—Steppie—the young soldier leaning through the window—"Nurse, I have a terrible pain." Like a kaleidoscope, the memories returned to Kenna with each mile traveled.

Then, one afternoon at three o'clock, the familiar word sounded from the train conductor's lips. "Atlanta."

Excitedly, Kenna stared out of the window. "Irish, I can't believe it. I'm actually home." She began to gather her things together as the train slowed.

"Not yet, Kenna," Irish cautioned.

"Well, in the next few minutes," she answered, her eyes shining with excitement. She would see Cricket and Verbena—and Johnsie. What a glorious time they would have that night—sipping hot chocolate and eating Verbena's stickies.

"Sit down, Kenna. We're not getting off."

"What do you mean, Irish? This is Atlanta. We're home."

He shook his head. "We won't be home for several hours yet."

Kenna stared at him in disbelief. "I'm getting off *now*," she said. But Irish, blocking her way, said, "No, Kenna. This isn't our destination."

"Well, it's *my* destination," she snapped. "I don't care where *you're* going. I'm getting off."

"You're my wife. And you go where I go."

The train started up again, and Kenna, trapped and furious,

sat down, her head turned toward the window to watch the rapidly disappearing Atlanta landscape.

Her fury grew with the clacking of wheels that took her farther and farther from Atlanta. Irish wouldn't get by with it. She would do something when the train finally stopped. If he thought she was going to spend her first night in a tent, or a gypsy wagon, he was going to be rudely surprised.

A carriage met them at the station. Kenna hadn't even heard the conductor announce the name of the town. Irish had awakened her after the train had come to a stop. The long trip had taken its toll and she was too exhausted even to care where she was.

The steady clop of the horses' hoofs on the cobblestoned street sounded in her ears. She didn't speak. She didn't bother to inquire where she was. Her resolve on the train had dwindled with each mile. Now all she wanted was a bed. She was past caring about anything else.

She shivered, and Irish pressed the woolen lap robe closer to her body.

The late afternoon sun, with its spiked rays jutting in all directions—a sunburst before her eyes—temporarily blinded her. And then the sun was blocked by stones of brown and a two-storied cupola rising toward the winter sky.

Kenna knew now she was in Macon. Brazenly, without the cover of darkness to hide their movement, they traveled down the broad avenue toward the house—the same one that Irish had forced his way into the night they had traveled in the gypsy wagon from the swamp.

She looked toward him. He ignored her castigating look. The carriage pulled to the rear and Kenna, almost asleep on her feet, tumbled from the carriage. Irish caught her in his arms and carried her to a shrouded chair inside and then saw to the luggage. By the time he had paid the driver and sent him on his way, Kenna was sound asleep.

He smiled, and lifting her in his arms, he took her upstairs to the master bedroom.

She slept for over twelve hours and awoke to the warmth of a roaring fire on the hearth. She didn't remember going to bed. She looked down at the gown covering her body. She

334

didn't remember getting undressed either. It must have been Irish who had done it.

Footsteps sounded along the hallway. Listening, Kenna wondered what would happen if it were not Irish, but the master of the house—returning.

"You slept a long time," Irish said, seeing her awake.

"It was a long trip," she reminded him. "Too long." And she climbed out of bed.

"Don't you want your coffee?"

"I'll be back," she said, disappearing into the hallway on bare feet.

In less than a minute she returned. Irish smiled as Kenna ran toward the bed and hopped into it, pulling up the covers after her.

"It's cold," she defended herself and her unladylike return.

"Then you'll want your coffee," he replied, handing her a cup of the steaming liquid.

"I'm hungry. Is this all the breakfast I'm going to have?" she inquired, seeing not even a piece of toast visible.

"You're acting like a spoiled lady of the manor this morning," Irish accused. "Just be thankful you have something warm now. You can fix our breakfast later."

She noticed he was dressed in a strange woolen robe—black to match the color of his hair. "And you seem to be usurping the lord of the manor's robe," she answered. Her gray eyes showed her seriousness. "Irish, we've got to stop this, you know."

"Stop what?" he asked.

"Breaking into other people's houses. We'll get into an awful lot of trouble."

Irish set down his coffee cup. "Are you finished?" he asked, coming toward the bed.

"Yes," she said, and swallowed the last few drops. He held out his hand for the cup and placed it next to his.

Kenna, her eyes mesmerized by the pagan-looking Irish Fitzpatrick, watched him remove the black robe. Before she could escape from the opposite side, he climbed into bed and took her in his arms.

335

"Would you live with me in the wagon?" he asked suddenly. "Summer and winter?"

"I don't plan to live with you anywhere," she answered, struggling against him.

His hands started their exploration of her body and he began to love her—not harshly, as he had taken her in the ship's cabin to spite Carlton—but tenderly, lovingly, as he had done in the deserted house on the night she thought they were both going to die.

"Irish, don't," she protested. But he paid no attention. He removed her gown and his mouth found the soft, velvet cleft between her breasts.

"Tell me that you love me," he murmured. "That you'll follow me wherever I go."

"No."

He continued to trace the curves of her body intimately, bringing her to the perilous edge of ecstasy. Feeling her stiffen, he said, "Don't fight me, Kenna. Not now."

She didn't heed his words. In an attempt to save herself, she pushed against him. But his hands knew too much.

She moaned. And despite herself, she weakened. Kenna entwined her arms around him as she felt his flesh upon hers.

"Tell me, Kenna," he demanded.

It was more than she could stand. The waiting—the agony. "Yes," she whispered.

"You love me?"

"Yes."

"You'll go wherever I go?"

"Yes, Irish."

In tenderness, he received her total surrender, and the sensual feeling spread over her, wrapping her in its overwhelming pleasure. For a long time, Kenna, reluctant to give him up, kept her arms around him, covering his face with kisses. She lay in his arms, totally his. She was Irish's wife in heart *and* body.

All at once, Kenna heard a noise downstairs. She lifted her head from the pillow and listened.

"Irish," she whispered. "I . . . I think the owner has come back." She reached for her gown, but Irish stopped her. "What will we do if he comes upstairs and finds us? Please, Irish. Let me put on my gown."

Irish laughed. "That isn't necessary, Kenna. The owner of the house knows every inch of your beautiful, silken body."

"Irish?"

"Haven't you guessed, Kenna?"

"But you can't be the owner of this beautiful mansion. You're a horse trader," she said.

"We'll have to discuss that over breakfast."

Hearing another noise, Kenna asked, "Then who's downstairs?"

"The cleaning woman, the window washer, and the gardener."

She sat at the table in the warmth of the kitchen. Her appetite matched her happiness. And she listened to Irish as he explained.

"My father was Judge Gerald Fitzpatrick—and it all started the summer that he married my stepmother. I was fourteen."

"And that's when you ran away and joined the horse traders?"

"Yes. When he finally found me, my father knew he'd made a mistake in marrying the woman. But there was little he could do about it except to send me to a private boarding school and let me continue to spend the summers with the horse traders.

"Then he died. He left the house to me—and my stepmother moved away. But the old house held such sad memories that I vowed I would never come back until I could find someone who could sweep the hate and gloom from the corners and fill the place with love again."

"I thought you had broken in," Kenna said, remembering the clandestine stop the first time.

"I know. It was a spur-of-the-moment thing. I had a great need to see you in my house, Kenna."

"And the ceremony? Were we really married that night around the campfire?"

"According to the clan. The chief joined us and blessed us

337

in his ancient Gaelic. That should have told you that I was no Irish horse trader," he said, smiling. "I would never have been allowed to marry outside the clan."

"But you let me go. You didn't tell me."

"It was hard, Kenna. I was so jealous of Neal. But I realized you either had to find him or put his memory to rest before I could claim you. I had no idea he was your brother—until that day at the château."

"I didn't want to leave him," Kenna said, sadly.

"You weren't helping him, Kenna. A man has to find himself. No one else can do it for him. It's better for you to be here with me," he added, a wicked grin spreading over his handsome face.

"But for how long?" Kenna asked. "Until summer when you go back to the horse traders?"

Irish hesitated. "I'm home, Kenna. The family mills I inherited have been waiting for me for a long time. But before I take on the responsibility of running them, I want one more summer of freedom. Then I'll be ready to settle down."

"And I'm to wait patiently for you?"

Irish shook his head. "You'll always be beside me, Kenna. I'll never let you leave me or be apart from me again. You'll dance with me at all the grand balls we'll be forced into attending, but before that, you'll dance with me one last time by the gypsy fire."

He stood, and drawing her tenderly to him, he said, "I love you, Kenna. From the moment I first saw you, I was obsessed with you."

"But you weren't very nice to me."

He touched her silver-blond hair with his hand. "I'll make it up to you, darling." Irish suddenly lifted his head—dark, proud, arrogant. "You hear it?" he asked. "The house sounds happier already."

Kenna wrinkled her nose and laughed. "That's the cleaning woman, singing."

Epilogue

APRIL. THE BLOSSOMING OF DOGWOODS AND AZALEAS HERalded the return of spring to Atlanta.

Through the streets the Irish horse traders came, with the king of the clan leading the stately procession.

Sleek, glistening horses, ridden by proud, arrogant, darkhaired men, pranced in the dust. And gaudy gypsy wagons followed behind.

In the back of one of the gaily painted wagons, Kenna sat, her large gray eyes excited as she fingered a gold necklace hanging from her neck. Her mouth curved in pleasure while she watched a playful white foal, the same color as Godrin, nuzzling its mother's side.

Kenna was conscious of a small quiver inside her own body—a delicate hint of new life to come.

She smiled. April 1919. The month and year were indelibly engraved upon her heart.

Acknowledgments

PHOENIX RISING BEGAN AS AN IDEA, UNSHAPED AS TO FORM
and substance. The idea became reality with the help of
many people whom I wish to thank: Professor Florian
Fleck, who served as guide, translator, and interpreter on
my pilgrimage to the trenches of France; Fort McPherson's
Public Information Office and post historian, for making
their files available to me; Fenton Dancy, for his gift of the
six-volume *History of the Great War*, found in the back corner of an old book shop; Ree Stamps, for digging out of her
attic the marvelous 1919 pictorial histories of the war; Jack
Barnes, for relating a true episode concerning his World War
I father; the staffs of Maud M. Burrus Library, Atlanta Public
Library, and Atlanta Historical Society, for helping to locate
elusive books and newspaper articles; and my editor, Mi-
chaela Hamilton, for challenging me to write *Phoenix Rising*.

Frances Patton Statham
Atlanta, Georgia
October 1980

About the Author